SAXON'S BANE

GEOFFREY GUDGION

First published 2013 by Solaris
an imprint of Rebellion Publishing Ltd,
Riverside House, Osney Mead,
Oxford, OX2 0ES, UK

www.solarisbooks.com

ISBN: 978 1 78108 136 5

Designed & typeset by Rebellion Publishing

Printed and bound by CPI Group (UK) Ltd, Croydon, CR0 4YY

SAXON'S BANE

GEOFFREY GUDGION

SOLARIS

ACKNOWLEDGEMENTS

THIS IS FOR the Gudgies; Deborah, James, and Sophie, who have not only tolerated a fundamental change in lifestyle, but encouraged me to keep going. My son James paid me one of life's purest compliments when he became so absorbed in an early draft that he missed two stops on the train. He has been demanding more ever since.

Many others have helped me along the way:

Early in this literary journey I discovered the Litopia online writing community, www.litopia.com. Numerous Litopians read and critiqued extracts at various stages, always constructively. I am particularly indebted to Lesley McLaren, Kristin Yates, Lisa Lieberman, and Lucy Lawrie, who were kind enough to critique the full manuscript. Their feedback was much-needed refreshment and direction.

Marcus and Susie Bicknell have been supportive beyond any calls of friendship. And if a little equestrian joy has crept into these pages, its inspiration grazes happily in their fields.

When I thought the book was ready, Debi Alper's professional critique not only showed me how far there still was to travel, she signposted the way forward. Her advice was fundamental.

The Verulam Writers Circle of St Albans accepted me into their talented group and provided invaluable feedback, writerly company, and the occasional libation.

My agent Ian Drury, of Shiel Land Associates, was willing to back an unknown author. He had the courage to believe that even in the current brutal market, the manuscript was publishable. Which it clearly was, but only with the help of some very good friends.

Finally, but only in the chronological sense, Jonathan Oliver and his wonderfully professional team at Solaris Books not only believed and enthused, they perfected.

"You touched the shadow world.
Very few people come back from that.
Maybe you make it easier for the shadow
world to touch this one."

Part One

Samhain

November

Chapter One

THE STAG IN the road would change everything.

Inside Kate's BMW, the sound system thumped out the kind of music that made Fergus feel invincible. Its tribal rhythm tightened the tension, and probably encouraged Kate to squeeze a little more out of the accelerator. She was nodding her head in time with the beat, flexing her fingers around the steering wheel, and holding the car tight to the turns as they climbed. Beside her, Fergus checked his watch, again, and made a mental calculation of their chances of being on time. Maybe. Just maybe, with luck, and if this ancient back road over the Downs didn't have flooded fords or flocks of sheep or any other obstacles that didn't appear on maps.

On the high ground the road straightened, and Kate floored the pedal so that the rain ran horizontally along the windows in the slipstream. Where they crested a watershed and grazed the clouds, ancient burial mounds lay humped in the bracken, half-seen through the mists.

Fergus's attention snapped back inside the car as it swerved.

"Keep your eyes on the bloody road, will you?" Fergus heard the tension in his voice. Kate was prodding the GPS, searching for routes. Wobbles at this speed were alarming.

"Then you work the sodding thing, you're the techie." Her voice was quite deep, with a purr-or-snarl kind of quality, and that had been a snarl.

Fergus tapped at the satnav screen, unruffled. He and Kate scrapped the way people can only scrap if they are confident with each other, as if the barbs were a form of verbal grooming. They were the best, him and Kate. Choreographed, professional, hungry, top guns in the sales league and determined to stay there. She did the pitch; he talked technology. Hearts and minds, vision and practicality, between them they had it covered. Fergus expanded the range until a cross-roads and the icon of a village started dropping into view, stepping down in minute increments.

Allingley.

A sudden gust of wind punched the car, making him lift his eyes as Kate briefly fought for control.

"Hey, slow down, for fuck's sake!"

Ahead of them a bend was approaching fast as the road dropped towards the woodland at the rim of a valley. Fergus could see a litter of freshly fallen leaves tumbling over the tarmac where the woods began, on a road scarcely wide enough for two cars to pass.

"Scared, huh?" Kate glanced across at him, smiling her challenge as she ignored the road and pulled the car round the first dropping curve into the valley, burning rubber in a blast of performance motoring.

"Shiiit!"

Their final words together were screamed in harmony; teamwork to the last.

The mind can do a lot of thinking in its final moments. Some strange corner of Fergus's brain had time to know that the stag in the middle of the road was magnificent. Shaggy-maned and bearing its antlers with all the poise of a medieval jousting helm, the beast had been staring downhill with its nose into the wind as if the last gust had carried the sound of a distant call. At the first thump and shudder of the brakes it turned its head towards them, and did not move. It merely glared at them over its shoulder so that the grizzled, moisture-matted pelt folded into its neck like the stole of an ancient king.

That same part of Fergus's mind, the bit that wasn't panicking and bracing his body for impact, wondered at the infinitesimal detail of the scene. A light fog snorting from a greying muzzle. Foliage, crystal sharp in the autumn patchwork of yellow-and-black, leaf-and-bark. The vibrations in a raindrop on the windscreen as the ABS juddered beneath them and they side-slipped over wet leaves with almost no check to their speed. On the edge of his vision the antlers turned to watch them glide past, but Fergus's focus had switched from the stag to the edge of the road and the drop beyond.

His first reaction was panic. The second was rejection. *This isn't happening, this isn't real.* But the verge still punched them nose-up into the air in a detonation of wheels and suspension, making the CD skip as they launched. Reality was a momentary hiccup in a digital scream. Weightless behind a whining engine, Fergus stared horrified at the canopy of an oak tree that loomed in front of them as the nose of the car started to drop. He sensed Kate's arms pushing away from the wheel as if to force herself backwards through her seat, but he didn't see her face. His eyes were locked on the trunk of the oak, a massive pillar of the woods that rushed at the centre of the bonnet. It filled the windscreen beyond wipers that counted them down to oblivion with their metronome beat. Three, two, one...

His final reaction was acceptance. Just before they hit, Fergus knew that the moment was real, that this was the instant of his extinction. And with that knowledge came three heartbeats of calm in which a great sadness dragged him downwards, a sadness so profound it was beyond weeping.

Chapter Two

ON THE OUTSKIRTS of Allingley, Dick Hagman felt the rain trickling off his yellow safety helmet, and hunched deeper into his donkey jacket. In front of him the mechanical digger belched diesel fumes, scooped another load of soil, and swung to dump the mess on the spoil pile. Hagman poked speculatively at the fallen slop with his shovel, watching for pickings. You never knew what might drop out from the stuff at the bottom of the old mill pond. Already he'd managed to pick out a couple of old coins, filched from the mud while the new owner's attention was elsewhere. If Russell saw him, and objected, he'd share the proceeds, fair's fair. But Russell was busy working the digger and might not notice.

The owner was up there now in the shell of the old Mill House, standing in the gap where the great axle had once connected the water wheel to the grinding machinery inside. Bloody incomer with too much money, Hagman thought, sneering at the sight of him mincing round a building site in a yachting anorak and those stupid cream chinos. At least he wouldn't come down into the mud dressed like that. The man started shouting at them and Russell killed the engine to hear.

"... deeper, I want you to do a proper job." Half a sentence spilled out into the sudden quiet. The accent sounded imperious, like a duchess on testosterone. Russell cupped his hand to his ear theatrically, forcing the man to repeat himself. Hagman hid his smirk by wiping the wet off his face onto his sleeve.

"Take it down deeper. There's no point in scraping the surface, it will only fill up again." The accent became clipped and strained as the man tried to establish his authority. He turned away as a loud crash of dropped planks came from within the house, and

Hagman winced as the noise jolted his hangover. He kept his face screwed into the collar of his jacket while the diesel restarted, waiting for the steady throb to anaesthetise his skull. Bloody Halloween party. Last night had got way out of hand. Bloody tight-arsed incomers lording it over us. Hagman wished he'd stayed nicely tucked up in a dry bed.

Hagman didn't want to waste time going deeper. Any good stuff would be nearer the surface, close to the edges where people could have dropped it, like from the earth bank where he stood. In the old days, this dam had given the Swanbourne enough of a drop to power the mill. When he was a kid, families had walked up from the village in the summer to picnic by the pond. Local children still played in the woods above it.

It ought to have gone to a local, this place, but no-one had the money. One of the old families should have taken it, kept it in the community, even if it meant the marsh stayed un-drained and the house had been left to crumble. It looked better that way. Natural, like. And Hagman would never have taken things from the ground while old Bert Millar was alive. Bert's family had always been there, ever since one of them was called 'Millar' because that was his job, running the mill. Now the ancient wheel lay in pieces on the bank, rotted beyond repair but saved from the skip while His Royal Highness decided how to incorporate the fragments as features in his garden. Still, there'd be lots of ways to string this job out and take some of that money off him before they finished.

In front of him, Russell reversed to the beginning of the trench, scowling, lips moving, and started again with another layer. At the limits of its reach the digger strained against the suction of the earth, tilting forwards with the diesel slowing to a near-stall at the effort. Hagman peered into the trench, wondering if some obstacle had snagged the bucket, but saw only black soil in a cut so saturated that the vertical sides wept. Then the ground yielded its grip with a sigh like the exhalation of a long-held breath, rocking the digger back on its tracks with the engine racing to recover.

Hagman shrugged further into his donkey jacket and hissed back at a pair of swans that were arching their necks at him from the bank. He guessed it was only the digger that stopped them attacking. Maybe this was their nest site. Hagman reached into the spoil pile, pulled out a sodden tangle of old sticks, and threw it at them before wiping the slime off his hands onto his trousers. He missed, and the swans pushed their beaks inquisitively at the fallen twigs before settling beside them. Hagman sniffed noisily and wiped his nose on his sleeve. He'd meant to scare them away, not calm them down.

The squall came from nowhere, thumping Hagman in the back and almost toppling him into the mud. More rain came with the wind, falling in great, heavy drops that turned into a chocolate cascade down the spoil pile. Hagman steadied himself and looked curiously at the swans, puzzled at their sudden calm. The sticks he'd thrown now lay curled around one bird, almost as if cradling it. As he watched, the rain sloughed away the surface dirt and a pattern of paler sticks began to emerge. With dry-mouthed disbelief Hagman watched bony digits appear, then an opposing thumb, all impossibly long in the absence of a palm. Behind them the twin bones of a human forearm emerged, splash by splash, from the covering slime.

"Russell!" Hagman's cry was a falsetto screech, the sound of a frightened child calling for a parent.

As the workmen in the Mill House gathered to gawp at the severed arm, the squall rushed over them towards the Downs, stripping the leaves from the trees in swirling eddies of orange. Two miles beyond the village, where the Swanbourne sprang from under the hill, it struck the steep-sided coombe like an unseen wave. As it sprayed upwards it danced grotesquely with the wreckage of a car tumbling end-over-end downwards through the trees, and ruffled the mane of a stag before fading to nothing amidst the rabbit-riddled barrows of the high country beyond.

Chapter Three

INSIDE THE WRECK, Fergus felt no pain. Not yet. Just a succession of brutal impacts that crushed the car ever closer around him. None of them, within his cocoon of airbags, was quite enough to grant him the blessing of oblivion. Even the final blow, a backwards slam so harsh that the car's rear must have cratered the ground, merely threw him doll-like against his headrest.

Silence. At first just the deafening absence of breaking metal, and for a fleeting moment Fergus had time to wonder that he lived. Sights and noises started to push into the jangling wrongness of his head. Gravel sounds of disintegrating glass. Further away, the heavy thumps of a wheel still bounding downwards through the trees. Crushed branches shedding wood and leaves. And above the collapsing airbags, the glimpse of shattered banners of windscreen that turned light into diamonds at the rim of a void.

Then the pain hit. It erupted through trapped and mangled limbs to fill his body, and when there was no flesh left untouched, it went for his mind. For a while he fought, thrashing, at the cliff-edge of madness. When he lost the battle, enough of his rational self remained for him to watch his own screaming fall and to despise what he had become.

By the time the sun was at its zenith above the clouds, Fergus had gone beyond the madness into a hinterland mapped more by faiths than by science, a place beyond pain, beyond even the memory of pain, beyond all substance. He was drifting down a slope, formless, an identity within emptiness like a balloon bouncing gently down a velvet roof in the twilight. Something had happened, something bad, something from which he was now released. The slope stretched to infinity but it too was formless, a spectrum of light from living white above to a black abyss below. He had belonged with the light but the light held the horror and the falling was so easy, so restful, even if the dark held menace in its unknown depths.

There were others above him, within the light. They too were formless, but it seemed natural to him that they should have identity, be individual in their formlessness. There was a man who was of the dark even though he was in the light, a man who wanted him to fade into the depths. There was another, shadowy identity beyond him, less substantial but larger and mightier, someone who watched his fall with regal indifference.

Then there was the woman. She was of the light and in the light, and again it was natural that this faceless identity should be able to smile, to offer encouragement. In response Fergus's mind braced against the slope but the easy downwards drift had become a current. The moment he turned his awareness towards the receding light he felt the pull of the dark. But with the shine of that unseen smile, the light now held more than pain, and at some unthinking level a decision was made, a mere stubborn refusal to let go. If this had been a battle of flesh and blood he would have leaned into the flow's force, bellowing his defiance as he staggered upstream. But Fergus was without substance, and nothing in his unremembered existence had been so hard as to counter that drag with just the will of his mind.

As if respecting his fight, the tide eased, relinquishing its hold. Slowly, with monumental effort, he started the limbless crawl back, accepting the light and the smile and the pain that it held.

Chapter Four

"So, Doctor Harvey, tell me what you see."

Clare Harvey shifted her position in the trench, placing her feet carefully clear of the body, and looked up to where her Head of Department stood on the bank. A crowd of onlookers lined the hedge behind him. Two workmen, the ones who had found the remains, were standing in the garden, near a policewoman who had stayed to watch even though there was no recent crime to investigate. Their faces were twisted into identical grimaces of morbid fascination. Clare's awkward position brought her backside into contact with the trench wall, and a saturating cold started to soak through her jeans. Miles Eaton, Professor of Archaeology and Anthropology, had spoken a little more loudly than was necessary, and put heavy emphasis on the 'doctor'. Clare guessed that the professor's overt use of her title had little to do with professional courtesy and a lot to do with massaging his ego. *See,* he was saying to the crowd, *I am important, important enough to patronise doctors.*

Clare looked down into the trench, hiding her anger. *Finish your posturing, you pretentious little prick, and let me do my job. And then let me publish a brilliant paper in the* Journal of Anthropological Archaeology *in my own name, or at least as Eaton and Harvey rather than Eaton et al.* Et al, *et alia,* and others; the undistinguished fate of those who laboured in the shadow of Miles Eaton, ME, the Mighty Ego. She looked back at him, forcing an engaging smile. *Don't blow it now, girl, this is a chance in a lifetime.*

"It's a bog body, of course, with the head very well preserved.

There is extensive decomposition down the left side. The left arm has been amputated by the digging machinery but we've recovered it from near the spoil pile..." Behind the Professor, one of the workmen looked queasy, and scraped his hand down his trouser as if to rid it of something foul. "There are leather bindings across the torso, and at the wrists and ankles, so we're probably looking at a ritual sacrifice."

"Yes, yes," the Professor interrupted. "All that would be obvious even to one of your undergraduates. Put the evidence in context. Describe the environment. What are the soil conditions?"

Clare waited before responding while an ambulance charged down the road, slowing and wailing its urgency when it reached the gawping crowd at the hedge. The policewoman wrenched her eyes off the corpse and spoke into her lapel radio. Clare was close enough to hear a burst of static and the tinny response. "RTA. Two casualties. Been there a while. Messy."

Clare stared up at the road, wondering about the injured people as the ambulance was obscured behind Professor Eaton's back. He'd turned away, muttering at the interruption. The pompous fool had come to an archaeological site in a tweed suit and bow tie. A *bow tie*, for heaven's sake. She supposed it was part of the image of the eccentric academic he'd been cultivating since his last television appearance. That would also account for the shiny yellow Wellington boots and the black fedora hat. The rain had stopped but he'd thrown a long coat cloak-like over his shoulders and was carrying a walking cane, the very image of a 1930s academic supervising his minions in their fieldwork. He turned back to her as the sound of the siren faded downhill through the village.

"The soil conditions?" he prompted, pointing his cane at the body and waving it in circles to emphasise his question.

Clare squatted in the mud at the bottom of the trench, examining its oozing peat wall. They'd rigged a petrol-driven drainage pump to clear the water but the soil around her was saturated for several feet above the level of the body.

"There are several soil horizons. He's lying in peat..."

"Of course, otherwise the humic acid would not have preserved the body."

Clare looked up at him, eyes flashing her frustration. Eaton was definitely playing to the crowd. He was also standing quite close to the trench, far enough back to avoid breaking its walls, but looking down in a way that told her he was enjoying the view down her shirt.

"... although the top layer of soil looks like alluvial silt."

Clare twitched her anorak closed over her chest and stood up, grabbing at the edge of the trench for support as her vision spotted and a wave of dizziness hit her. For a moment she regretted missing her lunch in her dash to reach the site, but she'd needed to stake her claim to be the field leader. As soon as ME went, she'd buy a sandwich.

"Do you think the peat bog is natural?"

Clare pushed her glasses up her nose and looked round the basin, absorbing the landscape. Upstream from the mill, the bog filled the valley floor between steep, wooded hills. She guessed the woods were ancient, clinging to hillsides that had always been too steep to plough. It would be a good place to go walking or running, about as wild as you could find in rural England. She could imagine quiet, mossy places, the kind that inspired you to pause and inhale a mighty peace.

"Doctor Harvey?"

Clare took a couple of deep breaths, blinked away the last of the light-headedness and focused on the immediate surroundings. Here, by the mill, it looked as if some prehistoric landslip had pinched the valley into a wasp waist, forming marsh above and open valley below.

"I think so. I'd guess this bit of the valley has been bog since the ice age. But the dam and mill pond are most likely medieval."

"You sound very confident."

"Allingley features in the Domesday Book but there's no mention of a mill." One of her researchers had fed her that information by mobile phone, and Clare enjoyed seeing ME blink as she went on the offensive. "So the top layer of silt is probably post-Conquest. He is lying well below that, in the peat layer, so I suspect his burial pre-dates the Conquest by several centuries. Carbon dating will give us a much better view, but I believe we'll find this guy is Saxon." Out of the corner of her eye Clare watched a pair of swans edge closer to the trench. Their necks were arched like cobras, threatening her as she stood with her head at the level of their feet. If they came any closer, she'd climb out.

"My dear girl, don't see what you want to see, just because you're a Saxon specialist!" Eaton sounded jubilant at the thought that he might have caught her out. "So how did you come to that rapid conclusion?"

"The peat has stained his hair orange. That could mean he was blond. If so, he'd be more likely to be a fair-haired Saxon than a darker Celt. But more importantly he's a big guy, much bigger than most Celtic remains. And if he's a Saxon I'd go further. Ritual killings would have finished with Christianisation, so I expect carbon dating to put him between the late fifth and mid seventh century. Do you agree?" *Come on, you old goat, let me prove myself right. Treat me like a colleague, not a freshman.* But the Professor ignored Clare's challenge, becoming preoccupied with making shoo-ing motions at the swans with his stick. The birds only hissed back at him and held their ground.

"So what next steps do you recommend, Doctor Harvey?" Eaton turned back to her with the air of someone who'd found such actions undignified.

Clare paused, gathering her thoughts.

"We should probably try and get the body out in one block, with its surrounding peat."

"Of course. Subject to the landowner's agreement." Eaton nodded towards the house, where the owner had given up his attempts to keep his men working, and was watching the dialogue from a gravel path. The man inclined his head.

"Best practice then would be to freeze-dry the body to inhibit decomposition."

"Quite. And what about the site, the area around the body?"

"We'll need to go through that spoil pile, there's probably all kinds of evidence in that. If we have the resources I'd like to dig some test trenches in this basin." Clare waved her trowel around the bog that had been the mill pond. The swans rocked slightly backwards at the movement but then crept a little closer. "There may be other bodies. Some of the other bog body sites have yielded multiple corpses."

"I suggest you also run a metal detector over the whole area as quickly as you can."

Behind her back, Clare gripped her hand into a triumphant fist at this first confirmation of her leadership.

"As soon as anyone hears the word 'Saxon' they will think of hoards of gold and this gentleman," ME waved towards the owner again, "will find his garden full of treasure-hunters."

Behind Professor Eaton, one of the workmen shifted uncomfortably, and then squinted as a stab of sunlight broke through the clouds. It angled into the trench along the line of its wall, marking the scooping lines of the digger in wavelets of light and shadow. In front of Clare it exposed a fleck of something harder than the surrounding peat, a smooth line about the size of a nub of pencil. Clare crouched, probing at the soil with her fingers. Above the level of the bog man's head was a thin layer of silt, as if the bog had at some time been briefly flooded before reverting to peat marsh. The object was embedded in the silt layer, just above and to one side of the preserved head, and Clare reached to pick it out of the soil with her fingers.

"Tooth!" Clare shouted, polishing it in her hand. "Human tooth!" She stood up triumphantly with the tooth pinched between finger and thumb, but she stood too quickly and her knees buckled. As she fainted, her vision dissolved into hissing fragments of colour, pure white wings mingling with black spots that became swans' faces. Yellow shiny boots disintegrated into stabbing beaks. Somewhere nearby people were shouting, but in the bottom of the trench Clare felt a dreamlike calm. To her, the great wings arched over her were protecting her, shielding her;

the hissing was directed at the men coming to her rescue. The sunlight through the wing feathers was as gentle as the inside of a linen tent on a summer's day, half-seen at the edge of sleep.

Clare's face lay beside the preserved head of the bog man, as close now as a lover on her pillow. His glistening mahogany features provoked no revulsion. In her disoriented state it was as if he was known, known intimately, even loved, so her eyes absorbed each detail of his face in dreamlike peace. Even the tiny cracks in his lips were preserved. He looked as if he were about to wake from his own deep sleep, with his forehead furrowed in the way of someone who was trying to recapture a dream.

As the cold and wet soaked into her clothes and her senses returned, Clare saw that the sun was illuminating a darker pattern under the peat-tanned skin. The shadow that she had thought was a frown radiated from the bridge of the nose out onto the forehead in a pattern too regular and fine to be a blemish. Fully alert now, Clare pushed her body out of the wet and turned to kneel beside him, ignoring the soaking cold around her knees. Gently she touched a finger to his forehead, illogically surprised to find his skin as chilled as the ooze seeping between the fingers of her other hand. Something so perfect should have blood and warmth.

Clare allowed her finger to trace the pattern under the skin, gradually mapping the outline of a stylised stag's head and antlers tattooed into the forehead.

Chapter Five

AT SOME DEEP, unconscious level Fergus knew that Kate was dead, long before they told him, but her death was part of the plot of this fictional world into which he had woken. You go to work one morning and you wake up in a living nightmare of fevered wrongness where you're weighed down by plaster casts and trapped in a spider's web of traction weights, a world of ritual indignity where you can't even piss without help.

There had been days he would remember only as jumbled fragments of time, less ordered than the flashes of passing fluorescent lights as his trolley was wheeled along. There were glimpses of faces behind surgical masks, faces that made no eye contact as he lay passive at the focus of their urgency. Otherwise his existence was bounded by the starched comfort of fresh linen, and hanging drips delivering the blessed relief of morphine.

There came a day when a doctor stood by his bed, talking softly, watching Fergus's face as he delivered the leaden fact that Kate died 'at the scene', but the knowledge was already there. It seeped out of a place his mind avoided without even acknowledging its existence. Fergus stared back, unable to respond, wondering if the doctor would interpret his lack of reaction as callousness. Kate's death was part of this new world of waking dreams. She still lived in the other reality, the reality of sharp confidence, of sales targets and business objectives, the reality to which he also belonged and to which he must return. He managed a blank nod of acknowledgement, going along with the fiction that was fact and the fact that was fiction.

The police came, probing his memories, reaching into the fog.

Yes, he and Kate were colleagues. His mind started to drift and they let him ramble.

"Kate. She becomes Katherine in front of customers, you know? Cool, professional. She charms them."

"You fancied her, didn't you?"

"Of course I fancy her. What man wouldn't? But she won't let a bloody good team be spoilt by a relationship. She's ace, really ace, good enough to sell well even without her looks, but they sure help." He stared up at the ceiling, smiling at a memory. " She has – *had* – a way of tossing her hair out of her eyes in mid-conversation, as if she's a bit irritated by it, like she's throwing aside her femininity, but somehow that makes her seem even more sexy, you know? Sometimes the buying signals start right then."

But a man can dream. You never stop noticing a woman like Kate.

"Mister Sheppard? Fergus?"

Had he slept for a moment?

"Can you tell us what you remember?"

"There was a traffic jam." A horn-blasting, expletive-spitting gridlock. That bit was clear. "We were late for a meeting, an important one. Tried a back road over the Downs."

"And was Kate driving fast?"

More fragments of memory solidified in his head. Rain flattened by the slipstream.

"Kate's a good driver. Was." He hadn't meant to sound defensive.

"Sure, but what speed were you doing?"

Fergus looked towards the place his mind avoided. There was something dark in there that he did not want to find, so he stayed on the edges, peering in, fearful.

"We swerved." But it can't have happened then. Working the GPS had given him a chance to admire the way her legs angled over the seat. GPS. He remembered the icon of a village. Allingley.

"Take your time."

"Leaves. Wind." And a road that curved down into the trees as if diving into the earth. Fergus could not force his mind around that corner. A horror lurked there. His memory disintegrated at that point like a damaged videotape. Losing patience, the police prompted him with what they knew. The marks by the roadside suggested high speed as the car left the road. They'd hit a tree, and tumbled further down the hill. The wreckage had been found some hours later by a couple on horseback, with Kate already dead at the wheel. They said that the emergency services had a difficult job to cut them free. The policemen placed slight emphasis on the plural 'them', watching him as if they were testing his knowledge of something which might trigger some extreme emotion. Fergus stared back, unsure what reaction they had expected. The facts they related were part of this new play in which he was acting. It was as if he had woken up in the middle of the first act and they were bringing him up to date on some of the lines he'd missed, but skipping others.

Fergus wasn't curious. He was relieved that they'd stopped trying to push him round the corner, but he wished that this new reality would go away.

"Visitor for you."

Fergus stared at the woman left standing by his bed as the nurse turned away. The woman was dressed in jeans and a short, well-worn, waterproof jacket that gave off an acrid, farmyard smell. She clasped a small posy of dried flowers in front of her; a dusty, fragile clump of orange too untidy to be shop-bought. He pulled his face into a half-smile, aware that his blank look might be rude.

"Hello." She spoke in the familiar tone of someone who already knew him, as if they already shared some history that needed no explanation. His puzzlement must have shown.

"You don't remember me, do you?" Her voice had the slight rural burr of middle England. He shook his head as she pulled up a chair.

"Sorry."

"I'm Eadlin."

The name meant nothing. Eadlin's smile was wide and confident, stretching freckles over her cheeks to give her a wholesome, polished-apple look. Her face was very slightly plump as if there was too much life inside to fit within the skin, the way a woman can look in the bloom of pregnancy. As she sat, Fergus flicked a glance downwards to where her anorak gaped open but there was no bulge to her belly. Early to mid-thirties, red hair, grey eyes, quite attractive. Whoever Eadlin was, he was glad she'd come. Her eyes held a gentle but intense focus, like some of the doctors, although he sensed she looked beyond the outward symptoms. More priestess than physician, perhaps.

Freckles. Some echo started to tug at the fabric of his memory, pulling at a corner of his mind that was hidden, and forcing him to acknowledge it. Fergus recoiled from that place, smothering the line of thinking before the nightmare could inhale its first scream.

"I found you. And your poor friend." Eadlin spoke matter-of-factly, reaching to put the dried flowers into an empty plastic water cup. "And if you don't remember maybe it's for the best. I brought you some flowers. Dried ones, I'm afraid, there's not much blooming at this time of year. Midsummer marigolds; they're supposed to be good for healing."

She talked on, filling the silence with sound. Fergus muttered his appreciation for the flowers, wishing he could think of something intelligent to say, and fearing his quietness might be ungracious.

"I heard you was out of Intensive Care. They wouldn't let me see you before, not being family, like."

"You're one of the riders." He had finally found his voice. The smell must be horses. "The police told me I was found by riders."

"That's right. Me an' Jake. He thought you was both dead. Luckily me and the ambulance men thought otherwise."

Jake. Another rip in the fabric. It was like trying to hold disintegrating curtains together against the daylight.

"So how are you feeling?"

"Actually I'm not feeling much at all at the moment." Fergus wiggled his fingertips at her from within their plaster casts, trying to keep the demons at bay with a joke.

"That's a bummer." Eadlin smiled at him again, with more humour than sentiment, but the smile was making the curtains in his mind crumble away. He replied unthinkingly, outrageously, anything to hold his head together.

"That's another thing I can't do for myself at the moment. Wipe my own bum." Fergus screwed up his face, becoming agitated within his restraints as he tried to keep his thoughts away from the mess. A fading voice of reason told him that he was being gross to a stranger.

"Are you all right?" Eadlin put her hand on his arm above the plaster cast, in a touch that was disconcertingly familiar, and the sudden look of concern on her face ripped apart the final shreds of fabric in his mind. As the memories flooded back he squirmed in the bed, eyes staring at horrors only he could see. Traction equipment jangled around him with noisy irrelevance as he writhed.

"Nurse!" Her shout was urgent, bringing help running.

Minutes later, as the injected sedative took hold, Fergus saw her leave. In the moment of clarity before oblivion he realised he hadn't even tried to thank her.

Part Two

Ostara

March

Chapter Six

FERGUS DROVE A long detour so as to arrive in Allingley from the south, avoiding the road over the Downs. He wasn't yet ready for that road, not on his first outing in four months. He drove with white-knuckle caution, ignoring the tailback of cars stacking up behind him as he eased around the corners, palms slick with sweat against the leather of the steering wheel. As the road rose towards Allingley there was a straight stretch where a youth in an ageing Ford overtook noisily and gave him the finger as he passed.

Fergus pulled into the side of the road where a church and a cluster of houses around a green told him he had reached the village centre. His hands were shaking as he exhaled and turned off the engine, resting his head forward against the wheel, eyes closed, absorbing the sense of achievement. Life advanced in minuscule increments, a progression of milestones marking banal achievements. Get in car. Solo. Turn ignition. Drive from A to B without crashing or disintegrating into a gibbering wreck by the roadside. If he'd learned one thing in the past four months, it was to keep facing the pain, keep pushing. Pain is an obstacle not a boundary.

Fergus opened the car door to the air, staying seated for a moment to let the daffodil chill of an English spring flood the interior and cool his sweat before he pulled himself upright. He dragged his crutches out of the back and braced himself against the car while he took in his surroundings. A warm tide of blood flowed back into his legs as they adjusted to the new position. Being out and on his own, with no watching nurse or physiotherapist, made him feel vulnerable.

So far, so good. First test passed. He could still handle driving a car. Now to find the woman. Fergus cringed at the thought of his reaction when she'd come to visit him. He owed her his thanks, at least, but the only clues he had were that she was called Eadlin and rode a horse. That probably meant she lived nearby, and Allingley was the only village anywhere near to the crash.

Superficially it looked a picture-book English village. 'Unspoilt', the guide books would say, despite the Forge Garage and its collection of sick cars at the edge of the green. 'Deathly quiet' would be the verdict of anyone looking for any sort of night out, except a trip to the pub. The village stores had the same air of struggling optimism as the 'Vacancies' sign swinging under the 'Bed and Breakfast' board of a nearby cottage. Next to Fergus the church notice board announced Sunday service times in peeling paint, alongside a new poster in big, colourful letters inviting the village to 'Worship With Us In Holy Week'.

It looked like the kind of place where the locals would make it their business to know everyone else's. Already net curtains had twitched in a couple of the cottage windows as residents watched the stranger. A pub would be the place to start. Landlords knew their neighbourhoods and were professional talkers. On the opposite side of the green, a pub sign with a white, richly-antlered stag and a coat of arms swung outside the 'White Hart'. It looked like a refurbished gastro pub with rooms, perhaps serving walkers and cyclists exploring the Downs. Maybe not that pub, today. Stags and Allingley were a bit close for comfort, but down a side street Fergus could see the sign of the 'Green Man'. It looked unpretentious, even scruffy, a locals' local.

Fergus swung towards the Green Man, persuading himself that this was a more likely place to start. He forced himself to walk as upright as possible and to use his crutches for balance rather than support. He'd get rid of the bloody things in a week or so, but at least they were a way of making people give him safe space. Today he didn't want to take the risk of falling over, not this far from help.

The saloon bar of the Green Man was empty apart from a sallow, paunchy man behind the counter who was reading the pictures in a tabloid paper. He looked up as Fergus entered, lifted one nostril and sniffed in a way that said the interruption was unwelcome. Fergus nodded and looked around, not sure how to begin. On the walls there were photographs of the local hunt and recent but framed newspaper cuttings with headlines that proclaimed 'Saxon Grave Found'. There was also a lethal-looking, two-handed sword padlocked to a wall. The sword had an oiled, newly-sharpened air as if it were more armament than ornament.

The man behind the bar made a noise with his newspaper and sniffed again to remind Fergus that he was expected to place an order.

"Do you serve coffee?"

"Nah. We only serve humans in here. No cats, dogs..." He looked Fergus up and down, staring at the crutches. "... or coffees. You could try the White Hart on the green." The lift of the nostril suggested that Fergus was a fool to think it was the sort of place that offered coffee.

"Orange juice, then." It arrived without comment. "Actually, I wonder if you could help me. I'm looking for someone, a woman."

"Aren't we all?"

"She might be local. Probably in her thirties, red hair, called Eadlin?" The man stiffened. "Rides a horse."

"Now why would you be looking for someone called Eadlin?"

Fergus felt his fingers flexing around the handgrips of his crutches, and swallowed the urge to tell the man to mind his own bloody business. Fergus had seen the reaction to the name, and he forced himself to stay calm. This man knew her.

"She helped me, last year. I wanted to thank her."

"You'd best ask the landlord. He may know."

"You're not the landlord?"

"Nah. Only helping out. Landlord'll be back later." Fergus stared at him, wondering why the surly manner was now almost hostile. Hanging behind the man's shoulder was a mirror, partially obscured by bottles, reflecting the pub's windows and the street outside. A woman was walking past, her long blonde hair flowing past her face in the breeze. There was something familiar in that hair and in the way the woman walked. He spun around, but too late to see her face.

"Who was that?"

"Who was what?"

"The woman who just walked past. Blonde hair."

"I didn't see no-one. And I thought you was looking for a redhead. Bit confused, are we?"

Fergus slammed some coins on the counter and grabbed his crutches, ignoring the snort of derision from behind the bar as he turned away.

The woman was turning the corner onto the green as he reached the street, disappearing from his view. Fergus swung after her but by the time he reached the corner, pulse racing at the burst of effort, she was half way across the green heading towards the Downs road. She was walking fast, faster than Fergus could manage, in the low-heeled stride of a woman with a mission and no time to spare. A stride like one he had seen many times before beneath a very similar cascade of yellow-gold hair.

"Kate?" At first Fergus saw nothing strange in his call. It was like catching sight of an old friend after months of absence, or an almost-certain glimpse of recognition in a foreign city. His shout was a cry of excitement and pleasure, which faded into hurt as the woman ignored his call and walked on without turning, hurrying her step. He followed in an awkward, limping gait that was the fastest he could manage, even with his crutches tapping either side to keep him steady. He willed her to turn around before she walked out of sight.

Fergus's pace started to slow as the woman reached the edge of the green and passed out of sight up the Downs road, and the illogicality of the moment dawned on him. He came to a halt where he could see up the road, already wincing at his own foolishness. The woman was letting herself into one of the last cottages in the village. The stranger's face that glared back at him from the safety of her own doorstep was middle-aged, old enough for the long, blonde hair to be an unsuitable vanity.

Fergus sagged as the reality of what he had done hit him, with the ache of unaccustomed exercise already tightening his limbs. He swore at himself and inhaled deeply, forcing himself to get a grip. His mind had tripped, the way he had stumbled at his first attempts to walk, and Fergus hung between his crutches, tossing his head as if insanity was a bothersome fly. The aches became welcome reference points of physical pain that mapped his healing body.

Beyond the cottages, the road climbed uphill between woods and a field for perhaps two hundred yards until it ran past a house standing alone in the narrowing valley. There were cars and a van parked outside the house and a bustle of activity. He focused on the hard reality of the people around the house ahead, welcoming the sounds of distant shouts and the solid thump of heavy tools being thrown into a van. It was as good a place to start as any. He launched himself at the hill, punishing himself with the effort.

Chapter Seven

TWO YOUNG MEN in muddy jeans and anoraks were loading digging tools into the van as Fergus approached the house. They seemed to be clearing up after a morning's work, although they looked too young, too clean, and too bearded to be workmen. A slender, bespectacled woman of perhaps thirty directed operations from the tailgate of an old estate car, where she sat pulling off rubber boots. She watched Fergus's laboured arrival with curiosity as the young men drove off in the van.

"You look bushed!" The woman's smile lit her face. After his sullen reception at the Green Man it was like a refreshing drink on a hot day. She held one bootless foot off the ground and rummaged behind her for footwear, trailing a garish sock from her toes.

"It was more of a hill than I thought." Fergus leaned into his crutches, breathing heavily. "I'm not very fit at the moment."

"So what happened to you?" She'd found a trainer, and waved it at his props.

"Car crash." He hoped that the note of finality in his voice wouldn't sound rude.

"There's a seat inside the gate if you want to sit down for a bit."

Fergus smiled his thanks and pushed through a gate with a newly carved 'Mill House' sign, and slumped onto a bench. His sigh of relief reminded him of his long-dead grandfather, and he forced himself into a more upright, youthful position. In front of him an unkempt garden sloped down to a stream, with a broad marshy area beyond. Rectangular trenches had been dug in the marsh, exposing black, peaty soil. The nearest and largest trench was surrounded by an improvised fence of chicken netting.

"You're not local, are you?" She called her question from her car, and Fergus answered over his shoulder.

"'Fraid not."

"I didn't think so. I must have seen everyone in the village while we were digging last year. They all came to watch." She appeared through the gate carrying a thermos flask. "So what brings you back?"

Fergus felt his shoulders tense. This conversation still loitered too close to the crash. He hadn't learned to talk about it yet, not in ways that didn't embarrass people.

"I'm looking for someone who helped me last year." Fergus tried to relax.

"Coffee?" She sat on the bench beside him, pouring. "I'm Clare, by the way." She clamped the thermos between her knees, held out her right hand to be shaken and offered coffee with the left.

"Fergus." Clare had a way of delaying her smile until after the handshake, as if she had seen behind any façade and was pleased at what she had found. It made the smile considered and genuine. Fergus found himself still holding her hand and looking at her until she ducked her head to one side, as if looking at him around an obstacle, while she waved the coffee cup in reproof. He took it, embarrassed, wondering if he'd met this woman somewhere before.

"What are you doing to your garden?" Fergus covered his confusion by nodding at the view.

"I wish it *was* my garden." Clare glanced at the house, which looked recently and expensively renovated. "This is out of my league. I'm just managing the dig. I'm afraid the owners are out, if you wanted to talk to them."

Fergus shook his head, not understanding. "Dig?"

"Hey, it was in all the papers, last November. Didn't you see the headlines about the Saxon warrior?"

"I must have missed it, but do fill me in." *And it's a good, safe topic*. He smiled but Clare seemed to need little encouragement.

"Imagine." She stood to find a better view of the valley, and waved her coffee towards the village with an evangelical enthusiasm bubbling in her voice. "Back then, this valley might have been the frontier between the Saxon migration and the indigenous Celts, you see? That knoll where the church now stands would have given them a defensible place, with fresh water nearby from the stream."

Fergus looked down the valley to where the church tower pushed the banner of St. George through the trees. Clare's eyes shone with excitement. "These woods would have been full of deer and boar to hunt, and they must have known that the land would be fertile. We even know the name of that first Saxon chieftain. Aegl. Allingley was Aeglingleigh in the Domesday Book. It would have been *Aegl-ingas-leah* in Anglo-Saxon, the clearing of the tribe of Aegl. Whoever Aegl was, he obviously decided it was a place to settle, somewhere to plant his generations."

Clare pronounced the name 'ay-gul' as if it were as familiar a name as 'Day-vid', and he found himself grinning at her. The elfin woman in the dirty jeans and wash-and-go hair was transformed by her passion for her subject, but she caught his look, blushed, and sat down. When Clare spoke again her voice was more controlled, her academic persona now keeping the romantic streak in check.

"Anyway, we got the body out in November, and pretty much stopped then." Clare took off her glasses and polished them. Now she looked like a schoolmistress on a field trip. "The trenches kept filling with water, see? We waited for drier weather in case evidence was washed away in the rains. Ideally we'd leave it longer but the owners want their garden back now they've finished restoring the house. My professor has done a deal; we send in busloads of volunteer students over the Easter vacation, and they get their marsh excavated and landscaped free of charge. We're planning how to do it today."

"What are you hoping to find?" Fergus wanted to reignite her excitement.

"No buried treasure, if that's what you mean." Still the academic. Clare pushed her spectacles back onto her face and wrinkled her nose to make sure they were in place. She left a streak of mud across her cheek and Fergus found that slight vulnerability appealing. Clare's small, gamine face made her look younger, but the first, faint signs of lines around her eyes told him she was at least a decade older than her students. "There wasn't even a buckle with the body, but that isn't unusual for finds like this. He was ritually sacrificed, you see, so they wouldn't have needed to honour him with grave goods. We've found some human bone fragments and teeth from the same period, so we know there was once at least one other body in the vicinity, a female." Clare touched the pocket of her jeans with one hand. The movement seemed instinctive, and perhaps connected with her mention of the female. "And if there were two bodies then there's a good chance there'll be more. The dig will tell us."

"Why the chicken wire?" Fergus nodded at the trench.

"There's a pair of swans who've been a bit aggressive, almost like they're defending the place. Hey, I've got to go. Let me run you back to the village." Clare stood up, throwing her coffee dregs towards the dig. Fergus gathered his crutches and stood to follow.

"I don't suppose you know a local woman called Eadlin? Red hair, rides a horse?"

"I remember seeing a redhead on horseback, but don't know her name. Try the shop or the White Hart, they'll know."

Chapter Eight

FERGUS DIDN'T NEED to ask again. As he lurched his way towards a pub lunch in the White Hart, he paused in the hotel reception to scan a large rack of handbills advertising local attractions. He pulled one out that had a silhouette of a horse and rider alongside the heading 'Ash Farm Stables' and which was, he read, 'Only 2 Miles from Allingley' and offered 'Riding Lessons for All Abilities with our BHSII Qualified Instructors'. He didn't know what BHSII stood for but it sounded impressive. 'Escorted Hacks in our Beautiful Countryside', it said, 'Contact Eadlin Stodman telephone...' There was even a map. Bingo.

Ash Farm Stables looked a fairly run down place at first sight. Or perhaps at first smell would be more appropriate, Fergus thought, sniffing the wind in its muddy car park. Two dilapidated barns beside the farmhouse presumably provided accommodation for the horses, while a third barn had been converted into a covered arena where a small group of women were having a riding lesson.

The front door of the farmhouse itself had an 'Office' sign hanging over it, but Fergus had no need to call. He could see Eadlin Stodman exercising a horse in an outdoor sand school, making it canter around her in a circle as she rotated with her arms outstretched like a circus ringmaster, both hands open towards the horse. The action lifted her jacket to her waist and his glance flickered over her jodhpurs, remembering that his only female company in the last four months had worn a uniform and arrived with a hypodermic. Eadlin's attention was focused on the circling horse and Fergus reached the five-bar gate into the sand school before it cantered between them and she noticed him.

Eadlin did a double-take and glanced at his crutches, her movements faltering. Behind her the horse came to a halt when her attention wavered, lifting its nose in Fergus's direction as if evaluating the stranger. Fergus grinned, embarrassed.

"Hello Eadlin. It's Fergus Sheppard. You came to see me in hospital."

"Fergus! Of course! Sorry, I didn't, like, recognise you..." Her accent reminded Fergus of something that he struggled to define, something homely and warm.

"I was a bit of a mess last time we met. I don't think my own mother would have recognised me then." He paused, wondering how to avoid making his next words sound trite. "I came to thank you. For... er... finding me. And to apologise. I didn't behave well the last time we met."

Eadlin laughed. It was an easy, natural laugh that wiped away his discomfort. "I don't normally have that effect on people, but you're excused! Did I bring back painful memories?" Her burr was pure country tea shop. He should be smelling butter over hot teacakes, not the acrid stink of horse. Eadlin opened the gate to let him through but Fergus almost stumbled when his crutches sank deep into the sand. He recovered, straightened with his legs braced apart for balance, and parked the crutches against the fence. The sand would cushion a fall, anyway, and Fergus found he was keen not to approach those jodhpurs like a cripple. He took the few steps towards her slowly, with his arms spread wide for balance.

"I couldn't remember a thing until you came." Fergus forced his voice to remain calm, as if walking without sticks was the most natural thing in the world. "I must have been blocking it out. Then I recognised you and it all came back. Sorry, it was a bit of a shock."

The horse ambled up to Fergus, sniffing at his pockets.

"He's hoping for a carrot. D'you ride?"

Fergus shook his head. "Never tried it." He started stroking the horse's neck, enjoying the texture. "It's like silk," he said wonderingly.

"His spring coat's coming through. Was it really bad, the stuff you had to remember?"

"We'd been there some hours by the time you arrived. It was an uncomfortable wait." Fergus knew there'd be some questions he couldn't avoid, not with the woman who'd found him. He kept stroking the horse, hiding his face behind its neck, needing the distraction. He found the touch unexpectedly comforting, like a distant echo of childhood, as if he was once again a hurt infant who had found a soothing presence that was large and gentle and warm. It unlocked barriers within him, freeing his tongue. His previous words now sounded flippant, almost disrespectful, so he took a deep breath and released a little truth. "I think I went a bit mad."

So far, no further. Fergus could feel the emotion welling up inside him. One day he would tell the story of the screaming time, but not now, not yet, not here. It was a story for a dark room and a bottle of whisky, with a friend who was close enough to watch him cry.

"He likes you." Eadlin watched his interaction with the horse, and seemed to understand the need to change the subject. "He's opening to you, accepting you, like. For him, that's unusual."

"How can you tell?"

"I know him. He's a rescued horse, a project of mine. He'd been really badly treated when I took him on. He was lame, starving, and injured, and he still doesn't trust people easily. He was going to be put down, but I saw honesty and courage in his eye so I accepted him and called him 'Trooper' because he reminded me of a wounded soldier. He's almost fit now, but I think he's got a bit further to go in his head." Eadlin paused her own stroking of Trooper's rump and glanced at Fergus. "His behaviour is still too, like, unpredictable."

"He's calm enough at the moment." Fergus stroked a spot behind Trooper's ears and the great head drooped in pleasure. He hadn't stood for this long without support since the crash.

"Trust takes a lot more than a good scratch."

Above Fergus the horse lifted its head and touched its muzzle into the angle of Fergus's neck, holding it there so that the warmth of its breath brushed over his skin. A strange sense of harmony started to fill Fergus's mind at this unquestioning animal contact. It made him feel naked, with the essence of his being visible to the animal. Not judged, simply known, and accepted. His eyes started to prickle with an unfamiliar emotion, and he dropped his hand and took a tottering step backwards, as alarmed as if the animal had developed the power of speech. In front of him Trooper simply lifted his head, stared into the distance, and waited to be led. Fergus's recoil from a moment of imagined intimacy was apparently neither alarming nor hurtful, it simply was.

"Are you sure you've never worked with horses before?"

Fergus shook his head, trying to work out whether anything had just happened or whether it had all been in his mind.

"Anyway, I've got to put him away now. I've a class of kids on ponies starting soon." Eadlin smiled in a way that suggested children on ponies weren't her favourite occupation. "Grab a seat over there," she lifted her chin towards some wooden tables and benches in front of the house, "and I'll make us some tea before the little darlings arrive."

Fergus lurched his way to a bench, trying to analyse what had happened with the horse. It had been beautiful and disturbing at the same time, as if the birdsong in the hedgerow had momentarily sounded like choral harmony. It was several minutes before Eadlin placed a chipped mug in front of him and swung her legs over the opposite bench. The steam from the mugs smelt floral and sweet. Indefinable flakes of herb floated on the surface.

"What's that?" Fergus looked down at the tea, studying it with rather ungracious suspicion.

"An old herbal remedy. Camomile, rosehips, and marigolds, sweetened with honey. Try it!"

He sipped suspiciously, deciding it wasn't unpleasant but no match for tannin-thick English Breakfast Tea.

"They're all healing herbs," Eadlin explained. "So are you back at work yet?"

"Next week."

"What d'you do?"

"Sales engineer for a software company. Kate – the woman in the car – used to sell the software, I had to show how it worked so that she could do the deal."

"Are you looking forward to going back?"

Fergus thought for a moment before answering. "I think the main thing for me has been to get out of hospital. All that charging around after sales is a little unreal at the moment." He hadn't admitted that to himself before. Perhaps it was easier to share thoughts with someone who had seen him close to death. He'd held too few real conversations in recent months; words became awkward around a hospital bedside, even with people whose company was normally easy. Friends from the cricket club would arrive, but soon be eating their own grapes and ogling the nurses while they struggled to recreate the camaraderie. "The doctors tell me I should do something physical for a while to rebuild my strength. Lots of walking or cycling. I'm going to buy a bike tomorrow, and start building up my legs."

Eadlin glanced at his crutches and raised an eyebrow.

"Oh, the crutches are just for balance, really. The muscles are still weak but the bones are about as good as they're going to get. They took all the plates and screws out a few weeks ago."

"D'you play sport?"

"I used to play cricket. Batsman. Only local league stuff but it was the main thing I did outside work, in the summer. Oh, and some squash to keep fit, but cricket was a bit of a passion."

"Was?"

Fergus tapped at his legs with a crutch. "They tell me I'm unlikely to sprint for the crease again, so if I can't run around I'd probably be useless as a fielder as well, and I'd be slaughtered on a squash court. Maybe I should take up rowing."

"You could try horse riding."

Fergus smiled, not wishing to be unkind, and sipped his tea while he thought of a polite answer. Across the yard a large, black horse was being ridden through the car park, its flanks heaving and its neck streaked white with sweat. Its rider was a powerfully-built man who sat very upright in the saddle, demonstrating his mastery by holding the animal into the proud curve of a dressage outline. Eadlin had twisted to watch at the sound of hooves.

"Talking of running around, that horse is pushed way too hard," she muttered, "but his owner is someone else you might want to thank for finding you. D'you remember Jake?"

"I remember there was a man with you. I'd forgotten his name."

Something in Fergus's tone made Eadlin look back at him, her eyebrow lifting again. On the far side of the yard, the man dismounted in an athletic vault, and looked hard in their direction as he tied his horse to a rail. Fergus could not recognise him, and wondered why his obligation to thank 'Jake' seemed theoretical when compared to the gratitude he felt to Eadlin. Maybe it was hormonal. He'd come to see the woman who had visited him in hospital, fresh-skinned, eyes sparkling with life. His mind had air-brushed Jake almost to insignificance.

"I remember enough to know that of the three of you, you're the one that I need to thank most. I mightn't have been showing much signs of life but I heard what happened."

Fergus watched the man she had called Jake march towards them. There was a touch of arrogance in the man's step. He'd seen the same swagger in top salesmen. Alpha male, handsome, king of the roost.

"Three? There was just the two of us, Jake an' me."

"Wasn't the tramp with you?"

"Tramp?" She frowned. "We didn't see no tramp."

"No? Weird looking guy, with long, light brown hair and a beard. He had a strange tattoo on his forehead." Fergus touched the point between his eyebrows. "I wondered if he'd fetched you. What's the matter?"

Eadlin had turned very pale, so pale that her freckles looked closer to him than the white skin around them. She did not answer. Beyond her shoulder, Jake had pulled off his riding hat to reveal dark hair plastered flat with sweat, which he finger-combed vigorously as he walked to lift it from his skull. In a moment he had swung his legs over the bench to sit alongside Eadlin, close enough to her to imply intimacy. As he sat, he grinned at Fergus, showing a line of white, even teeth, and caressed the back of Eadlin's neck between his thumb and forefinger. Fergus was not sure if the brief gesture demonstrated affection or possession. The man dropped his riding hat on the table and thrust a hand at Fergus.

"Jake Herne." Jake's handshake was stronger than necessary but his smile was amiable.

"Fergus Sheppard." Fergus faltered, unsure how to continue, and not understanding his own reticence. Perhaps it was an instinctive reaction to someone who was far too bloody good looking, and radiated a sexuality that hit even Fergus's male radar. Then maybe it was just the way Jake's handshake arrived palm-downwards, asserting authority as well as welcome. Fergus's boss shook hands like that. Jake looked sideways at Eadlin in a silent request for an explanation. Eadlin shuffled on the bench, putting enough space between them to assert her independence, but staying close enough to acknowledge a relationship.

"Jake, you probably won't recognise Fergus. He was in a bit of a mess the last time you saw him, in that crash last November on the Downs road."

Jake's head swung back to Fergus, his expression now curious.

"I remember. How are you?" His voice had the same slight burr as Eadlin's, but a stronger resonance, like an actor's.

"Getting fit, thank you." Fergus mumbled the platitude. "I came to thank you for rescuing me." His 'you' embraced them both.

Jake sat a little straighter and smiled. "You was lucky we rode past. No-one would have seen you from the road. But we never did hear how that crash happened."

"We swerved to avoid a stag." Fergus gave the minimum answer, feeling vulnerable, sensing the fracture lines in his composure. He wanted to return to the easy flow he had felt with Eadlin, but his answer gripped Jake's attention, making him sit forward, excited, staring. Jake's eyes were dark and deep-set, so for a moment they seem to peer through his face rather than be part of it.

"Fergus said he saw someone else at the crash, a tramp." There was a rush to Eadlin's voice, like a sudden nervousness, poorly masked. She too was staring, wide-eyed, and Fergus looked from one to the other, puzzled.

"At the time I thought he might have been a tramp. He looked rather unkempt. With hindsight maybe he looked more like a 1960s hippy. Long hair and beard, new age tunic, that sort of thing." Fergus heard himself falling into his usual trap of covering issues with flippancy.

"And the tattoo," Eadlin prompted.

"Yeah." It was time to filter what he said. Fergus felt himself teetering on the brink of memories that he tried not to acknowledge, let alone share.

It had been after the screaming time, when he began to drift in and out of consciousness. He would wake up, crying, aware that time had passed, and too far gone by then to feel shame at what he had become. One time when he woke, a tramp was standing by the crumpled mess of the bonnet on Kate's side of the car. The rain had stopped and there were woodland noises of birdcalls and wind through leaves, sounds of peace sighing over collapsed airbags that spread out like tablecloths in front of them. Bloody stains seeped outwards in the wet. Earthy autumn smells mixed with engine oil and blood. Kate's airbag was humped over the steering wheel, and she had fallen forward with her hair fanning out over the stains, gold tumbling onto rose.

Then there was the tramp, standing over her. From the wreckage of his being Fergus gathered the energy to speak. He could feel the pressure building up inside him, reaching for the critical point where sound would have enough force to be heard. "Help me," he might have said. "Stay with me." But even these simple sentences would not form in his head.

"*Please.*"

The syllable slipped from his lips in a bubble-burst of blood. Lumps of it flicked in front of his eyes as they arced away through the windscreen void to speckle the airbags with more crimson. As the tramp turned his head the tattoo on his forehead looked like a royal diadem, and in the coldness of the stare beneath, Fergus knew he was utterly irrelevant. It was as if his imminent death had been laid before a god to whom such deaths were meaningless, just the bloody game of mortals. Then the tramp turned back to Kate and stretched his arm through the void to touch her hair with the back of his hand.

"Fergus? The tattoo?" Eadlin brought him back to the present.

Filter. Filter hard. Lock it away. Fergus took a gulp of his cooling tea, if only to take time to collect himself. He gripped the mug two-handed to mask the shaking he could feel building in his hands.

"Yeah. He had a strange tattoo between his eyes," he jabbed a thumb at the spot, "like an inverted triangle. And a broken circle or a branch on each side above it. You know, it was a bit surreal because it looked like a stag's head, and that's what we'd crashed trying to avoid. But I was pretty far gone by then..."

His voice tailed away. They were looking at him in a way that he didn't understand. Jake listened intently, radiating an excitement that seemed almost sexual, but Fergus paid him little attention. He was fighting the quicksand suction of the memories. He dropped his eyes to stare at the table-top, its wood still slick with winter damp, but saw only fingers reaching through a void where a windscreen had once been. He could no longer mask the shaking in his hands. Eadlin looked away, over her shoulder to where Jake's horse was hanging its head by the rail.

"Jake, your horse should be sponged and rugged. He'll chill quickly in this weather."

"In a bit. I want to hear more."

"Do it now, Jake. While you're on my yard you'll treat your horse properly."

Fergus heard the steel in Eadlin's voice, but focused all his attention on the mug of tea, gripping it hard as if it was his only hold on sanity, watching the way the liquid danced and slopped. He knew that Jake was standing, staring at him, and that Eadlin was waving him away in a low, emphatic, chopping motion. *Go*. But Fergus was sliding into his own mental pit and was only vaguely aware.

There had come a time when even the pain faded and his eyes settled into a fixed stare, an unwavering line that had been determined by the angle of his skull where it had slumped back into the headrest. His line of sight passed uphill through a trail of broken bushes to where a woman waited above, holding two horses, one black, one chestnut. Fergus had been woken into a final flicker of consciousness by the touch of a hand on his neck, feeling for a pulse. A man's head floated in and out of the line of vision. In Fergus's memory it moved the way a hawk's head rotates and focuses down its beak at its prey. The eyes scrutinised him as dispassionately as a scrap of offal, then looked away as the man shouted back over his shoulder.

"This one's dead too."

The sounds penetrated Fergus's brain slowly, from a great distance. In time he decided that these words were something to which he should respond. Perhaps he should make some sign, announce his existence. While the scattered fragments of his mind were assembling, the picture in front of him altered. Now it was the man who stood with the horses and the woman whose face came into his line of vision. The result of all Fergus's effort to speak was just a tiny movement of his tongue, but the stretch of skin across his cheeks told him that his face was set within a hardened mask of blood. The blood was a sealing crust around his lips but was still salty-slimy within his mouth, and the taste distracted him. There had been something he had wanted to do, but now it was more important to savour the salt and watch the gentle, orange rain of oak leaves drift across his vision.

Strange how some things can be so clear. Sunlight after rain, falling leaves, and a freckled face that screamed into a mobile phone for an ambulance. Some things weren't so clear. A shouted argument about enough blood being spilt already; that wasn't clear.

And singing. Not the soothing softness of a lullaby, but more of a chant, a summons that demanded attention. Then came the smell and taste of unknown herbs crushed under his nose and pushed through the bloody crust into his mouth, a bitter sharpness in the slime. Finally just the chanting, the insistent call which stayed with him like a gentle drumbeat as the world faded.

"Fergus?" When he did not answer she reached across and gripped his wrist, hard enough to hurt. "Are you alright?" He managed to smile up at the freckles as she pulled him out of the pit.

"Sorry." Fergus wiped his face, glad to find that Jake had left them. "It's still a bit raw. School's out." He nodded towards the car park, where a noisy rabble of children was tumbling out of parents' cars, clutching their riding hats.

"My next class." Eadlin squeezed his hand again. This time the touch was gentle. "D'you have far to go?"

He told her where he lived, almost an hour's drive away.

"Don't drive any more today. Please. Stay in the village. The White Hart is good if you don't mind spending some money. Come back here tomorrow so we can talk some more."

Fergus liked the idea of talking more. Then children engulfed them with demands to know which ponies they could ride and could I please please please have Conker who was so sweet last week. As they shrieked they made sideways glances at the man with crutches who was sitting with his face turned aside and who might be crying. Eadlin sent them away to fetch ponies and turned back to him.

"D'you realise that horses can help people heal? Body *and* mind?"

Eadlin's words would have seemed preposterous but for Fergus's flash of chemistry with Trooper. His smile remained sceptical.

"Nah, seriously, and not just because you need to develop balance and co-ordination. Why d'you think Trooper responded to you?"

Fergus shrugged. "Maybe he was still hoping for a carrot."

"Nah. He, like, saw your pain. One damaged animal recognised another." She put some carrots on the table as she rose to look after the children. "Go and give him a treat. Come back tomorrow morning and we'll chat."

Chapter Nine

IT WAS BIZARRE how rapidly his mood could change. This new euphoria had to be unnatural, perhaps an over-correction to his earlier state of mind, but while it lasted Fergus was having a very good evening.

"It's choir night on Thursdays, love," the barmaid in the saloon bar said with easy familiarity, folding her arms and leaning on the counter so that her breasts bulged amiably towards him. "They have choir practice in the function room through there." She nodded towards a set of double doors off the bar. "It's got a piano, see? You'll find the lounge bar much quieter."

Fergus had chosen the saloon bar nonetheless. The lounge bar had a stag's head mounted over the fireplace. Not inappropriate, he supposed, for a pub called the White Hart, even if the one on the wall was a conventional, dusty brown. It had none of the majesty of the beast he had seen on the road, either; this was more of a Bambi with antlers. It stared at the room with an expression of mild surprise on its face, and he had stared back, eye to glass eye, until his demons faded. Face the pain. Always face the pain, but that doesn't mean you have to drink with it.

So he sat alone in the saloon, regaled with fragments of choral harmony, beside a blackened inglenook fireplace where apple logs blazed against an old iron fireback. To reach this seat he had needed to duck under beams draped with dried hops like parchment decorations, tapping his way with a newly-acquired stick in one hand and a pint of dark ale in the other.

Fergus was pleased with this stick. He'd selected it from a rack in the hallway, opportunistically placed there by the inn to sell locally crafted walking sticks to guests. It had a heavy ball of root wood for a handle which he was caressing as he sat, enjoying its polished texture and the pleasure of making a purchase. This was a man's stick, as muscular a walking aid as he could find, not some bentwood refugee from an old people's home. It had inspired him to jettison his crutches into the boot of his car a week earlier than the physiotherapist had recommended. He had become tired of the complexities of negotiating doorways with them, and more importantly, they left him with no free hands to carry things such as glasses of beer. Besides, his totter round the sand school had proved that he could manage without, at least for short periods.

Fergus lifted his glass in salute to himself, took another pull at his drink, and reflected that he had never before appreciated the warmth of the colour black. Black ale, thick with alcohol. Black beams, heavy with age. Black iron fireback, dusted with ash so that its pattern of a coat of arms showed in grey relief. Sparks rising bright against the dark from the crack and spit of the fire. A blackboard chalked with 'Today's Special – beef and ale pie', a slice of which had oozed black mushrooms onto a plate in front of him. Even, or perhaps especially, the barmaid's black skirt which stretched over her rump as she stoked the fire. His mood had swung to the state where he was deliriously happy to sit with good beef in his belly and a pint of ale in front of him. Easter anthems would not have been his first listening choice, but any live music was a bonus, even if it was interspersed with bellowed directions from a music director.

Full of bonhomie, Fergus supped and quaffed, feeling heady with freedom. There was the freedom to choose where he would sleep rather than in his allocated bed in a ward. There was the freedom to spend money, to drink ale, to spread newspapers across a table and then choose the time when he would go to bed. And tonight there would be no noises from nearby patients to disturb him, no low key lighting or the whispered routines of nursing shift changes. Fergus sipped more beer, and tried to guess the composer of the music being sung next door. His knowledge of classical music had improved a lot in the months in hospital, when he'd soothed himself with Schubert on his iPod rather than suffer the snores from the next bed. This composer eluded him, but he stretched his legs towards the fire with a sense of deep contentment.

A brick recess near his shoulder held a collection of dog-eared paperbacks and local guides. Fergus sifted through them, searching for reading material to pass the evening, and pulled out a small, card-and-paper booklet entitled *History of the White Hart*. 'Saloon Bar Copy – Please Do Not Remove' had been written on its cover in thick felt tip.

'There has been an inn on this site since at least 1532...' he read, *'serving travellers on the Downs Road, which was then a more important thoroughfare...'* Standard stuff. Local families, refurbishments, a proud tradition of serving the wayfarer... Fergus stifled a yawn as he flicked through the pages, feeling the ache of the day's exercise pull at his muscles.

'Hart' is Old English for 'stag', and the rare and beautiful white hart has been part of British folklore since time immemorial. In medieval times, the white hart was thought to be an animal that could never be captured, and like the unicorn they came to symbolise unattainable purity. In Arthurian legend, the appearance of a white hart inspired chivalric quests. Richard II, King of England from 1377 – 1399, adopted the white hart as his emblem, and the coat of arms on our inn sign is King Richard's.

However their reputation has not always been so enchanting. In pagan times the white hart was a harbinger of doom, a sign that a fundamental law had been broken, and that a terrible judgement or even death was imminent.

Fergus's mouth felt dry and he took a pull at his pint before breathing deeply and reading on, irritated by his own sensitivity. His euphoria had evaporated. Across the room, a middle-aged man in a battered tweed jacket and a clerical collar came into the bar and ordered half a pint. As Fergus looked up, the priest smiled in the confident way of someone well practised at being friendly with strangers. Fergus smiled briefly in response, and lowered his gaze to the booklet.

Today we know that there is a natural, if prosaic reason for white harts. A rare genetic mutation causes a condition called leucism which affects their pigmentation. We also know that they are no harder to capture than any other deer. Sadly, such is their rarity that they are valuable trophies, and any that are known to exist are rapidly targeted by unscrupulous poachers.

So if, in the mossy depths of our ancient woodlands, you spy a ghostly, antlered form, enjoy the privilege of an ethereal moment, but take care only to tell those who will also revere...'

"May I join you?" The priest was already pulling out a chair at Fergus's table. "It would be strange for two people to drink alone in the same room."

Fergus looked up, glad of some company but feeling an Englishman's reserve towards the priesthood. The dog collar was both a licence to talk and a barrier to conversation.

"John Webster, Vicar of St. Michael's over the road." The handshake was almost as firm as Jake Herne's, but Webster's smile reached to his eyes and crinkled them into fans of laughter lines. A touch of the same confidence, perhaps, but less ego. Webster had wiry, greying hair above an open, friendly face, and the physique of a retired rugby player. His fist made the half pint mug look like a toy. "I came to have a drink with the choir, after their practice."

"They're good, aren't they?" As Fergus spoke, a sweet harmony from beyond the doors was interrupted by a friendly tirade about diphthongs. Fergus furrowed his brow in puzzlement until the priest explained that it was something to do with pronunciation.

"They're worth an army of evangelists," Webster finished with a sigh of appreciation.

"You'll have to explain that."

"Ah. Our congregation has doubled since Tony Foulkes – he's the one doing the shouting – took over the choir. I give them theology, he gives them joy," he said with a modest smile, his eyes glistening. "People come to hear the music, and sometimes a little faith rubs off along the way."

"I would have placed his accent more in the Welsh valleys than Southern England."

"Tony married a local girl and they settled back here when he took early retirement a few years ago. So what brings you to Allingley?"

Fergus told him, in as few words as possible.

"I remember that day, only too well. A woman died, didn't she?" John Webster's demeanour was more alert, shifting from conversational to pastoral.

"That's right. Kate. She was a friend of mine."

"I'm sorry. I remember you were badly hurt. Are you recovering?"

"Getting there." Fergus felt himself retreat, sitting back in his chair and pulling his beer towards him. He'd already embarrassed himself enough at Ash Farm, so for heaven's sake let's talk about music or local legends. But the way Webster looked at him gave Fergus a glimpse of a great compassion hovering behind the half pint of beer and crinkling eyes, in the way a candle will throw a larger shadow than the physical object. After a long pause the priest spoke again, more softly now.

"If you ever want to talk, let me know."

Fergus swigged his beer and said "thanks", but put his mug down on the table with a click as crisp as a closing door. For a moment he stared at the booklet on the table by his hand.

"Actually there's something that's, well, a bit unsettling." He spun the booklet so the priest could read it. "This bit about white stags being harbingers of death..."

"Oh, that old wives' tale!"

"My crash... We left the road trying to avoid a stag."

Webster looked up from the article, his expression guarded.

"And was it a white stag?"

"Not really. Its mane and muzzle were fairly grey, but that looked like age. I think it was just a red deer that had been around long enough to go grey."

Webster looked down at the article again. "And had you 'broken some fundamental law', either of you?"

"Quite a few speed limits." Fergus grinned as the mood lifted.

"Well, there you are, then." The answering smile looked relieved.

"It's strange, though, that the first guy on the scene afterwards should have a tattoo of a stag on his face."

It was as if the conversation had stepped out over a void. The smile drained from Webster's face until he looked as if he was about to be sick, the way Eadlin had looked for a moment at Ash Farm. He searched Fergus's eyes, looking, Fergus guessed, for signs of falsehood. Finding none, he sat back in his own seat.

"Dear God, not you, too."

In a moment Webster had switched from being almost boyish and affable to seeming old, as if he had shrunk inside his jacket. Fergus realised that Webster was probably the kind of man whose face was an open book, making it hard to hide his feelings. Whatever he was thinking became transparent, and at that moment he was frightened.

"Are you going to tell me what's going on?" Fergus swallowed, feeling nervous. He'd never seen a frightened priest before. When Webster spoke, his voice was quiet, deadpan, coming from somewhere hidden inside him.

"Did you hear about the Saxon warrior they dug up on the day of your crash? He had a tattoo of a stag on his forehead."

Fergus stared at him while a fault-line opened in his mind. In front of him, everyday reality. Blackboard, menu. Black beams. A black priest's shirt beneath a clerical collar. Inside his head, the kind of grating discord of the early days after the crash, a tumbling wrongness with no points of reference, filled with fragments of a reality he wished he'd never known. A tattooed tramp. A golden fan of bloodied hair. *Please.*

The first reaction is panic. The second is denial. Fergus moistened his lips with his tongue, swallowed again, and reached for his drink.

"The guy I saw was no ghost, if that's what you mean."

Webster's face lifted, his expression hopeful.

"He was real. He moved." Fergus closed his eyes, trying to shut out the image of dirty fingernails caressing Kate's hair.

In the next room the choirmaster interrupted the singing again. Life continued as normal around them. "Cynthia, my dear," came through the door, "you have a lovely voice but the sopranos don't have the melody here. Give the poor altos their chance for stardom."

"I need another drink." Fergus pushed on his stick to heave himself upright. "Let me get you one, too." His steadiness on his feet surprised him, but Webster saw the challenge of the stick and leapt to his feet to help.

"You said 'not you too'," Fergus prompted as they carried their drinks to the table.

"Are you a Christian, Fergus?"

"Only nominally. Carol service at Christmas, that sort of thing."

"Like most of the population these days, sadly." Webster stared into his beer, his manner now care-worn rather than frightened. "This parish will probably be my last job before I retire. I was never destined to rise very far in the church. I was always too, too..." He fumbled for a word. Mentally, Fergus offered a few. Honest? Transparent?

"... straightforward. Not enough of the ascetic in me, you see? The bright ones get Deaneries or Bishoprics, but I was offered Allingley, and I was content. A rural idyll where the Vicar can play cricket for the village eleven on Saturday, and lead his parishioners to the pub after morning service on Sunday. A reward, perhaps, for twenty years in the inner city slums. But there have been times in the last few months when this quaint little backwater has felt like the front line in a very old battle."

Fergus let him gather his thoughts, surprised by the man's candour.

"When that Saxon was discovered, you see, there was huge media attention, much more than anyone round here had been used to handling. A kind of collective hysteria took over the village. Oh, things started innocently enough, school outings to Sutton Hoo, that kind of thing, but then it got out of hand. At first it was only children leaping out of the bushes dressed as Saxons and frightening old ladies, but then it became more serious. There are rumours of unspeakable rituals in the woods, things I thought had died out in the Middle Ages. Cynthia Lawrence's son – Cynthia is the soprano you can hear now – was nearly drowned when local boys tried to re-enact the Saxon's death by holding him down in the stream. There were even stories of the Saxon's ghost being seen in the village."

"Ah."

"Quite. Some of the sightings you can dismiss as being part of the hysteria, but others... Well let's just say they are sensible people. Members of my congregation. Christian teaching speaks of evil as a real, tangible force, but this is the first time I have felt the truth of that doctrine so powerfully."

Next door, the choir launched into an anthem, and as the harmonies of faith soared, the strain on Webster's face eased until he sat back in his chair, closing eyes that were starting to moisten in appreciation. A trace of a smile started to play around his lips.

"Don't tell anyone. Please." He sat upright in mid-verse, and looked directly at Fergus to emphasise his request. "They'll finish now. Please don't tell them about the man with the tattoo."

"Of course not, but why...?"

"I'd hoped that things were getting back to normal. There have been no sightings for several weeks, but some of the choir still won't go out at night on their own." In the background the music was building into a *fortissimo* 'Amen', the choral parts diverging from bass to soprano in a final, exquisite chord, and Webster waved towards the sound. "Let them keep this joy. Please."

"Some people already know. Eadlin Stodman, who found me..."

"And?"

"Jake Herne."

Webster's shoulders slumped and an expression of pain crossed his face. Behind him the function room doors opened, spilling a flow of chattering people into the bar. Webster stood, forcing a smile as they clustered around him, calling their greetings. On the far side of the room a large, florid man of perhaps sixty led the way to the bar and slapped the counter with his palm, demanding drinks for thirsty choristers. Fergus recognised the tones of the choirmaster, Tony Foulkes.

"Can you sing, young man?" Foulkes boomed at Fergus as Webster introduced them. Foulkes projected sound as if a performance was still in progress, with a rumble in his voice like the edge of laughter. Fergus suspected that the only time that Foulkes would be quiet was when he was looking at a piece of music where the tenor line was marked *pianissimo*.

Fergus shook his head. "People only ask me once."

"Well never mind, an inability to sing has never bothered this lot." The words were called without malice, as a broadcast tease that drew derisory responses from his choir. "Grab your drink and join us, if you want. The hard core musicians are about to have some fun."

John Webster's introduction had included a brief explanation for Fergus's visit, and the choir welcomed him into their midst as if the community of Allingley needed to make amends for his misfortune. Foulkes' wife led Fergus towards the function room, ensuring his inclusion. Julia Foulkes was a petite, fine-boned woman, elegantly groomed and still slender in middle age, with a porcelain delicacy that suggested chintz curtains and a heritage of Empire. She planted a gin-and-tonic on top of Bach and spread music across the piano, asking Fergus his preferences. Did he like Gershwin? Hoagy Carmichael, perhaps? So much more fun than Handel, don't you think?

"Are you joining us, John?" Foulkes laid his hand on Webster's shoulder, helping the priest to extract himself from conversation with Cynthia the Soprano. Cynthia proved to be a large, overdressed woman who was waving a port-and-lemon and enthusing about a holiday in Spain where she had become, apparently, "quite good at flamingo dancing."

"Thank you, Tony, no. I'll walk Mary home." A round, homely woman looked up from a pile of music, relief lighting her face, and smiled her thanks. She had the sort of arms that looked as if they would be more at home dusted with flour and kneading dough rather than sifting music, but there was a hunted, nervous look about her. Fergus had the impression that she had been sorting music to delay leaving. As Webster helped her into her coat, arms protectively round her shoulders, he stared at Fergus, his meaning written clear on that open book of a face. His look was a statement, a plea, and a warning, and said, *this is my flock. I am their shepherd.*

Chapter Ten

DICK HAGMAN WATCHED Jake Herne pull another pint in the Green Man. Jake was taking his time over it, teasing them, milking the story. All conversation had stopped, as if drawing a pint was now a novel and fascinating activity. Hagman squirmed in frustration on his stool in the corner of the bar.

"Well go on, then," one of the drinkers prompted, an edge of excitement in his voice.

"Like I told you, he saw him." Jake slid the pint across the bar, and scooped coins back towards the till. "Just like the others."

"Prob'ly saw it in the papers." That was Russell Dickens at the other end of the bar. Russell held his pewter tankard in a great, oil-stained paw as if it was a natural extension of his arm, the way he held his workshop tools. "Just like the others."

Hagman didn't know what had got into Russ lately. Wouldn't say boo to a goose, normally, a gentle giant who avoided arguments. Now he was needling Jake in a way that was more than a game, it was personal. Hagman was surprised Jake hadn't lost his cool before now. There were rumours that Russ had been making eyes at Jake's girl, as well. That'd be brave. Jake wasn't a man to cross.

"Nah. This guy thinks he saw a tramp, but he was spot on about the tattoo."

Another shrug. "Proves nothin'."

Jake just polished a glass in a nonchalant way, like he'd been keeping something back that would kill the argument.

"That car crash. This bloke says they crashed trying to avoid a stag in the road."

There was an intake of breath from the group. The line of faces along the bar between Hagman and Russell all stared wide-eyed and open-mouthed at Jake. Hagman shut his own mouth and straightened on his stool. Jake stood square to his bar, hands resting on the wood the way a captain might stand on the bridge of his ship. Proud of himself. In control.

"So what?" Russell again, determined to spoil the fun. "It was November, during the rut. There'd have been stags ranging all over the woods." There were murmurs of protest around the bar. People wanted to believe the spooky version.

"We made it happen, and you know it." Jake stared hard at Russell, his irritation finally showing.

Hagman looked around the bar, watching their faces. They'd all been there, that night, except for the old man by the fireplace.

"Bullshit." It sounded as if Russell was running out of words just when it got interesting, but there was a cackle and a "you tell 'em, Russ," from the old guy. Jake slapped the bar with his hand.

"Listen, you stupid sod. Remember we sacrificed a stag at Samhain. Are you too thick to make the connection?"

Hagman rubbed his hands together in his lap. This was getting nasty; maybe there'd be a fight. Hagman wasn't sure who'd win if it came to that. Jake was fit. He worked out a lot, and rode that horse of his, but Russell was bigger by at least two inches. Broader, too, and not fat. Probably stronger, but slower. It'd be an interesting fight.

"I remember you invited me to a Halloween party in the woods, but just because you can recite the Lord's Prayer backwards don't make you no warlock."

"Don't piss me off. You don't know what you're playing with."

"And you do?" The two glared at each other across the bar.

"Think about it, Russ." One of the drinkers tried to mediate. "It does seem a bit strange..."

"It was just a Halloween party that got way out of hand. Nice fancy dress, Jake, but the rest was mumbo-jumbo and I don't hold with slaughterin' a beast like that."

"But then we found the Saxon the next morning..." Hagman thought Russ was being unreasonable.

"We'd been told to dig there anyway."

"But think *where* it happened, Russ." Another attempt at persuasion from the crowd.

"And you think *what* happened. If we made it happen, and that's a bloody big 'if', a woman died, for fuck's sake. This ain't no joke any more, and I don't want no part of it."

Russell stared around the group. Some of the drinkers looked down but no-one replied. When Russell spoke again his voice was heavy with contempt. "Hey, you guys really believe this shit, don't you?"

In the silence that followed, Jake lifted his right hand, and for a moment Hagman thought he was reaching for a weapon, but Jake just jerked the cord of the ship's bell over the bar.

"Time."

"That's never bothered you before."

"This is now a private party, for my invited guests. And you ain't invited."

Russell looked around the room. Several men shuffled their feet, embarrassed. Russell was well liked.

"Jake, you always was a bit mad. Now you're proving it."

"Take your tankard with you."

Russell Dickens stretched out his arm and upended his tankard, sending a tidal wave of beer over the bar. The nearest drinkers recoiled, protesting, but Hagman on his stool couldn't move fast enough, and a stream of beer landed in his lap. "'ere, look out!"

Nobody took any notice of him. They were watching Russell's walk to the door. Most of them lowered their eyes as he passed.

"You too, granddad," Jake called to the old man in the corner.

"All right, I'm goin'." The old man struggled upright, muttering "bloody lunatics" under his breath, and followed Russell.

Jake mopped his bar into a spill tray with practiced ease. "This one's on me." He put a bottle of brandy on the counter.

"So are you goin' to have another party in the woods then, Jake?" Hagman liked Jake's parties. People lost their inhibitions when they put on a mask, especially the girls.

"They're not parties, they're sabbats, you idiot. And it'll be Ostara in a couple of weeks."

"Yeah, right."

"I still don't buy this." At least one of the drinkers was unconvinced. "I mean, it's a good story an' all, but are you really sayin' that we started all this Saxon stuff?"

"Well either that or it's a bloody big coincidence." Jake pushed the stopper back in the brandy bottle with enough force for the movement to sound like a blow.

"Careful, lads," a voice called from the back, "before someone else gets chucked out."

"Nah, we're all safe." Hagman mopped his trousers with a bar towel, wondering how far he could go with the banter. "None of the rest of us have been sniffin' at Jake's girl, have we?"

"I heard things are a bit rocky there. Is that right, Jake?"

Hagman looked up into the sudden silence, flickering his glance between Jake and the sceptic, and pushed the towel onto the bar as if it was a peace offering.

"'Ere Jake." The way Jake looked at him made Hagman wonder if he should shut up, but he ploughed on anyway. "If you've got this power, what are you goin' to do with it?"

"Just wait and see." It sounded as if Jake was still thinking that through. "Maybe it's time we put that priest in his place."

Chapter Eleven

IN HER FLAT near the university, Clare Harvey's sleep was disturbed. Twice now she'd woken up sweating, with her duvet over her face, fighting it back amidst dreams of being smothered. The first time, the dream had hovered on the edge of memory, fading as she became fully awake and saw the cold radiance of her bedside clock in the darkness. Fragments of dream floated away from her, something about swans and the trench, all tumbling away into the dark, like scraps of paper blown by the wind beyond her reaching fingertips. 1:43 the clock said, its dots blinking steadily in the night. Clare groaned and rolled over, pushing the duvet off her shoulders until the sweat cooled and she sank back to sleep.

IN THE UPSIDE-down world of dreams, she stands outside the protective mesh around the dig, but one of the swans is inside, in the bottom of trench, where Clare should be working. The swan has stretched one wing over the shoulders of a woman lying face down in the mud, almost as if it is comforting her, or protecting her body, or maybe even holding her down. As Clare begins to wonder how a woman's body came to be in her dig, the woman twists to look up at her. She is lovely, despite her muddy pallor, with a striking, high-cheeked, flaxen-haired beauty, but her eyes are wide and white and pleading. She holds a hand out to Clare, begging, and the lift of her arm moves the swan's wing to cover her face, so that her cry for help is muffled, seeming to come from within Clare's head.

So Clare reaches down into the trench to her, without wondering that the mesh is no longer there, but the woman's hand flails around blindly and grips her wrist as if she is drowning and Clare is her only hope of salvation. Clare braces against the pull but the draw is too strong, and she overbalances into a swirling chaos of feathers in which the Saxon's face sleeps serene in the fresh colours of life.

Some far recess of Clare's mind tries to tell her that he should be in her laboratory, eviscerated into post-mortem components, but she manages to dismiss the thought. He is there and he is beautiful, lying in pretend sleep while she holds herself above him, resting on her arms so that her hair cascades around his face. The strands make a tent that glistens in the sunlight; her gold tangled with crisper curls the colour of ripening wheat where it catches in his beard.

The same, distant, almost-conscious corner ponders the long, blonde hair but decides it is a minor irrelevance. He lies on his cloak in the forest, on lush grass not cold peat. The place is special to them; it is their tryst, a grove where the canopy of leaves breaks the mid-day sun into dancing fragments of light. The moment is complete in the afterglow of their love and the chance to trace her finger over the sacred sign on his face. No distractions can be allowed to intrude.

His eyes snap open. Grey, smiling eyes. Why should this be new and good information? He breathes, puffing her hair out of his face so that she giggles with the touch of his breath on her skin, and he moves. Swiftly, powerfully, he turns her on her back so that for a moment Clare wonders if he is going to cover her again, but instead he sits up, laughing, reaching for his pouch. He pulls out a bright red berry and shows it to her, making eye contact as he pushes a hole into the leaf mould beside her breast. He holds his middle finger rigid and penetrates the soil as if it is her body, and she giggles at this imitation of their play. He keeps his eyes on her face as he drops the berry into the hole and firms down the ground around it with his palm. Clare understands. Yew for war bows for the generations he has seeded within her. The thought makes her want him again, and she moves her legs and squirms as he bends to nuzzle her, but the tickle of his beard across her breasts becomes the drag of a duvet down her body and she wakes into the moist ache of his absence.

ABOVE HER ON the ceiling, near the window, a band of light shifted from green to amber to red as the traffic lights changed in the street below. Clare shut her eyes to the artificial, manufactured world and waited for sleep to reclaim her, seeking the dream, wanting to find again that moment in the forest.

IT WAS A good dream, a dream of sunlight and laughter and loving, but now Clare stands on the green reaching for it like a lost child. In front of her, an ocean of trees stretches all the way to the horizon in the black and yellow shades of late autumn. The air is chill, and heavy with the threat that builds behind her, rising above the Downs like the black thunderheads of a storm.

Children. Somewhere nearby there are children. As the threat grows Clare feels powerless, insignificant under its weight, and she starts to run. She must gather the children, protect them from this threat before it breaks over them all. But her legs will not move fast enough so it is like wading through liquid mud as the menace behind comes ever closer and the storm starts to break with the first heavy splashes of rain, rain that falls onto wood with the weight of an axe or scatters mud like a rock thrown into water. Then a goat squeals and thrashes, spurting blood, and the rain becomes arrows that hum outwards from the trees and part the air with impossible death. As Clare's legs struggle against the mud the screaming terror of the threat acquires a name.

Wealas.

5:38. BLINK. BLINK. 5:39. The milky greyness before dawn was outlining the window as Clare snapped on the light, making the outside world black once more as she stared at the mess of bedding tangled around her legs.

Wealas? Anglo-Saxon, a label of otherness, the word for 'those who are not of our tribe', foreigners. Clare knew her mind was analysing furiously in reaction to the power of the dream, seeking comfort in known facts. She kicked herself free and stood up, pulling the duvet with her and breathing heavily as if from strenuous exercise. Wealas. It was also the contemptuous Saxon label for the indigenous Britons. Over the centuries it would evolve into the English words Wales, Welsh. To have a dream containing a Saxon word was hardly shocking. What astonished Clare was its intensity. She squinted myopically at her reflection in the wardrobe mirror, standing naked and startled, and trailing bedclothes. The slightly unfocused view made her look pubescent, like some semi-pornographic Victorian 'artwork', the kind where the artist would paint his fantasies and make it art by calling it 'Nymph Surprised Bathing'.

Clare grabbed her spectacles from the bedside table and looked more closely, needing reassurance. Brown hair, cut short. Good. Not a hint of long blonde. Nothing voluptuous either. She thought she had a good body, an athlete's body, and she was proud of it and worked hard to keep it that way. Clare lifted a hand to a breast, finding comfort in its familiarity, its reality, in the way it had tightened in the cold air before dawn. She wondered what deep psychological need had made her dream herself into a body where she had felt the weight of her breasts shift as she moved, she who didn't even bother to wear a bra unless she was running. Even more worrying, there was no living reason for that maternal panic.

When analysis fails, go for a run. There's nothing better to clear the head than a solid 10K before breakfast. Ten thousand metres offers a lot of thinking time. Clare grabbed a juice from the refrigerator and reached for her running gear.

Outside the sky in the east was touched with the first hint of palest blue, and the light of the street lamps reflected a frost sugaring the parked cars. Clare set off in a pavement-pounding lope, knowing that in time the exercise would numb her mind like hypnosis and let any buried insight float free.

Chapter Twelve

SEVERAL HOURS LATER, the sun bathed the hills around Allingley with a light sharp enough to cut glass, shrinking the frost into shadow-bands of white beside the hedgerows. Fergus breathed deeply in Ash Farm's car park, squinting into the glare, and letting the purity of the morning dissolve his hangover. It was a day that rejoiced in the end of winter and inspired thoughts of robust, outdoor exercise.

If he'd been fit. Fergus took a grip on his new stick, still feeling insecure without a brace of crutches, and tottered towards the house. He moved in the unsteady way of an old man, taking short, nervous steps with his legs widely spaced, and prodding at the ground as he walked. But it was progress.

Eadlin sat behind the desk in the jumbled room that served as an office. Once, this room would have been the front parlour of the farmhouse, a place of dogs and heirloom furniture. Now the desk was angled across one corner, and the original leather armchairs spilt their stuffing onto a muddy, threadbare carpet. A fire of chopped logs had been lit in the open grate.

"I bought some carrots for the horses at the village store." Fergus waved a brown paper bag in her direction. "Can I scrounge a cup of coffee?" His greeting was a quiet, gravel croak that made Eadlin glance more closely at his eyes.

"Did you have a good evening?"

Fergus grunted, looking around the room while she mixed instant coffee. Large posters of horse breeds framed the fireplace, and a notice board informed him that 'Hat's Must Be Worn At All Times When Riding'. Eadlin grinned at him as she handed him a chipped, unsanitary-looking mug. Fergus sipped gratefully, more interested in the caffeine than the bugs that might come with it.

"So was it a late night?" she prompted.

"More like a liquid evening, and not a lot of sleep. I was led astray by some friendly choristers, then had a bad night trying to get my head around something." He parked his coffee on the arm of one of the old sofas and lowered himself into it, toppling the last few inches and grunting as he hit the leather. God, he sounded decrepit.

"You had an evening chasing choirboys?" Eadlin's smile was provocative and almost flirtatious. She had returned to her chair, and slouched back with her thumbs hooked into the pockets of her jodhpurs.

"These choirboys had grey hair and fine baritone voices. And I met your Vicar. Something he told me kept me awake last night."

Again, Eadlin raised a single, questioning eyebrow. Fergus would have found the mannerism cute if the subject hadn't been so troubling. He told her about his conversation with John Webster.

"Well, I guess we've either got an elusive tattooed tramp in the area or people are getting a bit, like, hysterical. Or maybe, just maybe, there's something in it." Eadlin leaned forward over the desk, her manner less relaxed.

"That's what's kept me awake." Fergus sipped coffee, hoping he didn't sound ridiculous. "That moment when the guy with the tattoo stood by the car, it's locked in my head. It's one of the memories that keep replaying in my mind and it's all so bloody real. It's never occurred to me that he wasn't... that he might not be..." Fergus didn't want to give the alternative a name.

"You said yourself you went a bit mad in the crash."

"True. But I hope I'm never sick enough to imagine some of the things I can remember. Shall we go and see some of those four-legged doctors of yours?" Fergus veered the subject away, not wanting to go near the pit again. Besides, it was easier to talk if there was a shared focus to look at, like a horse.

"Well if you're going anywhere near Trooper, you'll need to leave that thing behind." Eadlin nodded at his stick. "Troops has been beaten with a heavy stick at some stage. He's terrified of them. And whips, come to that."

Fergus looked down at his legs and spread his arms, wondering how to explain. A walk around the stables was slightly more ambitious than the previous day's few steps on soft sand.

"Come on." Eadlin stood and held out her hand to pull him to his feet. "I'll keep you upright."

Fergus swallowed his pride and accepted her support, letting her lead him arm-in-arm towards the barn like an old married couple.

"One thing puzzles me." They managed well together. Fergus just needed help with his balance, and he'd have enjoyed the close contact if it hadn't made him feel so inadequate. "You read about Victorian spooks or even Elizabethan spooks, but never about Saxon spooks. If such things exist, shouldn't they all have gone off to rattle their chains in Valhalla or wherever by now?"

"Who knows what they believed, back then?" Eadlin spoke quietly, as if considering her words carefully. "Most of the old knowledge was wiped out by the Christian church long ago. Perhaps they believed they could, like, bind a soul to a place, say to protect it or something. Are you religious?"

"You know, that's the second time someone's asked me that since I've been here but no, not really. Are you?"

"Nah, at least not in the Christian sense. Here's your friend Trooper." Eadlin paused while he made a fuss of the horse over the stable door. "Did you say your bones are mending?"

Fergus looked up, laughing as Trooper almost nudged him off his feet in his eagerness for more carrots. Eadlin's tone had sounded significant. "They're as straight as they are going to get. Like I said, it's the muscle that's still weak. Why do you ask?"

"Would you like to see what it feels like to ride? Not him," she added, seeing his look, "something really quiet to start with."

"Isn't it rather risky? I mean, I'm hardly fit…" His voice tailed away.

"You're in much better shape than some of our guests with Riding for the Disabled. I've just the horse in mind for you. She's bombproof." Fergus hesitated. Surely riding was a sport for teenage girls, the kind that went to private schools and had mothers who wore Barbours and headscarves? But Eadlin grinned and held out her arm to him, one eyebrow lifted in a way that was a challenge as well as a question, with a flirtatious sparkle in her eye.

Twenty minutes later Eadlin walked slowly out of the barn with Fergus balancing on one arm, and the reins to a docile mare looped over the other. A young stable girl in jodhpurs and riding boots passed them, pushing a wheelbarrow full of horse muck. She cast an appraising eye over Fergus, and smirked at Eadlin as if sharing a private joke.

"Do many, er, men ride here?" Fergus began to feel out of his depth.

"There are about half a dozen guys who keep their horses here, mainly members of the local hunt. There's a group of them hacking out over there." Eadlin nodded towards a quartet mounting up outside the other barn, with Jake Herne among them.

"I thought hunting was banned these days." The riders looked almost intimidatingly competent. Fergus let go of Eadlin's arm and forced himself to walk upright, dominating his limp.

"The farmers have to keep the fox population under control somehow, and there's no law against exercising your hounds. Sometimes a fox just gets in the way." She grinned at his expression. "Laws made far away don't always work out here. We've all learned just to get on with life and not to make so much fuss that people notice."

Fergus stumbled as the quartet of hunters approached, and in an instant of panic and shame he felt Eadlin grab him under the arm and save him from falling. Jake Herne's cheerful greeting from the saddle only added to his embarrassment.

"Take it steady." Eadlin pulled his arm into the crook of her elbow, and squeezed his hand in reassurance. "Jake seems to have taken to you." She stared after the group of riders. Fergus stretched himself upright and stood still beside her. The linking of arms had brought his forearm into contact with her breast and he savoured the softness until she walked him on towards the sand school.

Fergus wondered why Jake's goodwill felt superficial, then winced at his own ingratitude. "Does he work here?"

"Nah. He's landlord of a pub in the village called the Green Man. He usually rides in the mornings before opening up."

"I went there yesterday, looking for you. It wasn't a warm welcome."

"That was probably Dick Hagman. He's not the friendliest guy in the village."

In the sand school Eadlin stood beside the horse and made a basket of her hands, with her legs flexed at the knee, forming a human mounting block ready to launch him into the saddle.

"Put your left knee in this." The action pushed her breasts together, and as Fergus knelt on her locked hands their faces came close. Eadlin grinned at him with a sparkle of complicity in her eyes.

"Now you look where you're going, not at my cleavage, or I'll throw you all the way over!" There was no offence in her voice, just an earthy openness as she heaved him upwards.

Fergus had accepted the challenge to ride in the same way as he might accept a dare, not expecting to enjoy it, but half an hour later he was grinning like a lunatic. For four months he'd fought the frustrations of immobility. Now, even in his weakened state, vigorous movement became possible. Nudge with the right leg, and the horse moved left. Nudge with the left, she moved back to the right. Squeeze with both, and she started to trot, moving as fast as he would once have jogged. Trots were uncomfortable until Fergus learned to rise with them, matching his motion to the animal. The horse was a multiplier of strength, turning feeble signals into motion. For the first time since the crash he felt vital, liberated, and inhibited only by his lack of skill. It had been a long time since he felt so intensely alive.

"Sit up straight," Eadlin shouted at him. "Keep your heels down." The stream of instructions was non-stop. Then on one corner Fergus succumbed to his protesting leg muscles and sat back in the saddle, squeezing his legs harder against the mare's sides in an attempt to keep his balance. The motion changed. It was as if the horse had found another gear, a faster pace that was alarming as well as exciting, and he snatched at the reins to slow her.

"Whoa!" Eadlin stepped into the horse's path and brought her to a halt. Fergus, still unbalanced, started to roll forward over the neck until Eadlin reached up to brace him with her hand on his chest. Their eyes met and they grinned at each other, panting.

"That," Eadlin said, "was a canter, and you ain't ready for it yet!" She pushed his chest hard and Fergus slid back in the saddle, feeling mischievous and pleased with himself.

It was a short lesson. Fergus's leg muscles could only take so much. Eadlin walked beside his stirrup on the way back to the barn. Above her, Fergus sat upright and proud in the saddle, the grin painted on his face.

"You could be good." Her praise sounded genuine. "You've good natural co-ordination and balance. You're confident, probably too confident, but that will help the horse unless you do something stupid."

"I'm going to buy some of your lessons."

"Good! Actually, I've got another idea." Eadlin paused as if unsure how to say something. "Let's put the horse away and I'll make you another coffee."

Fergus walked taller as she led him back to the outdoor tables, hoping in vain for more contact along his forearm, and relishing the buzz of unfamiliar exercise. His muscles were shaking with the effort and he massaged his thighs while she made coffee. He was going to pay for this later.

"Yesterday you said that you'd been told to do something physical for the next few months." He hadn't heard her return.

"That's right." The conversation was going in a mildly alarming direction.

"How about helping out around here? You wouldn't believe the amount of work involved in looking after horses. I can't pay more than the minimum wage so people move on as soon as they find something better, and the teenagers can't help during school hours." Eadlin's speech was rushed, the idea formulating as she spoke.

"But you've seen the state I'm in. I can't even walk without a stick, yet, and I don't know the first thing about looking after horses." This was one crazy idea.

"You'll get better. You couldn't even walk without crutches yesterday. You could man the office at first, help me with things like the books and phones, so I could spend more time doing the heavy stuff, like." There was a note of slight desperation in Eadlin's voice, and Fergus began to feel guilty about his inevitable refusal.

"Eadlin," Fergus tried to find a way of saying 'no' without hurting her feelings, "it's a much more appealing idea than I would have believed an hour ago, but I don't think it's me."

"I know the money's crap but at least I could teach you to ride." Eadlin still had a hopeful expression on her face. She wasn't going to give up easily.

"Actually it's not about the money. I've four months unspent salary sitting in the bank, and an insurance cheque coming that might even buy me a house. But I'm a businessman, with a job to go back to. I live by looking at a computer screen and making technology work."

"Poor you. Ah well, it was an idea." She seemed genuinely disappointed.

"But I will come back for the lessons. I wouldn't miss all that shouting for anything."

A smile flickered across Eadlin's face but when she spoke it was with a note of caution.

"Don't expect everything to be the same back at work. The last few months will have changed you. Even if everything around you is the same, you'll be different. Give me your hand." Puzzled, Fergus held out his right hand. Eadlin turned it palm upwards, holding it between both her own hands and pushing at his skin with her thumbs. Her touch was firm but gentle. It could have been a physician's touch, but for the snags of hardened skin against his fingers from the calluses of physical work.

"Are you reading my palm?" Fergus was amused and slightly incredulous. Eadlin grunted, concentrating too hard for this to be a mere game or party trick. He bit back the urge to make some flippant remark about crossing her palm with silver like a fairground gipsy.

"Now give me your left hand." Again that focused scrutiny, held for longer than it would take to read a page. "Now hold them both up. Show me your palms." Eadlin watched the way his fingers splayed, and there was a look in her eyes that might have been concern. Fergus's smile started to fade as she took back his right hand, now dropping her face close to it to explore the fine detail.

"Take care, Fergus." The worry in Eadlin's face as she looked up at him was disconcerting. Whatever it was that she had found, she believed it and it alarmed her.

"What can you see?"

"I'm not sure. There are signs I've never seen before." Her uncertainty was more convincing than any confidence. Eadlin pushed again at the skin of his right palm with her thumbs. "You won't be the same, I promise you. Your life will take a new path, even if you don't know it yet. I see two crises, close together, as if the second is an echo of the first. It's, like, linked to it in some way."

Eadlin stared at him, reading his face as intently as she had read his palms. He returned her stare calmly, glimpsing something ageless within her, as if the freckles and freshness were merely a façade, and an ancient wisdom waited behind those grey eyes.

"I saw something in you yesterday, when you were with Trooper. I think you are open, sensitive even, in a way that you don't yet understand." Eadlin looked down at his right palm. Her mouth opened then closed without speech, as if she was unsure of what to say or how to say it.

"Tell me."

"I could be wrong. I've never read signs like this before." Another pause. "You're different. It's almost like you're still between the worlds. You've touched the shadow world, but you've come back. You have no idea how rare that is. It's like the shadow world hasn't let you go, not yet. I think you're still vulnerable. Take care, Fergus, please."

Fergus wasn't sure whether to be warmed by her concern or worried by her words, but before he could ask more there was a clatter of hooves as Jake Herne's party rode onto the yard. Eadlin let his hand drop, pulling her own back into her lap with a small smile of apology and a slight shake of the head. He parked her words in the same mental corner as the tattooed tramp, knowing his mind would probe the space the way his tongue might play with a broken tooth, hard and jagged, an irritating snag to his wellbeing.

Chapter Thirteen

FERGUS DIDN'T FIT anymore. His discomfort was more than physical, more than the embarrassment of his stick-assisted progress through the office cubicle farm. He used to feel sharp, on the ball, at one with the hum. Now the horizon of glass and aluminium felt as confining as the hospital ward. Oh, the welcome was warm enough. Lots of backslapping and arm pumping. One or two even had the grace to apologise for not visiting him in hospital. But hey, they said, he could remember how rushed it gets around here. Others would make eye contact and look away, their smiles fading, as if they had seen something in Fergus's eyes that unnerved them.

There was a shiny new laptop waiting for him, its password stuck to the screen with a Post-it note. God knew what had happened to the last one. Still spread over a hillside, probably. Fergus logged on, and looked around him while over four months of electronic vomit landed in his inbox. Near his workstation, the departmental notice board held the squash league, with his own name now the bottom layer of sediment.

Kate's workspace had been reallocated. Inevitable, really. There were different photographs pinned to its partition screens, and pressed male chinos stretched into the walkway where there used to be stockings and those distracting, untouchable legs. The owner of the chinos introduced himself in a California accent as "the new Kate". *The new Kate*. God, it made her sound like a piece of machinery that had broken and been replaced.

"You're the wrong shape," was all Fergus could think of in reply.

"Oh yeah." A laddish chuckle. "I hear she was pretty hot."

Fergus turned away. He had no words for this man.

"Take care," his cubicle neighbour warned him afterwards, "he's well connected. They call him the Rock Star, the best salesman in the States, flown in to plug the gap and learn about international markets. He'll be in the Boardroom one day." Fergus watched the Rock Star strutting around the office, radiating ego like a bow wave, and loathed him on sight. The new Kate was a Swing Dick.

The office routines still operated as if nothing had happened. The Sales Director gave his Monday morning team briefing, all exhortations and adrenaline as he strutted his stuff in the conference room. Behind him, a projection screen showed spread sheet graphics: sales achieved, 'must win' orders to reach the March quarter target, stretch objectives, failure not an option. One by one, the sales managers stood to commit their forecasts, their voices intense, religious in their fervour, devotees boasting their creed in values and probabilities. And with each commitment, the new Silicon Valley evangelist would punch the air and call "awesome", *uh-sum*. No-one else seemed to find it funny. Fergus looked around the room at the team, feeling an observer rather than a member. It dawned on him that he had lost his faith.

Fergus ignored his email queue. It was much more interesting to launch his browser and Google 'Allingley Bog Man' and wade through thousands of hits. National press, some of it, so the Saxon's discovery had been big news. He clicked on the most likely link, swallowing as the page loaded. There was something about his interest that was beyond morbid, it was almost prurient. One of the first web pages even had a photograph, an edge-of-the-trench shot where the Saxon's limbs were just contours of mud within mud, and the orange-haired, mahogany head was a grisly troll toy lying in the wet. The article told him little he did not already know. He clicked on.

A video clip from regional television had an interview with Professor Miles Eaton, the media face of archaeology, smiling at the camera, lecturing the public about the significance of 'his' find. Fergus could see Clare moving in the trench in the background. The clip cut to a close-up of the find's head, but there was nothing in that ginger-and-chocolate sculpture that he could relate to the figure he had seen by the car. Even if he froze the frame, there was just a shadow above the nose that might have been a tattoo, a mere darkening of shade.

Finally, within an academic publication, was a close up of the face in high resolution, under strong light. Fergus swallowed again, and shivered. He had a sense that he was looking at the world through a glass sphere, like a fishbowl. Outside the bowl, the office throbbed. Phone calls, printers, conversations laced with the tension of deadlines, progress, and pressure. Inside the bowl, he ran a hand over his eyes. His skin was cold and clammy under his fingers. He hadn't expected that reaction. He hadn't expected to find stark evidence, either. He reached out to touch the screen as if its cold hardness could confirm the reality of the image it showed. Quite clearly now, he could make out the inverted triangle of a stag's head with leaf-like ears, and a spray of antlers rising above each orange eyebrow.

For a while he stared at the ceiling, trying to reconcile the impossible. His computer had switched to screen-save mode by the time he pulled a pad towards him and tried to structure his thoughts on paper.

Crash tattoo = Saxon tattoo. Not a shadow of a doubt.

?possibilities? What the f...

1. *two men with same tattoo*. Yeah, like how many men had he ever seen with stags on their faces?

2. *must have seen newspapers after crash. Stayed in subconscious. Some kind of retro-fit into memory*. But he couldn't even pick up a newspaper for six weeks. *Television, then. There were TVs over the beds in the ward*. But surely he'd have remembered?

3. *Hallucinated or saw a ghost*.

At that he ripped the sheet off the pad, screwed it into a ball and binned it. Look further. There must be another explanation. He woke up the laptop again and ran another search. Allingley.

More web pages. The White Hart Pub. Local history and attractions. Car crash – woman killed. Strange how things creep up on you, buried between an estate agent's site and yet another press article on the Saxon. It was like reading his own obituary. *A woman was killed and a man seriously injured in a road traffic accident near Allingley last Tuesday, 1ˢᵗ November. No other vehicle is thought to be involved...* Three column inches and a photograph of Kate, laughing at the camera, sunlight on her face, dressed for a wedding or the races with a fascinator in her hair. Where had they found that one? Family, probably.

"That's her, right?"

The chinos stood beside him, their crotch at the level of his shoulder, intruding into the sphere of unreality. Fergus pulled his screen shut and looked up. The set of the shoulders within the starched shirt spoke of a confidence that crossed the border into arrogance. This man owned the space he moved in, even if it was somebody else's workstation. Fergus forced a smile and ignored the question.

"They tell me you're good." The Rock Star spoke slowly so his drawl sounded more Texan than Californian, and Fergus stifled the urge to laugh. Strap a Colt .45 on those razor-pressed slacks and the man could have been a gunslinger squaring up to a potential rival. Fergus demurred in an excessively British fashion.

"We're making a sales pitch together on Thursday." He named the customer. "This is the biggest deal on the prospect list and we're down to the wire. Close it and we not only make our March quarter target, we'll be half way to June's."

Which means you stand to make an obscene amount of commission.

"I'll send you the files. Dry run Wednesday."

"Awesome," Fergus muttered at his retreating back. Bloody Swing Dick.

The pitch didn't go well. They had no chemistry, no intuitive interaction. He and Kate had been a polished team, a double act, feeding each other the lines confident in their partner's ability to run with the ball, add value, and pass it back. The new man only wanted someone to push a computer keyboard to illustrate his solo performance. In any case, Fergus's patter was four months rusty, and after one fumbled remark, Swing Dick talked over any further attempt Fergus made to speak. Fergus's mind started to drift, and then at a crucial moment when his contribution was needed, he was staring out of the window.

Two worlds, Eadlin had said. And tramps with very specific tattoos didn't fit in this one. Beware, she'd said, you have touched the shadow world, you are between the worlds. So how could he have felt so intensely alive at the end of that riding lesson, with the vitality sparkling within him? Beyond the customer's office windows was a line of trees, their bareness no longer dead but latent with spring. Within a few feet of the window leaf buds were waving in the breeze, swelling from the stalk in a pure, water-drop curve that reminded him of the way Eadlin's arse filled a pair of jodhpurs. Earthy, somehow. Ripe with promise. Tactile...

"Fergus?"

Fergus's attention returned to the room. They were all looking at him, their expressions ranging from amusement to annoyance to the salesman's pleading desperation. Fergus smiled back, with the gentle smile of someone who doesn't give a damn.

They lost the deal. The Sales Director called a post-mortem review in his office, glaring at Fergus across the acreage of his desk while Swing Dick presented the case for the prosecution.

"Fergus, buddy." The Sales Director rose to his feet, marched round his desk and paced the room, swigging water from a plastic bottle. The transatlantic 'buddy' was meaningless, merely a device to make whatever followed appear reasonable. "I've had to cut you some slack in recent months, but I'm beginning to wonder."

"Excuse me?" Fergus noted that there was no invitation to give the case for the defence, even if he had one. "Just what slack have you had to cut me while I've been in hospital?"

"Well, precisely. I've kept your job open and carried your costs for nearly five months, and the team have had to pick up your work. At least I could fill the sales gap with a good guy." The Sales Director paused his pacing and waved his water at Swing Dick.

"I can't believe I'm hearing this." Fergus was bemused, almost as if he were starting to detach from the argument. Deep inside his mind, his self-control started to corrode.

"Look." The Sales Director's voice was now laced with anger, and he sucked water as if that was a means of keeping calm. "We're all sorry about what happened. Of course we are. But your crash cost me a key sales resource…"

"Kate." How mild and reasonable his voice sounded in his own ears, even as he teetered on the edge of the precipice. It would take only a word to nudge him over.

"… and badly dented our December quarter…" Flecks of saliva or water sprayed from the Sales Director's mouth.

"Kate. Not 'a sales resource'. Kate." The strain was tightening his voice and Fergus rapped his stick point-first into the floor to emphasise his point, but it was a gentle blow and the carpeted false floor deadened the sound. The pacing continued. Fergus struggled to his feet during the silence of a swig, and saw the first flash of alarm on Swing Dick's face. Good. Very good.

"… and I'm sure as *hell* not going to let you wreck my March quarter."

The sense of losing control was quite liberating, almost as if Fergus was no longer responsible for his own behaviour. There was a distant echo of childhood tantrums as he hefted his stick at its mid-point and slammed it horizontally onto the desk, gunshot loud. A flake of beech-effect laminate shattered under the root-ball handle and flew towards Swing Dick, who was already kicking his chair away from the threat. A cup danced and toppled, sending fingers of coffee reaching for the great man's papers. Fergus stared at the desk for a moment. Did he really do that? Then he turned towards the Sales Director, relishing the shock on both their faces.

"Kate." His voice was now piano-wire taut. "Her – name – was – Kate." Any second now he was either going to be in a screaming rage or a blubbering heap. Beyond the Director the office door swung open and his PA looked into the room, scanning their faces, her eyes wide and questioning. Fergus dragged the stick from behind him, and an engraved glass 'Top Gun' sales award fell to the floor. The bloody thing didn't break. Pity.

"She wasn't just a 'good sales resource', she was a person. She was my friend. And she took two hours to die, impaled on the mess that came through the dashboard." Fergus saw the shock on the PA's face soften into compassion and he fought against collapse. Dear God, let it be rage. No way did he want these shits to see him weep. "So you can take your fucking sales targets and ram them up your arse. If Swing Dick here isn't already in the way."

Fergus lurched through them to the door, avoiding the PA's eyes. One hint of tenderness now and he'd lose it. He braced himself against the frame, breathing heavily. In front of him the cubicle farm held regimented lines of heads, all facing towards him, like some smart-shirted herd of meerkats up on their hind legs with their noses twitching for danger. For a long moment they all stared at each other, until the silence was ruptured by an angry bark of command from behind him. For some reason the bluster calmed him, perhaps even elated him. Fergus gripped his new stick firmly in one hand, grinned wryly, and shook his other hand in the burnt-fingers sign to make light of the moment. It didn't work. He had broadcast his apostasy and the shock was written on their faces. A hand grasped his elbow, trying to pull him back into the room, but he shook it free. The office door slammed. Silently now, but with a sense of blessed release, he tapped his way through the staring faces towards his desk, trying to put as much dignity as possible into his step. It took him sixty silent seconds to collect his belongings and leave.

Behind the wheel of his car, still in the car park, Fergus started to shake. He'd never behaved like that before. Still shaking, he punched at the stereo and skipped through the CD changer until he found soothing music. He exhaled, feeling his shoulders drop, as sweet strings calmed him with a sense of innocence, hinting at a very English peace. Butterworth, 'Banks of Green Willow' the CD cover told him before he flicked it onto the passenger seat and relaxed into an aural massage. It made him wonder what the countryside around Allingley would be like in high summer. As the track ended he pulled out his mobile phone and dialled Eadlin.

Her warmth and pleasure at his voice was like a lifeline to a drowning man.

"That offer of a job," he said, "is it still open?"

Chapter Fourteen

"ARE YOU SURE this is OK? The job, I mean?" Fergus stood in the office at Ash Farm Stables, competing for Eadlin's attention with the office phone and the whines of a teenage girl who couldn't find some piece of tack. He felt pleased with himself; two weeks after he'd thrown away his crutches, he'd walked from the car park to the farmhouse without putting his stick to the ground. He'd limped, for sure, but it hadn't hurt much. It was just the way his legs worked, these days. A punishing exercise routine was working.

"OK? You're doing me a favour. The schools have broken up for Easter, I'm swamped by Pony Club children, and half my normal helpers have gone away on holiday with their parents. I'm running ragged."

"Maybe for a couple of months, until I get myself sorted out?"

Eadlin's reply was interrupted by another call, and she inhaled before picking up the phone. She handled the enquiry with brittle competence, running her eyes over his clothes as she spoke. As Eadlin replaced the receiver she lifted an eyebrow at his designer jeans and expensive trainers.

"D'you mind getting dirty?"

Fergus shook his head.

"Then let's get started." Eadlin looked pointedly at the stick in his hand, and he dropped it with a theatrical flourish into a rack of riding crops by the door. As she came round the desk he crooked his elbow at her, grinning in a way that he hoped was not too flirtatious.

"Sod that. If you can't walk without a stick you can stay behind the desk until you can. Could you manage a wheelbarrow? Let me introduce you to your new charges, it's time for their feed."

She was already ahead of him, calling over her shoulder. "So what changed your mind?"

"There's nothing like a touch of mortality to give you perspective."

Outside she started stacking a wheelbarrow with rubber feed bowls, each about the size of a small car tyre and filled with an unappetising muesli mess.

"So you resigned?"

"Sort of." Fergus told her about the row as she led him down a line of stables, dropping a bowl of feed over the door of each one. The wheelbarrow proved easy to manage, almost as if the weight was anchoring him.

"Were you and Kate very close?"

"Just good friends, to use the old cliché. We were comfortable with each other, flirted a bit, nothing more. But if I'd ever needed real help she'd have been the one I'd have called. I think she felt the same." He found it easy to talk in Eadlin's company. "You know, I think in a strange way I hadn't really accepted that she was dead until last week, not at a very deep level. It was as if the crash was only a bad dream and I would wake up and go back to normal life in the office. Kate was still part of normal life." His voice caught and Eadlin looked back at him as she hefted a feed bowl.

"Keep going. I think you need to talk about it."

Yes, he needed to talk, but he wished he didn't feel so emotionally incontinent when he tried. Fergus continued more quietly, ready to stop at the first sign of a crumble. "I cleaned out my car before I went back. There were two long, blonde hairs snagged in the passenger head rest. Sometimes we went to meetings in my car rather than hers. For some reason those hairs broke me up." His voice caught again. "They're still there."

Enough. Down the line of stables, horses' heads were stretching over their gates, all looking towards them. One or two started kicking their doors impatiently, eager for their feed. Fergus recognised Trooper further down the line, whinnying at them.

"I think Trooper is pleased to see us." Fergus had never thought his spirits would lift at the sight of a horse.

"Sorry to disillusion you, but he's pleased to see food. You won't get any sense out of any of them until their bowls are empty." Trooper proved her point by dropping his head into the feed, showing no sign of recognition. "So why did you come back here?"

Fergus watched Eadlin's jodhpur-covered rump as she bent, lifted, and dropped a food tray over a stable door. Some of his reasons could stay private.

"Well, I looked up your dead Saxon on the internet. There are pictures of the tattoo on his face. I know this sounds weird but I'm sure I saw him in the wreck. It's left a few loose ends in my mind that I want to explore, even if I don't know where to start."

Eadlin turned towards him with another feed bowl in her hands and a look of surprising intensity on her face.

"I think there are some things we'll never understand, but where we might get hurt trying to find out. I'd let that drop if I were you." The steel in her warning surprised Fergus. He opened his mouth to ask a question but she spoke over him. "Remember what I said about you being between the worlds, about being vulnerable. There are some doors you, of all people, shouldn't try to open."

Eadlin moved on briskly to the next stall. The set of her shoulders dissuaded him from voicing his scepticism about her palm-reading predictions.

"Actually, there *was* something else." Truth time. Fergus parked the wheelbarrow and hooked his elbows over Trooper's stable door, glad of an excuse to rest his legs. The horse looked up briefly before dropping his head to chase the remaining feed around the bowl. Fergus did not know quite how to put his next thought into words. Eadlin rested with him, giving him time to come to the heart of his answer.

"I had a glimpse of something, here. Something peaceful." His words were coming out slowly, spoken softly towards the horse. "Last time I was here, all I wanted to do was to get back to my old life, as if I could wipe away the crash and the hospital months. Then when I went back I kept on thinking about a moment in the sand school, with you and Trooper. I sensed something there, just for a moment. An instant of calm that was so powerful that it frightened me and I dropped it." The silence was comfortable between them, until Eadlin touched his arm in encouragement. "But back in the office, surrounded by all those egos, all that frantic pressure, finding a way back to that point of calm felt more important than any sales target could ever be. Am I talking complete drivel?"

Eadlin lifted her hand and laid it on his back. "You're probably talking more sense than your office mates will ever know." She smiled at him warmly, as if he had said something profound, and again he glimpsed wisdom behind her eyes. They reminded him of a Buddhist monk he had met on his gap year travels, a man whose serenity had seemed ageless, and before whom all the stresses of the world were but the petty squabbles of children. Then her smile became a grin and she was once again a freckle-faced young woman with her hand resting on his back, and he was sorry when she straightened and let it fall.

"This is good. You're asking good questions. You're like someone tuning in one of those old dial-faced radios, hunting for a signal. At least you're hunting, and when you find it you'll be receptive."

Eadlin started to move away but Fergus stayed, staring at the way the horse was snuffling and licking at the scraps in his bowl. Trooper had given no sign of recognition, no indication that for an instant, once, they had connected at an almost primal level.

"But my mind is all over the place." His truths were surfacing. "I swing from crying in public to childish euphoria over a pint of beer. I've just chucked in a good career in a spectacular flash of temper that I never knew I had, and I'm even starting to believe in some mental communion with a horse. I'm afraid I'm going gaga, that some of the damage to my skull has changed me."

Eadlin turned to look back at him, and he hoped his face did not look as lost as he felt. Outside in the yard, the repeater bell for the office telephone started to ring, but she ignored it.

"Has anyone mentioned Post-Traumatic Stress to you?"

Fergus shook his head. No, but he'd wondered about that.

"Because I think you've got it. And whatever label a shrink would put on you, you're going to feel a bit screwed up after that kind of experience. It's bound to change you, but not all change is bad. Come on; let me show you the office routines. How's your telephone manner?"

In the yard it was turning into the kind of spring afternoon when sunshine is a surprise and delight at an hour that used to be dusk. When the phone stopped ringing the silence was deeper, inspiring Fergus to stop and breathe. Beside him, Eadlin squinted at the sun, lifting her face to its rays.

"It'll be the equinox tomorrow." She sounded happy at the thought. "Ostara, it used to be called. It's the day when people celebrated the end of winter and prayed for fertility for their crops. It's always been a happy time."

"Prayed as in went to church?"

Eadlin giggled at the thought. "Nah, no way! Ostara's much older than that. Before the Christians came, Ostara was the festival of rebirth in the cycle of the year." Fergus stared at her. She had spoken as if the arrival of Christianity was still part of folk memory. Now she lifted her chin towards the car park, where Fergus's sporty Audi gleamed amidst the decrepit collection of yard workers' cars. His mountain bike was strapped to the roof rack. "Is that yours?"

"The car belongs to my ex-employer, so it'll have to go back in a couple of months, when my notice expires. I bought the bike to help me build up my legs, and it's working. I can manage a couple of miles, now, on the flat." For a moment Fergus wondered if he was doing the right thing to move away from the business world. He'd miss that car.

"D'you have somewhere to stay?" She interrupted his reverie.

"There's a woman in the village who lets out rooms. Mary Baxter. I got her number from the local tourist board, but apparently I met her that night with the choir. D'you know her?"

Eadlin nodded. "Nice woman, and it'll do her good to have you around the place." Behind her the telephone rang again, interrupting any further conversation as Eadlin ran to the office. Fergus bent to grip the wheelbarrow and grimaced as he lifted, enjoying the physical challenge, even relishing the complaints from his muscles. Some pain must be sought out so that horizons can expand. Tomorrow he'd cycle here from Allingley.

Chapter Fifteen

MARY BAXTER'S HOUSE was in a terrace of brick-and-flint cottages on the edge of the village. Each had a tiny, walled front garden scattered with spring flowers, like a line of slightly neglected old ladies holding out tea trays. Behind them their back gardens rose in narrow strips to the edge of the woods, a landscape filled with a productive litter of garden sheds and vegetable plots. Beyond the cottages, away from the village, the land between the lane and the woods widened into a broad common where children were playing a noisy game of football as Fergus arrived. He stood on Mary's doorstep and turned to watch the way the sun lit the underside of the clouds, feeling the satisfied exhaustion of physical activity even though he'd spent most of the day in Eadlin's office. He hadn't touched his stick all day. More progress.

Mary Baxter answered the door in a floral housecoat and fluffy slippers, wiping her hands on a tea towel, smiling in a way that was kindly but distant. Without the animation of the choir around her, her face looked too drawn for the homely bulk below. The smudges under her eyes were a similar colour to her hair, gunmetal streaked with grey.

"I've only two rooms that I let," Mary led the way into the house. "The large one at the back is already taken by Doctor Harvey from the dig." She spoke as if he'd know who Doctor Harvey was. "This one's free, though." She showed him a small room over the front door. It had recently been redecorated, and the framed prints on the walls seemed to be there to cover up the bare paint rather than being a natural part of their surroundings. "It were my son's room when he were a boy," she added in the same soft, teashop accent as Eadlin. The carpet was old and still had ink stains under the small desk. In the confined space her nose wrinkled slightly. "There's a bathroom at the back," she hinted. It was strange how quickly he'd become used to the smell of horses.

"It's fine, thank you, I'd love to take it."

Mary brightened and began to show him the rest of the house. She found going downstairs a challenge, rolling from side to side and grunting with the effort.

"It's me knees," she explained, looking over her shoulder to where Fergus side-stepped after her, grasping the bannister. "A right pair we make, don't we?" Fergus had explained his situation on the phone.

A cramped front room "for all the guests to use" was dominated by an old upright piano, crowned by a photograph of a soldier who grinned at the camera from under the maroon beret and winged insignia of the Parachute Regiment.

"Is that your son?" Fergus asked, picking up the photograph. She lifted the frame out of his hands tenderly, and polished his fingerprints off the glass.

"Yes, this is my boy." Mary replaced the photograph onto the piano like a priest placing a chalice on the altar. "He was killed in Afghanistan last year." The words fell from her mouth the way porcelain falls from a shelf.

"I'm so sorry, I didn't know..." Already she had turned away, waving her arm behind her to sweep away his condolences.

"Well now you know. You needed to know if you're going to stay here. So why aren't you going home for Easter?" she asked, leading him into a tiny kitchen designed for one to cook or two to eat in. A Formica-topped table with two bentwood chairs huddled against the wall opposite an old, enamel cooking range. "A young man like you should be with his family at Easter."

"My parents emigrated to New Zealand when my father retired, to be closer to my sister and her children."

Mary let out a maternal *tut*. "So you're going to work at Eadlin Stodman's place?" she asked rhetorically, as she showed him where to find mugs and milk.

"More like a working holiday. I'm taking a career break and getting fit at the same time."

"Eadlin's a good girl. Her family have been here for ever. She's what my dear mother would have called an 'old soul'."

Fergus smiled encouragingly. He thought he understood, but he wanted Mary to say more.

"Sort of wise, if you know what I mean. Fey." Mary had found another word. "Her mother and grandmother had the same gift. They knew about herbs and things. Healers, like."

Later, as Fergus was unpacking his suitcase, he heard the front door open and footsteps climb the stairs, treading with the light step and energy of a younger woman. A few minutes later there was a knock at his door. The woman outside was bespectacled, elfin, and familiar in a way that eluded Fergus for a moment. Then she held out her hand, smiling a little after the shake, and he recognised the woman who had offered him coffee on the day he had chased the illusion of Kate to the Mill House.

"Hello, I'm Clare Harvey, I gather we're housemates. Oh it's you! Hello, you're looking better. No crutches now?"

Clare stayed in the doorway while Fergus explained his return. He sat, as he spoke, in the single upright chair by the desk, resting his legs and feeling guilty at taking the only seat. Clare recognised his description of Eadlin as the red-haired woman who sometimes rode a chestnut horse past her dig.

"How's the dig going?"

Clare grimaced. "Disappointing. We've found nothing that you wouldn't expect to find at the bottom of a pond that's been filling up for a thousand years, mainly interesting scraps of very old rubbish. No more bodies, yet. The owners are happy because they'll get a nice clean pond for free, but I've got to keep a bunch of students motivated. They were mad keen to work on a site like this for their Easter vacation, but so far it's archaeologically tedious." As Clare spoke she looked idly at the clutter of Fergus's mementoes dumped on top of the chest of drawers.

"What's the photograph?" Clare picked up a framed, group photograph of a business team cheering at the camera. They were bunched together, several with one arm raised in a display of triumph. "And why are you looking all wilted while the others are cheering?"

"I brought that to remind me of what I'm leaving behind." Something in Fergus's tone announced that there was a story behind the photograph, and Clare looked up expectantly. "That was the sales team I worked with last year, taken on the day the financial results were announced. We came second, out of many, in the global sales league."

"Sounds good, but I still don't understand why you're the only one not cheering."

"Two weeks before the financial year end I broke a couple of ribs diving to catch a cricket ball. I missed an important customer meeting and we lost a deal. If we'd have won that deal the team would have topped the league."

"So?"

"The guy next to me in the photograph was my boss. He's a very focused guy, all deals, targets and testosterone. He insisted we went into that huddle for the camera, and put one arm around my back. As we cheered for the picture he squeezed my ribs. Have you ever had broken ribs?"

"No."

"It smarts a bit. Especially if someone gives you a bear hug. The camera caught me as my knees buckled."

"Nice guy."

"A Class 'A' shit, if you'll pardon the expression. We've just had a bit of a row, which is why I've resigned."

Clare looked back at the photograph and tensed. For some reason she had paled and was staring at the picture like a rabbit in the headlights.

"That woman the other side of you." She swallowed. "The one with the long blonde hair. Who is she?"

"That's Kate. She and I used to work together."

"She looks familiar, like I know her."

"Well you won't have met her recently." Fergus spoke quietly, his mouth dry. "Kate died in the car crash when I was injured."

There was a loud click as Clare let the frame drop back onto the chest of drawers, then turned away and left without another word. As Fergus struggled to rise, he heard her bedroom door shut in an emphatic way that said she did not want to be disturbed. Puzzled, he looked across the landing at her door then picked up the photograph. Kate smiled back at him, shoulders braced back, pelvis forward in a raunchy pose with both hands held at waist level in the thumbs-up gesture of success. God, she'd been lovely.

Chapter Sixteen

CLARE PULLS BACK from the edge of the grave, her dream-self wanting to flee from the blonde in the mud, crying "no, you're dead". The blonde's smile is kind, like a sister, and she flexes her arms at the level of her waist, shoulders-back as if reining in a horse, but she's tugging at Clare. The side of the trench crumbles so Clare pitches forward, but the arms that catch her are gentle, and fold into wings that have the pure touch of a pillow.

The threat is falling on them, rushing down the valley in a mighty wave. The Wealas' boots sound like the stones grinding on the sea shore on the day their ships' keels first touched this land. It is a low, hard, constant grumble whose note is changing as the Wealas pass the end of the marsh and fan out to form their line across the fields.

Clare holds children to her, pulling them into the shelter of the wall, gripping them tightly as if her arms alone could be more protection than the timber behind them. In front of her, men hurry to the palisade, buckling into helmets with their shields slung across their backs, each emblazoned with the stags-head emblem of their lord. One of them smiles encouragement at her as he passes. It is an older man, a veteran, the one with the pure voice who is always called upon to sing at their feasts. But an arrow strikes the bard in the face with a wet, meaty noise, knocking him backwards at her feet like a thrown sack of grain. He stares up the shaft with his mouth working until the shock on his face slackens and his limbs start to twitch. Taunts and shouts of triumph carry across the field from the trees.

Her lord is standing close, at the centre of the storm, shouting orders while he braces his bow against his foot and heaves to string it. In his face Clare sees the rage at being surprised, and the shame of failing his people. It is not the season for war, she wants to reassure him, none could have foreseen a raid now, with the harvest gathered and winter approaching. Tomorrow the blood month begins, the time for sacrifice and feasting on the livestock that will not last the winter. Who are these Wealas who dare to turn the cycle of seasons on its head?

Clare pushes the children behind her and stands, deliberately sharing her lord's danger, giving him strength as she reaches up to lace the cheek-pieces on his helmet. The sacred, stag's head sign of flesh and blood is now encased in one of gilded steel. As she finishes she touches his neck, feeling the pulse and the warmth of him through his beard, the vitality surging at the prospect of battle.

A horse is loose in the compound, its eyes rolling white with fear, its value protecting it from the archers. A child-woman has caught its trailing rope and is gentling it. The wild child, the tamer of horses. Their lord calls to the child in the half-mocking endearment that always makes her stand taller.

"Eadlin!" Little princess. The child's eyes are wide but strong; she takes comfort from the horse she has comforted. "I have a great task for you." How could he sound so calm?

He turns to Clare, and now she sees the depth of pain in his eyes. "The children. Strap them to her. Tell her to ride south to the hall of the Eorl."

He grips her shoulders hard as she starts to scream her loss, his fingers biting into flesh.

"There are too many." He jerks his head up the valley. "It is their only chance. Quickly now, before we are surrounded."

There is no time for farewells. The southern gate is cracked open and the horse leaps from stand to gallop with a single touch of the girl's leg. The children do not look at her as they race past. One is white-faced, his hands knotted into the horse's mane, while the younger screams her fear and rage from where she is strapped to the girl's belly. Above the rattle of hooves comes the thump of her lord's war bow as he picks off the Wealas running to intercept.

Clare stands unharmed in the chaos, her eyes following the path of the horse long after it has disappeared, feeling the despair weigh so heavily on her that she wonders that she can still stand. Behind her the sounds of battle change as the first rush reaches the palisade and axes meet shields. In a daze she turns, looking for her lord, and almost trips over the body of the warrior felled in the first volley of arrows. Clare bends to pick up his sword, a short single-edged weapon that feels powerful in her hands. It has neither the weight nor the length of the mighty pattern-welded blade on her lord's hip, the one Weyland made, but it would serve. Clare lifts it in front of her face, seeing her distorted reflection in the polished metal. Blonde hair. Anguished eyes that are starting to harden with resolve. She will not cower with the women. She is of the people of the swan and she will fight alongside her mate.

At the palisade, the first rush has fallen back, and one of her lord's warriors swings his spear shaft across his shield in a steady rhythm of challenge that is taken up all along the wall, until the air shakes with their defiance. Clare stoops to pick up the warrior's shield and walks to join them. It is all in the gods' hands now. If they so wish, she will live to see her children again. If not, then she will find such a death beside her lord as will be told around the fires of their people for all generations.

Chapter Seventeen

A HEAVY, RHYTHMIC thumping dragged Fergus from his sleep, making him flail about in the darkness, disoriented and panicking, not knowing where he was or what was happening. His arm connected with a bedside lamp, sending it toppling to the floor, and he lay panting until the shadows and the line of light under the door registered as his room at Mary Baxter's. The noise resolved into the steady banging of an unlatched window swinging in the wind, somewhere at the back of the house, which ended in a final slam and the rattle of a latch. Fergus fumbled for the fallen lamp and snapped it on, surprised to find it still worked. The bend to lift and replace it pulled at muscles still aching after the day's effort, and he stood to stretch. A moment later there was movement on the landing and a diffident, almost-unheard knock at his door.

Clare Harvey stood outside, pulling a dressing gown tightly around her, her eyes wide and round behind her glasses. She looked vulnerable, perhaps even frightened.

"I heard you moving around." She paused, her embarrassment clear. Fergus looked over his shoulder at his clock.

"Sorry to disturb you." A touch of desperation crept into Clare's voice. "I know it's late but I'm going downstairs to make a hot drink." She spoke faster now. "Would you like one?"

"Clare, it's the middle of the night..." Fergus struggled to keep his tone polite. If he'd known her better he'd have sworn.

"Please. I need to tell you something."

"Can't it wait until morning?"

"Please."

She turned away and Fergus followed her, muttering under his breath.

"Won't we wake Mrs Baxter?" It was hard for him to move quietly.

"She takes sleeping pills. Ever since her son was killed, apparently. Nothing wakes her at this time of night."

The reminder of their hostess's loss humbled him, blunting his irritation at being disturbed. In the kitchen he lowered himself into one of the chairs, hearing himself grunt like an old man as he slumped the last few inches and felt the sighing release of his limbs. He hoped this would not be a long conversation.

"So what's the crisis?"

Clare found a saucepan and poured in milk. Her shoulders lifted twice as if she was about to speak, then subsided with a sigh. Above her on the wall, a Palm Sunday reed cross was wedged behind a spice rack, its corn colour fading into grey and curling after twelve months of steam. Behind Clare, Fergus blinked away sleep and breathed his impatience.

"Sorry I left so suddenly this evening. I'm afraid your picture was a bit of a shock."

"It looked like you recognised Kate. But you didn't bring me down here in the early hours to tell me that."

"Yes, I recognised her." She tapped the wooden spoon on the side of the saucepan as if to emphasise her irritation.

"And?"

"This sounds really weird, but I'm having bad dreams about someone I've never met, but who looks like your colleague. And she's messing with my head." Clare poured hot milk into mugs and stirred in powder. Her movements were brisk, almost angry, but as she turned with the drinks her eyes were haunted. "When you said that she was dead I found that, well, spooky, so sorry if I was abrupt."

"No problem." Fergus pulled his drink towards him, wondering whether to risk upsetting Clare by leaving now. A woman dreaming about someone who looked like Kate was uncomfortably close to tattooed tramps and palm reading. That part of his head was already crowded.

"And I think you're part of this too."

He sat back in his chair, waiting for her to explain.

"The dreams started the day I met you. Then tonight, the next time I see you, they just got a whole lot worse. And they're not like some vague nightmare; they're very specific, very real. It's all mixed up with the dig, you see, almost as if I'm being shown things, however mad that sounds. But my subconscious must be making some of it up because I had put things from today into the dream."

"Such as?"

"In the dream there was a girl called Eadlin who rode horses, which must be because we were talking about Eadlin Stodman. 'Eadlin' is Anglo-Saxon for 'Little Princess', by the way. But the dreams are so intense it's like I'm going mad. There is a sense of dread, of fear building up in my head as if something awful is about to happen, so that I'm frightened to go to sleep. So I guess I'm trying to talk it through with someone who might not think I'm mad, and who seems to be involved in a way that I don't yet understand."

Clare rested her elbows on the Formica and blew steam off her drink, holding the mug two-handed. Fergus recognised that mannerism, and wondered if she was masking a shake. The eyes behind her glasses pleaded to be believed. Fergus was quiet for long enough for her to sip and put the mug back on the table. There was a slight rattle as it touched the Formica.

"A couple of weeks ago I might have thought you were crazy, but..." When Fergus didn't continue she tilted her head, prompting him to say more. Finally he inhaled, coming to a decision. He too needed to share a problem with a friendly stranger, to risk disclosure with someone whose disbelief would not wound.

"Actually, if we're sharing things that disturb us, I could tell you something just as weird." He breathed deeply again, trying to plan his revelation so that he kept the tone conversational, safely away from the pit.

"I think I've seen your Saxon."

Fergus expected at least to see surprise, but his revelation only triggered puzzlement.

"But he's not on display, yet."

"No, I mean I saw him standing by the car after the crash. I thought he was a tramp, but he had this strange tattoo on his forehead..." The scepticism in Clare's eyes silenced him, and Fergus felt a backlash of anger. She'd shared her own incredible experiences but didn't want to believe his. The stab of disappointment was almost physical. He forged on, almost stuttering as he struggled for words.

"The crash happened on the day you found the Saxon's body." Clare blinked but made no further comment, and he felt the crust over his mental pit start to crumble under his feet. "I'm told there are others in the village who claim to have seen him." This sounded lame. Clare was still listening, but he could see that only politeness was stopping her from commenting.

"He called Kate 'Olrun'." The memory leaped from brain to mouth, by-passing the protective filter. He saw Clare stiffen, suddenly more alert, but his mind was sliding towards the nightmare.

It was so clear, that time in the wreckage. After his last attempt to speak, that one word 'please' that had left him spent, the tramp had turned away. It was not even a dismissal. Fergus was simply not worth noticing. And from the depths of his loneliness, he watched the tramp stretch his hand through the windscreen void to caress Kate's hair.

Kate was not yet dead. There had been sounds, not long before, terrible sounds as if she was trying to vomit up the mess on which she was impaled. There had been movement too, pathetic fish-on-land flapping against the grip of the metal crushing their legs, although now she was still. But she was not yet dead, of that he was sure.

Olrun. As the tramp touched Kate's hair the name jumped into Fergus's brain as if spoken inside his head. It was said with infinite tenderness, a lover's greeting. Then the back-of-the-fingers caress had lifted in the kind of gesture a courtier might use to raise a lady from a chair for a dance. As he did so a deeper stillness settled over Kate and Fergus knew that she was dead.

Clare's scepticism had turned into alertness.

"Have you ever studied Saxon or Nordic mythology?" Her voice was excited now, an academic presented with new data. Fergus shook his head. The unexpected question helped him pull back from the brink. When he looked up, Clare was leaning forward across the table, hands gesticulating in emphasis.

"There is a well-known legend of Weyland, a magical blacksmith. He features in several surviving texts of that era, you see? This evening I dreamt that our Saxon wore a sword made by Weyland. In the legend, Weyland had two brothers, Slagfior and Egil, or Aegl. Remember I told you the origins of the name 'Allingley'? *Aegl-ingas-leah*? The clearing of the folk of Aegl? Anyway, in the legend the three brothers married three swan maidens." Clare wrinkled her nose under her glasses, and then pushed them back into place with her finger. She seemed to do that a lot when she was excited by her subject.

"Aegl's wife, the swan maiden, was called Olrun."

They stared at each other. Clare's eyes were now bright. Fergus felt he was trying to think though a surreal mental soup.

"What's a swan maiden?" he asked eventually, breaking the silence.

"Literally, a swan maiden was a shape-shifter, able to take on either human or swan form. But Saxon folklore was very strong on imagery and allegory, so the label 'swan maiden' might simply have been a way of describing a beautiful woman, see? There's another link," she said after a moment. "The legendary Aegl was a mighty archer. The muscles on the bog body tell us he was also an archer."

Fergus's head spun. His mind craved sleep and was not processing information. Clare reached into her dressing gown pocket and pulled out a small, silver pillbox, turning it over in her fingers.

"Every dig, I look for a token, like a talisman to connect me with the place, and I keep it with me. Nothing of intrinsic value, but some little artefact. A shard of pottery perhaps, or a broken piece of a bone comb. Once it was a rusty lump that had been an arrowhead. It's against the rules so I keep quiet about it, but I like to touch something that was touched by the people I'm excavating, you see? I need to create that physical link with the past. It helps me picture their lives."

Clare opened the lid of her pillbox, took out a stained tooth from a nest of cotton wool, and stroked it between her thumb and forefinger.

"This could be Olrun." She handed it to him. "The real Olrun."

"Looks like she's been to the dentist recently." Small drill holes and flake marks made pale wounds in the surface enamel. Fergus regretted his flippancy. Maybe he was too tired.

"We took several samples for radioisotope analysis, but we couldn't get a recognisable result, which is unusual."

"You'll have to explain that."

"Isotopes in tooth enamel are a way of finding out where someone grew up, see? That's how we know that the warrior in the bog was a first-generation immigrant, probably born somewhere around the mouth of the River Weser in what is now Germany. The woman's analysis was unusually vague, so we don't know where she came from. I can't remember ever getting results that are so meaningless."

"Maybe she flew in from Valhalla."

"Ha ha." She took back the tooth, caressing it. "She had children, you know."

"How...?"

"She managed to save them, before they were surrounded. Eadlin escaped on horseback with them strapped to her body." Clare's tone had tightened and she caressed the tooth with a strange, mesmerised intensity. Fergus didn't know how she expected him to react.

"Well, you didn't get that from isotopes." He was no longer sure of the ground rules for this conversation.

Clare looked at him as if deciding whether to trust him. "Can we keep this conversation between us?"

"Of course. I guess we're both suspending disbelief."

"Quite. Because this would totally wreck my credibility in the academic world if it became known." Clare took a deep breath before continuing. "If you think about it, we're always the actors in our own dreams. However bizarre the dream, we keep our identity. We don't go off and dream what it's like to be someone else."

"Unless we think we're Napoleon Bonaparte and we're in the loony bin."

"Huh." The tone said Clare didn't find this funny. "These dreams, the ones about the Saxon, it's me but it's not me. I have blonde hair, children and tits."

Fergus snorted at the unexpected vulgarity, but Clare had merely paused for breath, turning the pillbox over and over in her fingers and staring at it with morbid fascination.

"Clare, why are you telling me all this?"

"Because if I don't talk it through with someone, I think I'll go mad. And more than ever, I think you're part of this. Your blonde colleague. Seeing the Saxon. Olrun."

"Right now I'm struggling to keep up. Twenty minutes ago the only thing that disturbed me was seeing something that might have been an apparition, at a time when I was nearly dead anyway. Now you're talking about a whole mythology."

"But do you understand why I'm telling you? I don't know *why* this is happening to me. At first I really wanted the dreams. I even fell asleep hoping they would happen, because some of them were lovely. The Saxon and this woman, Olrun or whoever, they're lovers, see?" Fergus noticed that there was no conditional tense, no ambivalence. *They are lovers.* "And it really was like seeing the Saxons through their eyes. Literally, an archaeologist's dream. But now it feels like there's this huge weight of impending doom, like something terrible is going to happen."

"Do you think you might be getting too close to the project? Maybe you should leave that tooth behind." In response Clare closed her hand around the box and stuffed it into her dressing gown pocket.

"Maybe. Shit, I'm an academic. I deal in facts, hypotheses, evidence. Suddenly I'm confronted with something I can't prove to my peers, can't test against any scientific theory, and which would make me the laughing stock of the university if I tried to explain it. And after all, they're only dreams." Now she spoke too brightly, belittling her fears. Fergus stifled a yawn, feeling the drag of the day's efforts.

"Look, sorry, but I really must go to bed. We've both got more questions than answers." His body craved rest.

"'To sleep, perchance to dream; ay, there's the rub.'"

Fergus jerked his head back as it started to drop forward in sleep. He was vaguely aware that Clare had spoken, but he missed the words.

Chapter Eighteen

FERGUS PUSHED HIS bicycle up the lane to the stables, defeated by the incline. No matter. He'd set a benchmark and would now measure daily improvements. Besides, the world waking around him was so intense that he almost wanted to linger. Sunrise to a businessman was something that always happened on the other side of glass. It might be the glass of a windscreen as you stared at a morning traffic jam, or the glass of the office as you lifted your eyes from the overnight emails, but sunrise had always been wallpaper, a mere backdrop to life. It slipped past as part of the scarcely-noticed transition from night to day, less significant than the coffee. Fergus could not remember having smelt the sunrise before, that richness of newly turned earth in a morning so chill that there might have been a glacier beyond the Downs.

He paused in Ash Farm's car park, filling his lungs with the morning, letting his awareness expand. Fergus wondered how he could describe this moment to his former colleagues, then realised they wouldn't understand. They'd think he'd gone soft. Around him the landscape swelled as if some vast subterranean body had inhaled, tightening the earth over its curves. The land was female, fecund, as English as nut-brown ale, and rich with birdsong. No hum of equipment, no engine noise, just the dawn chorus and, at the edge of hearing, a sound that might have been singing.

Music. There should be music to mark the way the first lance of the sun was warming the hilltop woods from grey to brown. Elgar, perhaps. Something majestic. As his senses opened Fergus wasn't sure if the faint sound of chanting had been there from the beginning, or had just started, but it was there like a gentle undercurrent to the morning. There was something primitive about it, a tone signature from a time before music was written, sung in a rhythm that had the simple, insistent pace of a quickening heartbeat.

Intrigued, Fergus edged along the verge until he could look around the corner of the farmhouse towards the source of the chant. There, on grass that had once been a garden lawn, was Eadlin. She stood with her back towards him, facing the rising sun, with her arms stretched over her head so that her body formed the Y outline of a chalice, and she was singing a gentle chant in praise of the day. Rhythmic puffs of fog drifted from her mouth, fading from sharp light to nothing. Her forearms were outlined in a slender halo of gold where the downy hair stood clear in the cold against the rising sun.

Despite the morning chill Eadlin wore only a cotton shift, fine enough for the sun to hint at the silhouetted swell of a breast under her lifted arm. Her hair spilt down her back in a cascade that reached almost to her waist, auburn tumbling over white. Beyond her, horses grazed in the paddock with their breath steaming the grass. Behind her, her shadow stretched over the lawn until it split with the fork of her arms, one shadow arm running to his feet as if inviting him to join a dance. Eadlin's near-nakedness was no more sexual than the swell of the landscape around her, simply part of an act of raw worship that came from the dawn of time. Fergus stood transformed by the beauty of the moment, this instant of ethereal perfection. He felt that even if she had turned and seen him, their eyes could have met in pure appreciation.

It took perhaps ten heartbeats before Fergus realised that he was intruding, and a niggling sense of voyeurism made him back away. Embarrassed now, he edged back along the grass verge until he could turn and move quietly into a barn. As he started to breathe normally, horses' heads appeared over the stall doors, anticipating the morning feed and signalling the presence of a human by their whickering and movement. A little later, after his own morning communion with Trooper, the only sign that he had not dreamed the vision was the hairpin loop of footsteps in the dew across the lawn. As the sun rose further, soon that too was gone.

Jake arrived in the tack room later that morning while a stable girl was teaching Fergus the intricacies of bridles. He greeted Fergus by name, sliding one arm across his back as if they were lifelong buddies. His "heard you was back" was barked in the same tones that Fergus's former boss would have used to greet a favoured employee returning from vacation. Jake let his arm fall and pulled his face into a satiated, alley-cat grin. Fergus could smell alcohol on his breath. Jake, it seemed, had been partying.

"Morning, Jake." The stable girl looked at Jake from under lowered eyelashes, toying with a button on her shirt. Fergus was sure she had undone at least one button since Jake appeared.

"Morning, Emma." Jake smiled at her the way a rock star might smile at a groupie, and pulled his saddle off its peg. Fergus watched him leave, thinking that the guy had more charisma than was safe. God, it would be barely legal with this girl. How old was she? Seventeen, perhaps? The girl caught his look.

"He's gorgeous!"

"I think Eadlin's ahead of you."

She shook her head to dismiss his comment. "Won't last. Rumour is, Jake's been playing away."

By mid-afternoon, the sun had moved to the front of the farmhouse and Eadlin gathered a pile of tack onto one of the tables and showed Fergus how to clean it. They worked in amiable silence, working saddle soap into the stiffness of hard leather, while he formulated a question.

"Mary Baxter says you are a healer," Fergus began, struggling with a piece of leather.

"My Mum taught me how to use herbs, that's true." Eadlin smiled at him over her own pile of tack.

"In the wreck, when you found me, I remember you sang to me."

"You remember that, d'you?" Again, that lift of a single eyebrow. "You was almost beyond anyone's help then. It was only an old song to keep your attention, to stop you slipping away, like. Nowadays I gather first-aiders tend to shout at casualties and slap their faces to keep them awake. I just sang you a song."

"It had a strange rhythm, like an incantation."

"What's the difference? Incantation, prayer, song, they're just ways we give voice to something we want." There was a note of caution in her voice. The answer felt superficial.

"Well it worked for me, clearly. You could make a business out of it!"

Eadlin shook her head with a frown and a flash of what might have been irritation. "Nah. You can't sell what I do. It just wouldn't work. It's something my mother gave me, to use where I saw fit, in the same way that my gran gave it to her. If I ever have children I'll share it with them, if they have the aptitude. But it's a precious thing, more of a way of life, so you don't try and make a profit out of it. And you certainly don't want all the scrutiny and regulations that herbal practitioners have to put up with."

"You make it sound like a religion, almost like..." His voice tailed away.

"Like witchcraft, you mean?" Eadlin attacked a piece of leather as if it was responsible for such views. "It's funny. Healers in India chant as they cure people with herbal therapies, and the world gives it a fancy name like Ayurvedic medicine. Nowadays it's even acceptable in this country because it's exotic and we're allowed to be open to different ideas. Everyone forgets that we had similar knowledge here for thousands of years. The difference in this country is that a few hundred years ago they burnt anyone they caught doing it, so it went underground and a lot of knowledge was lost. But please don't call it witchcraft. That has all sorts of nasty connotations."

"So what *do* you call it?"

Eadlin looked at him and sighed, as if weighing up a decision.

"Well, if you're going to work around here you'd better know, so you don't barge in on any more morning prayers." Fergus felt himself blush. "Some people would call us pagans but even that's a label that the Christian church smeared us with, centuries ago. To us it's simply the Old Way. Mostly it's just traditions." She looked around for inspiration, and then waved her piece of leather at the freshly ploughed field beyond the paddock.

"Farmers round here will plant a cake in the first furrow that they plough in the spring. Whether you call that tradition or superstition, it's like a kind of respect to the soil that sustains them. Later in the year the same farmer will ask the Vicar to bless the harvest, and afterwards he'll join in the village harvest festival. You won't find the Vicar planting cakes in the first cut of a field, but he won't turn the farmer away from communion neither. Traditions and faith rub along together well, if you let them.

"But do me a favour, and keep what you see private, like. Around here we've learned to live peaceably together by not being too obvious about any differences. Even pillars of the church like Mary Baxter know that kindness doesn't have to wear a crucifix."

Eadlin's voice was even, with no undercurrent of mysticism, so she might as well have been talking about a church fete. Fergus had let his cloth drop onto the table, fascinated, but she waved a bridle at his pile of tack and reminded him that there was plenty more to do.

"So is this 'Old Way' a faith, or is it a way of healing?" Fergus was having difficulty concentrating on the stiff buckles in front of him. Eadlin put her own work down as if her answer was too important to be diluted with other activity.

"The Old Way teaches us that all living things are sacred, that there is a life force in everything and connecting everything." She closed her eyes and inhaled, so that her words seemed part of the vitality she described. "The life force is stronger in some places than others. Old trees concentrate it, so do springs and streams. Some places are naturally sacred, others are made sacred. The church in the village is sacred not because some priest scattered holy water in it, but because people have been worshipping there for at least a thousand years. You try going in there. Close your eyes and feel the peace."

Fergus felt that however bizarre this conversation would have been in the concrete of a city, it was strangely appropriate here in the countryside, surrounded by birdsong and blossom, the sounds and smells of spring.

"Isn't it a bit strange for a... for someone from the 'Old Way' to be enthusing about a church?"

"Nah, why not? To us it's simply a different way of saying the same thing. Christians pray to God for divine guidance. We chant to focus the energy of life, so our minds can find the spirit that's inside all of us. When you've had a few more riding lessons we'll hack out, and I'll take you to some places that will feel at least as sacred as a church."

"I think the Vicar might disagree. About it being similar, I mean."

"I'm sure he would. He'd probably think we're a bit too liberal in other ways, as well." Eadlin's eyes sparkled.

"In what way?" Fergus kept his tone innocent. He liked it when she flirted.

"Well I don't go along with it personally, but some people think that making love is a way of channelling energy." There were throaty undertones to Eadlin's voice.

"But you don't agree with that?" Now it was Fergus's turn to flirt.

"Nah. If the sex is that good, the last thing I want to think about is a cure for Grandma's lumbago." Eadlin chuckled in a rich, earthy way as she picked up a piece of leather and started polishing. Fergus caught himself flicking a sideways glance at the way her sweater moved as she worked, and he spoke a question as it came into his mind, without thinking.

"So is Jake a follower of this 'Old Way'?" He couldn't reconcile his high-energy, high-ego picture of Jake with Eadlin's picture of her faith.

Her mood changed as if some switch had been thrown. Too late, he realised that Jake's alley-cat look that morning probably hadn't been acquired in Eadlin's company.

"Jake," she said finally, "has chosen his own path."

Then she worked silently, punishing the leather with brisk movements, with her mouth set into a line. Fergus bit his lip and cursed himself for his insensitivity.

Part Three

Ēastre

April

The Paschal month... was once called after a goddess of [the Anglo-Saxons] named Ēastre, in whose honour feasts were celebrated in that month. Now they designate that Paschal season by her name, calling the joys of the new rite by the time-honoured name of the old observance.

Venerable Bede, *De Temporum Ratione* written in AD725

Chapter Nineteen

In HIS SECOND week, the week before Easter, Fergus's body was a collection of articulated aches, and he started to wonder if his exercise routine was too gruelling. At the end of the day he'd drag his bicycle through Mary Baxter's front gate, in urgent need of a hot soak and a large glass of wine, but one evening he paused in Mary's tiny front garden to listen to a woman's voice singing in a rich contralto. But for the mess a pianist was making of the accompaniment, it could have been mistaken for a radio performance. Someone, nearby, could sing. The pianist fumbled to a stop.

"Sorry." Clare's voice was followed by more, inexpert attempts at a chord. Fergus traced the sounds to the fanlight window of Mary's front room. Through the glass he could see Clare sitting at the piano, with Mary standing behind her, now humming her encouragement as Clare tried to find the notes. Fergus found it hard to believe that such a sound had come from Mary's frame. It should have come from an operatic dame, all bodice and bosom, not from dumpy little Mary. The music stopped as his key turned in the lock, and the two women turned towards the door into the hall as he appeared, smiling at him over the top of their spectacles in accidental co-ordination.

"Hi Fergus." Clare sounded genuinely pleased to see him. "We're practising Mary's piece for Holy Thursday."

"With the choir," Mary added. "I'm doing a duet with Cynthia Lawrence." Fergus had a vague memory of Cynthia as the over-dressed soprano with the loud voice.

"Do you like Pergolesi?" Clare asked.

"Love it. Especially with a little grated parmesan and a nice Chianti."

She stuck her tongue out at him. "Baroque church music. Mary's singing Pergolesi's 'Stabat Mater' and it's beautiful. I'm staying in Allingley until after the evening service so I can listen. Do come."

Which was how Fergus found himself in church on a Thursday, possibly for the first time in his life, and sharing a pew with Clare. Behind them people came through the doors in ones and twos and family groups, exchanging whispered greetings as they hurried to their pews. *Kiss, kiss, how's the family?* The church inhaled life as the evening fell, with people fluttering in from the fading day to mass in the church's candlelight like a horde of flightless butterflies. Beside him Clare craned her neck to study the church's ceiling, and interrupted his reverie.

"Imagine what the medieval peasants would have thought of this place."

Fergus sensed that Clare was about to launch into one of her imaginative descriptions. An easy companionship was developing between them; she was good company when she wasn't talking about dreams.

"Much the same as us, probably," he prompted.

"I doubt it. This would have been the only stone building for miles around. Put yourself in the mind of a serf who lives in a draughty, wattle-and-daub hovel. The priest would be dressed in a clean white surplice, and speak Latin, and you'd know yourself to be dirty and illiterate. His incense would make you realise you stank, and this," she slapped the great column beside her, one of a line marching down the aisle, "stamps his authority on earth."

Fergus looked around, impressed. Clare could conjure up the minds of the ancients. He could see no further than the plaques on the walls, and still only wonder at their lives. Near their heads, beneath a family crest and the badge of a distinguished regiment, was a simple memorial to Robert D'Auban, 2nd Lieutenant, Mons 1914, Aged 19. Albert D'Auban, Captain, Ypres 1917, Aged 24. *Dulce et decorum est pro patria mori.* Above them in the darkening glass a yellow-haired, infant Christ raised chubby fingers in blessing. How typical of the hubris of Empire, he thought, to show a blond Christ. It spoke of an age when God spoke English and had commissioned the British to civilise the world in their image.

Eadlin had said something about this church's atmosphere, about it being a holy, peaceful place. Fergus shut his eyes and opened his mind, trying to let the tranquillity come to him. There was something there, perhaps, some pervasive calm amidst the hushed movements of the gathering congregation, but nothing as powerful as his moment of communion that day with Trooper. It was elusive, calling to him like the scent of a distant flower.

"Can you smell it?" He turned to look at Clare, interrupting a comment about the Tudor roses on the ceiling. She lifted her nose like an animal testing the wind.

"Smell what? I smell musty books, wood polish, candles, flowers... Smells like a church to me."

Fergus shrugged. One minute Clare could have romantic notions about ancient peasants, the next she would deliver an academic treatise on medieval ceilings. Fergus tried to put his thoughts into words, surprised by his own candour.

"Peace. Centuries of peace."

Clare looked at him through the top of her glasses, then pushed them slowly up her nose as if she needed a moment to digest his comment. "Well," she said eventually, "this place has certainly been around for a while." She nodded over her shoulder at a painted board, listing 'Priests and Rectors of St Michaels Church' in an unbroken line starting in 1210. A footnote explained that records before 1210 were unreliable.

Fergus shook his head, lacking the words to articulate a concept that was only half formed in his own mind. He was wondering if a place could have an atmosphere that would survive the people within it, the way mellow brick could absorb heat from the sun and stay warm through a chill evening.

Still musing, Fergus stood, sang, sat and knelt through the service's ritualised choreography, as much a bystander as he'd been at that last sales meeting. His mind drifted back to another act of worship, when Eadlin had saluted the sunrise of Ostara on her lawn.

But gently, so gently that at first Fergus did not notice the shift in his mood, the atmosphere of the place started to take hold. As the light faded outside, the ceiling softened into a faint tracery, almost lost in darkness. Where it met the supporting columns, a line of stone angels gazed down. A trick of the eye and mind could easily imagine the music to be coming from them and from a celestial void beyond rather than the choir below.

In an expectant silence Tony Foulkes moved a music stand to the front of the choir stalls, and Cynthia Lawrence and Mary Baxter, in cassocks and flowing surplices, moved out to face the congregation. The cardboard edge of Mary's music folder shook a little as she prepared herself, her face tight with nerves. Beside and towering above them, a bare wooden cross had been erected as the church's only decoration this Holy Thursday night. Fergus glanced down at his service sheet, reading:

Pergolesi (1710 – 1736): Stabat Mater
Cynthia Lawrence, soprano, Mary Baxter, contralto

Stabat Mater dolorosa iuxta crucem lacrimosa dum pendabat Filius

The grieving mother stood weeping by the cross where her Son was hanging

The organ started its introduction, tracing simple chords whose melancholy commanded attention. Then Mary's voice opened, her deep contralto interweaving with Cynthia's higher soprano in a chord that reached for the listener's heart, squeezed, then pulled until the tears flowed. It was a performance of such aching beauty that all movement was stilled, and their music rang within a pure silence. For perhaps four minutes it was as if no breath was taken inside the church except those of the singers. Mary and Cynthia sang the same words, but it was a dialogue, an interplay of harmonies. Cynthia's angelic purity soared to the rafters with the love of a God who would submit to death. Mary's deeper tones stayed grounded on the marble, singing with infinite sorrow of a mother's love for a murdered Son, and all around them the congregation wept. As the music ended there was utter silence, and Fergus looked up to where the ancient rafters loomed in the candlelight, blinking his eyes and wondering how music could be so moving. Finally the silence was broken by a sniff and a ripple of quiet movement as hands reached for handkerchiefs. Fergus felt Clare take his hand, sharing a moment of exquisite beauty. She too was crying.

In front of the two singers, Tony Foulkes placed his baton on the music stand and made an almost-invisible circle of finger on thumb, the sign of perfection, before bowing his thanks. For those four minutes Mary and Cynthia had been transformed from individuals into channels for music, and now as they turned back towards the choir stalls they recovered their own identities. Cynthia Lawrence walked tall, smiling slightly, proud of a performance well executed, but Mary sagged, as if her gift had cost her dearly.

At the end of the service the congregation stood and moved towards the door in near silence, exhaling as they stood as if they had only just remembered to breathe. Many were still too moved for conversation. Watching them, Fergus tried unsuccessfully to reconcile this mood of sacrificial love with the naturalistic harmony he had witnessed on Eadlin's lawn at the dawn of the equinox. Across the church, John Webster swung open the ancient oak doors to release a congregation that had been touched with divinity on this eve of Christ's crucifixion.

The sound of a table overturning onto marble sounded like a gunshot in the hushed church, and the mood of serene peace disintegrated at the Vicar's cry of "for the love of God!" Ripples of consternation spread like shock waves through the mass of people from an epicentre by the door, where John Webster and the leading choristers were recoiling from some unseen horror in the porch. Using the column for support, Fergus climbed onto the pew to peer over the heads of the congregation.

During the service the church doors and inside of the porch had been daubed with fresh blood. It glistened in the porch light, staining the priest's surplice with crimson where he had brushed against the door. Over the shoulders of the semi-circle standing aghast behind Webster, Fergus could see a crudely-painted stag's head on the white plaster of the porch. Its antlers trickled new branches in running blood, and the snout drooled crimson onto the marble tiles of the floor.

Chapter Twenty

THE RHYTHM OF the village had changed the following morning. Fergus set off on his bicycle into a fog that deadened sound and smothered light, as if spring had reversed back into winter. He'd become accustomed to seeing the same patterns of movement. Village people, apparently, were as regular in their lives as commuters who caught the same train each morning. Clare, he knew, was a temporary feature as she packed in a morning run before returning home for the Easter weekend, but the slack-bellied men swivelling their heads to watch her run past would still be fetching their morning paper at the same time without the distraction of her body. Their faces, though, had a haunted look about them in the fog.

Tony Foulkes was also an early riser, usually striding out behind a Labrador and calling cheerfully to everyone he met. Today the Labrador was tied to the church notice board, whining for its walk, while Tony and John Webster scrubbed at the church porch, letting daylight show them the smears they had missed the night before. Above them the tower faded into the fog so that its castellation appeared insubstantial, and the banner of St George beyond was a mere hint of scarlet in the void. Both men nodded at Fergus, their faces tightening into smiles that did not reach the eyes.

Fergus paused on his bicycle and called a greeting, wanting to offer support but unsure what to say. Webster hoped that the daubing was a childish prank, perhaps by the same kids who had been frightening old ladies by leaping out of bushes with biro tattoos on their foreheads. Webster had decided not to wait for the police, wanting his church to be cleaned of the stain without delay. Foulkes wondered how many children had access to a bucket of blood. He had scraped a sample into a plastic medicine bottle and taken photographs. Neither imagined that the police would take the incident very seriously. Fergus left them to their task.

The fog could not deaden the sounds of a furious row that spilt out of the office at Ash Farm later that morning. Fergus paused in his task of mucking out a stable, trying to hear the words. The shouting ended in a metallic crash and he started moving towards the house, hefting a fork. Jake stormed out while he was still crossing the yard, slamming the door behind him and almost knocking Fergus over as he passed.

"Are you OK?"

Eadlin looked up from where she was gathering scattered rubbish from the floor, and nodded. It looked as if the waste bin had been kicked against the wall.

"Sodding man." She picked up a toppled desk tidy that had scattered a spray of pencils and slammed it upright, hard enough for more pencils to bounce out and rattle across the desk. "Sodding, bloody man. Can't think what I ever saw in him." Eadlin slumped into her chair, closing her eyes as if with a bad headache. "I need to let off steam. Let's go for a hack. It's time you rode out."

Outside in the yard Jake was swinging into the saddle, yanking at his horse's mouth to turn it towards the bridleway.

"If you think I'm ready." So far he'd only ridden in the sand school.

"You're ready, on the right horse. We'll keep it gentle, like." Fergus's attention was still on Jake. The horse was prancing under him in the car park, feeling its rider's tension, and Fergus winced as he saw Jake's riding crop swing backwards in a punishing blow to its rump. The horse bucked at the sting but Jake stayed glued to the saddle, perfectly balanced, and then struck again, hard.

"Bastard." Eadlin had seen the blows. "I can't believe he just did that."

Eadlin led Fergus out of the farm on a different route. She was quiet for the first few minutes, riding ahead of him up a narrow track towards the hills. Her shoulders were set and her horse was skittish, jogging in its impatience to run, so that its tail swished with the movement. Above it, Eadlin's hair flowed from under her riding hat, an auburn waterfall echoing the chestnut below. Then the path widened and she stood in her stirrups, turning back to invite him alongside.

"Sorry 'bout that. Jake, I mean."

"Do you want to talk about it?"

She breathed so deeply that her shoulders broadened as if she was about to hit something.

"Jake and I are history." She exhaled, her body settling deeper into the saddle. "We've been history since Ostara, even though he won't accept it. No woman dumps Jake, you see? His ego won't allow it."

"Was that why you were arguing?"

"Nah, today's fight was about the blood on the church. Things are getting way out of hand."

Fergus wondered what 'things' were getting out of hand. He was also surprised. He hadn't seen Jake as someone who'd daub blood on a church. "You think Jake did that?"

"Nah, not him personally, and he'll have a dozen cronies who'll swear he was in his pub all evening. But the stag mark tells me it'll have been done by one of his gang, someone who looks up to him, like that little runt Dick Hagman."

"You mentioned him once before."

"He's a local odd-job man. He's not the sharpest tool in the box but like one or two other Green Man regulars, he idolises Jake. If it's not Dick Hagman, it will be someone like him, so I hold Jake responsible."

"Look, it was a pretty sick thing to do, but why are you so upset about graffiti on a Christian church?"

As the track rose towards the hills the sun started to burn off the fog so that they rode in a bright, suffused light. For a moment the only sound was the wet brushing of the horses' hooves as they pushed through the grass. When Eadlin spoke she sounded calmer.

"The Old Way survived round here because we was quiet about our beliefs. People said we was just keeping quaint local traditions alive and we didn't, like, threaten anyone. Even the healing was done as a favour to friends. Now it feels like Jake wants to start a war."

"What's his problem? What does he want to fight about?"

"Y'know, I'm not sure? It's like he's just flexing his muscles, trying to prove he's king of the roost. But please, let's stop talking about him. He's spoiling my ride."

Fergus was content to be quiet and enjoy the novelty of being in the open on horseback. Ahead of them the Downs were taking shape through the cloud. Already the sky was almost blue overhead, fading to soft grey where mist swallowed the trees above the hedgerows. In front of them the path opened into a short valley that carved a green notch into the band of woodland beneath the Downs. A large bird of prey circled over the grass, making a high, plaintive, keening wail, like a farmer whistling for a lost dog. There was something unearthly about the call.

"Red kite," Eadlin said, pointing her riding crop at it, then grinned across at him, calmer now. "Let me show you somewhere special." She nodded up the valley to where its two-field width narrowed to one, which in turn ended in an angle under the trees, still opaque in the distance. Eadlin set off towards the trees at a canter, then let out a *whoop* and lifted out of the saddle to crouch jockey-like as she put her horse into a gallop. Fergus watched her little thoroughbred pull away from his docile mount the way a sports car accelerates past a truck. By the time he caught up with her in the angle of the field she had already dismounted and was grinning widely.

"Sorry 'bout that, leaving you behind, like." The smile and flushed face belied her words. "Horse therapy. It clears the mind. Hold the horses, I'll shut the gate. The farmer won't mind if we let them graze for a while."

Fergus lowered himself out of the saddle, reconnecting with his limp after the exhilaration of the canter. Eadlin led him on foot into the outskirts of the woods, following the banks of a small stream, and making no compromise for his pace of movement so he struggled to catch up. Where the hill steepened around them, the stream emerged from its source in a marshy tangle of roots beneath ancient trees.

"Come and sit." Eadlin patted a root lying along the surface, as thick as a tree trunk and furred with moss. "Mind the bluebells. They'll be lovely in May." The area was carpeted with the green starfish shapes of young plants. As Fergus sat, Eadlin squatted on her heels by the stream, folded over her riding boots, and splashed water on her face in a way that appeared to be more a cleansing ritual than refreshment. From her pocket she drew a crumpled paper bag and emptied the contents into the palm of her hand before scattering them on the surface of the stream. They looked like dried herbs, and a faint floral fragrance drifted up to him. Eadlin sang quietly to herself as she lowered her hands into the water, washing the dust into the stream.

"Some kind of offering?" Fergus asked as she sat beside him.

"Think of it as a mark of respect. Can you feel this place? It's probably been sacred since the earliest tribes came, long before Christ."

Fergus looked around him, seeing a woodland dell, mainly brown and bare but splashed with the latent greens of spring. He was not sure what he was supposed to notice, or feel.

"It's very pretty."

"Sod pretty. Relax, shut your eyes, empty your mind. Tell me what comes to you."

Fergus closed his eyes and breathed deeply.

"I hear things." It may have been his imagination, but his hearing felt sharper in this place. "The kite, a woodpecker. There's a breeze coming, clearing the fog. It's stronger above us, out of the shelter of the valley." He surprised himself with his eloquence.

"Good. What else?"

"The smell of the earth. Rich." Fergus decided not to mention the waft of animal droppings. "And I smell you. Horse smells and femininity."

"Thank you. Don't flirt, not now. Forget the senses you know about, what do you *feel*?"

Fergus let his mind empty. It was there, on the edge of sensation. It may have been planted by her suggestion, but he felt a hint of something old yet strong, a pure gentleness at the heart of all things.

"Vitality. Harmony." There was a note of wonder in his voice.

"That's it. Breathe it. Open yourself to it." Without opening his eyes, Fergus knew from Eadlin's silence that she too was absorbing the moment and the place. He felt he was being given a glimpse of Eden, and in his mind he reached for it but the vision faded, fragmenting beyond his touch as if it had been a reflection on a lake and he had thrust his hand through the water's surface.

"Don't try too hard. Open your mind, be peaceful, and it may come to you, but it can never be commanded. If it comes to you, and if you can find that focus, you'll find more wisdom there than in a whole world of books. You can open your eyes now." Below them the horses grazed quietly in the field, the kite was still circling, but they now all felt connected in a universal harmony. Eadlin's smile was wholesome and somehow at one with the landscape.

"I was right, you *are* sensitive. Maybe you've always been, but never discovered the gift. Maybe it's something that stayed with you when you touched the shadow world."

Fergus fumbled for words, unable to describe what he had glimpsed, but only one word fitted the moment.

"Peace..."

"Some people can find that peace anywhere. For most of us it's easier in certain places. Springs like this one, even churches. Some people never find it at all. I doubt if Jake has."

Fergus felt as if a fragment of distant music had called to him, but faded before he could listen properly. The silence became companionable; the sighing of the wind through the trees above them was all the communication that was required.

"You mentioned once that Jake had found his own path," he said eventually. He guessed that here, in this place, she wanted to talk.

Eadlin nodded. "His family were part of the Old Way, but we've always been a bit too peaceful for him. Last year he started experimenting with Wicca."

"Wicca. That's another name for witchcraft, isn't it?"

"I think its appeal to Jake is that Christians see it as the Enemy. He was caught stealing from the church, you see, when he was a kid. Long before John Webster came. He had form, as they say, so Jake did time in a young offenders institution. I don't know what happened to him there, but he came back hating the organisation that put him there."

"So what does Wicca involve?" Fergus was fascinated.

"Actually Wicca is pretty new. People are trying to re-invent something out of scraps of old knowledge. I'm sure some Wiccans are perfectly decent people, but Jake's found a darker form. Somewhere along the line he's picked up some pretty nasty ideas."

In front of them two pigeons strutted an elaborate courtship ritual on a branch overhanging the field. Their neck-rubbing and cooing was in harmony with the place in a way that talk of witchcraft would never be.

"Is that why you split up?"

"Partly. He started killing things. Sacrificing them." Eadlin started pulling at the crumpled paper bag in her hands, shredding it distractedly in her fingers so a fragment dropped into the stream and spun slowly away. "No follower of the Old Way would do that. We've too much respect for nature."

"So who or what are they worshipping?" This place made everything possible. A month ago he'd have reacted with derision.

"The Horned God and the Goddess." Eadlin paused, and swallowed. "Christians would call the Horned God 'Satan'."

In front of them the pigeons had started to mate, flapping furiously on the branch, their tails entwined. Fergus started to wonder what sort of world he had arrived in, where a woman would greet the sunrise half-naked on her lawn, then talk in matter-of-fact terms of Satanic worship as if it was as natural as the pigeons having noisy sex in front of them.

"There was something else." She balled the remains of the paper bag in her palm. "Wiccans believe that the Gods use people as proxies, like, so the priest and the priestess in a ritual actually become the Horned God and the Goddess." Eadlin paused. She seemed embarrassed. On the branch the pigeons had finished copulating and were sitting side by side. Fergus could swear one of them looked smug.

"Go on."

"In some of their ceremonies, the Horned God screws the Goddess. 'Ritual union' Jake calls it, which is a fancy name for a public fuck. Last year Jake asked me to play the part of the Goddess, at Halloween or Samhain as he calls it. Now I'll make love with someone because I love him, or maybe even if I only fancy him, but there's no way I'm going to have sex in front of others, particularly as part of some nasty ritual that I don't even believe in."

"I don't blame you. What happened when you refused?"

"We had a row, and I didn't go to his party, or sabbat as he insisted on calling it, but he found a substitute. Jake has never had a problem finding women. I told him if he ever did that again I'd chop off his balls."

One of the pigeons strutted nonchalantly down the branch and flew off across the field. Its mate watched its departure without apparent concern.

"Ostara." Fergus remembered Jake's satiated smirk the morning after the equinox.

"Yeah. 'Just a bit of fun' he says, but he's starting to take it very seriously. Especially since you arrived."

Fergus straightened on the root, alarmed.

"'Fraid so. At Samhain he killed a stag, you see, some poor beast he'd caught after it'd been injured in the rut. The next day they dug up the Saxon with a stag tattoo on his face. When stories started to go round about the Saxon's ghost being seen, Jake let rumours circulate that he was responsible, like he was some kind of warlock. Then you came back and told us that a stag caused your crash, so he's strutting round the place saying that's proof. You're his, like, trophy."

Fergus stared at the stream below them, his thoughts tumbling over themselves like water over pebbles. There was too much that he didn't understand. Seeing the Saxon in the wreckage. Hearing the power of Eadlin's chant. The memory of his fight back towards the light. A glimpse of pure harmony, in this place.

"Eadlin, I still believe that I'm only alive because you brought me back. Does Jake have power, in that sense?"

"You brought yourself back. I just helped a bit, and nah, no way does Jake have any special power. He doesn't have the aptitude. Whatever skills I have are handed down through the generations. It takes years of study, practice, and sometimes a bit of self-denial, and I have no idea how to do the things he's claiming to have done. I suppose Jake might have stumbled on something, but he sure as hell won't know how to use it. Maybe that makes him dangerous."

"Where's all this going, Eadlin? What does Jake want to achieve?"

Eadlin shrugged. "Dunno. Jake needs to control people. I think the blood on the church is like a challenge. The frightening thing is, these days he believes in his own power, and he's got enough ego for some people to follow him, 'specially the ones that are easily led like Hagman. But it feels like it's more than Jake; there's a tension building up all round us. It's as if the village is sickening with something so you know it's going to get worse even if right now there's only a slight headache, like. Places like this," she lifted her chin towards the source of the stream, "are the pulse of the land. You can feel its health. There's a place up the valley from Allingley, around where your car crashed, a place that used to be as sacred as this. But now Jake uses it for his rituals and it feels sick, even mad."

Eadlin hunched forward to squat by the stream, letting the water trickle over her fingers, with her body folded into a Z of riding boots and leg and torso, and her breasts pressed against the tops of her thighs.

"Thanks," she said, turning her face to him and resting her cheek on her knees.

"What for?"

"Listening. For not laughing at all these silly ideas. For being around. It helps."

A strand of copper hair had fallen forward across her face and Fergus reached forward to push it back behind her ear.

"Fergus, don't. Don't get too close, not in that way."

"Why not? We get on well."

"We get on too well, sometimes, but you don't belong to this place. I'll spend my life here, but one day soon you'll go back to being a businessman or whatever it is that you do."

"Maybe, but I like it here. Who knows what the future holds?"

"You're like a kid that's just been let out of school. You've barely been here a couple of weeks, and the weather's been good. Try running a stables in winter when you're sliding around in freezing mud earning the minimum wage for ten hours a day. Besides, our outlook on life is totally different."

"In what way?"

"You're used to having money. You need stuff like your flash car and those designer jeans you're wearing."

"Well, I used to earn a good income, so what?"

"People like you tend to want all kinds of things, maybe even think you have to have those things before you can enjoy life."

Fergus shrugged. Eadlin's comment was a bit stark, but not unfair.

"You think that you need all things to enjoy life. But I think you have been given life so that you can enjoy all things. It's the opposite starting point." Eadlin softened her words with a smile.

There was silence while Fergus absorbed what she'd said, a silence broken only by the distant scream of the kite.

"That sounds a bit profound for me, but even if you're right it doesn't stop us being friends while I am here."

"Fergus, I hope we'll be friends for a very long time, but I think we're more likely to be friends for a long time if we're not lovers for a short time. I know we flirt a bit, and that's good for my ego, but I don't want to lead you on."

Fergus sighed. "It seems to be my luck to fall for untouchable women."

"You haven't fallen for me. You just fancy me, and you probably haven't had sex for a very long time."

Fergus looked away.

"... besides," she continued, "for all you know, I might already be seeing someone!" Eadlin jumped to her feet and brushed her hands against her jodhpurs, suddenly energetic. "Come on, don't look so glum."

Eadlin pulled him to his feet and ran down the stream bank ahead of him, skipping lightly as if she had dropped a burden, and vaulted the fence into the field. Fergus followed more slowly, unbalanced on the uneven ground and grabbing at trees for support. When he caught up with her beside his horse, Eadlin put both hands on his shoulders and stood on tiptoes to kiss him on the cheek.

"Friends, right?"

"Friends. But you'll still have to help me up." Fergus nodded sideways at the horse and she dropped into her knees-flexed, basket-of-hands posture to help him into the saddle. Eadlin grinned at him and lifted an eyebrow as she crouched.

"I love it when you do that."

"Look, but don't touch." Eadlin vaulted him into the saddle and mounted her own chestnut.

"How do you like hacking out?" she asked.

"I could get a taste for this. Maybe with a horse that's a bit more, er, lively?"

"Good. I think it's time you tried Trooper, to give you the feel of something sharper. We'll keep you in the school for a while, until I'm sure you can handle him."

Fergus's grin as they rode off was exuberant.

* * *

SEVERAL HUNDRED YARDS away, in the trees above the far side of the valley, Jake Herne swore as he watched their departure through pocket binoculars. As they cantered out of the valley, he wheeled his horse with a vicious yank on the reins and trotted away in the opposite direction.

Chapter Twenty-One

EASTER TUESDAY. ONE month exactly since he first came to Allingley in search of Eadlin. No crutches today, no stick, just a walk like Quasimodo. Oh, and a few aches. Fergus decided to reward himself with a pub supper, and walked up the hill to the White Hart. His spirits lifted at the sight of Clare sitting on a bench near the church. She was staring over the green towards the Downs, with her head moving slowly as if she was scanning the landscape in search of a distant landmark.

"Good Easter?"

She turned to look at him. For a moment her stare was blank, until she snapped into focus and smiled.

"Sorry, I was daydreaming. Yes, thanks." Clare spoke as if her mind was still far away.

"Can I join you?" Fergus started to settle onto the seat, glad of the rest.

"What do you believe in, Fergus?"

Fergus paused in the act of sitting, surprised by the direct question.

"Why's everyone asking that around here?"

Clare turned her head away to look into the distance, more as if she were looking through the landscape than at it. "Because I've only ever believed in things that can be tested, things that follow a proven, scientific principle. Anything else is a hypothesis or a fairy story."

"Do I see the road to Damascus over there? What's changing your mind?"

The corners of Clare's mouth flickered briefly, showing more politeness than amusement as she took off her glasses and polished them on a handkerchief. For the first time, he noticed that she had flecks of green in mll eyes. They gave her a faint air of mystery, of something hidden.

"These dreams. I'm trying to work out *why* I'm getting them."

"A lot of people dream about their work. Maybe you're getting too close to it. Do many archaeologists carry pieces of dead people around in their pockets?"

Clare lifted her arm and let it drop back on her knee, as if irritated by his comment. "These are more than dreams. The detail is unsettling. Either I'm going mad or..."

"Or?"

"Or I'm being shown something, ludicrous as that might be for an academic to say." Clare pushed her glasses back onto her nose and stared at him, wide-eyed. He sensed her fear of ridicule. That gamine look was child-like and vulnerable, triggering an urge to help.

"And what are you being shown?" Fergus feared he was being sucked into a conversation he didn't need. Tonight he wanted wine and laughter, not spooks and visions.

"So far it's all logical. Archaeologically believable, that is." Clare waved over her shoulder towards the church. "I see an early Saxon settlement based around a great thatched hall where the church now stands. There's a defensive palisade around it stretching down to the bank of the Swanbourne, you see? And I could prove it. I bet if I dug a trench starting over there, I'd find a line of post holes marking the perimeter."

"An excavation that no-one's going to allow." Fergus had followed her pointing finger, which swept through the churchyard and a cluster of cottages before returning across the green. "In any case, if that's as logical as you say, it wouldn't prove anything."

Clare carried on as if he had not spoken. "No houses then, of course, and the valley was cleared for crops, so there was a clear view from here to where the Mill House now stands. No dam, though, just that spur of the hill."

"This all sounds very detailed."

"I told you, it feels frighteningly real. Real enough to remember the sound of rain striking metal helmets, and feel the weight of weapons."

"Shit!"

"I must have excavated a dozen Saxon swords in my career. They used a distinctive, single-sided blade called a seax, see? That's what gave them their name, Seaxons. Usually all that's left is a rust stain in the soil, but now I'm dreaming of the weight of one in my hand. She fought, you see, our Olrun."

"Clare, I really think you should talk…"

"I am. I'm talking to you. Do you know the sound of an arrow hitting someone's face?" Clare spoke more quickly now, an edge of hysteria creeping into her voice. "Sort of wet and hard at the same time, and it's as real and shocking as watching someone shot over there, today." She pointed towards the White Hart, where a tall, well-built man had just parked an old Land Rover. There was a flash of auburn hair from the passenger side as Eadlin got out and joined him. Fergus watched the pair go into the pub together.

"Why don't we…"

"And in the dream it feels as if the Saxon, Aegl, is my lover…"

"I'm told necrophilia is dead boring."

Clare's shoulders sagged. "Ha bloody ha. Look, take me seriously will you? I need to talk to someone about it and it's easier if you don't laugh at me."

"Sorry. It's a bad habit of mine. I get flippant about things that make me nervous, like dead Saxons. And I'm not laughing at you."

"Well, if this is making you nervous, think what it's doing to me. Tell me I'm not going mad, Fergus." Again that pleading look.

"I don't think you're mad. There's something weird going on that neither of us understands. But don't you think it would be better if you spoke to someone, um, professional about this?"

Clare shook her head emphatically. "That goes back to what I said at the beginning. If I'm not going loopy, I'm being shown something. If I see a doctor I'll be off the project and onto Valium, and I've lost all chance of working this out. For me, the question is not what I'm being shown, but why. It's just that I haven't worked out the message yet. And I wish you could understand what it costs for an academic to admit even the possibility of something so unscientific."

"It sounds like you need a drink." Fergus's eyes were still on the White Hart.

"Thanks. It might help me sleep."

"If my sparkling conversation hasn't had the same effect."

"Sorry, I'm not much company at the moment." Clare stood, and for a moment she seemed to be staring through the cottages on the opposite side of the green. "Last night…" She waved across the green.

"Last night what?"

"Nothing. I wanted to give you an idea of what it's like to be inside someone else's head. To think as they thought. When I'm in the dream, it's real, every bloody moment. Then when I try and put it into words…" Her voice faded away. Fergus put his arm around her shoulder and hugged.

"Hey, I believe you. And I don't think you're mad, any more than I am. But maybe we're both a bit screwed up."

Clare's eyes filled as they walked across the green, and she slipped her arm inside his elbow.

Chapter Twenty-Two

EADLIN HAD MANAGED to find a table. She smiled at Fergus across the crowded bar and spoke sideways to her companion before waving them over. The man beside her was a big, broad-shouldered individual with a mop of sandy hair, and he stood as Clare approached rather like a tousled bear rearing up on its hind legs. Eadlin introduced him as Russell Dickens, and as Fergus completed the introductions Russell enfolded Clare's hand in a great, oil-stained paw. Clare treated him to one of her pause-then-smile greetings, and Fergus could swear the man started to blush.

"Russell owns the Forge Garage on the green," Eadlin explained as they sat. "We was just discussing the May Day celebrations in the village. Russell's organising some of the events."

"Eadlin provides the horses and the wagon for the May Queen, see?" Russell spoke to Clare rather than the group. His voice had the same rural burr as Eadlin, but he spoke more slowly, almost shyly, as if he considered all his words before assembling them as speech.

"Wonderful! A traditional May Day festival!" Clare's stress had evaporated. "Some of those old customs go back centuries."

"Oh, we just do the usual stuff. May Queen parade, morris dancers, that sort of thing, then a bonfire and fireworks in the evening. It's a bit of fun for everyone. Plus there's always been a Jack-in-the-Green, although the Vicar's trying to stop that this year."

"What's a Jack-in-the-Green?" Clare's question showed more than polite interest. Fergus wondered whether he was seeing professional enthusiasm, or flirtation, or a mood swing. He knew about mood swings.

"Just a tent of leaves with garlands and May blossom, a bit like a Christmas tree with a dancer inside. The Jack dances round making fun of everyone, with a couple of helpers in green costumes. Some young women get their asses pinched, begging your pardon, but it's all pretty innocent. Anyway this year the Vicar's set against it. Pagan symbolism, he calls it. P'raps he's still upset about the blood on the church door." It had taken Russell a long time to say that, and he paused to hide behind his tankard.

"Jake Herne is well pissed off," Eadlin smiled and leaned forward, hugging herself, relishing the story, as if gossip like this was too good to wait for Russell's measured delivery. "My ex," she added, seeing Clare's blank look. "His pub is called the Green Man, see, and for years he's been the dancer in the Jack, so he's taking it personally."

Fergus lifted his pint. "Well, here's to the Vicar. Sounds like he's fighting back."

"You've lost me." Clare looked puzzled.

"We're pretty sure that it was one of Jake's group that daubed the church with blood," Eadlin explained. "There are a few of them who are daft enough to do it."

"This is starting to sound like tribal warfare."

"That's probably a good description." As Eadlin spoke, Russell looked at her in a way that had more meaning than a casual glance. A warning, perhaps.

"I need another pint. Let me get a round in." Russell interrupted the thread of the conversation and stood without waiting for a response.

"I'll help you carry." Clare followed him to the bar. Fergus and Eadlin watched them go, and then looked at each other. Eadlin lifted an eyebrow.

"Those two have hit it off." Fergus surprised himself by feeling a twinge of jealousy.

"Nah. Half the men in the village have been lusting after Clare since the dig started. It's the cute-little-girl-lost look; it makes them go all protective, like."

Fergus could understand that. At the bar, Russell and Clare were deep in conversation, Russell leaning over to listen, while Clare placed her fingertips lightly on his hand to emphasise a point.

"And she's enjoying the attention. But don't worry," Eadlin continued, "you're safe." She leaned back in her chair, eyeing the two at the bar, with a knowing smile on her face.

"Me? But Clare and I aren't…"

"Then you're a fool."

Fergus watched Clare lift a drink in each hand and turn towards them. Sensing his scrutiny, she lifted her eyes from the brimming glasses and smiled at him. He'd forgotten that her smile could light up her face. Had he been missing something?

"Eadlin, thinking of Jake," Fergus asked his question before the others could hear, "I'm still amazed that in the twenty-first century there are people who believe in this Satanic crap."

"You don't have to believe. You just go along for the fun, don't you, Russ?" she called the question to the approaching pair.

"Go along where?"

"Jake's parties."

Russell narrowed his eyes at her as he sat, and she made an almost imperceptible nod of reassurance, an affirmation of trust.

"It sounds like you know something, Russ." Clare grinned at him. Her question held a note of challenge.

"Well, sort of. Me and Jake used to be mates, see? He invited me to one of his parties, last year. Just the one, 'cause we sort of fell out after that. It was weird." Russell shifted on his seat and toyed with his beer, making wet smears in the wood, while the others waited for him to build the words in his head. "I thought it was just going to be a Halloween party in the woods, with Jake providing the fancy dress. There weren't many people there, maybe a dozen or so. I got the impression most of 'em had been before, and knew the ropes, like. It was almost like it was a club, and I was being tested."

"Tested in what way?" Fergus was intrigued, but Russell didn't answer his question directly.

"The fancy dress turned out to be cloaks and animal masks. Maybe it was the masks, or p'raps the mulled wine he was pouring was spiked. Both of those, most likely, knowing Jake. Anyway, people lost their inhibitions." He glanced up at Clare from where he was staring into his beer. This time, the blush was unmistakable. "It was like you could hide behind the mask, pretend you was someone else. Things got a bit out of hand."

"They know about the stag, Russ."

"Right." Fergus wondered if Russell's relief hid more secrets than a sacrificed stag. "Well, I left soon after Jake hacked the head off this beast with that bloody great sword of his. It sort of sobered me up. All of a sudden it seemed like reciting the Lord's Prayer backwards wasn't just a party trick."

"I can see why he's an 'ex'." Clare was round-eyed as she looked at Eadlin.

"He wasn't always like that. A bit wild, maybe, but not cruel."

"But I still don't see the connection between a Halloween party," Clare wondered, "and this tribal war with the church that you're talking about."

Russell inhaled a couple of times as if he was about to speak, or was wondering how to say something.

"Spit it out, Russ." Eadlin put her hand on his arm and squeezed her encouragement.

"There are rumours that Jake's going to try black magic against the church, to get back at the Vicar. Have a ceremony with a funny name. Not a sabbat, but an es… es…" he fumbled for the word.

"Esbat." Eadlin's eyes were hard. "It's used for a ritual curse."

"And the people in this club of his will go along with that?" Fergus thought the conversation was bizarre. "They actually believe he has some kind of power?"

"I don't think they believe, not all of them." Russell sighed and fiddled with his tankard. "Leastways, they didn't at the beginning. For most of them it started as an excuse for that kind of party. There's something about those masks and the drink and the chanting that makes it feel right to behave... differently." He shuffled in his seat. "I know some of them. Now Jake's calling it a coven, and I think they're finding it's hard to leave, like they're bound together with their own sordid secrets. But Jake believes. Jake *really* believes. He's convinced he's got power, and the rest are beginning to wonder.

"I think some of them feel frightened as well as dirty, but they're too scared to get out."

Chapter Twenty-Three

"HOW'S IT GOING?"

The following day, Fergus leaned over the gate at the Mill House to watch Clare hunched over a plastic bowl, scrubbing at unidentifiable lumps of matter with a toothbrush. He was pleased with himself for walking up the hill from the village without a stick. A month before, he'd barely made it on crutches.

"Zilch." Clare wiped the back of a gardening-gloved hand over her forehead where she had started to perspire in the warmth of the afternoon. "Not a thing, apart from bottom-of-the-pond rubbish. If we don't find something exciting soon, the mud monkeys are going to lose interest." Clare waved her toothbrush towards a troop of students who were nibbling away at centuries of soil with trowels and spades. The bowl of the pond looked like an open cast mine, with heaps of soil being trundled up a path to a waiting skip. From the top of the old dam, the owner was diverting some loads to a new pile as part of a landscaping exercise, to the clear annoyance of the students.

"As it is, some of them didn't come back after Easter. We have to finish this week because term starts next Monday, but we'll be pretty much done anyway."

Fergus felt a stab of regret. He'd miss her company. "I was worried about you this morning. You looked a bit frayed." That was an understatement. Clare had blinked at the morning with bloodshot eyes, and set off for her run looking as if she'd already finished a marathon.

"I think you were right. I'm getting too close to this dig." Clare rocked back on her heels and looked as if she was about to say more, then closed her mouth as a student pushed a wheelbarrow up the hill towards them. "Fancy a walk?" She peeled off her gloves and tossed them down beside the toothbrush.

"If it's not too far. I'm getting fitter but…"

"I'll drive you up the road. There's a level bridle path a bit further up. Do you have time?"

Fergus hoped Clare hadn't seen his hesitation. The Downs road snaked away into the dark country of his mind, towards the place he pretended did not exist. Any lie would be justified to find another path.

"Sure." Face the pain, always face the pain.

Ten minutes later Clare parked a mile above the village, at a point where a bridle track forked away into the woods that fringed the valley. Fergus paused for a moment beside her car, looking up the road as it climbed away from them. His relief that he hadn't had to pass the bend above the trees felt like cowardice. One day soon he'd make that journey. He'd been avoiding it too long. His mind would not be fully healed until he could stand tall and composed above the oak tree. He breathed deeply and walked after Clare, trying to minimise his limp.

"This bridle track runs around the valley, pretty much following the contour line." Clare spoke in the brisk way that he thought of as her 'academic' voice, the one that declared facts. "There's a sort of hairpin bend at the end before it comes back on the other side. The hillside gets pretty steep up there. I've been here running a few times, see?"

"I sense you wanted to talk," Fergus prompted.

"Hm. I suppose I'm frustrated at the lack of progress. Not just with the dig, but with the story behind the dig."

"You mean the dreams?"

"Sort of. I've spent my working life piecing together ancient lives from fragments of evidence. Suddenly I'm seeing it all as vividly as a Hollywood movie, whether I want to watch or not, but I haven't worked out the plot yet. After we wrap up and go, I think I'll have lost the chance."

Fergus let her talk on. A few hundred yards from the road the track forked again, with a rutted path branching off towards the valley floor. There was a padlocked five bar gate across it, hung with a dirty, hand-painted sign saying 'Private'.

"I'd like to explore down there." Clare paused and waved at the gate, as if wondering whether to climb over.

"Why's that?"

"We're near the end of the valley. The Swanbourne must have its source down there. Springs were often sacred to the Saxons." She looked down the path into the valley, clearly tempted.

Fergus had rested against a tree. "You should have a talk with Eadlin about that sort of thing. She might take you to a few places, provided you weren't going to dig them up."

Clare shrugged and walked on. Beyond the gate, a rusting barbed wire fence bordered the path on the valley side. On the downhill side of this fence, towards the stream, rhododendrons had grown into a thick screen which masked their view. On the uphill side of the track there were signs of active woodland management where the alien rhododendrons had been cleared, preserving an undergrowth tracery of native elder and hazel.

Clare stopped again at a gap in the bushes where the rhododendrons had been crushed in some way. Broken ends of branches were sprouting new shoots of furled green leaves while thick, nut-like flower buds covered the undamaged plants. A tangle of fresh barbed wire had been laid in the gap. The trail of broken undergrowth led down into the valley.

"Do you notice something strange?" Clare turned slowly through a complete circle.

"What?" Fergus was starting to shiver. The sunlight still touched the trees high above them but here where the valley narrowed into a steep, shadowed cleft it seemed unnaturally chill.

"No birdsong. It's early April, birds have been singing all along the path, but here it's quiet."

"Apart from the crows." A harsh, grating call sounded from below them.

Clare started picking her way through the barbed wire, lifting strands away from her jeans as she made her way through the gap in the shrubs.

"I think that's private." Fergus was uneasy. Suddenly the whole excursion was a crazy idea.

"Come on, this may be my last chance to explore. We can always say we got lost." Clare seemed to have forgotten the state of his legs. Fergus looked round nervously for anyone who might object to their trespass, but Clare was already through the wire so he followed, picking his way cautiously downhill through the leaf litter. His muscles were aching; he should have brought his stick.

In the valley bottom the gap in the shrubs opened into an oval, grassy clearing between the trees and the stream. At the village end of the clearing a rutted track led back towards the padlocked gate. The track forded the Swanbourne beside the clearing, and ended at a gate into a meadow that was empty apart from a wooden store and field shelter for horses. Tyre marks in the mud and grass by the ford showed recent signs of a thickly wheeled vehicle turning.

At the upstream end of the clearing a shallow, reed-fringed pond marked the source of the Swanbourne. Between the track and the pond, in the centre of the clearing, a boulder was embedded in the ground as if it had fallen from the heights around them and impacted thickly in the grass.

"This place looks cared for," Clare whispered. The atmosphere inspired whispers rather than confident speech. "No undergrowth. The shrubs have been trimmed back, and people have walked on this grass, recently." Spring grass was starting to grow in the clearing, but it had been trampled back to mud around the scorched site of a fire in the centre. "And that boulder didn't come from round here." She started walking towards it.

Fergus turned a full circle, feeling a cold sweat start to form.

"I know this place," he whispered, but Clare was already crouched over the boulder. Fergus looked back up the gap through the rhododendrons, towards the bridle path. As he looked, small movements flitted between the trees on the hillside above them, the way shadows move at the edge of vision in the dark, but disappear when you look directly at them. Fergus could feel his heart start to pound, pumping adrenaline so that his vision and hearing surged into sharp focus. He knew that Clare was crouched in front of the boulder and that her hands were running over it. She was a beacon of excitement on the periphery of his awareness, oblivious to the threat growing around them. Small sounds, no louder than the rustle of a blackbird among dead leaves, echoed the movement in the trees, coming closer.

"Rune stone!" Clare started shouting in her excitement, so that he wanted to shush her but her enthusiasm was blind to his growing panic.

"It was here. The crash. Right here."

"It's a rune stone. This is incredible. Come and look!"

Now Fergus's eyes flicked from movement to movement, always too late to see anything for certain. The motion might have been the turn of a falling leaf, which in the blink of an eye became nothing but the green dusting of spring growth, but still the rustles crept closer, watching.

"Clare, please, let's go. Now." His line of sight up the gap in the shrubbery now held the memory of a drifting orange rain of falling leaves, and a corpse-cold face that mouthed 'this one's dead too'.

"You have no idea how important this is." Clare hugged herself with excitement as she jumped to her feet and turned to him. "What's the matter?"

Now the movement was inside the rhododendrons, tumbling down the slope. It crept in little falling rushes, always where Fergus wasn't looking, but it was there, it watched, it guarded, it threatened. On the verge of panic he grabbed Clare's forearm and pulled her from the clearing. Angrily she shook herself free where the clearing met the track and he almost fell, but he kept his staggering flight going towards the gate.

Fergus couldn't run but he managed a tottering step up the track, as if by almost-overbalancing he could force his legs to move fast enough to catch up with his will to flee. At the gate he was briefly defeated by the padlock and heavy chain until he managed to climb over and fall onto the ground on the far side, like an exhausted soldier finishing an assault course. Somehow the gate was symbolic, a boundary that was more than physical, where Fergus re-entered the real world. The demons were no longer outside of him and attacking, but were part of his shock, a product of his mind, still terrifying but less threatening. As he lay panting Clare vaulted over, landing lightly beside him on her toes.

"What the hell's the matter?"

Fergus stared at her, his mouth working. He didn't understand her irritation. He flapped a hand back towards the clearing.

"My crash. The wreckage, it finished there. That's where Kate died."

Clare squatted in front of him, searching his face. Something she saw in his eyes softened her expression into compassion. "God, was it that bad?"

Fergus had no reserves left, no strength to hang on to the filters. He screwed his eyes shut, and began to thump his head backwards against a plank of the gate, making a little pain to hold the big pain away.

"I just wish," thump, "I didn't have to remember," thump, harder now, "the screams." Another thump, making lights burst in his head.

"Was she terribly hurt? Do you want to talk about it?" Clare's hand gripped his shoulder in both comfort and restraint, and Fergus stilled his head to stare at her, willing her to understand without him spelling it out.

"Kate couldn't scream." Fergus waved his hand vaguely over his belly. "Stuff had come through the dashboard. It... she... stomach... " He took a great sobbing breath. "Kate couldn't scream." He started banging his head again, slowly. "The screams I want to forget are my own."

Geoffrey Gudgion

"Oh, Fergus," Clare sat down beside him in the mud and put her arm around him, pulling his head into her shoulder, and with that tenderness he felt the pit in his mind open.

"I tried so hard." The first sob filled Fergus's body and he had no strength left to repress it. "I really tried." His legs drew up into a foetal crouch, and he twisted into her so the words he mumbled into her breast became meaningless. Clare rocked him, shushing him gently as if he was a child, pulling him into herself. Eventually Fergus's body stilled and reality started to seep into his awareness like the wet soaking into his jeans. When he had been quiet for a time Clare eased him away with a gentle kiss on his head.

"Oh God, I'm so sorry." Fergus pulled himself up the gate and stood leaning on it, braced against his hands with his head bowed into the collar of his anorak. "I'm so ashamed."

Clare stood and slid her hand up his back. "Don't be." She tugged him away from the gate, back towards the village, leading him away from the focus of his horror with her arm still protectively around him. Where the track neared the road, foresters had carved a seat out of a fallen tree trunk and Clare sat Fergus down, holding his hand in the intimacy of compassion.

"Were you like that for long?"

"I don't know. A few hours, maybe." Long enough for the blood to dry into a thick crust on the outside, but still be slimy and salty in his mouth. "But I probably wasn't conscious for all of that time."

"You said you tried so hard... Tried to do what?"

Fergus took a great, gasping breath that had the catch of another sob before he answered.

"To keep in the screams. You grow up being told that real men don't cry, so at first you do anything to keep the sound inside you. You even bite lumps out of yourself, anything to keep it in." The words started to spill from his mouth in an unstoppable torrent. "But the madness pulls you down eventually, and as you fall you despise yourself because you haven't the strength or the guts to hold on. And once you've started you can't stop,

161

because screaming helps, you see. However much you loathe the thing that you've become, you turn yourself inside out with the effort to push more pain out of your mouth. You even resent breathing because when you're sucking in air you're not bellowing out the pain."

Fergus fumbled for a handkerchief and buried his face in it until another spasm of shakes left his body, smoothed away by the hand stroking his back. When he straightened, his eyes focused on the view as if he was seeing it for the first time. Late afternoon sunlight touched the tops of the trees on the opposite side of the valley, warm greys dusted green with the first signs of leaf. Blood and pain and death did not belong in this place, not with the day's fading warmth around them. Fergus started to push the thoughts back up the valley, confining them in that dark glade around the stone, in the way he used to seal them behind the nightmare door in the attic of his mind. The nightmare now had a home that was not inside his head.

"Have you ever told anyone before?" Clare gripped his arm as if he was an invalid that might fall over, and she shook it slightly when he did not reply.

"You can't, I couldn't... I knew I'd end up making a fool of myself. Back there I panicked when I realised where I was and it all came out before I could stop it. Sorry." Fergus breathed deeply, swallowing and fighting for composure.

"Don't be. Those things needed to come out."

"You know, when I got back to the office, it was like a void between me and everyone else. I looked at them scurrying around in their pressured little lives, and I thought 'what's the point?' All this manufactured stress, running around after the next deal, the quarterly targets, the commission cheque, and for what? In that wreck I would have swapped every deal I've ever done for one single minute of pain-free existence, or for one friend to hold my hand. The next time I die I want to have friends around me, good friends who don't want to lose me. I want my life to have meant something more than a bank balance."

Clare let go of his arm and fumbled in her pocket for her own handkerchief. His hand fell onto the seat like a dead weight. His tone was becoming more conversational but Fergus still spoke as if to a point in front of them, making no eye contact. The temperature started to fall as the shadow line of the setting sun climbed out of the valley.

"I've started to wonder what happens, afterwards. I mean, where do we go, after we die? Do we simply cease to exist? Whether you go peacefully in a hospital bed or screaming mad in a car wreck, is that the end? I still think I saw your Saxon, which is impossible unless..." His voice tailed off.

Clare squirmed on the seat. "I need a shower." Her tone was suddenly practical. "Then let me buy you dinner in the White Hart. I think we both need a drink. After that I can tell you about the rune stone."

"Rune stone?"

"That boulder in the clearing." Clare pulled him to his feet. "It's a great find, maybe as important as the Saxon's body. I'll tell you later because right now I've got a wet bum and I need a shower and change."

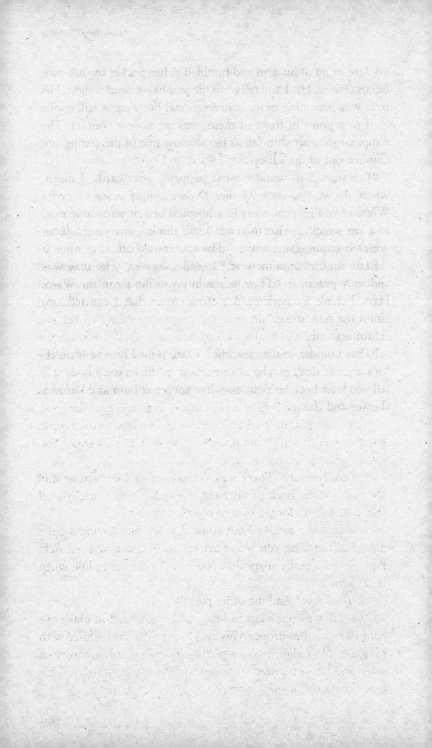

Chapter Twenty-Four

"ARE YOU OK?"

Clare rested her hand on his back. Fergus stood at the White Hart's bar, savouring a large gulp of the heaviest wine on offer. Its bite held a hint of oiliness and promised alcohol, lots of alcohol. As its comfort spread within him he rolled the glass against his forehead, letting the cold affirm reality. Fergus nodded and followed her to a table near the fire, unsure how to behave. How could he clink glasses and have a normal conversation after letting himself be seen like that? He chose a seat on the opposite side of the table, resting his arms on its neutral surface.

"How do you feel?" Clare's eyes were wide and concerned behind her glasses. Fergus looked away, unable to hold her gaze.

"Exposed. Numb. Embarrassed, as if I've just thrown up in front of you. It's a bit humiliating to be seen in that state. You must think I'm pretty pathetic."

"Of course not." There was vehemence in Clare's tone and she touched the back of his hand in emphasis, but briefly as if she, too, was no longer sure of the ground rules.

"It was going to come out some day. It's like having a belly ache and knowing you won't get better until you've been sick. Part of me is really sorry that you were in the firing line when it happened."

"'Part of you.' And the other part?"

"Well, if someone's got to hear it," Fergus tried to make eye contact again, but dropped his eyes to the table and fiddled with his glass, "I'm glad it was you." He managed an embarrassed smile and Clare reached across to squeeze his hand again. This time the touch lingered longer.

"I think we're propping each other up."

Fergus covered her hand with his, sandwiching it for a moment before pulling back. The pit in his mind still yawned close by. "So tell me about this rune stone." There was little enthusiasm in his voice, but he needed distraction.

"It's a boulder carved with runic script, see? It's really rare, probably from the same period as our Saxon." Clare watched his eyes, holding back her enthusiasm. "How much do you know about runes?"

"Not much. Early writing, isn't it?"

"Sort of. The Saxons were story-tellers rather than letter-writers, you see. When they wrote something down it had great significance, so runes could be both a script and potentially a charm, or a spell." Clare's words became more animated as the subject took hold. "The word 'rune' itself means 'secret' or 'whisper'. Take this one, for example. It's on that stone back there."

Clare spread a paper napkin on the table and drew a symbol with a vertical line and an equal-sided triangle half way up on the right side. Her movements were brisk, betraying her excitement. Fergus tried to concentrate but the gut-churning shame of his collapse filled his mind.

"Looks a bit like a 'P' with an extra line on top." He pushed himself to show interest.

"True. But this one sounds like the English 'th' sound, not a 'p'. It's called the 'Thorn' rune. It can be used to spell something as part of a phonetic script, or it can be a symbol in its own right."

Silence. It was only when Clare covered his hand with hers, again, that Fergus realised he had drifted off into his own world. He wondered if the touch was a sign of intimacy or whether Clare was trying to attract his attention. She leaned forward so that she could look up into his eyes.

"Hey, it's OK." Clare's face was close and Fergus smelt perfume, an unexpected splash of femininity that made her nearness appealing. "It really is OK."

"Sorry. Keep going." His voice sounded gruff. One more hint of compassion and he'd start crying again. He shuffled his chair around the table towards her, angling his neck so that he could watch her drawing.

"Runes as symbols are very conceptual." Clare spoke slowly and clearly as she thickened the lines of her rune symbol. Fergus sensed she was giving him a lifeline back to normality. "Depending on the context, the Thorn rune could mean a mighty strength, or conflict, or even male sexuality." Clare looked up and they both retreated slightly at the closeness of the eye contact. A faint blush coloured Clare's cheeks.

"So what does your rune stone say?"

Clare shook her head with slight impatience, as she might with a slow student.

"Even if the runes were clear, that stone would absorb months of expert analysis, and I'm not a runes expert. You don't simply walk up to a rune stone and read it as if it were a few lines of Shakespeare, you see." Clare's speech gathered pace again, and she wrinkled her nose under her spectacles. Any moment now she would... "It's the sort of thing that academics will be writing learned papers about for several years." ... push her glasses up her nose with her finger. "And those runes are so weathered I doubt if we'll ever decipher the whole stone. It's too decayed. And why are you looking at me like that?"

Fergus's head had settled onto his hand, fascinated as much by the life in Clare's face as the words she was speaking. Archaeology ignited a passion within her. Her eyes shone in the firelight and he noticed Clare had applied some makeup while they changed at Mary Baxter's. He wondered if he should feel flattered.

"Sorry. You had me enthralled." Fergus wondered if she ever became this animated about subjects other than Archaeology and Anthropology.

"Interesting phrase to use. In Old English, 'thrall' meant 'servitude' or 'bondage'."

Perhaps not. "I think I'll give the bondage bit a miss. Sounds far too kinky." Fergus could feel his mood swinging back on

167

the rebound. From depression to euphoria in a single glass of wine; the speed of change was frightening. The phrase 'post traumatic stress' crept into his mind but he managed to kill the thought. Much more important to enjoy the moment. He felt he'd dropped a burden and was starting to soar. "Fancy another?" He waved his glass.

"Let me get those."

As his mood lifted, he became aware of Clare's physicality, and turned to watch her as she stood at the bar. She had changed into a tight, enticingly tactile, cashmere sweater which emphasised the slender figure inside it. He wondered why he hadn't noticed before. Fergus was still admiring Clare's figure when she turned and smiled. He managed to lift his eyes to her face in time, and smiled back innocently.

"There was at least one other rune that was clear, though." Clare settled into her seat and started drawing on the napkin again, before turning it towards him. The design she had drawn was like a Y with a spray of three lines above the central point. "This is the Algiz rune. When used as a symbol it means elk, stag, or deer." Fergus sat forward, senses alert. "Normally it's associated with defence, or guardianship against evil, maybe even of some link with the gods."

"Normally?"

"This elk rune was carved upside down, which has negative connotations, usually opposite to the normal meaning. It could mean anything from a hidden danger, to a curse, or divine damnation."

"But you say it all has to be read in context."

"Exactly. I'm going to go back with a camera before I leave, but I think we'll need specialist equipment to trace most of the runes. Frankly, I don't think we'll ever read the full inscription."

"Take care." Fergus's mind recoiled from the thought of going back to the clearing. His euphoria started to fade.

"Well, it's on private land, so we'll need the owner's permission anyway before we can do anything officially, but the stone will be big news in academic circles." The excitement in Clare's voice told him the find would do her career no harm at all.

"Why's it there? I mean, what was it for?"

"Rune stones were usually memorials to a chieftain, but they could also be boundary stones, or associated with a sacred site. The early church destroyed all the signs of paganism they could find, see, which is why they're so rare in this country. But there's something in that clearing that gives me the creeps."

"The whole place gives me the creeps, but it sounds as if you've found something else."

"That clearing looks maintained. Shrubs trimmed back, no undergrowth coming up through the grass, that sort of thing. And there's a lot of blood on the stone and at its base. Dried blood, but quite fresh. Something died there, fairly recently."

"Jake Herne's party place."

"Precisely."

"A fox might have caught a rabbit." Even as Fergus spoke, he realised how limp his alternative sounded. Clare shrugged in dismissal.

"Animal kills are messy. The kill is pulled apart by the predator and scavengers. Something was slaughtered there, something at least the size of a goat or a sheep."

Fergus shivered, despite the warmth of the fire, with the dawning fear that his paranoia in the clearing might have been more than the memory of trauma. What was it Eadlin had said? Something about a place that used to be sacred, but which now feels sick or mad.

"I think we should talk to Eadlin. If that's where Jake has his sabbats we should plan the next step rather than rush in."

Fergus wondered if Clare noticed how naturally he'd started saying 'we' rather than 'you'.

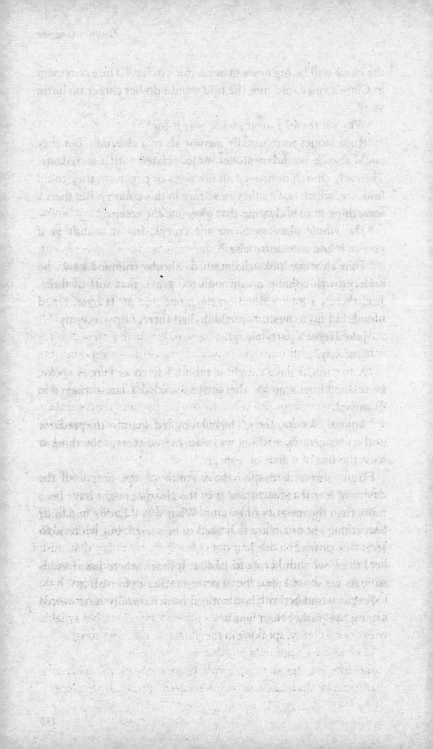

Chapter Twenty-Five

THIS DREAM IS good. Enough awareness remains for Clare to know that it is a dream, but tonight she is herself. The absence of a threat, the joy of knowing a dream-self that is herself, is like a cool cloth after fever. She runs through the woods in a steady lope that eats the miles, on a path that is grassy and firm and dappled with sunlight. The track runs near a lake where Fergus is feeding the swans and smiling at her. "I can't run," he calls, "you go and have fun, and I'll stay with Olrun." So Clare runs, content, feeling the stress dissolve with each footfall onto the grass. The track disappears into the distance with the hill on one side and the rhododendrons on the other, so when a woman steps out of the bushes in a business suit Clare is cross because this is her dream, her run, and the conditions are perfect. Besides, the woman looks like Fergus's friend Kate in the photograph, and Clare's happiness fades as if the sun has hidden behind a cloud.

"You're dead," she tells Kate in the same tone of reproof she might use to tell a student that they're late for a class.

But Kate smiles at her like an old friend with news to tell, so Clare slows her run to listen. Kate has a way of flicking her head to keep that mass of blonde hair out of her eyes, but rather than push her hair back with her hands she spreads them wide as if she is striking a pose for a speech or a performance. As Clare stops, Kate looks directly at her with gentle warmth and speaks, but her words are meaningless. She enunciates each incomprehensible syllable with crystal clarity, speaking in the lilting cadence of a song.

Ef ek sé a tré uppi váfa virgilná,

She lifts her hand to forestall Clare's questions. This is a performance that can not be interrupted. Ef ek... If I... Norse.

171

The woman is speaking Old Norse.

Svá ek rist ok i rúnum fák,

Something about runes. One hand now waves downhill towards the rune stone.

At sá gengr gumi ok mælir við mik.

Now the words are spoken as if they had awful significance. Clare stares at her in confusion until Kate smiles again and repeats the words, speaking with the soft patience of a teacher reading a poem in a class. Then Kate puts up her hand, palm outwards, in the universal sign to *stop, stay, do not follow*, before she turns and walks down the hill towards the clearing.

CLARE WAS INSTANTLY awake. No fumbling transition from sleep, with the dreams fading in the dawn or already lost. She threw back the covers and reached for a pen and paper, shivering naked in the cold but desperate to record the words while they were fresh in her mind.

The suspension of disbelief, Fergus had called it. Clare had just dreamed about a dead Englishwoman talking to her in Old Norse. Old Norse, for heaven's sake, not even Anglo-Saxon. She didn't even understand the language beyond a rudimentary vocabulary, but she had seen those words somewhere before, in one of the old poems. Pulling a dressing gown around her, Clare opened her laptop and logged on to the internet.

An hour later she had found it. The epic *Hávamál*, when the God Odin talks of the power of runes.

Ef ek sé a tré uppi váfa virgilná,
Svá ek rist ok i rúnum fák,
At sá gengr gumi ok mælir við mik.

If I see a corpse hanging in a tree
I can carve and colour the runes
So that the man can walk and talk with me.

An answer answerless, Clare thought, stretching back in her chair and rubbing her eyes. The only common link was runes. It was like staring at a crossword puzzle for too long. She snapped off the light, staring out through the window for inspiration. Already it was light enough for the trees to be outlined against the sky, and from somewhere nearby came the grating call of a vixen in heat. Clare was learning to recognise the sounds of the country. The first signs of a new day reminded her that she still needed sleep.

Chapter Twenty-Six

SHOWING OFF TO Clare was a mistake. Fergus had seen her car arrive while he was riding Trooper in the sand school. Perhaps he succumbed to a macho need to impress her. Maybe he wanted to show himself in a fit and vital light after the gut-churning embarrassment of the previous afternoon. Either way, he failed.

There was an exercise that Eadlin had taught him that morning, using a single low jump set up at one side of the riding school. The trick, Eadlin said, was not how high the horse can jump, but how well you can move with him as he jumps. So she persuaded Fergus to drop the reins and come over the jump with his arms out to the sides, forcing him to find that point of balance where the rider flows with the horse's movement. Next she'd told him to do the same thing with his eyes shut. Listen to him with your legs and bum, Eadlin said. Read his movement, become one with him. Trust him; let him be your eyes. Now flex with the jump, don't jump it for him.

For Fergus the buzz was more than the exhilaration of the canter, that ability to move at speed in a way that made the injuries to his legs irrelevant. The joy was in the sense of partnership with the animal. Point him at a jump, feel him commit, and know that he will take you over. So as Clare came to the fence around the school to watch him, Fergus turned the horse towards the jump, felt him surge forward, and in an almost infantile display of 'look, no hands', Fergus winged his arms to the sides and closed his eyes.

The whiplash sliced the air in a sharp hiss of noise, a single stroke that should have finished with an impact and a scream but which stopped as silently as a knife cut. Beneath Fergus the horse lurched sideways like an antelope evading a lion, and as Fergus's eyes snapped open the ground leaped up to smash him in the face so swiftly that he was hardly aware of the fall. A glimpse of Clare standing open-mouthed at the fence shattered into fragments of light as he bounced and rolled.

Sand. Wet, gritty sand ground against his teeth as the world reorganised itself in his head. Fergus rolled over, sat up, and grinned foolishly at Clare, who was already squatting beside him. Either he'd missed a few seconds or she could move really fast. While Fergus tried to work out what had happened he gathered a disgusting mixture of sand, dried horse shit, and saliva in his mouth, and spat.

"Sorry. We must stop meeting like this." The humour seemed to relax her. Beyond her Trooper had backed against the far fence, trailing reins and blowing heavily.

"What the hell happened?" Eadlin arrived at a run.

"Sit still for a moment, get your breath back." That was Clare. To need her ministrations twice in two days was doubly embarrassing.

"I'm OK, really." Fergus started to get up, frustrated at the way the world tilted and spun. He swore and stood grasping Clare's arm until the riding school organised itself into its proper equilibrium. Trooper came into focus, ears back, and the whites of his eyes showing. If the horse had been a dog, it would have been cowering with its tail between its legs, and probably whining.

"That man," Clare nodded towards the car park, "cracked a whip. I never knew a horse could spin so fast."

"That's Jake Herne, and I'll deal with the bugger later." Eadlin glared across at Jake, who stood at the tailgate of his Range Rover with a long dressage schooling whip in his hand. Jake sneered at them and walked off towards the barns as if the little drama was beneath his notice.

"That," Fergus said, flexing his limbs, testing for damage, "was childish, and bloody stupid. Trooper's afraid of whips," he explained to Clare. He was steady on his feet now, brushing off sand.

"Now let's try that again." Fergus braced himself and walked over to Trooper, who backed away as if expecting to be hit. Clare started to follow but Eadlin put her hand on her arm and shook her head.

"You're not going to let him get back on, are you?" Clare sounded incredulous.

"Let him be." Eadlin watched the interaction between man and horse, nodding approvingly as Fergus approached it with slow, open movements until he could pick up the reins, and the horse would let itself be touched.

"What are they doing?" Clare asked after Fergus had spent a long time stroking the horse's neck and whispering in its ear.

"Calming each other. Trooper's been frightened and he knows he's hurt his friend. He needs reassurance."

"*Trooper* needs? That fall could have set Fergus back months!"

Eadlin glanced at Clare, lifting an eyebrow at the concern in her voice.

"That horse is healing him faster than any doctor could manage," Eadlin said quietly. "They, like, understand each other at a very deep level." On the far side of the school the horse's head started to droop, until it bent to nuzzle Fergus in the angle of his neck. "They're both carrying a deep well of remembered pain." Now it was Clare's turn to look sharply at Eadlin, wondering if she too had witnessed a collapse like the one in the woods, but Eadlin's focus was on Fergus and Trooper.

"The difference," Eadlin continued, accidentally answering Clare's unspoken question, "is that one day Fergus will be able to talk about it, if he finds someone he'll let get that close. The horse can't." Now Trooper stood motionless while Fergus laboriously climbed the fence to mount. Both women watched in silence as he circled the horse, launched into a canter, and put him over the jump. This time he kept his eyes open and a firm hold on the reins.

"That's enough," Eadlin called. Beside her, Clare let herself breathe again. "Finish on success. Now put him away and come and man the office for a while. I want to keep an eye on you, in case you have a touch of concussion."

Eadlin strode back towards the office, her shoulders set with anger. Fergus noticed Russell Dickens waiting in the doorway, watching. Russell was at the stables a lot, these days.

"Feisty, isn't she?" Clare returned Russell's wave as they walked Trooper to his stable.

"She's the boss. It's her yard, and her horse. Do you ride?"

Clare shook her head. "I tried it once. The horse and I didn't get on. I decided that if I ever wanted sixteen hands between my thighs again, they probably wouldn't belong to a horse."

Fergus's laughter was cleansing, even if it did make his head hurt. He'd done too little of that in recent months. There had been times of happiness or even euphoria since he left hospital, but he couldn't remember the last time mirth had erupted into a good belly laugh.

"Pity." Fergus indulged a brief fantasy of Clare in jodhpurs. Her rump would fit into a saddle the way he might warm a brandy balloon in the palm of his hand. Then he checked himself, mentally pulling back at the memory of the previous day's humiliation.

"Are you all right today? Apart from collecting air miles on horseback, I mean."

"Fine." Fergus spoke with a 'let's move on' finality. "It's good to see you here. Something on your mind?"

"Apart from being worried about you, you mean?" Clare looked hurt.

"Sorry." Now Fergus felt guilty. "Look, I didn't mean to be brusque. It's probably a reaction to yesterday. No-one's ever seen me like that before. And to answer your question, I feel a bit flayed."

Clare touched his arm, accepting the apology. "Don't go into a shell. I think you'll need to talk about it again. You might find it easier with someone who already understands."

Fergus led Trooper into his stall and buried his face in the horse's flank while he loosened the girth. He called his thanks from within that warm smell, glad of the bulk between them. Finally he straightened to pull off the saddle, wincing at new bruises.

"I tried telling this guy, once." Arms full, Fergus nodded at Trooper, who was tugging at a hay net. And what a humbling experience that had been, a grown man weeping into the neck of a horse. "But he's not a great conversationalist."

"Actually there *was* something I wanted to talk to you about." Clare picked up the bridle and followed him towards the tack room. "Your friend Kate, did she speak any languages?"

"Not that I know of. Why?"

Clare told him about her dream. "I'm back to the same problem," she finished. "Either I'm a bit screwed up, or someone's trying to tell me something."

"So what does this tell you, apart from Kate taking a post-mortem course in archaic languages?" Fergus smiled to soften his words.

"I think the dream is like the runes themselves. Abstract, conceptual, a rune of runes, see?"

"Not really. You've lost me."

"That poem; I don't think I'd have imagined it on my own. I read it years ago as an undergraduate, but now it's something I had to be pointed towards. If it was in my head it was buried really deep."

"So what's the message?"

"I've been reminded that the Saxons believed runes could have great power, such power that Odin said that he could carve and colour runes to raise the dead. Maybe my subconscious is just making connections between Aegl and the rune stone, but on the other hand..." Clare handed him a tangled mess of bridle and reins. "I need to see that rune stone again."

Fergus's gut lurched at the thought of the stone. Eadlin's warning about the Saxon, made so emphatically on the day he first returned, had suddenly become significant. "Look, Clare, I'm not sure that I can..." He struggled for words that said 'count me out'.

Clare didn't seem to have heard him. "I tried this morning, and took my camera, but there was someone there. The gate was open and I could see a Range Rover down the track. It might have been Jake Herne."

"I'd take great care if I was you. Come and talk to Eadlin; she may be able to tell you more about it."

In the office, Russell Dickens filled one of the old armchairs so that his weight squeezed the stuffing out of the splits in the leather. Russell heaved himself upright, smiling, as Clare entered. If he'd have been wearing a cap, Fergus thought, he'd clawed it from his head and crumpled it in front of his belt. Clare declined his offer of a seat.

"Look, I don't mean to intrude, but can I ask your advice?" Clare looked at Eadlin and Russell in turn, including them both in her question. "Yesterday evening Fergus and I went for a walk in the woods. We strayed off the path a bit..."

"... and found the clearing where I crashed last year." Fergus continued. He saw Eadlin and Russell exchange looks. "We think it's where Jake has his gatherings..."

"There's a stone there," Clare interrupted. "With traces of runes carved into its surface. It's very old. Do either of you know anything about its history?"

"It's called the Blot Stone," Russell spoke kindly, like a protective uncle, "and Fergus is right about what happens down there. I'd leave that clearing alone, if I were you." Russell had stayed standing when Clare refused his seat and now he didn't seem to know what to do with his hands, so he stuffed them into the pockets of his overalls.

"But archeologically, the stone may be really significant, see? Surely the owners would understand that. Who owns the land?"

"From the bridleway up the hill to the road it belongs to the Forestry Commission," Eadlin explained, "and below the bridleway, all the land in the valley down as far as the mill is owned by the D'Auban Estate. But the woods around the spring below the bridle path, plus the field at the end of the valley, that's all been leased out to Jake Herne."

"... and you've got as much chance of him allowing a bunch of outsiders down there," Russell added, "as you would of persuading the Vicar to let you dig up the churchyard."

"Then I'll have to go on my own, when he's not there." The anger in Clare's voice hardened. "This could be the archaeological find of the year and I'm not going to let that prick get in the way."

Clare pushed herself off the wall and left abruptly. Fergus spread his hands at the others in a gesture that might have been despair or apology, and followed. He called after her but she outpaced him, striding away until she reached the fence beside the sand school. There she waited with her hands gripping the top rail and her shoulders lifting with her breath.

"Sorry. That was a rather ungracious exit," Clare said as he caught up with her.

"It must be frustrating."

"It's bloody infuriating. That rune stone is a fantastic discovery. It might tell us more about the Saxon. And the man who controls access to it is round here, somewhere." She waved her hands around the yard.

"You could still ask. Wait until he says 'no' before you do anything. But I wouldn't approach him yourself. After that nasty little incident with the whip he probably associates you with me, and all of a sudden I seem to be unpopular, for some reason. Have some fusty old professor write from the university."

"I have someone in mind. Incidentally," Clare continued, "the name 'Blot Stone' is curious. 'Blot' is an Old English word meaning 'blood sacrifice'." She smiled wryly at him. Beyond the car park a full moon was rising over the trees, pale and almost transparent in the setting sunlight.

"It will be a clear, bright night." Clare nodded at the moon.

"If you're planning some illicit research in the woods, I'd leave it. If you're caught there's no chance he'll agree to access."

Clare smiled and squeezed his arm in reassurance as she left.

181

Chapter Twenty-Seven

CLARE PARKED HER car where the bridleway joined the Downs road, and checked the pockets of her anorak. Digital camera, freshly charged. Notepad, biro. Mobile phone. There was even a pair of compact binoculars from a previous walk. And in her hand, a large, police-style torch, powerful enough to throw a light across the face of the stone that would emphasise the shadows of carvings, even under a camera flash. Clare snapped it on, and the beam speared into the trees like a motorcycle headlight, throwing everything else into shades of blackness.

Too much. The torch was a harsh, manufactured intrusion. Without it, the moon reclaimed the night, filling the air with silver and making the landscape itself shine in shades of pearlescent grey. Clare stood by the car to let her eyes adjust to the dark, wondering at the night sky in the deep country where the stars are fatter and set in a continuous orb that hangs close to the earth. Below the road, a fox trotted purposefully across a field, one with its moon shadow.

In front of Clare the bridleway was a pale ribbon between the between the trees. Even here, she did not need the torch, although the woods faded into blackness either side of her. Small, furtive movements scurried away from her in the darkness as she walked. Clare froze, shivering, as an animal screamed nearby, the victim of an unseen kill, and her ears searched the following silence.

Sound carries a long way on a still night. At the edge of hearing was a murmur that might have been a road or a crowd. Clare walked on towards the sound until the reflected glow of a fire touching a distant branch, gold on silver, confirmed her fears. Still Clare kept going, intrigued, reasoning with herself as she walked. Their eyes would be dazzled by the fire. She could hide in the shadows if anyone came. She could outrun anyone in the village if needed. She wanted to see what they were doing.

Clare's resolve faltered at the second fork, where the gate with its 'Private' sign hung open. By now the noise could only be people, a jumbled sound that might have been a celebration or even a fight, a discordant intrusion into the night. Where the track crossed the stream below her, a line of 4X4 vehicles reflected the glow of a fire. Beyond the screening bank of rhododendrons, the inebriated giggle of a woman was shushed and a lone male voice cried out in a strong baritone, the words indistinct through the bushes. The call prompted an answering bellow from many voices, call and answer repeating in a parody of a church service, priest and congregation, bidding and response. Above the noise of the ritual, Clare's own breath was loud in her nostrils, pulling in oxygen that was laced with wood smoke. She kept walking along the bridleway, slowly now, placing her feet with care, watching for the gap ploughed through the bushes by Fergus's car.

The gap was too narrow, the bank of bushes too deep. Clare could only see a strip across the clearing below, and that was partly obscured by leaves. Her view sliced across the edge of a circle of figures that faced inwards towards the unseen fire, towards the rune stone. Clare swallowed and felt her heart begin to pound as she realised that the figures were inhuman. The outlines of the two forms that were in full view were obscured by dark cloaks, but both held flaming torches in front of them and the wolf's head on the nearest was clearly visible. Clare stared at it, dry-mouthed, until she saw that the hands that emerged from the cloak to grip the torch belonged to a man, not an animal, and that human hair was falling beneath the hawk's head on another. Her rational side over-ruled the instinct to scream and flee. The sounds filling the air were human voices, repeating the same indistinct words over and over in a ritual chant. Clare backed away, her heartbeat slowing.

By the time she reached the open gate down to the clearing, Clare was berating herself for her panic. In front of her, the bridle path stretched back towards the village, a line of moonlight through the trees, a clean route out. Down the track, the glow reflecting on the cars told her that she would have a clear view of the ritual from the bottom of the track. Just one look. Clare had a brief mental image of her dream where Kate had held up her hand, palm outwards in the sign to stop, but she brushed the image aside. They were only people, after all, just people in animal masks.

She moved to the side of the track, into the deep shadow under the bushes, and crept down the hill. The noise of her foot crunching a layer of dried leaves sounded deafening and she froze, holding her breath. The pattern of sound was changing, gathering menace, but there were no signs that anyone had heard. Clare exhaled, lifted her foot as gently as she would extract ancient pottery from the soil, and placed it behind her. She stood in clear moonlight on the track, no longer sure. Beyond the bushes the chant changed tempo, gathering pace and volume like an engine of hate, as if the ritual was moving towards a climax. Below her she noticed a gap in the shrubbery, a narrow passage where moonlight reached to the ground, snaking towards the fire. It enticed her in, absorbing her into the shadows. Finally, from deep within the bush, Clare could crouch into a position where she had a leaf-dappled view of the whole clearing.

Eleven figures, all focused on the rune stone. There was movement beyond, partially obscured by the fire, and eleven became thirteen as two more masked forms appeared, dragging an animal with ropes that had been tied to its horns. Clear within the chanting she heard the terrified bleating of a goat. Clare pulled at a small branch to find a better view, and saw the goat pulled into the rune stone so its chest was on the side away from the fire, with the ropes from its horns stretching its neck over the stone's top and forcing its chin down onto the carved face. The bleating became strangled and the beast's hooves thrashed frantically at the ground on the far side.

A figure wearing a goat's head mask with curving, scimitar horns separated from the circle and squared up to the stone, hefting a massive, two-handed sword. Clare's hand flew to her mouth, releasing the branch, so she didn't see the blow, but the sound was a wet, meat-cleaver thump, immediately followed by a spade-like noise as the sword-tip hit the turf. The sound resonated with her nightmares and she squirmed in her hiding-place, but still grabbed at the branch to clear her view as a roar of approval spread through the group.

It took a moment for Clare to realise that the jet of black liquid in the air was blood. An analytical corner of her brain wondered at the pressure that could force such a spurt, but what caught her attention immediately afterwards was the pattern of the blood as it flowed down the stone. She released the branch, reached into her pocket for her binoculars, and crouched awkwardly to peer through a lower gap in the leaves. The headless body of the goat had fallen out of sight, but the flow of its blood down the carved surface was separating, spreading into individual trickles that found channels on their way to the ground. The chanting had ceased, and cloaked figures were moving in the clearing, passing across her line of sight. All Clare's senses screamed that it was time to go, but the pattern of blood demanded her attention. As she focused the binoculars on the stone, one line found the elk rune, flowed down its shaft, and paused, swelling, until it split to explore the three tributary branches, colouring the rune with blood. Algiz reversed. Hidden danger. Divine retribution.

The bush shook as a body crashed into it and Clare stifled a scream, shocked into immobility, her eyes swivelling to search for the threat. A few feet away, a cloaked figure in a mask that might have been a squirrel or a rat began to back into the bush.

"... don't wanna do it on the ground. Too friggin' cold." A woman's voice, apparently drunk. "There's a branch in 'ere. Jus' the right height." Clare hadn't been seen, not yet. She started breathing, forcing herself to take shallow, quiet breaths. She eased out of her crouch and began to back out of the bush, placing one foot behind the other, ready to freeze at the first crackle of a dried leaf. Beyond the woman another figure blundered into the foliage.

"Where the fuck are you, then?" Male, probably middle-aged, also drunk. A mask that might have been a wolf's head was pulled off and a face peered into the body of the shrub. Clare tugged the hood of her anorak over her face and tried to become as still as the leaves around her. Giggles and a lecherous chuckle came from nearby. The revellers had found each other. Clare guessed that a heavy movement of the bush was the woman being lifted onto a branch. More giggles, followed by the fumbling noises of clothing being unfastened.

Clare was locked into an unnatural crouch that she knew she could not sustain; already the ache was building in one leg. When she heard sucking sounds and a small, female moan Clare looked up, hoping she might have a chance to slip away. They were close, too close. The woman would only have to look over her shoulder and Clare would be in clear view, but the rat mask was looking downwards to where the man's face was buried in her breasts. As gently as a T'ai Chi exercise in slow motion, Clare eased the police torch into her hand and straightened, rocking backwards onto her rear foot. Good. Now another step.

The mask swivelled at Clare at the crunch of the leaf, its nose pointing directly towards her, and the woman squealed.

"There's somebody there." She pulled her cloak protectively over her breasts, and kicked the man in the back with her heel. "There's a fucking peeping Tom in the bushes."

The man lifted his head from her body. Clare snapped on the police torch, blinding them, and burning a grotesque instant in her mind: the rat- or squirrel-masked woman had her legs wrapped round a paunchy man with his face screwed up against the light and his trousers and underpants around his ankles. Clare spun round, and burst out of the bushes onto the track as if the starting pistol had just been fired on a hundred metre sprint. Behind her she could hear the woman screaming, with male voices now calling out in alarm.

Stupid bloody girl, Clare berated herself as she ran. *Curiosity damned nearly got you in deep shit.* But no matter, they wouldn't have recognised her. Clare eased out of the sprint into the kind of pace she could sustain for a mile, resenting the weight of the anorak and the bounce of equipment against her body.

Headlights cut the night behind her, swinging in rapid arcs as a vehicle was manoeuvred to follow. Clare did not turn, but stretched back into a sprinting pace as she heard the pursuit climbing the track towards the gate. She was still close enough to hear the angry revving of its diesel. Clare knew this sense of impending disaster, this inability to outrun doom. It went with meat cleaver sounds of weapons hitting flesh. She could have covered no more than half the distance back to her car when the headlights swung off the lower track onto the bridleway, and she dived into the woods before the beams could mark her position. No way could she outrun pursuit and reach her car first.

It was dark under the trees, and switches of hazel whipped at her face, impeding progress. Clare stumbled over a fallen branch and stayed low as the first vehicle went by, no more than twenty yards below. Panting, she squatted in the undergrowth and watched. More vehicles drove down the bridle path beneath her, their lights and sounds fading downhill towards the village. One turned uphill, and soon afterwards passed above her on the Downs road. One set of lights did not fade, but were extinguished somewhere the other side of the intervening woods, and she guessed that a vehicle had stayed where the bridleway met the road, waiting for her. Clare huddled deeper into her anorak, shivering as the sweat cooled on her body, swore quietly to herself. They'd recognise her car. Maybe it was a good job that the dig was ending. She settled down to wait.

Half an hour later, other noises that Clare could not identify carried through the night. They sounded like blows, and the tinkling sounds of breaking glass. Shortly afterwards the hidden vehicle moved away, but Clare waited ten more minutes before emerging from under the trees, rubbing her arms for warmth as she stepped onto the bridleway. She stood at the edge of the shadows, listening and watching, until she was sure that there was no human movement nearby. Some mad corner of Clare's mind suggested she return to the rune stone, but she shuddered at the thought and started walking towards the road. She'd had all the excitement she could handle for one night.

Clare was near the end of the bridle path, and relishing the thought of surrounding herself with familiar metal, when the lights of another car stopped on the road. She was close enough to hear the slamming of its door. The bastards hadn't given up. A minute later a torch started moving towards her, and Clare climbed back into the undergrowth, cursing.

The figure passing beneath her was moving strangely. The walk was hesitant, almost limping.

"Fergus?"

The figure on the path yelped, and its torch spun and probed the bushes.

"Jeez, Clare, you frightened the shit out of me." His voice sounded high and strained.

Clare scrambled out of the undergrowth, holding her hand up against the glare of the torch. "What are you doing here?"

"I was worried about you. I guessed you'd gone to the rune stone when you didn't come back." Fergus was gabbling. Clare could see he was seriously spooked. "Then I found your car and I thought…" Fergus waved down the bridle path towards the clearing. He was wide-eyed and breathing heavily. More than spooked, he was terrified. "Someone's trashed your car."

She swore. "Badly?"

"Tyres, lights, windows. They've scratched words into the paintwork."

"You came back for me." Fergus's face told Clare what it must have cost him to come to this place, on his own, in the dark. She stood on tiptoes and kissed him. "Thank you." He stared at her, too rattled to respond, so she slipped her arm inside his and walked him towards the cars.

"What happened, Clare?"

"I blundered in on Jake Herne's esbat." She told him the story of the evening.

"But why was it so important for you to go there tonight? That stone isn't going anywhere."

"But I am. The dig's finishing this week."

"I'll miss you."

Clare squeezed his arm a little tighter.

"Come and see me. I'll show you the Saxon, if you want."

"We might have different ideas of a wild night out, but I'll come anyway." The tension seemed to be leaving him as they reached the road. "I'll walk back there with you, if you like, tomorrow. To the stone, that is. In daylight." His voice sounded unnaturally light, as if he was forcing himself to make little of the offer. "Keep watch from the bridleway, perhaps, and make sure you aren't disturbed."

Clare paused before answering, guessing what the offer must have cost. "Are you sure?"

"It took me by surprise, the first time. I'll be prepared now, and I don't like boundaries. Especially the ones I build in my own head."

Clare might have kissed him again for that offer, but she'd just seen the state of her ancient Volvo, slumped on four flat tyres and crying tears of glass and cable from its lights. She felt Fergus's arm move to hug her round the shoulder.

"You can borrow mine, if you want." Fergus nodded at his little Audi. "I hardly use it, these days."

"Fergus, I'm frightened." Clare held him more closely. She could make out the words 'GO HOME BITCH' scratched down the side of her car. "What have I got myself into?"

Chapter Twenty-Eight

As the sun rose Tony Foulkes pulled his front door shut behind him, lifted his head and sniffed the morning air. His Labrador dropped her nose into the grass, moving with the happy urgency of a dog bombarded by the scents of overnight trails. Tony's more elevated nostrils relished damp earth and blossom, the crispness of ground frost in the hollows, and the promise of a fine day. It was a day to lift the spirit, a day to rejoice in this cerulean lightness at an hour that had been locked in darkness only a few weeks before. This was Tony's favourite time, the time when the village began to stir, an hour he shared only with a few of the doggy fraternity and the van delivering to the village shop. Out on the farms, the day would already be well advanced, but here in the village the early risers were a small communion of friends whose faces lit with their daily greetings.

Tony whistled the dog back to him as he climbed the hill and turned into the churchyard, following his new morning routine. Ever since the blood on the church door he'd started his morning walk with a turn around the church, just to be sure that all was well. Besides, Tony thought, it was an opportunity to perform small services of care among the graves. To pull a weed or to set a tumbled jam jar of flowers right was as much an act of worship as the way his Julia polished the brass eagle lectern in the church every week. There was a quiet joy in small, unseen acts of giving.

This morning something made the dog nervous. She ran off as usual with her tail sweeping moisture from the long grass, but came back to him rapidly, whining, with her tail now clamped between her legs. Tony crouched to pet her, looking back along the double line her paws had made through the dew as she slunk back from the yew tree corner of the churchyard. Along that path a Victorian stone angel spread its wings, marking the grave of long-forgotten gentry, and it was a monstrosity in Tony's eyes. Why not a Christian cross, or a simple headstone, he wondered, or even the proud embellishments of a heraldic tomb. Anything but the stone emotion of weeping angels. Today there was something new there, something his eyes could not interpret, a bright flash of scarlet hanging high and partly hidden by the marble wings. Puzzled, Tony walked closer, trying to decipher what he was seeing in the shadows beyond the angel, back where the yew's ancient darkness bordered the churchyard wall.

At first Tony thought he was looking at a hobby horse, the old-fashioned child's toy with a stylised horse's head on a long stick, but this hobby horse had a disproportionately large, red tongue sticking out of its mouth. Then he noticed the horns on the animal's head and felt the tightness across his chest as the shape resolved into a severed goat's head, impaled on a stake and staring at the church with its glazed, dead eyes. Tony now saw that the impossibly large, scarlet tongue was a church hymn book which had been stuffed into the beast's mouth.

Bellowing his anger, Tony rushed at the stake and wrenched at it, but the tightness across his chest focused into an ache that sank into his left arm so he heaved again, one-handed with his left arm trailing, consumed by the need to throw the vile thing beyond sacred ground. But his growls of effort became a groan of agony as his chest exploded in crackling filigrees of pain, and Tony staggered, leaning on the stake for support. For a moment he stayed there in obscene intimacy, eye to eye with the severed head until his legs collapsed involuntarily, making him appear to kneel in homage with his head bowed and his hand still clasped around the stake. Then another spasm creased him over and Tony fell, tumbling on his side between the graves. As he let go of the stake it sprang away from him, shaking the desecrated book free from the goat's mouth.

The dew-soaked grass bathed his face like a touch of grace and for a moment the pain subsided. In front of his nose a damp, limp *Hymns Ancient and Modern*, the tool of his chorister's trade, had fallen open at a verse.

Just as I am, of that free love
The breadth, length, depth, and height to prove,
Here for a season, then above,
O Lamb of God, I come.

Not yet, Tony tried to say, not yet. Then pain gripped his chest and his soundless cry was not for his God but for his wife. His outstretched hand clutched at air, wanting not the hand of his Saviour but the comfort of his soul friend.

Chapter Twenty-Nine

FERGUS WATCHED HIS own car arrive at Ash Farm and winced as it mounted the verge before Clare corrected the steering. He left his barrow load of hay, and walked to meet her as she stopped at an angle in the car park. He decided that her parking was no better than her driving. The face that emerged to look at him across the top of the car was wide-eyed and pale.

"Tony Foulkes is dead." Clare was unable to say more, and flapped a hand in front of her as if the words she needed would not come. "It... goat..." She grabbed at his shirt as he came close, pulling it fretfully until he folded her into his arms and shushed her as he might a child. Her shoulders began to shake as the tears started. There must be more to this than the death of a man she scarcely knew.

"I found him, in the churchyard," Clare sobbed into his chest. "Lying between the graves. Heard his dog as I came back from a run. She was beside him, howling."

Fergus stroked her back. "D'you know how it happened?"

"They killed him. Herne's lot." His hand slowed until he held her loosely, feeling that a trapdoor had just opened over an abyss. Fergus lifted his hands to her shoulders and pushed her away until he could look into her eyes. The fear he saw there softened his voice.

"What makes you say that?"

Fergus could see the struggle in her face, the academic need to present data pushing aside a more basic, emotional instinct. "It's called a nithing pole. Pagan cultures used them as an extreme form of cursing. They'd sacrifice an animal and jam its head on a stick, see, then point it towards an enemy with curse runes carved into the stake. Sometimes they'd put something the enemy valued into the beast's mouth to strengthen the curse."

The confusion must have shown in his face. Clare hit his chest with her fist, not hard enough to hurt, just enough to show her frustration. "Last night they killed a goat. I saw them do it. This morning Tony died underneath a goat's head nithing pole with a hymn book stuffed in its mouth."

Fergus stared at her, feeling his face slacken as acceptance numbed him. "The police?"

"They arrived just after the ambulance. I tried to tell them about last night but they seemed to think I was mad. I don't think dealing with Satanic rituals is in their instruction manual."

"But the... pole thing?"

"They took it away with them. One of them pointed out that I can't prove who put it there, and they don't think anyone could prove it caused Tony's death. The ambulance men said it looked like Tony had a heart attack."

Behind Fergus the repeater bell for the office phone jangled over the yard. He ignored it.

"It might be a coincidence. Natural causes."

"You didn't see that poor beast slaughtered. What's going on, Fergus?" He stared at her, finding no words to take away the fear in her eyes. The repeater bell snapped off as the call diverted to the answering machine.

"He's here." Clare tensed and looked past his shoulder. Jake Herne was walking out of the barn towards the office.

"He rode early this morning. He was in a foul mood."

Herne saw them and paused to stare, then jerked a hand upwards towards Clare, middle finger extended into an insult, and mouthed 'bitch'. The repeater bell started again, insistent.

Fergus felt his control start to slide. He recognised the feeling now, the sense that events were driving him, that he was sliding towards rage beneath outward calm. He had as much power to halt his lurching march towards Herne as he would have to stop a dive from a cliff into the sea, despite Clare's pleas for caution from beside him. Only the nature of the impact was undecided.

Eadlin overtook Fergus, running towards the office, muttering something about "answer the bloody phone, can't you?" as she followed Herne through the door. Normal life continued as a backdrop to the coming collision.

Fergus stopped in the doorway, unsure how to start. Herne looked up from where he was writing instructions about his horse's care in the livery book, and glared as Clare pushed into the room behind Fergus. The look was unpleasant but not abnormal, and the realisation hit Fergus. *He doesn't know.* Eadlin was standing by the desk, talking into the telephone.

"Hi Russ... No I haven't..." Her stillness became palpable. Eadlin stared at Herne, mouth gaping in shock. "Yes, I'm still here... Russ, I heard you... Jake's with me now. Call you back." She replaced the receiver slowly.

"What?" Jake's tone was aggressive.

"Oh Jake, how could you? A sodding nithing pole in the churchyard? What got into you?"

"So fucking what?"

"So Tony Foulkes died this morning, right beside it, that's what." Clare's voice shook. Good girl, Fergus thought. Scared half witless and she's still standing up to him.

Herne's face widened in surprise, then stretched into the kind of rictus grin that Fergus had seen on salesmen as they receive the news of a major, unexpected win. The expression of conquest was almost sexual as he pulled his arm into a clenched fist of triumph.

"It fucking worked!" His elation seemed mixed with wonder.

"Jake, what's happening to you?" Eadlin was stunned by his reaction, and her voice rose into a shout. It was the first time Fergus had seen her lose her composure. "Listen to yourself, for fuck's sake! A man's dead."

"Now that priest won't dare mess with me." Herne ignored her, and strutted around the room with his arm flexed, making short, punching movements with his fist. "It fucking worked!"

Fergus felt the remains of his self-control slip away. Until this moment he'd kept violence in check because he knew that Herne would beat him to a pulp if it came to a fight. Now Fergus looked around the room for a weapon. Beside him, at the door, was the rack of riding crops and schooling whips, flimsy things as weapons but in their midst was his wooden walking stick, discarded since his return. Fergus pulled it out, momentarily exploring the thick, root-ball handgrip before he held it lightly by its tip, with the heavy end swinging by his leg like a club. The threat was unmistakable. It was strange how calm he became as he discarded the conventions of normal behaviour.

"You've caused the death of a decent old man, and you're happy about it?" Even his voice sounded calm.

"You don't frighten me, you little spastic."

"Nithing poles were always thought to be an underhand way of fighting." Clare moved to stand alongside Fergus. "They were the last resort of cowards who would not confront their enemies in open combat." Fergus had not heard that steel in her voice before.

"Fuck off, you interfering little bitch, this is nothing to do with you. If you keep poking your nose into other people's business, you'll end up with a lot worse than slashed tyres. And you," Herne waved back-handed at Fergus, close enough to his face to multiply the insult, "can get the fuck out of here."

"I'll go when Eadlin says I should go, not you."

"Fergus, stay where you are, please."

"So that's the way it is, is it? Does this little spastic want to get inside your knickers?"

"It's no business of yours, but he's a friend and that's all, but a better friend than you'll ever be."

"And right now it looks as if Eadlin needs a few friends."

Herne stepped up to Fergus, moving inside the swing of the stick before Fergus could lift it, and jabbed him in the chest with his finger. As Herne spoke flecks of spittle sprayed into Fergus's face and he turned his head in disgust.

"I told you to get out, boy. Don't ever come between a real man and his lover." That was a strange choice of word, Fergus thought. He would have expected 'woman' or 'girl', but not 'lover'. It was too soft a word, too tender. Perhaps it was a country thing.

"Real man? Lover?" Anger tightened Eadlin's tone into a snarl. "You were never my lover. You just rutted, like an animal. Your idea of foreplay had as much sex appeal as a snuffling pig."

Herne crossed the room in two strides, moving surprisingly swiftly for a man of his bulk, winding his shoulders for a blow. The movement opened the range and Fergus took a half step forwards, preparing his own blow, but Jake moved too fast. Herne uncoiled in a back-handed swipe across Eadlin's face that snapped her head to the side and lifted her backwards across the room even as Fergus hefted his stick and swung. He tracked the swing of Herne's hand the way he would track a cricket ball bowled wide and high in a predictable trajectory so that it could be swept safely to the boundary. The stick's club grip and Herne's hand connected with cold precision and a sound that held the faint, wet gravel noise of breaking bones. It was as satisfying as hearing the cricket ball hit the sweet spot, knowing it would fly for six. Herne howled and kept spinning, folding as he spun to nurse his hand in his stomach.

"You little shit!" Herne crouched over his hand, cradling it in his other arm as he squatted on his haunches. "You broke my fucking hand!"

Fergus stared at him, stunned by what he had just done. His anger had burst in that single blow, leaving him with an illogical instinct to apologise. He looked down at his stick, resisting the urge to throw it away. "I think you'd better go."

"I'll fucking murder you." Now Herne was on his feet, pacing the room with the hand hugged under his arm, bowing his torso repeatedly as if in some arcane ritual of dance.

"Get out, Jake." Eadlin rested against the desk, moving her jaw experimentally. She wiped her mouth with the back of a hand, and looked down at the streak of blood that it left. "Get out, and take your horse with you." Her voice was muffled by the bloody slush in her mouth. "I want you off this yard as soon as you can move your horse."

The look Herne gave them was pure malice. "You'll regret this, all of you. I'll have you begging for mercy before I'm finished."

Fergus rested his backside against the desk as his reaction to the moment weakened his knees.

"Not before we've made you beg Julia Foulkes for her forgiveness." Clare's voice still held that note of authority. "The pity is that she's so Christian that she'd probably give it."

Fergus gripped the stick harder to mask the shakes that were building in his hands. He realised that this made him look more aggressive. "Just get out."

"You have no idea who you're messing with. And what."

Clare shut the door behind him. Fergus took one hand off his stick and stared at it. It was becoming a pattern. Rage then shakes, and a sense of guilt or failure.

"What's happening to me? I haven't hit anyone since primary school."

"He deserved it." Fergus heard the mess in Eadlin's mouth and turned to look at her.

"You OK?"

Eadlin nodded, massaging her jaw. "Thanks. He wasn't always like that, really." There was desperation in her voice, as if she needed to apologise for her former boyfriend. "He's changing. It's like this thing is taking him over." She wiped blood from her mouth onto a handkerchief. "And I think you've made a serious enemy. Jake won't forgive what you just did."

"Something tells me I'm lucky that the dig's finishing and I'm moving out." Clare had slumped into one of the leather armchairs. She stared at Fergus and he understood. *But I still have no answers.*

Chapter Thirty

CLARE ROLLS HER head against her pillow as if in a fever. Woods encircle her, imprisoning her, grey shapes in a mist that drips menace. At their margins, spreading onto the fields, warriors stand with their spears upright, lethal saplings fringing the forest. Then the woods start running towards the settlement but it is warriors not trees, and leading the charge is Tony Foulkes who bounds over the tussocks of grass shouting a war cry. Clare wants to call to him to take care because he will give himself a heart attack, but Tony is helmeted and cross-gartered and carries an axe and wants to kill her.

Aegl's arrow takes Tony square in the chest so that he slides forward a full pace on his knees under his own momentum, and as he falls a great groan of loss stumbles through the Wealas ranks. Their spears sink back to the edge of the woods the way a wave retreats from a beach, until Wealas and Saxon stare at each other across open land where a king lies dead, a goose-feather flower blooming from his heart.

Five men leave the trees, four warriors with sheathed weapons walking in a square around an old greybeard with the robe and staff of a druid. In the opaque, drifting rain they march like an honour guard of ghosts come to collect their dead. The old man leans on his staff as if overtaken by infirmity, while behind him the four warriors make a table of their shields and lift their king onto their shoulders. In silence they bear him from the field, giving him honour with their dignity, until the druid stands alone. He stares at the settlement with the wind flapping his cloak around his knees and blowing drips of water from the fluttering ends of his beard, and the druid's presence strikes them with more force than any king's. When he speaks it is in their own tongue, with the lilting accent of his race, and a voice that carries to the wall with the clarity of a bard so that all can hear.

"Every man will die, but one. Your women will become the playthings and slaves of our warriors. This is sure. But you," the druid points his staff at Aegl, "your bane is that you will not die. For you there will be no balefire, no release. You will spend eternity lost in this world and even fifty generations hence you will still yearn for the halls of your ancestors."

He speaks with calm dignity, the way one tells an inarguable truth, with none of the screaming passion of a curse. Such utter certainty is chilling. Then he turns and walks back towards the woods, leaning heavily on his staff as if he has expended much power and is drained. When he reaches the trees the grey, flapping cloak is swallowed among the trunks and the tightening ring of warriors.

Chapter Thirty-One

"ARE YOU OK with leaving your car here?" Clare parked Fergus's car off the road, above the bridleway, where it could at least be partially screened by bushes. Fergus shrugged. He was more concerned about walking back to the clearing than about what might happen to his company car.

"What's happening to your own car?"

"Russell's fixing it for me. And hey, who have you been seeing?" She reached past his shoulder and pulled a long, blonde hair from the passenger headrest.

"That'll be Kate's. I hadn't the heart to throw it away." Clare stared at the thread in her hand as if it held the answer to some profound question, the way he had seen her stare at Olrun's tooth.

"And you think that *I'm* morbid? May I?" At Fergus's nod of permission, Clare coiled the hair into the silver pillbox from her pocket. "I have a theory I'd like to test."

Fergus heaved himself out. Clare had just saved him the need to throw the hair away. That had always seemed too symbolic. Clare followed, opened the boot of Fergus's car and pulled out a rucksack. "Are you sure you want to do this?"

"Sure." He knew he spoke too brightly. "Why the bag? It looks like you're mounting an expedition." Clare was tying a blanket to the rucksack.

"It's a lovely afternoon. I brought a bottle of wine and some sandwiches. I thought we might have a farewell picnic afterwards, if you want." Clare also spoke too lightly, in a way that failed to hide a deeper significance.

"Good idea. I, er, brought my stick." Fergus lifted it in superfluous illustration. "To beat off the bad guys."

"Do you realise you've become quite a hero with Mary Baxter and the church crowd? Tony's death and your run-in with Herne are the only topics of conversation in the village." Clare shrugged into the rucksack as they started walking.

"Very gratifying, but I'll still avoid dark alleyways for a while. I don't think he's going to forgive and forget."

"I'm probably just as much in the poo. He chased me down this track after I took a peek at his party."

"What exactly *did* you see? I was a bit distracted the other night." And a bit distracted now, come to that. The track ahead of them darkened where it entered the shadow of the hill, then darkened again as it reached the rhododendrons. *Face the pain. It is an obstacle, not a boundary.*

"Not a lot. It looked as if killing the goat was an excuse for an orgy. I'm not sure which was worse; fighting off cramp in my legs or watching Squirrel Nutkin being screwed by a wolf. The last I saw, the wolf had his hands over his eyes, his trousers round his ankles, and *way* too much excitement in between. Are you all right?"

Fergus breathed deeply, forcing himself to stay calm as they approached the shrubbery that screened the clearing. He started to shiver as they left the sunlight. The gate to the side track, the scene of his collapse, stood open with the padlock and chain hanging free. Down the hill, where the track crossed the stream, they could see Jake Herne's Range Rover. Herne's horse was in the meadow at the end of the valley, and as they watched Herne himself appeared from the store by the animal shelter, dragging a block of hay one-handed. The other hand dangled across his chest in a plaster cast and sling.

"So that's where he's taken his horse." They both moved until the bushes screened them from Herne's view. "I hope it bloody well kicks him."

"I guess we won't be going down there today." Clare sounded disappointed. "I wonder how he's managing to drive?"

"One-handed, I suppose. He wouldn't have to change gear with the hand I broke."

"Shall we go back and find somewhere else for our picnic?"

"Let's go on." Fergus nodded forwards, needing to prove to himself that he could walk past the place without panicking. He faltered as they reached the trail of the car's wreck, and he felt her grip his hand. On the far side of the gap he stopped, turning his head as if smelling the air.

"It's not just me, you know." Fergus spoke almost to himself, feeling the chill of a light sweat bloom across his forehead. "There's something here, something nasty."

Fergus reached inside himself for the awareness that he had sensed sitting beside the source of another stream, on the day he rode out with Eadlin. The more he tuned out the everyday world, the more he became aware of a deeper resonance. There was a wound in this place, an absence of harmony, as if the fabric of nature was torn and bleeding.

"Apart from Jake Herne, you mean?" Clare looked around nervously.

"I thought it was me, the last time, panicking when I realised it was where I, where it..." Fergus waved a hand vaguely, lacking the words to describe the root of all nightmares. "But it's more than that. There's something malicious here, something evil."

"Come on, let's walk." Clare tugged him onwards, keeping hold of his hand, forcing him to move briskly until they had rounded the end of the valley. She turned onto a footpath that ran uphill on the eastern side of the valley, setting a pace that had him struggling to keep up. Only when the path broke clear of the trees and they stood in sunlight did she stop and turn, searching his face. Whatever Clare saw there relieved her, and she smiled and touched his face.

"For a moment back there I felt I'd lost you. It was like you'd checked out."

"More tuned in than checked out." Clare's fingers on his face were soft, making him want to touch her in return. Gently, she lifted on to her toes and kissed him on the mouth.

"Thank you."

"What for?" Fergus hoped that he didn't sound too stunned.

"Coming to that place with me. It meant a lot."

"I'm simply facing my demons. Quite literally, it seems." Fergus reached for her again but she had turned away and he found himself trying to embrace a rucksack.

"Let's take the long route back. How are your legs?" Clare called over her shoulder. Fergus watched her stride uphill, admiring the way her backside moved. Peachy. Perfect.

"Absolutely fine." Something in his tone made Clare look at him, but he ignored her implied query as well as his aches. She was grinning as she turned back to the path.

"Something I saw at Herne's orgy gave me an idea."

"Sounds exciting."

"Not that sort of idea. Do you remember me mentioning an old poem, the *Hávamál*, where Odin says that he could raise the dead by colouring runes in the right way?"

Fergus grunted. He was still enjoying the way her arse moved but the hill climb was hard work. He had no breath left for conversation.

"Well, the day before Tony died, Herne and his cronies managed to colour the runes with goat's blood."

"Tony probably had a heart attack, nothing more. And as far as we are aware there are no newly resurrected ghosts running round the churchyard."

"And the night before we discovered the Saxon they had probably coloured the runes with stag's blood."

"You're not seriously starting to believe that stuff, are you?"

Clare paused and turned as they crested a rise. Fergus lifted his eyes from his own view and grinned at her, but her eyes had become hunted, even frightened.

"I had another dream last night. It was very real. Like I was there."

Fergus was too breathless to respond.

"It was as real as packing up the dig this morning. More frightening than anything else because it felt as if they, we, were all going to die, see? In my dream I actually saw someone die. I have to tell myself it was only a dream."

Fergus touched Clare gently on the shoulder, turning her to face him. Her arm inside her sweatshirt felt fragile, like a bird's wing. He put his arms around her and hugged her, awkwardly reaching around the rucksack until he settled his arms above it, behind her shoulders.

"What's happening to me, Fergus?" Clare mumbled into his chest. "Am I going mad?" Fergus whispered reassurance into her head. "I'm dreaming about stuff that might have happened fourteen hundred years ago and, yes, I'm starting to believe it. I have a dream about a dead woman talking to me in Old Norse and I react as if I've made an archaeological discovery. I'm an academic, for heaven's sake, I'm supposed to be professional, logical, to respond to reasoning and not to fairy stories. Or dreams."

"Are you going to carry that wine back with you? Because I think we both need a drink. This is as good a place as any for a picnic, and my legs need a rest." He swept his arm across the view. Beneath them the valley of the Swanbourne opened onto rolling farmlands that faded into the distance towards the sea. The field with Herne and his horse was out of sight beneath the curve of the hill.

"Do you want to tell me about it? Your dream, I mean?" he asked, as they sipped wine from plastic cups. She breathed deeply for a moment, and then spoke in her academic voice, the one that had echoes of the lecture theatre.

"A Celtic war band comes over the Downs late in the year, after the fighting season is supposed to be over, you see, so they take the settlement by surprise. The pollen grains found in the Saxon's clothing tell us he was killed in late autumn."

"So you knew the timing already."

"Quite. I could just be lifting that bit out of my subconscious."

Fergus stared at the road on the far side of the valley, tracing where it left the open Downs and disappeared into the trees. He looked away, squinting at the light as he forced himself off that mental track. The afternoon sun was warm on his face.

"Why would they attack after the fighting season is over?"

Clare shrugged. "Perhaps there had been a drought and the crops had failed. They might have come raiding for food or for cattle, for meat to feed their families in the winter. Maybe they were trying to eliminate a particularly troublesome warlord by catching him off guard. Who knows?" She was calmer now.

"So the settlement was over-run?"

"Probably, although I haven't seen – *dreamt* – that. There was a druid with the war band, and I'm afraid of him. Even now, wide awake, I'm afraid of him, almost as if all the threat is concentrated in him. My dream stopped when he told the Saxons they would all die except Aegl. Aegl would be denied burial rites and would be cursed never to reach the halls of his ancestors."

"Sounds like a friendly guy, your druid." Fergus took a bite out of a sandwich and chewed thoughtfully. "What might Aegl have done to upset them? Apart from being Saxon, that is."

"Maybe Aegl killed the wrong man. Maybe the druid had other plans all along, because no-one knows for sure why bog people were slaughtered that way. Quite a lot of bog bodies are high caste, ritual killings that are found on a boundary, you see? Perhaps their religion had an idea that you could create a ghostly watcher on the border, a sort of spirit guard to hold back the enemy."

"You said Aegl would be denied burial rites. How does that fit with you digging him up from under the mill pond? It looks as if he was buried anyway."

"The important thing to a Saxon would probably be the rites rather than the burial itself. And he was killed by ritual drowning, with no burial. Actually you're giving me an idea." It was Clare's turn to pause and think. "I can't believe a serious academic is saying this, but maybe we should give Aegl a Saxon funeral."

"Oh, and do you have a spare longship to hand? You know, so we can re-enact the Sutton Hoo burial?" Clare's smile stayed half-serious despite his teasing. "Don't you think your university might object? And what exactly were the Saxon burial rites?"

"Of course no-one is going to let us bury the body. It would be like letting go of Tutankhamun's mummy. We'd have to steal him." Clare looked at Fergus mischievously over the rim of her cup, her eyes sparkling. "And we know too little about Saxon rites. They're mentioned in passing in epics like *Beowulf*, but it's not like having the Saxon Pagan Prayerbook to hand."

"Maybe you should ask Eadlin. She knows a lot about old traditions." Fergus thought the idea was preposterous but he was content to humour her. This sparkling, impish Clare was better company than her serious, academic persona.

Clare turned to lie back against her pack, angling her face to the sun. "You'd never believe it's only April," she said, shutting her eyes against the glare. Her position lifted her sweat shirt and stretched it across her body, and Fergus fantasised for a moment about putting his hand on Clare's belly and sliding it gently upwards. He propped himself on one elbow beside her and took the licence of her closed eyes to appreciate her figure, until Clare opened one eye and grinned at him conspiratorially.

"It would be fun, though, wouldn't it?" She giggled.

"What would?" Fergus felt himself blushing, as if Clare had read his thoughts.

"Stealing the body. My professor would have an apoplectic fit!"

Clare's laughter was sexy and he tilted his head towards her tentatively, fearing rejection, but she lifted her face to him until their lips met, and parted. She tasted of wine, filling Fergus's mind with the heady sense of her femininity. As they kissed he touched the side of her face and let his fingertips explore downwards, tracing her outline through the sweatshirt until her nipple hardened under his palm like a button under velvet. Gently, reprovingly, Clare lifted his hand away and sat up.

"Let's walk."

"Can't we just sit here and talk? I never knew body-snatching could be so interesting!"

Clare grinned and nodded at the scenery. "And half of England has a grandstand view of us." She stood and stretched as Fergus repacked the rucksack. "Let me show you something I found on one of my morning runs."

She set off along the footpath, grinning back over her shoulder. He could swear there was more swing to her hips since they had rested. The path crossed the spine of the hill out of the valley and led gently downhill, still angling away from Allingley as it plunged into the trees fringing the escarpment. By the time Clare stopped beneath a massive yew tree Fergus's legs were aching badly and he was using his stick in earnest. Fergus flopped down with his back against a nearby tree, stretched out his legs and sighed at the opportunity to rest.

Opposite him Clare caressed the bark on the ancient yew, savouring its texture. Its once-mighty trunk had hollowed at its centre, growing outwards in an interwoven ring of lesser trunks, like a colony of offspring around its former girth. It formed the shape of a royal crown rooted into the leaf-mould of the forest, feathered with dark green leaf. Some of its remaining branches had bowed low towards the ground and were resting on timber supports guyed into position by the foresters, so that the tree looked like an elderly warrior asleep on his crutches.

"This must be unbelievably old," Clare said reverently, tracing the folded bark. "It was almost certainly here when the Normans came. It was probably a sapling when the Saxons came. It might even date from around the time of Christ."

"Can any tree be that old?"

"There's a yew in Scotland that's been dated to at least three thousand BC. I doubt if this is half that age, but it must be one of very few in England to have survived the Middle Ages. They cut them down for bow staves, you see." Clare turned to look at him. "Don't settle down yet, I want to show you something." Reluctantly, Fergus let her pull him to his feet. She held his hand and led him round to the far side of the tree, to where the woven ring of trunks had left a lozenge-shaped gap into the hollow centre. The sides of the lozenge were polished by the passage of people through the ages.

"There's a way inside, see?" Clare dropped on all fours and started to crawl slightly uphill, disappearing through the gap. Fergus followed behind her, with the aches in his legs becoming irrelevant as her crouch let her sweatshirt hang loose below her body, and his view stretched from waist to neck.

"What do you think?" As Clare pulled him upright inside the tree Fergus found himself within a gnarled circle of wood where strands of yew had twisted and fused to leave a void perhaps three metres across. Here and there were gaps like spy-holes but the ring was almost continuous until the trunks separated at around head height to spread their individual paths of greenery. The base of the circle was flat, higher than the surrounding forest floor, and covered with a deep litter of fallen leaves that rustled as they moved.

Fergus closed his eyes, feeling insignificant in the presence of immense age, and tried to listen to nature in the way that Eadlin had taught him.

"Is there any of that wine left?" Clare asked, tugging at his shirt, and Fergus's eyes snapped open into the moment.

They made a nest with the blanket inside the tree, where Fergus worshipped at the altar of her body. When the need became too strong and their bodies blended, he looked down at her, searching Clare's face as he savoured the miracle. Her gaze was over his shoulder, up into the crown of the yew, almost as if her mind had slipped away from their intimacy into some distant reality.

Afterwards they lay nested together like spoons, curled up on the rug with her back to his belly. Fergus let his fingers caress her body, savouring the dry silk of a lover's skin, before he reached over and cupped her breast. He could hold it entirely within his hand, feeling it nuzzle at his palm like a tiny captive animal, exquisitely delicate and feminine.

Suddenly Fergus felt Clare tense, holding herself very still, and he froze with her as a mouse appeared from some crevice in the base of the tree. It moved slowly, one cautious step after another; their motionless forms apparently too vast for the beast's comprehension. As it walked its spring-lean body balanced precariously on the dry leaves, with its nose and whiskers twitching at the unfamiliar smells. Fergus lifted his head slightly as it passed out of sight behind Clare's shoulder, and suddenly recognising their presence, it was gone in a brown blur. Clare turned over to him, laughing.

"He looked so... pompous!"

The laughter made her breasts move and desire surged back so that they coupled a second time, with urgent hunger now, in a tumbling, laughing tangle where the giving is the taking and the taking is the giving. As they rocked together Clare made a small cry and Fergus held himself still within her, poised in the tender power of possession. He cradled her face between his palms until their eyes locked, and at that soul-to-soul moment they spilled together into a helpless time when it felt as if some other life had surged into creation between them. It was of them both and of itself, leaping joyously and independently so that for a brief while it owned its creators, leading them in the dance of utter union. Then, gradually, they became just two people again, with their loins fluttering together in gentle aftershocks like the rumbling echoes of fading thunder.

Chapter Thirty-Two

IT WAS TWILIGHT when they reached the edge of the woods, with the horizon still darkly clear against a fading sky, and the lights of the village standing out bright and warm in cottages that were already softening into shadows. Ahead of him, Clare jumped for a low branch and swung from it, giggling, until Fergus beat his chest, made gorilla noises, and slipped his hands inside her sweatshirt. He crushed her to him and lifted, but they collapsed into a laughing heap when his legs folded under their combined weight. Within a few breaths the giggles had quietened while they kissed as lovers kiss before Clare jumped to her feet, dancing backwards out of reach. Fergus lay there, watching her, filled with emotion but letting the exhaustion hold him to the ground. Clare was silhouetted against the last blush of the day, beneath a sky already speckled with the first stars, and he wondered if the world's colours were truly richer tonight. He reached for his stick and hauled himself upright. The world was fresh and wonderful but his legs hurt like hell, and the path to the village green was stretching into the longest quarter mile of his life.

"Race you to the pub." Clare still walked backwards, teasing him.

"First one there buys the drinks."

"In that case, let me help you." She moved alongside him and slipped an arm through his.

"If there ain't a seat, I'll lie on the floor."

"I still need to fetch your car."

"Leave it. I'll cycle up there in the morning. Can't manage the hill tonight."

There was not only a seat; there was a table where Fergus could stretch his legs to his sighing content. He guessed he'd just walked four miles. Five weeks before, he'd bought this stick, thrown away his crutches, and sat at the same table talking to John Webster. Today there were smiles of recognition from around the bar, and moments later the black-skirted barmaid arrived with a bottle of wine and two glasses.

"Landlord says it's on the house." She nodded over her shoulder at a grinning host.

"Tony Foulkes was well loved round here," the man called, dismissing their thanks.

"Local hero." Clare poured and touched glasses.

"Let's hope there isn't a price to pay." Fergus felt his euphoria deflate as he saw a hand-written notice on the doors into the function room saying 'Choir Practice Cancelled'. Next to it, a printed sign announced 'Function Room Reserved For Committee Meeting Tonite'.

The bar was filling up. A steady trickle of people walked through, some staying by the bar, others going straight into the function room. John Webster walked through and nodded towards their table. He managed the brief, flickering smile of someone whose mind is elsewhere, but did not speak. Cynthia the Soprano followed soon afterward, tick-tocking over the flagstones in gold shoes and black stockings like a walking ormolu clock. Her face wore the distant, dutiful pride of a Committee Member.

"How are the legs?" Under the table, Clare ran her hand down the inside of his thigh.

"Stiffening up."

Clare laughed, then sat back and beckoned as Russell and Eadlin came in. Russell beamed at the sight of her.

"Good to see you." There was a touch of shyness about his grin. "I thought all you university lot had finished today."

"My mud monkeys have gone, but I'm staying on tonight." Clare stood and kissed them both on the cheek while Fergus waved a tired greeting.

"Bring some glasses; the wine's on the house."

"Thanks, but I can't stop." Russell nodded towards the function room. "I'm on this Committee."

"But I'm not." Eadlin pulled up a chair as Russell left, and smiled at Clare in a knowing way. "Unless I'm intruding?"

Fergus looked at Clare, wondering what Eadlin had seen. That glow to her skin, that sparkle under lowered lashes, was it so obvious? The look the two women were giving each other spoke of a sisterhood to which men could never belong. Eadlin reached across the table and picked a flake of leaf out of Clare's hair. Clare blushed as she shook her head in answer.

"Not at all."

"So what's this committee all about?" Fergus nodded towards the function room.

"The May Day Committee. The Vicar's trying to persuade people to drop the Jack-in-the-Green this year. Too pagan, he says."

"So why is this Jack-in-the-Green so bloody important?" Fergus was bewildered. "I mean, it's just a bit of fancy dress, isn't it?"

"It's important because John Webster and Jake Herne have made it important, and neither of them want to back down."

"Does that mean Jake Herne's coming tonight?" Clare looked worried.

"Him? Nah, he's not a Committee man, and there'd be a fight if he turned up in here. But at least two of his little group are in there. If it comes to a vote, it'll be close."

"Why's that? Surely people will react to Tony's death?"

"Not everyone links the Jack-in-the-Green to Tony's death, leastways not directly, and some of the people that do make the connection are scared. Jake's friends have been dropping hints that anyone objecting too strongly might find a nithing pole in their front garden one morning. A lot of people believe Jake Herne has real power, now."

"Do you think so, Eadlin?" Clare reached for Fergus's hand as she spoke, gripping it too tightly for mere tenderness. The esbat and nithing pole seemed to have rattled her badly. Eadlin thought hard before answering.

"Nah." Eadlin shook her head. "Jake knows some of the old words, but that ain't enough. Like, I could learn to say the 'Hail Mary', but that wouldn't make me a Catholic, let alone a Cardinal."

"But what if he coloured the runes with blood?" Clare leaned forward, eyes wide behind her glasses.

"If that's significant, it's accidental. But Jake really believes he's a force to be reckoned with, and I'm afraid John Webster's chosen the wrong battleground." Eadlin sipped her wine. "Like I said, people don't link the Jack with the goat's head. The Vicar might as well try and stop the kids dancing round the maypole. That ain't Christian, neither, but all the mums and dads want to see their kids dressed up. May Day's just a bit of fun, and the village will need a laugh after Tony Foulkes' funeral next week. He was well liked."

"I'll come back for the funeral." Clare was thoughtful for a moment, toying with her glass before speaking carefully into her wine. "I wonder what sort of funeral the Saxon might have expected, before the church arrived?"

Fergus could feel Clare's leg against his, and gently increased the pressure against her thigh.

"I thought that was your speciality, you being an archaeologist, like."

"We don't know enough about Saxon rituals." Clare returned the pressure. "They didn't write much down."

"So if you don't know, what makes you think I might?"

"Clare's got an idea," Fergus spoke quietly, looking at Clare for a nod of permission. "She wondered about giving her Saxon a pagan funeral."

"Seriously?" Eadlin sat back in surprise, and then clapped her hands with excitement. "Go, girl!"

"It's only an idea. It seems so unfair to keep him like a specimen in a drawer, see, or worse still, in a museum case for ghoulish people to gawp at. If he was a relative, say, of yours, how would you bury him?"

"It depends on what sort of beliefs he had. I don't know if what I believe is what he believed."

"So what do you believe, then?"

Eadlin paused, closed her eyes and breathed as if she was inhaling the answer, with her palms turned upwards in her lap in a posture that was almost yogic. She opened her eyes and smiled as she found the words she needed.

"I believe we're only truly fulfilled when body, mind, and spirit are in harmony." Eadlin spoke in a soft, measured way with breaths between each phrase, an oasis of calm in the midst of the noisy bar. "When the body dies, the mind fades away with it, but the spirit is eternal. Christians think that the spirit keeps its individuality, but the Old Way teaches us that the spirit is absorbed back into a stream of life that connects all things. Sort of like raindrops, which are separate for a while but fall to earth and are absorbed. The water remains, but will never again group together into that particular raindrop."

As she spoke there was a subtle radiance to her skin as if the life within her was illuminated by her convictions.

"So what about ghosts?" Clare asked. "Does that mean you don't believe in all this talk about the Saxon?"

"I believe that there is something of ourselves that survives death for a while, like an echo, which stays separate until it's absorbed back into the stream. Some people would call that a ghost. Maybe something stops them from joining the flow, like a really traumatic death, or p'raps they just don't want to let go. Sometimes, though, I think they're kept here by something outside of themselves."

"Like a curse." Clare was listening intently.

"Could be, but if the power of how to do that ever existed, I mean *really* do that as opposed to simply wishing evil on someone, then the knowledge has been lost."

"So how would a pagan funeral work these days, then?" Fergus brought Eadlin back to the original question.

"Sadly, the law has very strict rules about how to dispose of bodies. We'd probably have a standard cremation then scatter the ashes with a small ceremony. Sorry if that's not what you wanted to hear."

"It doesn't sound as if your rituals would be the same as the Saxons', anyway." There was disappointment in Clare's voice. "They also believed in the individual surviving into an after-life. The warrior feasting in the halls of the gods, and all that."

"Maybe the actual words aren't as important as the honour we give to a dead person, or the blessing we wish on his spirit. Next week the Vicar will bury Tony Foulkes and I'll go to the funeral, but no-one will see anything sacrilegious in that. It's a way of showing respect for Tony and support for Julia." Once again Fergus glimpsed wisdom in Eadlin's eyes, something ageless behind the grey. "Maybe we all find what we believe in. I hope Tony has his eternity as Tony in a Christian heaven. When it's my turn I'll be content simply to be a part of a universal spirit."

"A pulse in the eternal mind, no less." Clare smiled to herself.

"Rupert Brooke!" Fergus exclaimed, his face lightening.

"You've lost me." Eadlin looked from one to the other.

"'Gives somewhere back the thoughts by England given.'" Fergus was on a roll.

"Will one of you please explain what you're talking about?"

"Rupert Brooke, First World War poet. I had to learn it at school," said Fergus.

"Come on then." Clare's smile hardened into a challenge.

"And think, this heart, all evil shed away

A pulse in the eternal mind, no less

Gives somewhere back the thoughts by England given..." He faltered.

"Her sights and sounds; dreams happy as her day..." Clare prompted,

"And laughter, learnt of friends; and gentleness,

In hearts at peace, under an English heaven."

Fergus and Clare finished the last two lines in chorus, to laughing applause from Eadlin.

"You two are good together." Eadlin looked over her shoulder as raised voices broke through the murmur of debate from the function room. "Sounds like the Vicar's having a rough time."

"… I believe a real and tangible evil has entered our community…" John Webster sounded cornered.

"… come on, Vicar, this is the twenty-first century."

"… but the goat's head in the churchyard…" Cynthia the Soprano's voice lacked confidence.

"… is nothing to do with the Jack. We've always had a Jack."

"There's no need to shout."

"… and no-one knows for sure who put it there, anyway…"

"… take a vote…"

John Webster's face said it all when the meeting broke up. He and Cynthia walked through to the street door with tight-faced dignity, the first of the crowd that emerged into the bar. Russell just shrugged his shoulders as he joined them.

"Bunch of sheep." His tone was contemptuous. "It was the God Squad – the Saint Michael's crowd – versus the rest. Half of those were in a funk and the others just want a quiet life."

"So you voted with the Vicar?" Clare sounded approving.

"Yeah, but not because I liked his argument. I just don't like being threatened, especially by Jake Herne. And oh," Russell changed the subject, "your car is going to take several days to fix. Need to order in the parts, see?"

If it wasn't for the way Clare's fingers were linked with his under the table, Fergus could have felt jealous about the spark between Clare and Russell. There was a touch of the 'little girl and puppy dog' about it, even if the puppy dog was more of a bashful man-mountain. Within a minute Clare had asked Russell if he'd give her a lift up the road to fetch Fergus's car, and Russell had accepted as if she'd thrown him a stick to chase.

"Don't worry." Eadlin interrupted Fergus's thoughts as he watched Clare and Russell leave.

"You're very relaxed about it."

"Like I said once before, you're safe. Leastways, you are from Russell. Sure, he's sweet on her, but it's a protective thing; he's not chasing her. And you, my friend, are a lucky man. It should have happened weeks ago."

"Are we that obvious?"

Eadlin picked up a flake of leaf from the table. "You're shouting from the rooftops. But take care of her. I've got a nasty feeling that Jake's planning revenge. He'll hurt both of you if he can."

Chapter Thirty-Three

ST MICHAEL'S CHURCH was filling rapidly for Tony Foulkes' funeral. Clare and Fergus chose a side aisle by the wall, placing themselves at the edge of the hierarchy of grief radiating outwards from Julia. Around them individuals and families filed into the pews quietly, muttering subdued greetings before they bowed their heads in prayer or sat in quiet contemplation. A slow peal of bells reverberated through the church from the tower behind them, ringing out alternately with sharp clarity then heavier, softer tones as if through a wall of cloth. Fergus heard a fellow mourner whisper that they had muffled the bells.

In front of them the stained glass window of the lady chapel was a Victorian complexity of reds and blues and golds, its colours too rich for the moment. Its central panel depicted a winged angel in knightly armour, presumably Saint Michael, raising a sword to strike at a devil at his feet. The artist had given the saint's face the same honest frown of a hero in some pre-War children's story book, the kind of book where a clean-limbed young man would be drawn seeing off the cads and bounders with a righteous fist. Grouped around the saint was an adoring circle of lesser angels with androgynous, vaguely female figures. Their faces all had the same lean, finely chiselled look, as if they were a chorus of identical Clares. An irrepressible, irreverent corner of Fergus's mind was wondering if angels came equipped with naughty bits when a chord from the organ announced the arrival of the cortege, and he started guiltily.

There was a terrible sense of mortality as the coffin was carried in. Apart from Kate, death had always been an impersonal event, reported off-stage like a Greek tragedy. Even Kate's death seemed part of a nightmare, still not fully resolved. Today death arrived shoulder-high and feet first, awful in its reality, borne with ritual dignity to be laid on trestles between ranks of weeping choristers.

The choir did not give their best performance, and they knew it. Their voices faded into near silence as ripples of grief shook their singing. Even Cynthia Lawrence's pure soprano was almost inaudible. It was only when John Webster walked forward to stand in front of his friend's coffin, after all the hymns had been sung but one, after all the words of praise from the family's oration, that the mood started to change.

"Today," he started, "must be one of the hardest days of my priesthood." He paused, gathering his strength.

"Priests are supposed to develop an emotional distance. We have to learn to share moments with sensitivity and feeling while avoiding the full emotional burden. Our role is to help others in their grief or happiness, and not to talk over-long about their personal emotion. But today I cannot do that because we are burying a beloved friend and brother in Christ. And more than that, a friend who has become a casualty in a very old battle.

"Oh, I have no doubt that Tony's death will be recorded officially as 'natural causes', but many in this congregation today will know of the evil that has entered our community, focusing its hatred on this church, an evil that has taken its first life. It is a blow beyond description for Julia, who has lost her soul mate, her friend, and her lover. For almost forty years the hearts of these two musicians have beaten to a shared rhythm. It is also a terrible blow for the church because the church's strength is not in these mighty stones around us; it is in the people, the communion that worships within its walls. And I cannot imagine a greater wound to this church than the loss of this dear and decent man.

"So we have two priorities in the coming weeks. Firstly we must support and pray for Julia and comfort her in her loss, and secondly we must pray for our church, that we might find the strength and the means and the champions to fight this war. I do not doubt that with the help of Christ we will find that strength."

John Webster's voice shook with emotion. Now he paused, and drew a folded piece of paper out of his pocket.

"The hymns we are singing today were chosen by Tony. He and Julia have known for some time that he had a heart condition, that his time with us might be limited." A ripple of surprise ran through the congregation. "Earlier this year he wrote to me with very clear instructions in the event that he left us suddenly, with no time to prepare. Some of his letter is private, but let me read you his final paragraph.

"'Marrying Julia was the best decision I ever made, and not only for the joy of our life together, but because she brought me to Allingley. I have been made so welcome in this wonderful community that I have felt little yearning to return to Wales, to the 'Land of my Fathers', so to speak. But I would like to be taken out to the sounds of the valleys and that wonderful tune 'Cwm Rhondda'. And, my friend, ask them to belt it out, will you? Especially the basses. Give it some wellie, as they say. Don't be too sad; if the Good Lord is merciful, there will be another tenor in heaven.'"

John Webster was unable to continue. Slowly, he folded the letter and replaced it in his pocket, breathing deeply several times before he managed to straighten his back and speak.

"So now we will sing our final hymn, number 214, 'Guide me, O thou great Redeemer'. And while we grieve with Julia and for ourselves, let us also rejoice that there is indeed another tenor in heaven."

The first lines were scarcely audible above the organ. Only Mary Baxter of the choir, strong little Mary, managed to put some power into her contralto voice. In desperation John Webster moved to stand on the chancel steps, opening his arms wide in command so that his surplice spread like wings, shouting the hymn with little thought for harmony.

I am weak, but thou art mighty;
Hold me with thy powerful hand:

Behind him at least one tenor and a bass swelled in support.
Fergus could almost hear Tony Foulkes' rumbling laughter that
first night in the pub, when Tony had introduced him to the
choir.

"Tom Caister and Allan Bullock," he had said of the two
men. "Just think of them as Castor and Bollocks, the Heavenly
Twins."

Bread of heaven
Feed me now and evermore.

As the organ played the introduction to the second verse
Webster shouted again,

"Sing, for the love of God, sing!"

Then he stayed with his arms raised while the volume grew
like the rumble of an approaching avalanche and the pallbearers
turned the coffin behind him. Only when the final verse started
in muscular force did he lower his arms and step forward, his
face streaming with unashamed tears as he led his friend's coffin
out into the churchyard.

When I tread the verge of Jordan
Bid my anxious fears subside;
Death of death, and hell's destruction,
Land me safe on Canaan's side:

At last the choir engaged, singing the part harmonies with the
bass line ringing out as well as at any Eisteddfod. There was
a sense of defiance, of a congregation marching to war, as the
final triumphant lines thundered to the roof.

Songs and praises
I will ever give to thee.

As the coffin passed them Clare put one hand over her eyes and held on to Fergus with the other, staggering so that he feared she was on the point of collapse. When he turned to her, supporting her, she simply gestured across the church.

"The warrior. They carried him from the field on their shields. It's the warrior, all over again."

Not understanding, he looked over her head, following the line of her arm, but saw only the coffin being borne shoulder-high from the church. When he turned back to her she sank into her pew, head folded over her hands as if in prayer, and shook her head to silence his whispered concerns. Confused, he knelt beside her in ritual piety, waiting for the moment when it was polite to rise and follow the family into the churchyard, when the silence could be broken. A shaft of sunlight broke through the cloud outside and shone through the stained glass window in front of him, throwing multi-coloured splashes of light onto the plaster walls. Through lowered eyelids he watched tiny motes of dust floating against the black chequered marble of the floor.

He never afterwards managed adequately to describe what followed. He would only ever try with a very few people. He was as fearful that the moment itself would be tainted by scorn as he was nervous of the scorn itself, because some experiences cannot be condensed into words. It was enough that it happened.

It started with a sensation that was almost a shiver, like a touch of clean, spring air and sunshine on winter-whitened skin. Then the blessing – he would always think of it as a blessing – broke over him in a wave, engulfing him and filling him with a sense of unutterable joy. He had a moment to wonder what was happening, and so knew the sensation came from outside of him, not within him, before he surrendered to a glimpse of divinity. It was pure light and colour and smell, and it rooted him on his knees, oblivious to the congregation rising and leaving. All that was good and fresh in creation condensed into a presence that was around him and in him, one with him but not of him, that flowed to every fragment of his being. Then slowly, as slowly as falling swan's down, it started to recede, leaving him to open his eyes on a world where dust motes still floated in the sunlight, in air that was now filled with the smell of flowers.

He sat back in his seat like a man waking from a deep sleep, with a sense that time had passed although the patterns of light from the windows seemed not to have moved. He looked around, needing solitude to absorb the unsought benediction. The church was almost empty. The last of the mourners was leaving, and Clare stood waiting in the aisle, looking troubled by his unexpected piety. Beyond her, on the far side of the church, Eadlin was watching him and for a moment he thought he saw an expression of immense tenderness on her face, the kind of look Romantic artists would give an angel gazing on redeemed mankind. Then when he focused on her it was gone, so swiftly he wondered if it was his imagination.

Eadlin's words by the spring echoed in his mind. *You are sensitive... Maybe it stayed with you when you touched the shadow world.* He closed his eyes for a moment, feeling more aware of himself and the physicality of the world around him than he had ever known. When he opened his eyes Eadlin had left. Only Clare remained, looking at him with her head tilted on one side as if to say 'well?' Rather shakily, he stood and walked over to her.

"Are you all right?" She was fretting nervously at a handkerchief.

"Did you, can you... I mean..." He struggled for words. "Can you smell flowers?"

"Of course I can. It's a funeral, silly."

"Of course. Sorry." She slipped her arm inside his, and he allowed himself to be led outside. There was something he had meant to ask her, but it could wait. He felt like a tranquil island in a whispering sea of grief, but in that slow-stepping, silent walk to the grave, he was coming to accept that all we see is not all that is. He was not yet sure what he was expected to do with that knowledge, but the certainty of an otherness was humbling and wonderful.

He stood with Clare at the edge of the crowd around the grave, dazed but with all his senses acutely tuned. Eadlin moved to stand the other side of Clare, and slipped her arm through hers as if Clare were the one needing comfort, not Julia Foulkes. Eadlin glanced at Fergus across Clare's head, lifting an eyebrow in an unspoken question. He shrugged, unsure whether her uncertainty was about him or for Clare, and inhaled the richness of newly dug earth and the smell of imminent rain.

Between them, Clare slipped clear of their arms, bent over, and picked up some loose earth spilling from the pile beside the grave, rubbing it in her fingers and sniffing it.

"Fire layer," she muttered, her words almost inaudible above John Webster's prayers. "There's been a large fire here, a long time ago." She moved to peer between the mourners towards the grave, and Fergus guessed that she was trying to see how the soil stratified. A gust of wind blew across the graveyard, making dry debris tumble between the graves, and billowing out John Webster's surplice behind him. Clare straightened, suddenly, and spun into Fergus, holding him urgently so that the force of her hands gripped through his jacket, hurting his side where her nails dug through the cloth.

"Not real." The note of hysteria was back in her voice. "Can't be real."

He looked down at her, unable to understand her panic, but her face was buried in his chest and he could only stroke her hair, instinctively soothing her the way a parent would comfort a child. Eadlin was watching them, her face taut with concern. Fergus looked over Clare's head for something that might have triggered her reaction, wondering if it had anything to do with the way the freshly dug earth smelt like her excavation. In front of them, John Webster's surplice fluttered gently in wings of purest white, like a swan's.

Part Four

Beltane

April/May

Chapter Thirty-Four

FERGUS TOOK TIME off from the stables to deliver Clare's car back to her from Russell, and to collect his own. Clare kept promising to show him the Saxon, as if this was an experience he'd want. He supposed it would be difficult to avoid it, and seeing the Saxon would be a price worth paying for an afternoon and evening with Clare.

She greeted him in the foyer of her faculty, standing like a petite beacon of beauty in breathtakingly ugly surroundings. Fergus had expected an environment with more character, perhaps a patina of age and ivy, not a structure that had been provoking gag reflexes since it won its first design award.

Clare wore her academic persona. Smart shoes, clean slacks, and make-up had replaced the dirty jeans of the dig site, although the swoop in his stomach at the sight of her felt just the same. The sparkle in her eyes reassured Fergus as they kissed cheek-to-cheek, betraying no raw material on which the campus gossips could feed, and he whispered in her ear as their faces touched.

"I've missed you."

Clare led him down a corridor, allowing a brief fluttering together of fingers as they flashed the private smile of lovers.

"Are you OK?" Fergus was concerned. Clare's face was drawn and shadowed despite the sparkle.

"Bit short of sleep."

"More bad dreams?"

"Getting worse. And before I forget, Jake Herne has refused the university permission to examine the rune stone on his land. His letter also included a threat to prosecute anyone found trespassing."

"That doesn't surprise me."

"Nor me, but I *will* find a way of looking at that stone. Let's go in here and say hello properly." Clare glanced around her to ensure they were not observed, and opened a door marked 'Professor of Archaeology and Anthropology'. After a surreptitious check inside, she pulled him into a spacious room furnished with an imposing mahogany desk, a large leather sofa, stacked shelves of books and endless photographs of the same individual. In an instant it was as if Clare had opened the door to another mood; she become a schoolgirl raiding the headmistress's study.

"I recognise this guy," Fergus exclaimed, "he's on the television." The photographs showed Professor Miles Eaton talking to camera, Miles Eaton receiving awards, and Miles Eaton shaking hands with celebrities.

"It's my boss's office. Now show me how much you've missed me."

"What if he comes in?" Fergus asked as they broke.

"The old goat is lecturing for the next hour." Clare turned to lock the door behind them. "I've always thought that sofa is wasted on tutorials…"

Later, as they lay tangled and flushed in each other's arms, she kissed him on the nose and giggled.

"Meetings in here with that egotistical bastard will never be the same again."

Fergus caressed her rump, luxuriating in its texture, in the way it was ripe with promise.

"Stroking your bum is like eating dark chocolate after a feast." Fergus let his hand settle more firmly on one cheek, and squeezed. She lifted her head and looked at him quizzically. "That moment when you're replete but still manage to find room for one last pleasure."

Clare giggled again and rested her chin on his chest. "Fergus, I've been thinking."

"I hope your thoughts are as exciting as mine."

"About why I'm having these dreams."

Fergus let his hand lay still.

"Look, Clare, can't we...?"

"Like if someone's trying to tell me something."

"Clare, please. Why can't we be like other couples, and talk about music or sex and then go out to a film or something? We've just made wonderful love and you're talking about ghosts and we're on our way to see a corpse. Can't we just be us for a while?"

"Sorry." Clare toyed absent-mindedly with his chest hair. "But you're the only one I can talk to about it. Please?"

Fergus let his hand drop. The feast was over.

"So what's on your mind?"

"Maybe they're all trapped, somehow. Aegl, Olrun, possibly even Kate."

"Or it could just be bad dreams that you could fix with a good holiday."

"But perhaps I can give them peace, help them move on."

Fergus did not want to think about that, not now, not in the midst of such intimacy. Nightmares should not be allowed to intrude on beauty.

"And just how do you think you can do that?" He felt drawn in despite himself.

"Well... Shit!" Clare leapt off him and reached for her clothes.

"What happened?"

She nodded at a clock on the wall. "His lecture is nearly over. Let's go. Do you still want to see Aegl?"

Fergus shrugged, the mood of love already broken. He'd hoped she'd have forgotten the idea. Given a choice, Fergus would rather have gone for a walk with Clare or found somewhere private without the fear of being caught *in flagrante delicto*. Now he found himself more in fear of seeming afraid than of seeing the body.

"OK." Fergus spoke to her back as she repaired her makeup. Face the pain. Always the same mantra. Face the pain.

Clare led him into a laboratory, empty of people but cluttered with equipment. "Still sure? He's not a pretty sight."

"Keep going." Fergus was not going to back out now. "Don't we have to get dressed up in overalls and masks and stuff, like the pathologists on TV?"

"No. He's in a climate-controlled case. He's been freeze-dried but we're taking no chances about introducing him to modern bacteria or moisture. Here." Clare pulled back a green baize cover from a trolley to reveal a coffin-shaped perspex box that trailed electrical cables to a socket. Fergus was startled by the suddenness of the movement. He had been expecting more ceremony, more of a build-up, and more reverence.

"Red hair," was all Fergus could think of to say. Somewhere inside him there was a rush of relief that he could not recognise this artefact as the tramp beside the wreckage. This body had skin the colour of old mahogany, with fiery, dark-orange hair trailing bizarrely from the scalp and face. Fergus could remember pale skin with the broken veins of wind-burn in the cheeks, and a beard and hair the colour of dried straw.

"It's the tannins in the ground," Clare said. "It darkens the skin and dyes the hair that colour, you see? He was probably blond."

Fergus forced himself to look at the face. But for the darkened skin, nothing in the features suggested death. The Saxon's character was still clear in the full mouth, slightly fleshy nose, and a brow furrowed with wisdom lines. Only the faint tracery of the stag tattoo was familiar, near-black within the brown. He might have been a man asleep, or perhaps a wooden carving, if it were not for the impossibly-coloured hair. It was only when Fergus allowed his eyes to travel along the body that the reality of a corpse hit him. Below the neck, the detailed perfection of the face disintegrated into a flattened chest which looked like the folded leather of a discarded jacket.

"His chest was probably crushed by the weight of the bog." Clare seemed to read his mind. "Look, you can see a wound in his shoulder, though." She was still talking as if to a student, pointing out the long gash in the left shoulder like a cut in the leather. "Probably an axe wound, which we know happened shortly before death because there is no calcification of the bone, but it was not the cause of death. Nor was he killed by the stab wound to the leg, which was powerful enough to slice into the thigh bone but missed the major arteries. See?" Clare pointed with professional distance towards a tear in the skin on the upper right leg. Fergus tried not to look beyond it towards the decayed mess on the cadaver's left side. "He was almost certainly drowned. He was staked down, alive. You can see the leather thongs on his wrists and ankles."

Fergus looked at the corpse's right hand. The fingernails and even the tiny patterns of folded skin on the fingers and palms were perfectly preserved. The severed left arm was lying loose beside him, a mere bundle of sticks ending in a claw with no soft tissue remaining.

"Why the difference?" he asked, waving his own hand between the left and right side of the Saxon's body.

Clare shrugged. "Probably because of variations in the soil conditions. Rotting peat makes bog acid, which pickles tissue like vinegar. If there's poor drainage then the soil becomes anaerobic, which means no oxygen. It's the combination of bog acid and no oxygen that kills the bacteria and stops decomposition, you see? There was alluvial silt just above the layer where we found the body, which suggests a flow of fresh water soon after he was put in the ground. That might explain the partial decomposition."

"Wouldn't the stream have oxygenated the site?"

"Good question. We think the basin silted up fairly rapidly, and that the stream flowed along one side of what had become a marsh. It probably wasn't channelled to create a mill stream until the early middle ages, and he'd have been deep in peat by then. Anyway the flow would have been at the surface level only, not at his depth."

"Thank you, professor." Fergus tried to make light of the moment. Something in this scene felt wrong, even beyond the macabre object of their attention. Clare spoke as if she was delivering an academic treatise.

"I told you that there was another body above him in the silt layer, but nothing remains of that except a few teeth and some bone fragments. We know it was female and contemporary with the Saxon, but not much more." Clare's voice softened. "I think it was Olrun."

Fergus gestured towards the Saxon. "It must be pretty rare, finding something like this."

"Actually he's not so unusual. I guess several hundred bog bodies have been found across Northern Europe. All of them were buried in cold weather, so the natural embalming started before decomposition set in." The academic voice was back, but it was tightening and becoming brittle, as if Clare was forcing herself into a role.

"We can work out quite a lot about him. We know he was aged around 38, and we even know what he ate for his last meal, despite the poor state of the lower stomach and genital area..." Clare waved her hand at that part of the corpse then turned away, resting both arms onto a workbench and allowing her head to drop forwards between her shoulders.

"Shit, I can't do this anymore."

"Hey, what's the matter?" Fergus put his arm around her shoulders.

"Those dreams," Clare said quietly. "I know him. I mean really know him, as a person." She shut her eyes and breathed deeply, forcing oxygen into her lungs. "Here, he's a bog man, an exhibit, soon to be sent off to a museum where he can be gawped at by thousands. But I've dreamt of him alive and vital, with blood and life surging through him. To me, he's Aegl, an arrogant, lovable, inspiring chieftain." Clare dropped her voice even lower, so that he had to strain to hear her. "And in those dreams, he's my lover."

Clare straightened and turned, allowing him to fold her into his arms and stroke her back so that her next words were spoken into his chest.

"It's like I'm living in two worlds. There's this one, with you and the university, and a future. The other world, the Saxon one, the dead one, is so real that I think I must be going mad. And there are times when the two worlds are getting muddled, as if the boundaries are fraying. I see echoes of my dreams in everyday life, almost like I'm making stuff happen."

"Maybe you should get away for a while. Like I said, take a break. Let's go on holiday together."

Clare sniffed and hugged him without answering.

"Hey," Fergus lifted her chin so she had to look into his eyes, "I've had to compete with an older man before, but never one this old!" Clare's flicker of a smile was merely a polite acknowledgement of his attempt at humour. "Or," he said looking at the corpse, "quite that ugly." He pulled the baize covering back over the case.

That night they made love in her flat, but their lovemaking had no fire and seemed an act of comfort rather than passion. Afterwards they lay together on her bed, legs entangled under her duvet, while he watched the shifting patterns of orange light on the ceiling from her lava lamp in the corner. There was a brighter band of light near the window where the traffic lights outside cast their steadily changing colours over the curtains, creating kaleidoscopic confusion. Clare's head was on his shoulder and Fergus could feel the gentlest touch of a breast on his chest as she breathed. Around them, the clutter of her life gleamed a more constant orange in the shadows; family photographs, a bean bag, and a dressing table so piled with files and journals that there was no room for cosmetics. Clare, he decided, inhabited a space in a utilitarian way; she did not project herself onto it.

Loud music started in the flat below, thumping its rhythm through the floor. Muttering at the intrusion, Clare pushed herself up and sat cross-legged facing the lava lamp, pulling the duvet cloak-like around her shoulders. Fergus twisted to lie in her lap with his head on her thigh, and looked up at her as a wave of joy surged through him at the intimacy of the moment.

"What are you thinking about?"

Clare was silent for a long moment before answering. "I'm going to do it. Take Aegl, that is."

"If you're caught, your career is finished."

"I'll probably be in prison as well, but I'll risk it."

Fergus shuffled to settle his neck more comfortably, still looking up at her. "How are you going to do it?"

"I'll need help. And in case you were thinking of offering, I need someone who is strong on their feet. And might have to run. Sorry." She spoke matter-of-factly.

"No problem." Fergus was only half concentrating, anyway, watching instead the way the lava lamp touched the underside of Clare's breasts with gold. He slid a hand up her body to caress them, wondering anew at their texture, feeling them duvet-warm and soft under his palm. The noise from the flat below had settled into a steady rhythmic thump, and as Fergus cupped a breast he could feel her pulse fluttering birdlike in his palm.

"Your heart is almost *in tempo* with the music."

"Make sure you resuscitate me when it stops."

"Rely on it. Mouth to mouth." Fergus turned to kiss her belly before continuing. "You're trusting whoever you ask with your future. Choose carefully." He rolled her nipple under his thumb.

"Russell would probably do it. He won't let me down. Anyway getting Aegl out shouldn't be difficult. It's not like he's some hoard of gold in the safe. It's what to do with him afterwards that worries me." Clare was calmer now, closing her eyes as if her announcement had been a release. Fergus felt her nipple tighten and swell.

"But I can't let him be sent off to the museum. If he'd died recently, if he was someone's father, we wouldn't treat him like that." Clare's voice took on a slightly husky quality, encouraging Fergus to let his hand slip downwards, across the plain of her belly, to tease her with his fingers. Clare started to move with him, swaying in time to the music from below. "I mean, how long does someone have to be dead before they lose the right to some respect?"

Fergus ignored the question. Clare's musty fragrance was filling his senses and dampening his thinking like an opiate. He turned to kiss the source of that feral scent and she gasped, tensing. Suddenly Clare moved to straddle him, kneeling above him and rising to guide him. The moan as she sank onto him might almost have been the groan of a mortal wound.

Fergus had not known her like this. There was brutality in Clare's movements, as if by taking him she could fix herself in this current reality. He tried to calm her, holding her close to slow her. It almost felt that they were fighting until she shuddered and let out a sound that was more a wail of loss than a cry of fulfilment. Clare collapsed onto him, wordlessly, as if she were trying to pin him down and imprison him with her body. Fergus pulled the duvet over them and caressed her back, knowing that he needed to soothe her. For the first time there had been no giving in their loving. The act felt like a response to some unspoken need in her that he did not yet understand.

In a little while Fergus felt a tear drip onto his neck and cut a warm track over his shoulder. Confused, he reached inside himself for the point of calm that Eadlin had tried to teach him, but he was blind to whatever was troubling Clare. For some unknown reason an image of his crash leaped into his mind. There had been a time, before the screaming time, when he had sunk his teeth into his own flesh, compounding pain with pain in an effort to keep his sanity. Fergus squirmed at the memory. He hadn't had a waking flashback for days. Why now, when he opened his mind in search of intuition? In the fractured silence Fergus forced the memories back into that private box in his head, and hugged her more tightly in his own need for comfort.

Beside him Clare breathed deeply, and as she slept she made small noises of fear or pain until he soothed her again, watching her face as it softened and the furrows between her eyebrows faded into the sighs of deep sleep. Softly, tenderly, Fergus pushed a strand of hair back over her temple, and laid a hand on her breast. He touched her with a gentleness he did not know he possessed, wanting to savour the wonder of her form but still to leave her sleeping, yet even at this lightest touch Clare groaned and rolled away from him.

Chapter Thirty-Five

CLARE RESISTS THE fall into the nightmare but the arm around her shoulder holds her with tender insistence, in the way a loving friend might help a condemned woman towards her execution. At that thought Clare tumbles, flailing, until her fear becomes surprise and then triumph at the sight of the blood that her sword sprays through the air at the end of her stroke.

For she has killed, and she glories in the killing, in these final moments of their people. The palisade is breached, too few are left for a shield wall, and all around her is the chaos of separate combats, three against ten, one against three. These are men she knows like brothers: the heroes, the bards, the drunkards, the fathers, her lord's bravest and best bellowing their defiance and dying on the point of a spear because none of the enemy dares come within the swing of their axes and give them equal fight. Yet there is a wild liberation in this battle, in the brotherhood of men who have accepted death and so have nothing left to lose except the honour of their dying.

In the melee Clare knows the exultation of her first kill, slashing her blade across the throat of a Wealas boy who thinks he can play with her. The boy sways away from her thrust easily, taunting her, but she sees his concentration waver as her breasts lurch within her clothes, so he misses her snarl as she starts her backswing. In an instant the check and drag of her blade across his throat earns her full membership of this bloody brotherhood.

The boy stands rigid for a full heartbeat after her blow, a frozen moment of time in which their eyes meet and she knows him. In that heartbeat Clare knows the boy in the man who cries *not fair* in his mind at the shock of the wound. In that heartbeat she knows the man in the boy and his axe-fighter's surprise at the speed of her lighter blade. In that heartbeat she feels the rage of the warrior who knows himself bested by a woman. And as the fatal pulse gathers, Clare wonders if this child-man with jewels of blood in his wispy beard also knows her, the swan maiden who has become the she-wolf with a dripping blade.

Then the blood erupts from his mouth in a gush of crimson vomit, and as the boy drops to his knees she leaps and spins, whooping in the mad joy of the warrior, with her blade spraying an arc of garnets around her.

Clare had not seen her lord wounded, but he staggers towards her, shield gone, shield arm hanging loose, and a stream of blood flowing from where an axe has struck clear through his mail coat into his shoulder. There is an awful hesitancy in his step, a burden greater than the wound, and the sorrow in his face tells Clare it is time. There are worse things than death. Better to die at his hand, with honour, than to submit to what must come to all the women. Slowly, ignoring the madness around her, she steps towards him with her arms opening wide so he can strike true, willing him to know her acceptance.

Clare senses rather than sees the thrown spear, but she hears the sickening sound of its impact as it punches his leg into the mud. It knocks him sideways with the spear's length flailing at the sky, and sends his sword spinning away in the dirt. Screaming her rage, Clare runs forward to pull out the spear and turn him.

"Please. Together." Weeping now at the end of things, Clare pushes her own blade into his hands and braces its hilt against the mail coat on his stomach. Swiftly, she kneels astride him and raises herself above him, guiding the point under her ribs in a grotesque parody of union. With their eyes locked in this ultimate bond, she sees too late the axe swung flat-side into her temple, sweeping her aside in shattered fragments of light.

* * *

WRONGNESS. A SENSE of wrongness fills Clare's head as if an army of warriors were humming the same, deep note. Her eyes flicker open at Aegl's groan; already he is bound. How strange that they should both want death, and want death for each other, yet each see the other's face lighten as their eyes meet. Across the dirt, through the passing Wealas legs, he calls to her.

"Olrun." His voice has their private gentleness. It is a tone that belongs with piled furs and whispered endearments behind their screen in the hall, not with dirt and death. "Whatever happens, in my heart you are pure. You are my woman, my swan, my sword-sister..."

Clare's own hands are pulled behind her and bound, and Aegl's words become a futile bellow as a hand reaches inside her clothes and gropes at her breasts. Clare squirms against the violation but a beard is at her ear and its voice mutters Wealh words whose meaning is clear. *You are mine.*

Aegl faints when they lift him, strapped to a spear shaft like a stag taken in the hunt, mercifully insensible from the moment his shoulder takes the weight of his body. The survivors are herded together at spear point to follow. Most of the women are there, huddled together in a frightened clump, weeping for their men. One of the Wealas lifts the skirts of his tunic and waves his penis at them, calling out in a tone that needs no translation. Three of Aegl's warriors are there too, hanging their heads in shame that they live. Clare does not blame them. They are young, these last few, and the lust for life runs strong in the young. The old ones, the veterans, all died fighting and cursing, choosing a swift passage to the halls of the gods with Wealas blood on their axes. But among the young men, the ones whose beards are still fine with youth, these three chose a few more hours of life when the point of a spear was at their throat.

For some reason Clare does not understand, the druid makes the women carry empty wicker baskets. Every basket in the settlement must be there, together with their tools for tilling the fields. One of the Wealas makes to untie her hands so that she too can carry a burden, but the druid stops him.

"Not you." The druid smiles at her in a way that holds no humour. She had forgotten that he speaks their tongue. "You fight!"

She hopes it will be swiftly over, before he wakes, but they lay him in a hollow scraped from the bog, and the cold and the wet revive him so they have to stand on his limbs as they tie him down. Only when the druid directs the women to fill their baskets with earth and block the stream does Clare realise what is going to happen, and she screams, so the Wealas know that she is his woman. One of them moves behind her and rips her clothes open at the neck, pulling the rags down to her waist so that her breasts are bared.

"Hey, saeson!" the Wealas calls across her shoulder. Clare knows that Wealh word. Saeson, Saxon. The Wealas reaches around her and grabs her breasts, waving them at Aegl, and calling to him in taunting words that can only mean *I am going to have your woman*. Clare feels his genitals harden against her wrists where her hands are tied, and she grabs them through the cloth of his tunic, digging her fingers into his testicles and crushing with all the strength she can find. The Wealas squeals and spins away but she holds on so that she is pulled over before she loses her grip. Clare can hear her persecutor howling on the ground behind her while his companions laugh, slapping their thighs with the hugeness of the joke.

But still they make her watch, while the women and the three captured warriors pile their loads across the stream, avoiding her eyes, building up the earth wall long after its height becomes superfluous and the water spreads outwards from its base towards the hollow. There the druid stands bare-legged, cursing in an arcane tongue that becomes a rhythmic, hissing menace at the edge of their hearing, endlessly repeated as the waters rise.

As the day fades to twilight a cold stillness fills the air, forming into a grey mist that settles over the marsh and curls cat-like around the druid's legs. Not even the Wealas will touch that mist, retreating up the hillside so that once again their spears blend into the forest. When the water reaches the edge of the hollow, the first spear shaft is struck against its shield in a slow, merciless rhythm, and Clare calls to him as the beat is taken up around the valley: words of pride and endearment and hopeless strength, but not of farewell. Never farewell.

It starts with a trickle into the hollow, which becomes a tiny waterfall, and then the end comes swiftly. When the water finds him, the drumming on the shields gathers pace to a continuous roar, and Clare screams one final message, loud enough to shake the rafters of Valhalla.

"Wait for me."

Spluttering now, Aegl lifts his face clear of the water and nods. "At the glade." Aegl holds her gaze until the mist floods the hollow, swirling in with the water as if it had been sucked down by his final breaths.

Clare will not weep. She will not allow them that victory. She understands what will happen now, but she is a princess of the people of the swan and she will walk to her fate with her head high, and shame them with the grace and dignity of her kind. Soon she will join her mate.

AN ETERNITY LATER, in the black hour before dawn, Clare wakes and pushes her mind out of the place where it has hidden from the damage being done to her body. Like a child lost in the forest at night she has backed into a soft corner of her being, folding into herself while she waits for the light and for love to return.

Clare recoils from the pain but uses it to force herself into reality. They have not even troubled to bind her, thinking her beyond movement. Against her side is a wall of the hall and she uses its support to grope her way upright, biting her lip until the blood flows in her need to stay silent. She pauses, standing, waiting for her brutalised body to accept that her mind is once again in control, and for her senses to feed her mind with awareness.

She is inside the hall. One or two rush lights still flicker in their brackets and there is a glow of embers from the fire pit to illuminate the mass of sleeping bodies. Slowly, Clare starts to move through the snoring Wealas, biting herself again to stifle her instinctive cries. A warrior tenses in his sleep, strains his body, and breaks wind. She freezes, but the warrior merely scratches at a louse, licks his lips and slips again into debauched oblivion.

Clare takes a cloak, needing not its warmth but its concealment. The robe she wears is pale and will draw the eye of any still awake. One of the Wealas had thrown it to her when the muddied, bloodied thing that she had become could no longer arouse desire. Perhaps even the Wealas could feel compassion. Once it had been a fine thing, made from cloth brought on a perilous voyage from far to the South. Brought, it was said, from a land even beyond Rome where the sun was so fierce it could kill a man who stood too long in its glare. It was lighter than any wool, and fine, and had been bleached until it was almost white so that her beauty had been sung in praise songs at their feasts. It was the robe of a princess, the woman of a mighty lord, but two Wealas had fought over the gold and garnet brooch that had fastened it, and so it had torn. Then the scraps of something beyond price were thrown back to her in the dirt, damaged goods for damaged goods.

Clare also takes a broken spear shaft from the wreckage, needing its support to walk, but still her progress is slow. It demands reserves that come from deep inside her, so that she reaches the new dam through will-power, not through the strength of muscles that cry out for the punishment to cease.

At the edge of the dam Clare pauses, taking in the new landscape. In the east the sky is already pale, so the forest is no longer a black mass but starting to reveal itself as individual trees. The stream is in autumn spate and the new lake has filled swiftly, a flat expanse of lighter grey, mirroring the sky, where yesterday there had been a bog-filled basin. At its borders, oak and rowan stand black in the opaque light, with their feet in the rising water. Their trunks look strong and permanent, denying the death seeping around their roots. Soon the water will lap to the top of the dam, and cut a new channel through the earth and debris until the barrier is washed away. Within a few moons little will remain.

Clare bends and picks up a stone, wincing at the movement. Lifting the hem of her robe, she drops the stone into the cradle of her skirts and hefts its weight. She chooses another, adding more until their weight makes it hard to stand. Then she stoops and kneels, resting the mass on the ground while she ties the garment high around her shoulders. The rocks grind into her belly as she stands, hauling her weight up the spear shaft, and the dark cloak falls away. Now the cold air touches her where only her husband should ever have touched her. Clare gathers her strength for a moment, leaning against the grounded spear shaft, before staggering out onto the dam. She needs to reach the place without falling on the loose surface. If she falls, she may not be able to rise.

He is close. She can feel him. She knows the way to him even when he is dead, the way the North Star stays constant in the skies while the heavens turn. It is gentler now, this yearning, as if his star is low in the sky and faint as on a summer's evening, but still it fills her, calls for her, needs her. Clare turns towards the settlement, where the thatched roof of the hall rises into the sky, six times the height of a man and more. They will burn it, she knows, before they leave.

A breeze is coming, autumn-chill. She feels it lift her hair and she inhales its scent, hoping impossibly to smell a trace of the milky warmth of infant bodies. They are out there, somewhere, and they are safe. She knows it with a mother's certainty. *The gods keep you, my children. Forgive what I must do.* But the breeze is autumn-rich with leaf mould, and laced only with salt from the distant sea. She turns back towards the water.

Slowly, awkwardly, Clare sits on the edge of the bank and slides down to the water's edge, ignoring this last pain. There she stands, leaning heavily on the spear, and steps out into the water. She grimaces as its chill bites at her legs, but she keeps moving outwards, planting the spear shaft carefully for support. Each step drops her steeply lower into the water and she can feel the loose soil tumble around her ankles in small landslides, racing her to the depths. As the water laps higher Clare gasps, then sighs as its icy touch numbs the rawness between her legs.

For a moment she pauses, leaning on the spear shaft, taking a final moment of almost-pleasure in the absence of pain. In front of her the mirror images of trees in the water are broken by the ripples of her movement, but something else slides across the reflection as if flakes of snow are drifting through the sky. Clare looks up, searching for the source. Already the sky is the grey of a dove's wing, but now there is a glimpse of something paler, something clean that soars across the grey. And another. The glimpses became great wings of purest white that caress the sky with their grace, gliding smoothly downwards until they too are mirrored in the surface, and swoop to meet their own reflections in a bubbling rush of water. In the milky dawn of her widowhood, the swans have come for Olrun.

"Welcome, sisters," she murmurs across the expanse of water. "Come, share the mystery of my death." But the swans just fold their wings in the expanding ripples of their landing, and wait.

"I cannot fly with you, my sisters. I am defiled. No wings can bear the weight of my shame."

You are of the people of the swan, her own mind replies. *The stain is of men, not of swans.*

"I chose man-kind. I chose a man as mate, he is my lord."

Your lord is dead.

"Aye, dead, and with no balefire to honour him, no grave goods to mark his greatness. His sword will be taken in triumph to the halls of the Wealas."

There will be other swords. Your son will be king, and will raise stones in his praise.

"There is a curse. I feel its power. His spirit may be bound forever in this place. He may never reach the halls of his gods."

It is not given to us to change such things.

"But it is given to us to choose. I cannot give him the proper rites nor honour, but I can give him myself. I will be his companion in death as I have been in life."

Sister, there is no renown in this. No men will know the manner of your passing, nor of his.

"But there is love. Remember me, sisters."

Clare spreads her arms as if to fly, and tilts forward so that the water rushes up her body and closes over her head. As she soars downwards the robe billows out behind her in fluttering streams of white, until the weight of the stones anchors her to the lake bed. Desperately she reaches around her, searching for him, but as her breath gives out and she starts to choke, her fingers close only on the silt washing down off the dam.

Chapter Thirty-Six

THE SOUND OF a great, gasping breath intruded into the depths of Fergus's sleep and he stirred, unsure for a moment where he was. His eyes fluttered open, fighting against the comfortable drag of the pillow, and registered an unfamiliar ceiling where a pearl-grey dawn pushed over the curtains into the fading glow of a lava lamp. There was the sound of breathing beside him, the fast breathing of exercise or fear, and he turned his head to see Clare lying on her stomach and braced on her elbows, lifting her face clear of the bed. She was staring at the crumpled white expanse of the pillow with a strange, wide-eyed expression. Fergus smiled at her with the intimate smile of a lover, enjoying the tantalising glimpse of breasts.

"Good morning."

Clare did not answer, but turned on her back, panting as if they had just finished a mighty coupling, and pushed the duvet down her body, away from her face. The exposure enticed him and he reached out to caress her arm in gentle invitation. Clare twisted on her side, almost as if she was avoiding him, and swung her legs out of the bed to sit on its edge. Fergus lay still for a moment, enjoying her silhouette in the soft light and ignoring a distant alarm in his head that told him all was not well. The way her waist swelled into her rump occupied his attention. It begged to be stroked, but she was beyond his reach so Fergus rose and knelt behind her with one knee each side of that alluring backside. He put his arms around her, tenderly, and let one hand cup a breast as he whispered in her ear.

"Are you OK?"

Clare tensed at his touch, her body rigid. "Hey, what's the matter?" He hugged her more tightly, allowing his erection to nudge at her backbone.

"No!" Clare flung her arms up violently, breaking his hug. She leapt to her feet and ran into the bathroom, slamming the door behind her. Fergus rocked back onto his heels, stunned. As he tried to work out what he might have done wrong the sound of the shower came from beyond the bathroom door. Then, as his shock gave way to hurt, he heard the unmistakable sound of a sob.

The bathroom door wasn't bolted. In Clare's one bedroom flat, the door didn't even have a bolt and Fergus opened it gently. Clare's face was screwed up against the rush of water and she seemed unaware of his presence. What alarmed and hurt him even more than her rejection was the way she was scrubbing between her legs, punishing herself with a flannel so violently that her skin was already pink and raw around the dark vector of her crotch. Fergus stared, horrified, unable to associate this self-inflicted brutality with the passion of the previous day. It was as if she wanted to cleanse herself of all trace of him.

"Clare, why...?" Fergus had no words to formulate his question. At the sound of his voice Clare spun away, trying to squeeze her body into the corner of the shower unit, with her arms crossed protectively over her breasts.

"What on earth's the matter?" The water was cascading in tiny ripples over the ridges of her backbone until it formed a miniature torrent between the cheeks of her backside.

"Leave me alone. Please."

"But what's all this about? Last night you were all over me, literally. This morning you're screaming if I touch you. What's going on?" Fergus's concern was starting to be laced with anger.

"Just go. Please. Just go." Clare dropped into a crouch in the bottom of the shower.

"I don't understand. Tell me what's the matter."

Clare didn't answer. The blast of the shower was now onto her head, making it hard for her to breathe, and she sank back onto her haunches. She hugged her legs with her face buried in her knees but her shoulders were shaking and Fergus knew that she was crying.

"Clare, what have I done?" She was beyond reach, both mentally and physically now that her body was jammed against the folding door of the shower. Fergus had a fleeting sense that the previous evening's passion was something he'd imagined, as if the intimacy had been a dream.

"Go away."

For long moments Fergus watched her, now rocking backwards and forwards in the shower. He tried putting his hand on the door, letting it push gently at her body, but at that slight pressure she flinched away, squirming. Then his anger took over and he spun away to grab his clothes, dressing with furious tugs at zips and belts, but his anger was fleeting. Fully dressed, Fergus filled time with the banality of making coffee in a kitchenette that was filled with glimpses of a life he didn't yet know. A pin board cluttered with lists and tradesmen's cards and holiday postcards from friends. A framed photograph of a family group sitting on a lawn in the sunshine, caught in a moment when a pose became real as parents and a sister and a younger Clare dissolved into laughter at the antics of a dog. Family. She needed help. He needed help, and he didn't even know where to start looking.

Chapter Thirty-Seven

"I THINK IT'S already dead." Eadlin stood at the stable door, watching Fergus muck out. He'd been attacking the compacted shavings with the kind of brutality that would win an infantryman points at bayonet drill, driving the fork in deep and heaving the bedding into the air until the sweat plastered his shirt to his body. He could have managed without the stink of horse piss and manure, but the pain of protesting muscles was good.

Fergus paused, panting, waiting for Eadlin to say more. He didn't feel communicative.

"Leave that and come and tell me what the hell's going on."

"What do you mean?" Fergus had time to feel uncomfortable about snapping at Eadlin while she marched him towards a paddock fence, out of earshot of the yard.

"You're bloody-minded, snarling at everyone, and if you aren't winding up the rest of the staff you're staring into space with your mind elsewhere. Plus you've got the longest face in the yard, and that includes the horses." Eadlin nodded at the herd in the paddock.

"Sorry." Fergus hadn't realised it was so obvious. He took a deep breath, feeling the pent-up frustration ready to burst. He gripped the top rail of the fence hard enough to hurt.

Fergus made several false starts at explaining, staring out over the paddock, before he looked at her. The calmness of Eadlin's gaze sliced through the mess in his head, and finally he spoke sense.

"I'm worried about Clare. I think she's a bit screwed up, and now she's cutting herself off so I don't know how to help her."

"Did you have an argument?"

Fergus shook his head.

"She's been having nightmares. Bad ones, about the Saxon and a woman she says died with him. I think last night was particularly bad. I slept at her flat for the first time, and this morning she'd changed. I couldn't get close to her. Eadlin, believe me, I..."

"Nah, I know you well enough. You wouldn't do anything to hurt her."

"But she's traumatised. At first she wouldn't even speak to me, then she just wanted to be left alone. She curled up crying on her bed and wouldn't let me touch her. I gave up when I realised I was making things worse, and now she won't answer her phone. I've had one text saying 'sorry, bad dreams' but that's all, and I'd guessed that already."

"Do you want me to try and talk to her? She might respond to a girlie shoulder."

"Would you? I'm out of my depth here."

Eadlin touched his arm reassuringly. "I'll give her a call, ask if she'll let me go and see her. You might have to look after things here for a few hours."

Fergus felt so pathetically grateful that he couldn't speak. Eadlin leaned over the fence beside him and they watched the horses in silence for a few moments.

"You're in love with her, aren't you?"

Was it love, this turmoil inside him? "I suppose I am, though I haven't even told Clare that, yet. Do you think it would make a difference if I did?"

"I'd guess she probably knows, but on the whole, girls like to be told."

"I did tell her what happened in the crash though, the bad stuff. It came out one day. Caught me by surprise. It's quite a heavy thing to put on someone. I don't want..." Fergus paused, gripping the rail again, struggling to find the words. "I don't want our relationship to be based on pity."

"'She loved me for the dangers I had passed, and I loved her that she did pity them.'"

"That sounds like Shakespeare." Fergus hoped his surprise was not too obvious.

"Othello."

"You're strange, Eadlin. You spend your life buried in horse muck, yet you quote Shakespeare."

"I like reading, even if I haven't discovered Rupert Brooke. I've got to do something in the evenings, and it's cheaper than the pub. Anyway, who says you can't have a brain and ride?"

Fergus shook his head. "Well, if you see her, there are a couple of things you should know. Whatever horror she has dreamt will be as real as if it's actually happened to her."

"And?"

"She believes she's being shown things for a reason, so something is expected of her."

"Ah. That could be trickier. Let me see what I can do."

Eadlin turned to rest her back against the paddock fence with her elbows hooked over the top rail. Her attention was elsewhere, towards the car park, and Fergus caught himself staring at her, puzzling over the enigma that was Eadlin. There were times when, to use Mary Baxter's phrase, she seemed a very old soul. There were also times when she radiated a sexuality that challenged even his feelings for Clare.

Like now, when Eadlin stared past his shoulder towards the car park, and unfolded her arms to lay flat along the top of the fence. The movement stretched her shirt over her figure, revealing a light scattering of freckles across her chest that faded towards the swell of her breasts. Fergus twisted to follow her gaze, and saw Russell Dickens ambling towards them.

"I'll call her," Eadlin promised as she left. She walked to meet Russell half way. *Lucky bastard.* Strange how you can be in love with one woman and still feel jealous when another plants her affections elsewhere. Fergus wondered if Jake knew. Russell had been in and out of Ash Farm's office so many times that they might have been building the May Queen's cart rather than borrowing it.

Russell and Eadlin stood out of earshot, close enough together for his bear-like presence to dwarf her, but without touching. Only

Eadlin's body-language suggested any intimacy. It was a long discussion, with more than one glance in Fergus's direction. As they finished speaking Russell nodded in agreement and turned towards Fergus, while Eadlin continued alone to the office.

"Mornin'." Russell took Eadlin's place looking over the fence. Fergus waited, wondering what was coming. Between the four of them, the link between him and Russell was the weakest. A sisterhood was growing between the women, but the men treated one another with amiable caution. Fergus wondered if his attraction to Eadlin was as obvious as Russell's to Clare.

"Eadlin says you're doin' well with the horses. Learnin' fast." Russell nodded towards the herd in the paddock. Fergus muttered his thanks, waiting for the real reason for the talk. He still didn't feel sociable.

"Never could get the hang of them, myself. Always felt too clumsy. I'm better with mechanical things, tractors and stuff." Russell looked down at his hands, turning them over to stare at the oil ingrained in the lines of his palms, as if seeking inspiration. He lowered his voice. "There are whispers goin' round the village. Something's brewing." Now he was coming to the point. "Think you ought to take care."

"What do you mean, Russ?"

"You've made a bad enemy in Jake Herne. Humiliated him. He ain't goin' to let that rest."

"You mean I might find myself staring at a nithing pole, one morning?"

"I mean he'll use you as the next goat, if he can get away with it."

"Seriously?"

Russell looked at him directly. "Since Tony Foulkes' death Jake's been acting like he's got some kind of divine authority. People are frightened and he's enjoying their fear. When you broke his hand you didn't just dent his ego, you told people he's still human. So yes, I think he'd kill you if he could get away with it." Russell paused to let his message sink in. "Jake'll try and pay you back in a way that the police won't pin anything on him, but the right people will know it was him that punished you."

Russell's sincerity was clear. Above them the sky was building into a thunderstorm, and the sunlight lancing under the cloud painted the landscape in sharp contrasts of light and dark, bright green and angry cloud, brilliant enough to narrow the eyes. It was a scene of such majestic peace that it made threats of revenge hard to take seriously.

"D'you have to stay here, in Allingley? I mean, you'd be a lot safer if you was out of his reach, like."

"This sounds like the old 'get out of town' cliché."

"Well, maybe you're right. The way I see it, you can choose to disappear and take yourself off, or you can stay here and Jake will make sure you disappear. And it's not if, it's when."

"Thanks, I appreciate the warning. Let me think about it."

"Well while you're thinking, don't go out alone at night. Stay with the crowds. Oh, and if Clare comes visiting, keep her close. He don't like being put down by a woman, neither, especially one who's trespassed on his land and messed up his party. He wants to teach her a lesson, too, and none of us want Clare to be hurt, do we?"

The rail shook as Russell pushed himself away from the fence. In the paddock, Trooper lifted his head from the grass at the noise and stared at them. Fergus watched the horse, trying to digest Russell's warning. Leave? To where? To do what? He felt the stubbornness stir within him, the same bloody-mindedness that had made him refuse to accept the boundaries of his recovery. He closed his eyes, trying to find that point of calm that Eadlin had shown him, and wondering if his desire to stay was bloody-mindedness or madness.

It was there, as Fergus opened his mind; an instinct or wisdom beyond words. His eyes snapped open as the blessing in the church became one with this moment, a moment when a horse that was also a friend strode through shining grass towards him, beneath a sky bruised purple by thunderheads. The vitality of the land was tangible, and he knew himself to be part of it.

The clouds covered the sun at the first roll of thunder, and as he waited for the horse to reach him a chill rush of wind spattered the first heavy drops of rain in his hair and onto his shoulders.

Chapter Thirty-Eight

IT WAS LATE afternoon before Eadlin returned. Her battered Land Rover splashed into the car park as Fergus swept a line of water and muck from the yard after the downpour, working as if his energy could push Herne off the face of the earth. He rested on his broom and watched her walk towards him. Eadlin's face was enigmatic, perhaps puzzled, offering no sign for him to read.

"Well, I saw Clare."

"And?"

"Dunno, really. Some good news and some not so good news." Eadlin looked around at the activity in the yard, and then glanced up at the sky. "The weather's clearing. Put a saddle on Trooper and let's go for a hack so we can talk quietly."

This sounded ominous.

"FIRST THE GOOD news." Eadlin did not wait to be asked, but started her debrief as they left the yard. For once Fergus wished that Eadlin had simply taken him to one side for a quiet chat rather than taking out the horses. Trooper had picked up his tension and was jogging underneath him, disrupting his concentration.

"I think Clare feels the same for you as you feel for her." As Fergus exhaled the horse softened under him, mirroring his mood. "But that was one of the weirdest conversations I've had for ages. She's in quite a state, as you said, and she's not making much sense. At least that's what I thought at first." Eadlin paused to order her thoughts. "Clare summed it up herself. Either she's going a bit loopy and needs better qualified help than I can give her, or she's being shown something."

Fergus grunted as Trooper danced sideways in his enthusiasm to be off. Restraining him was like keeping a dog on a leash in open country, except that this dog wore a saddle and weighed nearly seven hundred kilos.

"Eadlin, I'd have tried a lot harder to make her see a doctor if I hadn't seen that Saxon myself. I believe her."

"Well, I don't think Clare's mad, neither. Sit deep, shoulders back, keep your hands still." Eadlin illustrated her advice with her own posture. Fergus liked it when she braced her shoulders back. "She also thinks the only way to fix things is to give the Saxon a pagan funeral."

"What do you think about that? She's risking her whole career."

Eadlin shrugged. "Her career's her own problem, but there's no reason why we shouldn't help her with a little ceremony. Apart, that is, from the slight legal problem of theft and improper burial. But if someone's really stressed, the best thing can be to help them find their own solution. Let's help her do it, and it doesn't work, then maybe she'll see a doctor. The thing is, Clare believes it. This mess in her head is real."

Fergus wondered what *was* reality. The rhythmic brushing of horses' hooves through wet grass, that was real. Jake Herne's face saying "this one's dead, too"; that had been real. But a tramp or a Saxon who had held out his hand and called Kate 'Olrun'; had that been reality or part of his madness inside the wreck?

"So is that all the bad news?"

"Nah, 'fraid not. She says these dreams are a lot worse when you're around, and, yes, last night they included rape."

"Shit. That makes me feel really good."

"Clare said to tell you she's sorry. She knows you must be upset."

Fergus nearly swore again. "Why can't she do that herself?"

"She's terrified of another nightmare if she speaks to you."

Ahead of them the track disappeared into a stand of trees that was spiked along its margins with white candles of horse chestnut. Something in the palpable health of this land might have rescued him from madness. Fergus wished he knew how to give Clare the same peace of mind. He caught Eadlin looking at him, and he saw understanding behind those grey eyes. Perhaps it wasn't only the land that was healing him.

"There's more." Eadlin paused to bring her own mount under control. Both horses were fizzing with excitement, impatient to run. "The bit that really worries me is Clare's seeing echoes of her dreams in everyday life. What she dreams happened to the Saxons actually happens, like now, in Allingley. She claims she saw the death of a bard before Tony died. She was also going on about swans, and there was something about dead warriors being carried on shields, but I didn't understand that bit."

"Maybe she really should see a doctor."

"I tried that. No luck. The scary thing is she's just dreamed about rape and murder. She's frightened something just as bad will happen around her, soon."

The significance of Eadlin's words took a moment to sink in. "So what we can do to help?"

"Sorry, but you can do most by staying out of the way for a bit. The rest of us have a plan." Eadlin relaxed her reins as her horse quietened, accepting the walking pace as the woods drew closer. "Early on Monday morning Clare and Russell are going to steal the Saxon's body. It's the May Day holiday so the university will be quiet. Then in the evening while Russell is entertaining everyone with the fireworks at the bonfire, the rest of us can give that Saxon a decent, pagan burial." Eadlin sounded excited by the adventure.

"Just like that? I take it Clare's sure she can get him out? And where are you going to bury him?"

"Clare says all she'll need is something to put the body in, and a quiet moment. We'll probably bury him near that spring where I took you riding soon after you arrived. It's a peaceful spot, the sort of place that would have been sacred to the Saxon." There was a slight lift at the end of the sentence, as if Eadlin might have added 'as well'.

Fergus snorted. The whole plan sounded surreal. It also excluded him.

Eadlin reached across and touched his arm. "Cheer up. You'll see her on Monday, but Clare wants to keep her distance until the burial. She wants to be with you, but you might have to take things gently for a while."

"Tell her, I mean…" He didn't know how to say what he wanted.

"I'll give her a hug for you."

They rode in silence while he absorbed the news.

"Russell told you about Jake Herne's threats?" Eadlin's question was rhetorical. "Have you decided what you're going to do?"

"Sure. I'm staying. This place," he gestured at the scenery, "gets under your skin." Fergus faltered when the poetry in his mouth seemed too rich to be spoken, even to Eadlin. He'd been about to blurt out a musical analogy, about how the scenery had been an Elgar landscape when he first arrived, strong and showing its bones in the way the flints streaked the shoulders of the fields with white. Soon it would be a Vaughan Williams landscape, a sweeter place of larks hovering over crops and trees dozing in the sun.

"Take your time," Eadlin prompted him.

"Time, exactly. Pace here means the thump of hooves on turf. It used to mean the speed at which I could clear emails."

"Allingley isn't the only beautiful place in England. But it's probably the only one where someone wants to kill you."

"I know I've only been here a couple of months, but Allingley is starting to feel like home. Besides, I'm bloody-minded when I'm pushed."

"Well, make sure your stubbornness doesn't get you killed. I don't want you to go, but this ain't your fight. You came here to get fit and I'd say you've done that. There's no comparison to how you were nearly two months ago."

"Actually there's something else, something I don't understand yet." Fergus was silent for several strides of their horses. The freshly-washed atmosphere after the thunderstorm helped him to think, bringing his mind into sharp focus like the countryside around them. The path led into the stand of trees, and as they entered the cavern of leaf he found the words.

"When you showed me that place where you're going to bury the Saxon, it was as if you had given me a glimpse of something good, a harmony that connected everything." Eadlin nodded. "Well there was a moment like that in the church at Tony's funeral. It was as if all that harmony had concentrated and found me, even touched me."

"I told you, you're sensitive." Eadlin showed no surprise at his revelation.

"Psychic, you mean?"

"Nah. Just sensitive. Receptive to things most people don't see. It's a gift."

"So what am I supposed to do with this gift?"

"Only you can answer that."

"Well that moment in the church is the other reason why I'll stay. Maybe even the main reason. Here I'm connected, like I'm part of the story. My life has meaning here, even if I don't yet know what that meaning might be."

"Maybe that explains what I saw in your palms when you first arrived."

"You've lost me."

"You touched the shadow world. Very few people come back from that. Maybe you make it easier for the shadow world to touch this one."

Fergus had the sense that he had just learned a profound truth.

"So Clare might be right about me giving her nightmares?"

"Could be. Who knows? But if you stay, remember what I said about you being vulnerable. Watch your back."

"Right now I feel very much part of this world." Ahead of them, the late afternoon sunlight broke through the cloud, angling through the far edge of the wood in a mosaic of green and gold.

"D'you remember how I cantered away from you that day when we rode to the spring?" Eadlin's voice lifted, changing the mood.

"And I lumbered after you watching your bum disappear into the distance. Yes, I remember. It inspired me to deserve a faster horse!"

"Sometimes, a blast of speed is a great cure for stress." Eadlin watched him carefully, evaluating his riding. "You're managing Trooper ok, but straighten up, relax. Listen to his motion. Imagine you're taking his pulse with your legs. Now nudge him sideways. Play with him." Trooper sidestepped neatly until Fergus's and Eadlin's legs were touching.

"Like that?" Fergus smiled at her, enjoying a little harmless flirtation.

"OK, I guess he's listening." Eadlin edged her horse away. "Sensitive, isn't he? Do you think you could handle him in a gallop?"

Fergus's grin was enough of an answer. At the edge of the wood the track emerged into a broad, ploughed field bordered by a margin of untilled turf. Both horses picked up the pace, becoming restive.

"This farmer's a keen supporter of the hunt," Eadlin nodded at the view, "so he's left a riding track around his crop." Her little thoroughbred started cantering on the spot, although Eadlin stayed balanced at the centre of the movement, at one with the energy beneath her. Trooper started snorting and throwing small, eager bucks. The rocking-horse movement was alarming, like sitting on a volcano and not knowing quite when it would explode.

"Walk him forwards, relax a little. It's about a four hundred yard run to the gate into the next field. Then about three hundred yards uphill into the far corner by the woods. Sit deep, listen to him, become one with him."

There was a skin-tightening, almost Zen-like moment as Fergus felt that he and Trooper had bonded, like two cogs engaging. He felt the horse's head drop, arching downwards, giving him leadership, no longer fighting to go but waiting for his signal even though dancing with impatience. The sense of raw animal power contained by the reins in his fingers gave

Fergus an irrational surge of confidence, as if he had spent his life in the saddle.

"Brilliant! Now you've got him. Let's take it steadily at first." Eadlin nudged her chestnut into a trot. At first, as she looked across at him, she seemed only to be demonstrating, encouraging him to find that point of balance where the energy can be held with the lightest touch. But then that shoulders-back, eyes-in-contact posture acquired a mischievous element of near-sexual challenge. Both horses picked up the pace, bounding in anticipation of the inevitable command.

"I think we should let them run." Now Eadlin's grin and challenge were explicit.

It took the lightest touch of the leg and a giving of the hands to launch their power into the evening. Trooper gave one mighty leap of joy and surged forward into the adrenaline-charged madness of a gallop, with the wind of his speed drowning all sound but the thunder of hooves.

Eadlin lifted and crouched, jockey-like, with her face close to her horse's mane, grinning like a lunatic, eyes squinting into the wind, with her backside poised over the saddle. Beneath Fergus the great muscles in Trooper's shoulders bunched and flexed, and the pounding of hooves tightened the tension like the rattle of drums at a military display. Into this delirious madness a bird flew up out of the grass, flapping frantically between the horses. It seemed suspended between them, unable to fly fast enough to escape, each feather perfectly visible and its beak half open in its panic. Then it gained height and arced away over their heads into the hedge, and they both whooped into the wind with the exhilaration of knowing they were riding faster than a bird can fly.

Eadlin started to draw ahead and turned her head sideways to shout at him, something about giving with the hands, let him carry your hands in his mouth, but the words were lost. Then Fergus looked up and rushing towards them was the gate, standing open but dangerously narrow for two horses to pass through simultaneously at a gallop.

For a moment Fergus considered reining in, conceding the race, and following Eadlin's jodhpurs through the gate, but in a moment of invincible lunacy he pointed Trooper at the hedge. He felt the dialogue with the horse, sensed him check, lock on and commit to the leap, and when the surge and soar came it was as if they had grown wings and taken flight. The glorious bond of a working partnership was physical poetry, a moment of divine exhilaration, a rush that made him want to go back and do it again, and again, and again.

Eadlin had pulled back, alarmed at what he was doing, so that when Trooper landed Fergus was able to overtake her, giving no quarter. With a laughing yelp she gave chase, pulling back alongside as they charged up the hill where her horse's lighter build gave her the edge, so the two pairs were neck and neck as they approached the corner of the field. The exit into the woods was a sharp, narrow turn, impossible to achieve even in a canter, let alone a gallop. Finally Eadlin called "Enough! It's a draw," laughing as she reined in, but Fergus had to win.

He pushed on until Trooper could see no track and braced his forelegs out, bouncing into an emergency stop. Fergus was still half out of the saddle and the sudden deceleration sent him rolling forward over Trooper's neck to lie whooping and giggling on his back in a thick pile of grass and cow parsley at the field's edge.

"You alright?"

Fergus reassured her with an air punch and another whoop while wet grass saturated his clothes. Eadlin slid from her saddle, holding out a hand to pull him up.

"Stand up gently in case there's any damage."

On his feet Fergus held on to Trooper's stirrup leather for a moment while they both panted, breathless, sandwiched between the heaving flanks of their horses into a hidden world that was only themselves, surrounded by the earthy stink of horse sweat.

"You're an idiot!" Eadlin's eyes sparkled with laughter, her face glowing with exertion. Fergus could never remember feeling so intensely alive. It was the most natural thing in the world for their faces to edge closer, mouths parting, until her hands came up in between them and pushed him away.

"Mustn't." She didn't sound convincing.

"Sorry." Neither did he. Eadlin pushed him on the chest again, quite firmly, but without anger.

"The rules haven't changed, and I'm nobody's substitute!"

"Sorry," Fergus said again, almost meaning it this time. A kiss would have been natural in a moment of sheer, exuberant joy. Now he was starting to feel like a naughty child.

"Don't spoil things. Clare deserves better than that. Now let's get you back in the saddle, and you look where you're going." Eadlin spoke without rancour as she formed her basket of hands for him. Fergus accepted the help even though he felt he could leap into the saddle in a single bound.

Eadlin was right, of course. It was the *and*-ness of things that confused him. For a moment his feelings for Clare had felt completely compatible with Eadlin's earthy sexuality. As Eadlin led the way into the woods Fergus admired her rump nestling into the saddle, and still he did not find the attraction inconsistent. The adrenaline of the gallop was still pumping in his veins, sharpening the moment as their horses walked through the cathedral-column trunks of a stand of beeches. Around them blackbirds had started their evening songs and a rich, liquid chorus came at them in overlapping waves like an echoing harmony of nature's choir. Eadlin stood in the stirrups, turning back to him.

"If you're staying in Allingley, does it mean that you're going to stay on at the stables?"

Fergus guessed that Eadlin had switched to practicalities to break the mood.

"I will for now, if I may, but you're probably right about not spending my life shovelling horse poo. I'd like riding to feature in whatever life I do build, though. What we've just done was wonderful." Eadlin lifted an eyebrow at him. "The gallop, I mean." Fergus swallowed, realising he was digging himself in deeper. "One day I'd like to be good enough to compete. On horseback it doesn't matter that I can't run properly. I can be as good as the next rider if I try hard enough and have the right animal."

"You two would make a good competition partnership." Eadlin nodded at Trooper, who was blowing hard but still breaking into periodic jogs with excitement. The implied offer was humbling but before Fergus could respond, Eadlin reined in at the junction of two paths, waving her riding crop at the track ahead. Fergus recognised the spot from his walk with Clare on the day they had become lovers.

"Allingley's just over the next hill, but we'll turn off here. Let me introduce you to a king."

"A king? I'm not dressed for royalty!"

"Come and see."

Eadlin led the way uphill and halted in front of the ancient yew tree. "Meet King Arthur!"

"Oh, the tree." Fergus had a sense of anti-climax. "Why 'King Arthur'?"

"The Victorians called it that. Someone had an idea that it dated from around the time of King Arthur, so that was the name they gave it. To the village folk it has always been the Sweethearts' Yew." Eadlin dismounted, but Fergus stayed in the saddle, uncomfortable to be in this spot with her. The almost-kiss after the gallop had been a moment of wild joy, in Eadlin's domain of horses. In this spot he finally felt guilty, and watched Eadlin as if she was trespassing as she led her horse towards the far side of the tree. Bizarre that it should have a name like that.

"There's a way in round here. It looks like a woman's..." Eadlin blushed slightly before she disappeared from view. Out of sight, she found a polite description. "Girlie bits." Fergus remembered the lozenge-shaped gap between the folded trunks. Her voice now came disembodied from behind its bulk. "There was a healing rite, once," it sounded as if the 'once' was an afterthought, "which had sick people passing head-first from inside to the outside. Yews have always been associated with rebirth."

"Perhaps you should bring Clare here."

"The patient needs to believe in the tree. Come and have a look."

"King Arthur and I have already met." He would not enter the tree with Eadlin, whatever healing she was offering.

"Oh." Eadlin sounded disappointed. "It's also been used as a tryst by village couples for centuries." She emerged from behind the tree, still leading her horse, but her smile faded as she looked at him, trying to interpret the expression on his face.

"I guess I already graduated."

At that Eadlin laughed, as if life was bubbling through her body, and swung herself back into the saddle.

"Well maybe you really are becoming one of us."

Chapter Thirty-Nine

ON THE EVE of May Day the sun settled towards the horizon through scattered cloud, promising the kind of sunset that would inspire onlookers to give the Almighty a round of applause. Fergus sat at one of the tables in front of the farmhouse, with the peak of a baseball cap tilted against the glare, enjoying a glass of Eadlin's home-made wine. It tasted of flowers and herbs, as different from the shop-bought variety as her tea, and he could feel the oily warmth of its alcohol suffuse his body. Fergus slouched in a chair with his feet up on a bench, wondering what preparations Clare might be making for the theft of the Saxon's body.

Eadlin hadn't mentioned his indiscretion after the gallop, but the ambiguity still lurked in Fergus's mind, disturbingly warm as he sipped her wine and enjoyed her unspeaking companionship. You needed to be good friends to be comfortably silent with someone. Perhaps he was becoming more horse-like. Horses graze together, tuned to each other, but need no more affirmation than presence.

Eadlin had covered a table with scraps of greenery, and sat binding flowers and leaves into posies for May Day. She sang quietly to herself, one of the old songs that have more rhythm than tune, the kind of song whose words are soon lost but leave a lasting scent of ancient earth. She crafted each nosegay with care, placing a spray of delicate white flowers on a bed of oak and ash leaves, and laying out pieces of bark with which to bind them. Fergus watched, intrigued, as Eadlin opened a bottle of dark ink and started to paint a sign on a scrap of bark with a fine, pencil brush. Her song acquired the intensity of a chant, and he stared, mesmerised, as her brush made the symbol of the Thorn rune that Clare had drawn for him in the White Hart.

"What are you doing?" Fergus pulled his feet off the bench and sat upright, focused on what was taking shape under her hands.

"Making posies for tomorrow." Eadlin smiled at him innocently, wrinkling the freckles over her nose. "Oak, ash, and thorn for May Day. The flowers are May blossom. Some people call it hawthorn or whitethorn."

"But the sign..." Fergus waved at the bark, trying to remember Clare's description of the Thorn rune. Something about strength, or was it male sexuality?

"That's from me. It's a kind of protection." Eadlin rolled the bark around the nosegay so that the rune was hidden, and tied it with a red thread. "Wear it for me?" She held the finished posy out to him, looking directly into his eyes. The intensity of her look required that Fergus lean forward to take it, but he felt uncomfortable and held the flowers between them as if the gift was not yet accepted.

"Thanks, but I'm not one for buttonholes, really." Fergus hoped he didn't sound ungracious. In the back of his mind was his lingering guilt at the attempted kiss. He wasn't sure that he should be taking flowers from Eadlin.

"Please. We're all going to wear one." Eadlin waved at the other bundles.

"All?"

"I'm making one for Clare, as well as for Russell and me. Think of it as a lucky charm. Tomorrow's a big day."

"Ah yes, of course, Clare's stealing the body."

"Nah. I mean tomorrow is Beltane. If Jake's going to make a move, it will be tomorrow."

"Beltane?"

"The spring festival. It's half way between the equinox and the summer solstice. It's always been a feast day, when country folk pray for fertility for the crops they've sown. Mostly it's a good excuse for a party, a happy time. It sort of helped the Old

Way that the day was taken over by the socialists and called May Day, or Worker's Day, or whatever, because the authorities stopped asking why we wanted a bonfire."

"So why would Beltane be so important to Jake?" Fergus still held the posy limply between them.

"If you worship the Horned God, then Beltane is a fire festival, one of the great sabbats of the year. It's a time when the shadow world is closest to the living world, like it is at Halloween. If Jake wanted to make a point to his gang, then Beltane is the time to do it."

"And this bunch of flowers will help?" Fergus hoped his scepticism didn't show too much.

"Please. If you still have any connection to the shadow world, Beltane is also when you're most vulnerable." The fervour of Eadlin's plea made Fergus relent. He passed her his baseball cap.

"OK. Why don't you sew it to that?"

"Tomorrow," Eadlin said, as she threaded a needle with the same scarlet thread, "we'll shut at lunchtime so everyone can go to the festival. I need to go earlier with the draught horses so that they can decorate the wagon, but please come in with the stable girls, not on your own. Russell and I will watch your back, but make sure you stay in the crowds."

Fergus was only half listening. Watching her sew that ridiculous bunch of foliage to his cap reminded him of the stories of knights of old, whose ladies stitched their favours to their champions' helmets. Except, of course, Eadlin was not his lady, even though the *and*-ness still confused him. As she tugged at the thread she seemed strong, alluring, unattainable, and *different*, centred in a world he would never fully understand.

Chapter Forty

"EADLIN SAYS IT'LL keep us safe." Russell held the posy between them like a lovelorn suitor.

"Oh for heaven's sake, Russ, I'm an academic! That's pure superstition." Clare had waved the flowers away before she heard the tetchiness in her own voice.

"I thought superstition was partly why we're here. Give him a pagan funeral, and all that."

She laid her hand on his arm. "Sorry, Russ. Bit short of sleep. You wear it for me, if you want."

Russell lifted the lapel of his overalls and showed her his own posy hidden underneath.

"Maybe later, then. I don't want to attract attention on campus. Anyway, it's time for you to hide." Clare lifted the tailgate of her Volvo estate as if she was inviting a dog to jump in after a walk. Was she really doing this? So much subterfuge, meeting at a remote woodland car park, just to let Russell leave his own car and hide in her boot without attracting notice. It was unreal. Clare threw a rug over Russell and the large, pine blanket box that Eadlin had provided from the farmhouse. Already they were acting like a pair of criminals.

Clare's mouth felt dry as she drove onto the campus and parked beside a back door to her block. She stood by her car, scanning the windows around her. Laboratories, offices, lecture rooms, all empty. No security cameras. She could still back out, apologise to Russell, and say it was all a mistake. In the morning light the nightmares felt less real. Reality was a pedestal ashtray outside the faculty door, awash with dirty water and floating cigarette butts. Clare tested the door and her movement disturbed some pigeons on an overhead ledge. A feather floated down, pearl grey, the colour of the dawn when the swans came for Olrun. Was the dream a sign of madness? Or was madness the way she left the locked door and walked round to the main entrance, leaving Russell shut in her car?

"Morning, Tom." The security guard looked up in surprise and softened at the sight of her. Dear old Tom. He was like an elderly, family friend who wished he was thirty years younger and single, and Tom always wanted to talk. Yes, she was very dedicated to be in so early, and on a Bank Holiday. No, no-one else was around, not even a research student. And yes, she was fine, Tom, really, just a bit tired. Clare could see herself in the mirrored surface behind the reception desk. God, she looked awful. Pale face, eyes smudged dark, hair going lank. The only fresh thing about her was the loose, man's shirt stuffed into her jeans. By the doors into the passage Clare turned and waved, just to make sure Tom had stayed behind the desk. He could be too friendly, sometimes. Tom beamed back at her, pleased by her gesture.

Clare stopped beside the door to smokers' corner, breathing deeply, scanning the frame for any trace of an alarm system. None. With the sense that she was pushing her career out over a void, she pulled on a pair of surgical gloves, pressed the emergency exit bar, and let Russell into the building. He also wore gloves. Criminality starts here.

"You OK, Clare?" Russell pulled the door shut behind him, carrying the blanket box. Clare nodded, not quite able to believe that the moment was happening.

"Let's get you out of the corridor." She pulled out her keys and led the way to the laboratory, locking the lab door behind them.

"Hey, my friend." Clare's voice was tender as she pulled off the baize cover and opened Aegl's case, ignoring the sounds of disgust from Russell.

"Do you need a hand?" His tone begged her to say no. Clare shook her head. This was a service she wanted to perform for Aegl herself.

So light. There was no substance left to him. Clare lifted Aegl's body in her arms, supporting the neck and head the way a mother might cradle a child, inhaling the smell of old leather and mushrooms. So dry, so rigid. Clare gasped as both legs separated and fell back into his case with a noise like falling books.

"I'm so sorry." She spoke to Aegl, distress prickling her eyes. This was far, far worse than breaking ancient pottery. This was wounding a friend.

"Get on with it, Clare." Russell spoke in the strangled tones of someone trying not to vomit.

She laid Aegl's head and torso tenderly in the nest of wood shavings that Eadlin had prepared in the blanket box, and touched his face. The skin beneath the beard had the hard coolness of the laboratory work surface.

"Someone's coming. Move." Russell pushed her aside and dumped the legs into the box without ceremony. Clare started to arrange them into a dignified position, but the skeletal arm was almost thrown on top and she glared up at Russell, eyes flashing her anger. Aegl deserved better. Only when Russell put his finger across his lips did reality hit her.

Footsteps were clicking their way down the corridor in a slow, measured tread, and Clare knelt on the floor of her own laboratory, surrounded by scattered wood shavings and the evidence of her crime. She stared at the frosted glass panel in the door, incapable of movement, with the panic rising like bile in her throat. It was Russell who had to throw the baize cover back over the trolley and push it into its corner, but the outline of a figure beyond the glass galvanised her into sliding across the floor until her back was against the wall. Russell had hefted the blanket box and was trying to stand in a corner in so that his shape would not be visible through the door. They both held their breath while the handle rattled.

Tom, on his rounds. Just don't try and unlock the door, Tom. When the footsteps moved on, Clare almost wept with relief. Russell exhaled, placed the blanket box on the floor so gently that even Clare did not hear a sound, and started to screw down the lid. Clare restored the lab to its normal appearance, hoping that it would be days before anyone noticed Aegl's absence, then pulled a perspex box out of a drawer, and emptied the contents into a manila envelope.

"Olrun," Clare explained as she stuffed the envelope in her jeans pocket. Russell looked blank. "His wife. Now let's get you both into the car."

Five minutes later Clare walked alone through reception, clammy-skinned and sick with apprehension, carrying a large roll of paper and a box of drawing materials. Tom smiled his affection. "Are you starting an art class, Doctor Harvey?"

"Have you ever been brass rubbing, Tom?" Tom shook his head. "Well I've found an old stone with strange carvings on it, and I'm going to take a rubbing. Watch." Clare put a coin on the counter, unrolled a corner of paper over it, and rubbed the paper lightly with a ball of dark wax. A perfect image of the coin appeared on the paper.

"Cor, that's clever."

"And with luck it will pick up the carvings on the stone so I don't have to bring the whole thing back here."

"You sure you're all right, miss? You look proper poorly."

"Been working too hard. Bye, Tom!"

In the eyes of an ageing security guard, Clare had arrived alone, and left alone with nothing larger than a roll of paper. Aegl slipped from academia as unobtrusively as a stag crossing a forest clearing.

In the woodland car park she let Russell out of the boot, and stared at the blanket box.

"I've blown it, Russ."

"Nah, no-one saw."

"My career. They'll know it was me."

"No, they won't." The encouragement sounded limp. "Anyway, there's no going back now." The lost look in Clare's eyes made him give her an awkward hug, until she stood on tiptoes to kiss him on the cheek in thanks. Russell blushed as he turned towards his car.

"Best you follow me to Allingley."

Allingley was alive with preparations as they drove through the village an hour later. A maypole had been erected in the centre of the green, where teachers from the primary school were arranging coloured ribbons ready for the dancing. Near Russell's Forge Garage, two of Eadlin's horses stood harnessed to an old farm cart, tossing their beribboned heads at the flies, and surrounded by a crowd of children. A working party of parents was tying freshly-cut whitethorn boughs into a hoop behind the carriage seat, and decorating a throne for the Queen of the May on the bed of the cart. As Clare and Russell drove past the green, Eadlin handed the reins of her horses to a parent and followed the cars into the garage's servicing bay.

"Hello gorgeous!" Russell pulled the doors closed behind them and gave Eadlin a surreptitious squeeze. "You look stunning!" Eadlin was dressed for her carriage-driving role in polished riding boots, skin-tight white jodhpurs, ruffed shirt and a tricorn hat.

"Success?" Eadlin asked, as she disengaged from Russell. "Hey, come on girl," something in Clare's eyes made Eadlin fold her into a hug, "we'll sort this out together, tonight."

"I know it's the right thing to do. I just hope it doesn't cost me my job," Clare mumbled into Eadlin's shoulder. She stood back after the embrace. "Love the costume. You make me feel quite dowdy."

"Fancy dress is not obligatory. Here." She took her own whitethorn posy from her hat and pinned it to Clare's shirt. Behind her, Russell spread his hands and shrugged.

"Can we put Aegl somewhere safe, until tonight?"

"Use my office, if you like." Russell nodded towards a booth in a corner of the service bay. "I can set the alarm."

Clare insisted on carrying the blanket box herself, cradling it like a parent with a child's coffin. After Russell had locked up she stood staring at the door until Eadlin touched her arm and she started.

"Sorry, I was dreaming. I brought Olrun as well." Clare patted her pockets. "I'd like to bury them together."

"Olrun? Oh, she's…" Eadlin's voice faded away in puzzlement. "You're going to have to take me through this later, step by step. Maybe it didn't all sink in, like, the first time. Right now it's chaos outside, and any minute there'll be a squeal when one of my horses steps on a child. Hey, if you want a laugh, take a look in the yard of the Green Man," Eadlin called as she pulled open the door. Clare decided not to tell her about Russell's large, dirty hand-print now decorating one cheek of her jodhpurs. "Jake's in a foul temper, trying to find a way of strapping himself into his Jack-in-the-Green costume without hurting his hand!" She giggled as she left, leaving Clare looking thoughtfully after her.

"What's on your mind, Clare?"

"How long before the parade starts?"

"Ages yet. Why?"

"If Jake Herne's busy here, the rune stone will be quiet." Clare's faced creased into her first real smile of the day.

Chapter Forty-One

D ICK H AGMAN LEANED against the gate into the Green Man's delivery yard, looked up the lane towards the village green, and excavated his ear with a finger while he watched the flow of activity.

"His girlfriend's back."

Behind him the struggles inside the Jack-in-the-Green costume stopped. Hagman looked back over his shoulder and stifled a laugh. Jake Herne didn't like to be laughed at; he needed to be the jester, not the fool. In an hour or two his face would be covered in green greasepaint, decorated with leaves, and leering out of the costume with sinister merriment. Girls would shriek, toddlers would scream and hide in their mother's skirts, and the merriment would begin. But at the moment, Jake's face revelry sweating and pinkly ludicrous as he struggled with the straps inside.

"What?"

"His girlfriend's back. I saw her car go past." Hagman scrutinised the contents of his ear and flicked his fingernail into the yard. Jake swore loudly.

It had been a morning for swearing. Getting Jake Herne inside the Jack hadn't been the problem. It fitted over his shoulders in a harness like a bell tent, festooned with foliage and may blossom, with an oval cut out for his face. Jake could shoulder the burden easily, and he was fit enough to dance inside it as he led the maypole dancers and the morris men. The swearing had begun when he tried swinging the costume one-handed in a practice dance. Both hands were definitely needed. Hagman had helped Jake buckle his plaster cast to one of the harness's handles. It worked, after a fashion, but it hurt, and with every twinge Jake had sworn revenge.

"So what if she is?"

"Well, what if we can't get him on his own?"

"Then we'll have to find a way of keeping her out of the way. Slip her a spiked drink, cosh her, or whatever, we only need a few minutes."

Hagman wasn't sure if Herne was joking. Still, he had a score to settle with that little archaeologist; she'd interrupted the esbat just when it was getting interesting. Hagman licked his lips at the memory of the naked woman on the rhododendron branch, all curves and shadows in the moonlight, in the moments before the hysterics started and the torch shone in his eyes.

"Are we still going to do it, then?"

"Of course we bloody are." Jake rested the costume on two tables either side of him, and crawled from under it. "Shut that gate, you never know who's listening." Hagman pulled the double doors closed behind him. Their height made the small yard seem cramped. The space was normally occupied by Herne's Range Rover but it was now dominated by the costume perched between the tables. Around them the walls were lined with beer kegs and stacked crates of empty bottles, a rack of weight training dumbbells and an exercise mat, the debris of Herne's existence.

"You sure about this, Jake? Couldn't we just rough him up a bit? Scare him away, that sort of thing? I mean, it's murder, innit?"

"That bastard's going to suffer for what he did to me."

"Yeah, but I don't think the others will go along with killing someone."

The speed with which Jake could move stunned Hagman. One second Jake was flexing his plastered arm, the next his good hand was around Hagman's throat, lifting him against the doors so that he could feel his jowls pouched out above Jake's thumb and forefinger.

"Then don't fucking tell them, you pillock." Hagman struggled to get his toes to the ground to relieve the pressure on his windpipe. Jake let him drop and patted his cheek, suddenly calm. "We'll just let the word spread, afterwards, when they can't stop it and can't prove it. And maybe by then they'll have more than a missing cripple to think about."

Hagman massaged his throat, eyes lowered, sullen. "What d'ya mean?"

"I sacrificed a stag and we got the Saxon. I sacrificed a goat and the choirmaster died. Now we're going to give Him a man. Let's see what He does with that."

Hagman shivered. He didn't like this new certainty in Jake. When Jake spoke like that, a frightening look came into his eyes, the sort of look that made Hagman want to hide. Jake's hand came back again and Hagman cringed against the doors, whimpering, but Herne folded his third and fourth fingers under his thumb to make the sign of the Horned God with his index and little fingers, and pushed the sign under Hagman's nose.

"We're going to do this and we're going to do it well because it's His will. If you let Him down, He'll make sure you'll regret it for all eternity." Jake's chilling intensity softened and he slid his good arm around Hagman's shoulders. Now when he spoke, it was like a parent encouraging a child.

"Stay strong. You'll find He has a way of helping out. Now, I've got a job for you." Hagman looked up at him gratefully, like a beaten dog that suddenly receives a pat from its master.

"I'm going to do this properly, robed and masked," Herne continued.

"What, in front of everyone?"

"Especially in front of everyone. Now take my car keys and fetch my hood and gown."

"But I'll miss the parade…"

"Nah, there's ages yet. I want you back here in time for us both to get ready. Remember, you're crucial."

Hagman puffed himself up and reached for the keys. He liked driving Jake's Range Rover.

A few minutes later he stopped where the bridleway met the Downs road, and furrowed his brows in thought as he stared at Clare's parked Volvo. Some people never learned, did they? The question was, what to do about it? Hagman pulled out his mobile phone and called Jake.

A minute later, Hagman eased Jake's car forwards onto the bridleway, and parked it a few hundred yards from the clearing, where the bridleway widened enough to turn around. He wouldn't want to scare her off, now, would he? But maybe the boyfriend was with her. At the thought of Fergus's stick, he pulled a folding shovel out of the boot. It was best to be prepared.

CLARE KNELT IN front of the stone, with her roll of paper in the grass beside her, willing the pattern of runes to emerge from under the surface mosaic of orange and white lichen, grey stone, and dried blood. This would be even harder than she thought. Once, the stone had been intricately carved, but now whole patches of the surface had flaked away, and she doubted if even laboratory techniques would uncover what once had been in those areas.

Faint sounds of movement in the undergrowth made Clare look around nervously. The glade felt wrong, as if something malicious lurked in the bushes. Fergus's reaction to the place still spooked her. Clare shivered involuntarily, and then relaxed as she saw a blackbird rustling the dead leaves under the bushes, hunting for worms. *Get a grip, girl.* She pushed her fears to the back of her mind, and forced herself to think analytically.

Start with the context. Rune stones to proclaim a chieftain's prowess were normally set up where people could see them, not hidden deep in the forest. In this hidden glade, with a spring, this one was more likely to have a sacred meaning than to be a boundary stone. So if this is its original site, she could expect the runes to have both literal and mystical interpretations.

Clare allowed herself to trace the runes with her fingertips, touching the stone so lightly that only flakes of lichen would be disturbed, and then drew each rune on a pad on her knee.

Two runes close together were clear. Perthro, then Eihwaz, as meaningless in isolation as taking any two letters from a modern inscription. The Perthro rune looked like a buckled staple on end, and might represent a cup, or something contained within a cup. Secrets, perhaps, or hidden meanings, maybe something female. Eihwaz, an angular 'S' of three straight lines, enlightenment, endurance, or strong purpose.

Or, literally, a yew tree. She sat back on her heels, trying to assemble the fragments of the puzzle in her mind. Under the rhododendrons the blackbird bounced and stabbed, then was still after a gobbling swallow, but around her the rustlings continued.

Perthro, Eihwaz, Algiz. Clare traced the rune she had spotted on that first day with Fergus, the day he'd collapsed. Algiz, the elk rune with its spray of three lines like antlers. Strength, divine protection, but here it was reversed to imply a negative. Hidden danger, perhaps, or even the loss of the gods' protection. In any context this would be a powerful warning, but against what? Clare sat back, thinking, with the dream of Kate and the runes running through her mind like background music.

For a moment Clare felt a sense of presence, a silent scream of warning so powerful that she looked around the clearing, half expecting to see a tumble of golden hair, but there was only the natural greenery of the woods. The warning clamoured in her mind. Algiz reversed. Kate and the dream poem. Dream poem, the *Hávamál*, no longer strange to her because Clare had read it many times since that first morning. Another verse leapt into her thoughts.

That er thá reynt,
er thú að rúnum spyrr inum reginkunnum,
theim er gerðu ginnregin ok fáði fimbulthuir,
thá hefir hann bazt ef hann thegir

That is now proved
what you asked of the runes of the potent famous ones

which the great gods made and the mighty sage stained
that it is best for him if he stays silent.

Clare rose on her knees in front of the stone, as if kneeling
at an altar, mouthing the words of the *Hávamál* while she tried
to decipher its arcane meaning. The verse could mean 'leave
this alone', but that wasn't what she wanted to hear. Around
her the sounds of the glade were crowding in, no longer merely
blackbirds but a presence that made her twist around with a
sharp intake of breath. But she was too late to avoid the shovel
that swung flat-side into her temple, sweeping her aside in
shattered fragments of light.

HAGMAN LOOKED DOWN at Clare's body, excited and frightened
by what he'd done. *Keep her there, out of the way,* Jake had
said. Now she lay on her back with her arms tumbled upwards
beside her head as if in surrender, and her eyes half closed. The
position had pulled up her shirt, exposing her belly button,
and Hagman knew she wasn't dead because her stomach was
moving as she breathed. He thought she looked rather cute and
vulnerable like that. It made him feel powerful.

But Hagman didn't know what to do next. Jake would
have known. Hagman bit his knuckles and took a few steps
back towards the lane, but then turned around, squirming in
indecision. A trickle of blood explored the crevices of Clare's
ear, overflowed, and dripped into her hair. Hagman started
justifying what he had done to himself, muttering that she
shouldn't have been trespassing, who knows what she might've
been up to. She might've broken into the field shelter and stolen
stuff.

Field shelter. Robes. Got to get the robes. That was what he'd
been sent to do. Mustn't go back without those. As Hagman
started moving towards the shelter the woman groaned and
one arm flopped downwards before she fell still and silent once
more. She might wake up and still get back to the village, and

then all hell would break loose. Swiftly now, he trotted to the shelter, returning with a hank of nylon twine that had once bound a bale of hay. *Think like Jake. Pretend you're Jake. Do what Jake would do.*

CLARE HATED THIS part of the dream. She hated it for what it was, and she hated it more for what would follow because it was the overture to madness. Clare didn't understand where she was, but knew she must be lying on the ground because there were feet near her face. There was something wrong about the feet this time. The dirty trainers and jeans didn't fit the dream and she puzzled at the sight while a hum of wrongness filled her head like an electric charge.

Clare's arms were pulled behind her and bound. That part fitted, and she tensed in anticipation of the hand that slid inside her shirt and pawed at her breasts. She squirmed against the violation but although she tried to scream, the only sound that emerged was a low moan. The touch was different; she'd expected the hard, overt grope of a conqueror, not this furtive feel as if the perpetrator was afraid to be caught. Clare wasn't sure which was more loathsome. She managed to roll over, groaning, and the hand withdrew.

"Bit choosy, are we?" came the voice in her ear. "Well there's not enough to get hold of, anyway."

Clare started to thrash around on the ground, but her legs were bound until she was securely trussed. As she was lifted there was a new explosion of lights and pain in her head, and she passed out again.

CLARE'S EYES OPENED on a landscape on its side, framed by a doorway, out of focus. She became aware of a wooden floor, hard and coarse against her ear, and she squinted to try and make sense of the view. She must have lost her glasses somewhere. The view looked like the field at the end of the valley, with Jake

Herne's horse grazing in the distance. This room must be part of the animal shelter. The door and its fittings looked unnaturally heavy, as if this room had been adapted for additional security. Awareness returned and Clare struggled against the twine binding her limbs.

A foot stepped over her, pulling her attention away from the field. He was carrying a large swathe of cloth over his arm, a dress maybe, or a cloak. Something trailed from his other hand, but before Clare could focus on it her attention was drawn to the line of animal masks high on the wall, each with a similar drape of material hanging below its peg. All the faces of the masks were angled downwards, scrutinising her as she lay on the floor. This hadn't been part of the dream. Nor was the man who now squatted in front of her face. Clare knew him from the waking world. She'd last seen him with his trousers round his ankles. He belonged with the wolf mask. And he must be the letch who'd groped her.

"I've gotta go." The Groper spoke with bizarre normality, his voice ringing false like a bad actor speaking his part. "We're gonna have some fun with your boyfriend now, but we'll have lots of time to get to know each other later, around midnight. Tonight's Beltane, see, and we're going to have a party. Jake says you're invited." He touched Clare's cheek with his fingers, and traced them down her neck until they touched her nipple through her shirt. He licked his lips and smiled at Clare in a way that made her want to scream but no sound broke its way through the hum of wrongness in her head.

In the pocket of Clare's jeans, her mobile phone began to vibrate and she rolled on top of it, instinctively trying to smother the sound that she knew would follow. But the jangly music swelled with each unanswered ring, strident in its demand for attention. The Groper turned her over, rifling her pockets, and spilling the phone onto the floor alongside the envelope with the bone pieces. He tossed the envelope aside, wrinkling his nose in distaste, but grabbed at the phone, peering at its screen.

"It's your boyfriend. Ah, bless." He dropped the phone onto

the floor, and the ringtone died as he ground the phone into fragments with his heel.

"We wouldn't want you calling for help, now, would we?" The Groper smirked as he rose to leave. A look of indecision crossed his face as if the actor's mask was slipping, and almost as an afterthought he bent to cut the twine binding her hands. "You can manage your legs yourself." Now his voice sounded whinier, almost apologetic.

Hagman stood silhouetted in the door, with the goat's head mask hanging from his other hand, its long sabre horns trailing towards the ground. The silhouette of his arm, the hanging robe, and the horns formed the rune of Algiz reversed and Clare fought back rising hysteria as the door closed. There was the sound of heavy duty locks being snapped shut on the far side.

Clare still had no power to scream, but the screams would come later. Who was it who'd spoken about the screaming time? Her own screaming time came after the sacrifice, she knew that. Olrun had shown her. But she couldn't remember whether it was Fergus or Aegl who was going to be sacrificed. Clare focused on the thin line of light coming under the door, hoping that its beacon would illuminate the turmoil of pain in her head. That light hadn't been part of the dream before, either.

Chapter Forty-Two

FERGUS SAT OUTSIDE the White Hart, enjoying a pint of ale with the choir. Some of them had carried the function room's electric piano out into the sunshine, and were entertaining the May Day crowds with barbershop singing. The choir clustered around Julia Foulkes, who had brushed aside their protests and insisted on playing the piano "because Tony would have loved this." Tony's Labrador was tethered to her chair, its nose on its paws, eyes darting from point to point as if it was still hoping to see Tony stride out of the crowds. Julia played with fragile poise, a throwback to an Imperial age that prized resilience in adversity above all qualities. She appeared to draw energy from the crowd's laughter as the Heavenly Twins sang Gilbert and Sullivan comic songs.

The flowers that bloom in the spring, tra-la
Breathe promise of merry sunshine

The maypole on the green had long since been swathed with multi-coloured ribbons by dancing children, and the bargain-hunting fervour of the crowds around the produce stalls was fading. Eadlin had left half an hour before to take her horses back to the stables, and the attraction of the moment was the pig roast that wafted rich smells over the grass. Fergus wondered if he was paranoid to wear Eadlin's protective posy in his hat, and to sit with his stick resting against his leg. The village green on May Day must be the safest place in the world. All he needed was Clare's company to enjoy it.

She's around, Russell had assured him. Just a bit stressed after taking the Saxon. She's probably still at the stone. Fergus tried

Clare's mobile again, but it rang through to voicemail, again, and he left another message, concern tightening his voice. He scanned the crowd for a glimpse of her, but he could see nobody he knew apart from Cynthia Lawrence, picking her way across the grass towards them and stumbling as her high heels sank into the turf. Cynthia nursed a bottle of champagne in the crook of her arm as if it was a baby.

"I won the Guess The Weight Of The Pig competition," she called, beaming her triumph, then winced as a whine of electronic feedback cut across the music. Russell was having mixed success at mending the public address system. As Cynthia found a chair amongst them a drum started thumping out a steady marching beat around the corner in Green Man Lane, and there was a collective groan of "Oh, not again!" from the group around the piano. After a four beat introduction, an accordion struck up a tune, and the Jack-in-the-Green came dancing round the corner. The Heavenly Twins struggled on bravely for a few bars,

As we merrily dance and we sing, tra-la
We welcome the hope that they bring, tra-la
Of a summer of roses and wine...

but faltered to a halt, unable to compete. Julia Foulkes smiled her apology at their audience and closed the piano lid with graceful restraint.

"Some jokes become tiresome with repetition," she muttered. At another group of tables, the morris dancers recognised the accordion as a call to perform, and streamed off the terrace. One of them let out a mighty, beer-fuelled belch as they squared up on the green, and lifted his ribboned hat in mock apology. Better out than in.

"Infuriating behaviour," Cynthia spoke loudly enough for her words to carry onto the green. "They've had far too much to drink."

"It looks as if someone's giving it away." Fergus nodded at one of the Jack's attendants. The figure was dressed in a green hunchback costume like the old cartoon character of Punch, with foliage sown into his hat and clothes and his features obscured by greasepaint. He'd been prancing round the morris men for most of the afternoon, almost as if he was part of the dance.

"He's called a bogeyman, and he's got a firkin of beer under that hump," one of the Heavenly Twins explained. "He hands out free beer to show there's no hard feelings about the practical jokes. And brace yourself, Cynthia, he's coming your way. I think he heard you."

The bogeyman capered over to Cynthia's table, and lifted her hand to his lips in mock salute.

"Oh, do go away." Cynthia waved her hand at him imperiously, the way she'd shoo a persistent fly. The bogeyman grinned, exposing a line of teeth that shone white in the green-painted face. He pulled a plastic, disposable cup from a pouch, held it under a tube which ran over his shoulder from the firkin on his back, and offered her a squirt of beer.

"I do *not* drink beer, thank you." Cynthia spoke with regal disdain. The bogeyman lifted his nose in the air, crooked an elbow as if to carry a handbag, and minced around her in a parody of her airs and graces. Even one or two of the choir laughed. In the middle of the laughter the bogeyman snatched Fergus's cap from his head and placed it on his own to embellish the mockery. Fergus made a good-humoured cry of protest and lumbered after him, but the man was too nimble. The bogeyman danced away backwards, out onto the green, holding the cap out in front of him, taunting Fergus to come and grab it. Each time it was almost in reach it was whisked out of his grasp, always moving further away from the inn.

The joke became boring. Fergus stood still and looked around him, realising he had been drawn to the edge of the green near Green Man Lane. His stick was still by his chair. On the far side of the green the public address system made another feedback scream before the voice of John Webster interrupted the afternoon to announce that the May Queen would now draw the prizes for the raffle. Throughout the crowd heads either turned to watch the Vicar, or dropped to rummage for raffle ticket stubs. For a moment Fergus and the bogeyman stared at each other, alone in the crowd. The man's eyes glared white, like the teeth, within the anonymous mask of greasepaint. Fergus threw up his hand in a dismissive gesture and turned back towards the inn.

"Keep it."

In an instant the green figure was in front of him, its manner conciliatory as it filled another cup with ale and held it out to Fergus.

"No thanks."

Now the cap was offered, see-sawing backwards and forwards in the opposite hand in a clear mime message. *Drink my beer and you can have your cap.* Reluctantly Fergus took the cup and sipped, finding the taste strong and salty. The creature's hand mimed a palm-upwards, lifting motion, still holding the cap out of reach until the drink was finished. Only then did it bow theatrically, flash the teeth within the green mask, and return the cap. It was strangely comforting to wear Eadlin's token again. Fergus ignored the bogeyman and stood looking for Clare from this new direction. If Russell and Eadlin had not been so emphatic that he should stay with the choir, he'd have gone looking for her. The heat of the sun was warm on his back, and he stifled a yawn as he watched.

There. A slender figure, shorts and sweatshirt, half-seen in the throng. It might be her. Fergus started to walk after her, weaving to try and keep her in sight. He could feel his heart racing.

The stumble was unexpected. It was like stepping off a curb that he didn't know was there, and Fergus stood still for a moment, wondering why he was swaying. He hadn't drunk that much. He tried to walk towards the crowd but his leg folded, dropping him onto one knee with a hand braced in the grass. From somewhere nearby a voice Fergus knew announced that over two hundred pounds had been raised towards the church tower restoration fund, but as he lifted his head the tower itself was starting to tilt. As his other leg buckled, his arm was dragged around the shoulder of the bogeyman, pulling him upright. The man stank of beer and sweat, and the metal edge of the barrel under the hump dug into Fergus's arm.

"Had one too many, have we? Let me take you somewhere you can lie down quietly." As Fergus was turned towards Green Man Lane he tried to cry out in protest, but the words emerged as meaningless mumblings. He felt a surge of hope as Mary Baxter hurried past towards the raffle draw, and he made another ineffectual attempt to call.

"Fergus Sheppard, look at the state of you. You should be ashamed of yourself." Mary carried on past them without pausing. "And mind you don't come into my house until you've sobered up." Fergus's cries became an inarticulate growl. His head felt too heavy to support and lolled forward, tipping his cap onto the ground. Eadlin's flowers crumpled under his toes as he was dragged into the lane.

The Jack-in-the-Green followed them into the Green Man's yard, masking their departure with its bulk. Fergus was dumped onto an old wooden Windsor chair, but slid sideways until he was grabbed by his shirt and hauled back into place. Somebody passed a rope around his chest, tying him to the chair's back. The seat was screwed to two carrying poles like an antique sedan chair, and Fergus's fuddled brain struggled to work out its purpose. Out of the corner of his eye he could see the bogeyman peering through a crack in the doors, watching to see if they were followed.

Jake Herne put an empty crate on end in front of Fergus, and sat looking at him with a smile of pure malevolence. His green-painted face and neck projected bizarrely from a white, sweat-saturated muscle shirt.

"How do you like my little cocktail? It's useful with the girls." Fergus heard the words but was starting to feel more detached than frightened. "Though sometimes they don't remember how much fun they've had." This was all happening in another place and to another person. His mind started to float off on its own meanderings until Herne slapped his face with his good hand.

That hurt. Must concentrate. Got to find Clare.

"Did you ever hear about revenge being a dish best served cold? Wrong. I'm going to take mine hot, very hot." Herne enjoyed gloating. "You see, every year we burn the Jack-in-the-Green on the bonfire, and tonight we're going to wrap you up nice and tight and put you inside it."

A silent scream started to grow in one corner of Fergus's mind. A gentle euphoria was spreading over the rest. His head had slumped forward and he watched, helpless, as a string of drool escaped his lower lip and landed on his trousers.

"The pity is that I'm going to have to knock you right out, so you won't feel nearly as much pain as I'd like. That's the trouble with these fast-acting drugs, they don't last long enough. It will be a few hours before we light the bonfire, and we wouldn't want you waking up and causing a fuss, would we?" Why did the bastard sound so reasonable? Herne's face came into view as he ducked his head to make eye contact. "It's going to mean getting up at dawn to clear up any bits of you that are left over, but it'll be worth it."

Fergus tried to speak, but the sound came out as a mumble.

"... mad..."

"Mad? Nah. I've found the best boss ever." Herne leant forward so that his mouth was close to Fergus's ear and the stink of his sweat filled his nostrils. "He gives me what I want, I only have to ask. I want to hurt that meddling priest, and He gives me the choirmaster. Even better than I'd hoped. I want to teach you a lesson, and you come to me so easy it's like picking an apple."

Fergus's eyes closed. Didn't want to look at Herne. Maybe sleep a bit. There was the sharp sting of another slap across his face, and he opened his eyes.

"One more thing. I've saved the best until last. Mister Hagman here has excelled himself today. He's got your girlfriend safely locked up by the Blot Stone. She's probably got a bit of a headache, but we've got a special night lined up for her." Finally Fergus managed to push back the weight of sleep that was dragging him down, but his attempt to launch himself at Herne merely resulted in a pathetic moan and a lurch against the rope so that his backside started to slide off the seat. Herne heaved him back into place, and stood to pass another length of rope around his body.

"We're going to celebrate High Beltane tonight, after the bonfire," Herne continued, speaking over Fergus's shoulder so the heat and smell of his breath brushed across Fergus's face. "Just a few of us, the ones I can trust. And in case you didn't know, High Beltane includes the Horned God coupling with the Goddess. Tonight your cute little friend is going to be worshipped as a goddess. So die knowing that I'm going to fuck your girl. I won't even have to tie her up, just give her some of the stuff you've had. And when I've finished fucking her, I'll drop her into that pond by the Blot Stone and hold her under. Who knows, maybe in a thousand years someone will dig her up like the Saxon and wonder how she died."

Fergus's mind processed the words, but his mind glowed dimly, like a dying torch. Someone was growling but the flickering bulb in his head was being smothered under a great weight of tiredness.

"Search him. Take his phone, wallet, anything metal and anything that would identify him."

"Jake, I don't like this." Was that the bogeyman?

"You're already in it up to your neck. When you're done, cover him well with this, then the Jack. Make sure nothing shows. Then let's go and get cleaned up." A large blanket was dumped in Fergus's field of view. The working part of his mind had shrunk to a terrified point of light even before the needle stabbed his arm.

Chapter Forty-Three

CLARE GROANED AND rolled over onto her back and stared up into the gloom with an avalanche of pain filling her head. The line of animal masks stared back at her, implacable. The cloaks had been pulled down from beneath several of them. That would explain the cloth beneath her and balled under her head. She couldn't remember untying her legs, either. A rational, feeble corner of her mind waved a flag labelled 'amnesia'.

The vomit erupted almost without warning, leaving Clare with barely enough time to turn her head to one side to spew over the floor, and with each spasm her head tightened into a sheet of agony. When her heaving subsided she wiped her face on a cloak and dropped it over the mess. The line of light under the door beyond was fading; already the sun must be out of the valley. Clare lifted a hand to explore a prickle under her chin, and felt the posy that Eadlin had pinned to her shirt in the garage. She pushed her nose into it, hoping to mask the smell of her own vomit, and found comfort in the token of friendship. Thanks, girl, but it didn't work, she tried to say out loud, but her tongue seemed too big and no words emerged.

Water. The need for it filled Clare's mouth the way the pain filled her head. As delirium reclaimed her she wondered if they'd let her drink before the horrors began.

"YOU SHALL NOT drink." The most frightening mask above her has the face of Professor Eaton. "You stole the Saxon." The line of masks either side of Eaton is an infernal jury that stares down at her, merciless in their judgement. "Guilty," pronounces a rat.

"Guilty, guilty, guilty," they all intone in turn. "He shall die," the wolf calls, as strident as any Inquisitor.

But the body that swings from the pole as they carry him to his execution in the marsh is not Aegl but Fergus Sheppard.

Chapter Forty-Four

THE CROWD ON the green was thinning out. Now the lure of the raffle was over, families were drifting home to rest between the day's delights and the evening's fireworks. Already Russell could see clear across to where Eadlin's tricorn hat weaved through the stalls on the far side as she searched. His phone call had brought her back in a rush.

Fergus? The Heavenly Twins had paused to think. Oh, he was fooling around with Dick Hagman in his bogeyman costume. He'll be back; his stick's still here. But thank God the Jack-in-the-Green has finally gone. That ghastly man Herne has been pestering us all afternoon. It made Julia Foulkes feel quite ill. The Vicar's taken her home…

Russell ignored the rest of the conversation and scanned the crowd, senses tuned. The debris of the day showed more clearly across the grass as the festivities drew to a close. The village's immaculate green was now littered with crumpled napkins, paper plates and plastic forks, tumbling scraps of raffle tickets, and a discarded lump that might be a baseball cap. Russell turned it over in his hands, sniffed at the bruised nosegay of May blossom, and lifted his eyes in time to see Dick Hagman let himself out of the Green Man's delivery yard and slam the gate behind him. Hagman was still dressed in his bogeyman costume, but stood more upright now, with the hump hanging flaccid down his back where it had been relieved of its firkin. Hagman turned away from the gate, wiping greasepaint off his face with a bar towel, and froze when he saw Russell watching him from the top of the lane.

"Dick! I need a word!" But Hagman ignored his call and scurried away in the opposite direction, glancing back over his shoulder as he went. Russell let him go, more concerned with what, or who, he had left behind him. Russell pulled out his mobile and called Eadlin.

"I may have found him."

The Green Man was too quiet as they approached. The village's second pub should have been as packed as the White Hart. Eadlin pushed at the door, and peered through the glass, puzzled by the notice taped inside. 'Closed for May Day.'

"What pub closes on a holiday, for heaven's sake?"

Russell rattled the locked gates into the delivery yard, and looked upwards. They were too high for him to jump up or climb over. "Jake's up to something, that's why. Fergus is in there, I'm sure."

"Then you'd better give me a leg up." Eadlin stood back, looking up, planning her climb.

"But that must be seven feet!"

"Easy. Make a basket." Eadlin demonstrated her posture for helping riders to mount, and stepped into his hands.

"If I wasn't so worried I'd be enjoying this." Russell's voice was muffled.

"Just get your face out of my chest and heave." Eadlin held herself with her stomach balanced across the top of a gate until she was sure the yard was empty, then rolled over and climbed down the gate's frame on the far side. She held her finger across her lips as she let Russell into the yard, and pointed towards a frosted glass window on the first floor. A shadow moved beyond the glass, and a rush of water came down an outside pipe as a toilet was flushed.

"Bugger, it's locked." Eadlin tried the door from the yard into the pub, and they both looked around for inspiration. The sound of a shower started above them.

"Oh God, no." Eadlin stared at one corner of the yard, where the Jack-in-the-Green stood on its stretcher, ready for its procession to the bonfire. "Surely he wouldn't..."

They both pulled the Jack off its stretcher, working with feverish haste as they realised the truth of the tightly wrapped bundle bound to the chair inside. Eadlin swore quietly and continuously under her breath, *bastard, bastard, bastard*, as they laid Fergus out on the ground, pausing only to lay her hand on his neck, feeling for a pulse.

Russell opened his mobile and started dialling.

"What are you doing?"

"Calling an ambulance, what do you think?"

"Wait a bit." Eadlin leaned forward to smell Fergus's skin, and lifted his eyelid. "He doesn't need an ambulance. He needs to sleep it off."

"The police, then. For fuck's sake, Jake was going to murder him. This has gone too far."

"But Jake will say he was only trying to frighten him. Claim it was a practical joke that got out of hand." Eadlin lowered her voice as the shower sounds ended above them. "Give me your keys. I've got an idea."

Chapter Forty-Five

PEOPLE FLOWED DOWNHILL as the sun set, drifting from the green towards the common on the outskirts of the village, almost as if some human tide had turned. Farmers on the green packed their produce stalls into the backs of Land Rovers, yielding to hot dog stands on the common. In the fading light Jake Herne led the Jack-in-the-Green through the village, waving his good hand theatrically to acknowledge the ribald cheering, as if his place had always been to lead the Jack rather than carry it. Jake kept his plaster cast hidden under a swathe of cloth. Behind him, Russell Dickens had volunteered to take his place as pallbearer, ahead of Dick Hagman.

Hagman had sweat trickling down his face, mingling with the beer sprayed over them by the crowd. He'd deliberately picked up the heavy end, stretcher-style, in case the big oaf in front of him questioned the weight, and he was fighting to keep the Jack upright. Unsighted behind its pyramid of leaves, Hagman heaved a mighty sigh of relief when he finally felt grass beneath his feet and knew that they were on the common. He even managed to join in the cheers and banter as the Jack was laid on the platform of wooden pallets that had been prepared for it.

"Bury it." Jake's whispered instruction needed no repetition. Hagman kept stacking wood around the Jack, even though some in the crowd objected, shouting that they wouldn't see it burn.

"Paraffin?" Russell sniffed at a bundle of wood in his hand.

"It got wet in the rain." Hagman's voice was high with tension, but Russell shrugged and kept building. It was fully dark by the time the bonfire was finished, and Russell started to move the crowd back behind the safety tape that had been staked out perhaps seventy yards from the bonfire and the line of firework frames.

"Come on, you lot," Russell shouted, "we can't start until you're all behind the line," and slowly the crowd obeyed, muttering about "bloody killjoy 'Ealth and Safety".

Jake savoured the moment. It was his traditional right to light the bonfire, as the dancer in the Jack, but this year he made a spectacle of it. He held aloft a flaming torch, staring at it as if it were a talisman, before lowering it slowly towards the pyre, then pushing it in like a sword thrust.

The bonfire caught quickly. At this signal Russell and Hagman lit other corners, and the little blazes ran along prepared lines of oil, linked together, and flared. Within moments the bonfire was a solid mass of flame.

Hagman started to panic when the smell reached him. Soon afterwards the stench brushed a coughing path through the spectators as the smoke drifted across the common.

"What the hell are you burning in there, Jake?" someone called from the crowd.

"Smells like old boots!"

"Or the leftovers from the pig roast!"

Hagman covered his nostrils and looked nervously at Jake, surrounded by the stink of his guilt, but Herne merely gestured behind him into the bushes and nodded. Hagman understood the signal, knowing what was hidden there. He pulled a cardboard tube from his pocket and threw it into the edge of the flames on the side nearest the crowd. It was a simple pyrotechnic, designed for theatrical effect. All that the watchers behind the tape saw was a momentary, dazzling flash and bang, followed by a ball of smoke that rose up from the fire. It was enough to distract everyone's attention, and as their eyes readjusted to the darkness they saw a new figure beyond the bonfire.

Even Hagman was impressed, and he'd known what was coming. The figure stood motionless, flickering in and out of vision as the flames rose and fell. Its body looked wholly black, so that it would have appeared as an absence of light rather than a presence but for its monstrous goat's head and scimitar horns, with its eyes reflecting the red light of the flames. Its silhouette showed no limbs, but gave the impression that the infernal head was supported on a wedge of blackness whose broad shoulders tapered towards the ground.

In the crowd there was nervous male laughter and isolated screams from some of the women. The figure radiated a sense of evil that went far beyond the mummery of a May Day bonfire party. As they watched, the wedge supporting the head changed shape as its unseen arms slowly lifted, spreading the robe into bat-like wings. As the robe lifted, its sole decoration was revealed in the firelight as an inverted cross, the antithesis of a Christian symbol, gleaming in some silver material on the front of the Satanic chasuble.

Count to twenty, Herne had said. *We'll shock them and end it.* But Hagman was distracted. There was a shout of "No, for the love of God, no!" as John Webster ducked under the tape and strode towards them, bellowing "Stop this obscenity!"

From another corner of the common, Julia Foulkes also brushed aside the tape, her scream of "murderer!" slicing through the air. All her famous poise and control had snapped, and as she started to run towards the fire Hagman had no doubt that this fragile woman was at that moment capable of violence. Hagman turned nervously back towards Herne, wondering if Jake had gone too far with the goat's mask.

"Chuck it, you fool!"

Hagman swung his second pyrotechnic back-handed towards the fire, but his aim was poor and rushed, and it arced into the furnace heart. The explosion released a wall of heat across the grass and sent a volcano of burning debris tumbling outwards. In the centre of the fire a final slab of blazing wood fell away, releasing a cascade of smouldering material that ignited in a crackling eruption of flame. Inside this new flare was the shape of a human torso and head, burning furiously with much of the skin already gone and the jawbone hanging open in a silent scream. Within seconds the body slid out of sight, collapsing into the flames as the fire settled and a new shower of sparks erupted into the sky.

Ten yards from Hagman, Webster and Julia stopped in their tracks, the certainty of what they had seen written over their faces.

"Sweet Jesus, what have you done?" Webster cried, making the sign of the cross.

A short distance upwind, Russell swore emphatically and ignited the opening sequence of the firework display, sending the first mortar coughing into the air. It exploded above them with a punch that hit Hagman deep in his panicking chest, scattering distraction in a perfect parabola of colour.

Beneath the bursting fireworks circles of people radiated out from Hagman and the fire. An outer ring of the crowd looked upwards, murmuring their "oohs" and "aahs" in ignorance of the drama. A closer arc of watchers at the tape stared towards the fire, whispering their uncertainty about what they had seen. There had been something in the fire, some trick of the heat perhaps. Whatever it was, Julia Foulkes had been shocked out of her rage, and was speaking into a mobile phone with the crystal authority of an English gentlewoman.

Beyond Julia was an inner ring of people, a pentacle spaced almost equally around the fire, but there was no consistency in their behaviour.

Dick Hagman backed away from the heat, whimpering.

Russell Dickens launched fireworks with furious urgency, rushing the display into a continuous, frenetic finale.

Jake Herne had jettisoned his mask and robe, but stood with his arms outstretched, palms upward in supplication, chanting in an ugly, incomprehensible tongue. His theatrical air had evaporated with that momentary exposure of the body. Jake Herne was begging.

Almost opposite him, John Webster sank to his knees and implored the Almighty's blessing on whichever poor soul had been in the fire. His words met and battled with Herne's in the crackle of the flames.

Unseen by any of them, Eadlin Stodman stood in the fringes of the woodland. She too held her arms outstretched with palms lifted and hands open to receive. Her chant resonated with the earth and folded itself into the plume of smoke rising into the night.

From high above the village, the sound of detonations rushed up the valley, panicking a sleeping horse into a mad charge across its field. The thunder funnelled between the narrowing hills until it hit the field shelter and shook Clare's delirium like the clash of a hundred spears against their shields. Clare woke into darkness where the pain in her head flickered in colours of purple, shot with the acid yellow smell of her own vomit. Thirst clogged her mouth in crumbling cascades of brick red but she tried not to acknowledge it. There would be water, later, she remembered that. It was the horrors that came before the water that Clare didn't want to remember. On the floor of the store she squirmed herself tighter into the nest of Satanic robes, and winced as the spears hit the shields again.

Far to the south, beyond the undulating farmland, blue flashing lights were called into life when Julia snapped her mobile phone shut. As the firework display ended and the May Day bonfire began to collapse in on itself, police sirens converged on Allingley.

Chapter Forty-Six

THE POLICE INSPECTOR was inclined to believe the Vicar, even though there wasn't any evidence. At least, not yet. Vicars tend to be sensible people, not given to wildly exaggerated claims. If it had been only the woman, the Inspector would doubt the existence of a body, but the Vicar backed the woman's story like it was the Creed.

Besides, every fibre of the Inspector's instinct told him something was wrong. There'd been more call-outs to this village in recent weeks than there should be in as many years. It had started with reports of graffiti on the church, and then there was a vandalised car and the business of the goat's head. That had been downright nasty. Something was going on.

The Inspector could see the smouldering remains of the bonfire in the wavering beams of the police torches, still steaming under the spray of a hose they'd run out from the nearest cottage garden. Not that there'd been much left to put out by the time he'd arrived. Still, he doubted if the remaining charred timbers were substantial enough to hide a body. He'd seen burnt bodies before, all twisted and blackened but still recognisably human even after intense fires. He'd smelt them, too, and the smell had put him off his Sunday lunch for weeks. But so far nothing here looked like a body, even though there was a lingering smell that might, perhaps, have been one.

The Inspector pointed his torch at the people he'd selected for further questioning, and tried to work out the relationships between them. He'd a habit of attaching mental labels to the players around a crime. It was easier than remembering names. He'd singled out six, this time, and they were sitting in three pairs on the tree trunks that edged the common, each establishing their distance from the others as if to prove that they weren't together. There was the Vicar and the woman who'd made the call, the one he'd labelled Laura Ashley. They were sitting with their heads together, hands clasped as if they were praying. Those two believed what they'd told him and they weren't in a hurry to go anywhere. Beyond them, the unnatural pulses of blue light illuminated his men as they worked their way through the crowds, looking for witnesses who would corroborate Laura Ashley's story.

On the next tree trunk there was the big, slow-speaking guy he called the Bear, sitting with his arm around the woman he thought of as Puss in Boots. Puss was a pretty thing in jodhpurs and long leather riding boots, and all his men wanted to be the one to interview her. Those two were nervous, much more nervous than innocent people had any right to be, even when confronted with police lights and sirens. They knew something but were acting dumb. The Bear was one of the organisers and had been pointed out as someone who'd built the fire, so he'd have to stay.

Then there were the last two, the ones who'd also built the fire. One of them, the Weasel, cowered away from the beam of the torch, almost shaking with fright. The Inspector kept the beam on the Weasel's face, watching him wince at the scrutiny. There's the weak point. If anyone was going to crumble under questioning, it would be that one. The Weasel had denied seeing anything, gabbling his responses with the panicked defensiveness of a child caught with his hand in the sweetie jar. Guilty as hell, of something.

Which left the arrogant one, the one with the plaster cast on his arm and his shoulders braced back as if he were some tribal chieftain who demanded deference. Smart Arse. The Inspector knew the type. As soon as the heat went on, so to speak, he'd refuse to say anything without a solicitor. He'd probably even call him 'his brief'. Now Smart Arse turned his head away from the torch, staring into the distance as if all this commotion was beneath his notice. The Inspector would bet a week's pay that this man had form. If they did find anything in the fire, he'd probably have a story ready which would blame everything on the Weasel. The Inspector came to a decision and beckoned over his sergeant.

"Tape it off." He waved his torch at the fire. "Treat it as a Scene of Crime. Let's wait until daylight before we go blundering through the ashes. In the meantime I want statements from those two," he flashed the beam at the Vicar and Laura Ashley, "and then they can go if they want. These four must stay here."

"Am I under arrest, Inspector?" God, how the Inspector hated Smart Arses who knew their rights.

"No Sir, you're not under arrest. I'm simply asking you to stay here to help us with our enquiries. But your arrest can be arranged if you'd prefer."

Smart Arse simply blinked at him.

By the time there was enough light to examine the ashes, the crowd had long since dispersed. Just the three couples remained, plus an enterprising burger van that had stayed for the gossip while he sold coffees and bacon butties to the police. The Inspector was glad the Vicar had stayed, even though he'd been free to go. Otherwise the other four would probably have kept silent about the goat's head mask and strange cloak that one of the constables had found in the bushes. Tempers had flared for a while amidst accusations of Satanic practices, but they were still no closer to an answer. Nothing would surprise the Inspector any more. He'd been a copper in this county for over twenty years, and the goings-on in the rural communities had lost their power to amaze him.

Finally, the Inspector waded clear of the pond of ash and charcoal, and walked up to the Vicar and Laura Ashley. As he peeled off rubber gloves and overalls he made it clear what he thought about half his force being called out in the middle of the bloody night to nothing more than a bonfire. No normal bonfire, he said, would totally destroy a body. There'd have been something left to see. So do me a favour and check your facts, next time, will you? The couple reacted with stunned disbelief, as if he'd told them that their church had collapsed, and he found his indignation fading. They believed what they'd seen, and they too would be humiliated in the aftermath of the night. But most of all in that moment, the Inspector dreaded Smart Arse's crowing.

The Inspector wasn't prepared for the surprise and relief on the faces of the remaining four as they were released. Even Smart Arse's bluster was half-hearted. They didn't seem to be working together, but each pair believed there had been something to find in the fire. The Inspector's internal alarm system went into overdrive.

Furiously, he marched back to the site of the bonfire, making wind-up signals to his men. In the centre of the pile of wet ash he turned, searching the scattered pieces of charred timber for any sign that would support his screaming instinct that he was missing some vital clue. In frustration he kicked at the pile of debris, dislodging a metal object that rolled away from his boot. The Inspector bent to pick it up, but it was just an old hinge, the kind that would have fitted on the door of a cupboard or the lid of a box. Swearing, he tossed it towards the other metal debris they'd found, which included, incomprehensibly, some dumbbell weights.

As the Inspector drove away, he wondered why the couple he'd thought of as the Bear and Puss in Boots still sat on a tree trunk, watching, even though they'd spent the night without sleep and had been told they were free to go. Their behaviour set his mental alarm going again. Later he'd be told that they'd sat there until the last policeman had left.

But no-one saw how the couple then pulled a bucket and a shovel from the back of a Land Rover, and brought them to where the Inspector had stood. Quietly, almost reverently, they filled the bucket with ash.

Chapter Forty-Seven

"Can't we get some sleep first?" Hagman slumped in an armchair in Herne's flat above the Green Man, clasping a large brandy from the bar downstairs. His eyes were red with tiredness, and now that he knew he wasn't about to be arrested for murder, he only wanted to drink and sleep.

"You whine like a school kid. 'Mummy I wanna go bye-byes,'" Herne taunted as he emerged from the shower, towelling himself one-handed with the kind of care an athlete might give to his body before a contest. He strutted around the room naked, flaunting himself, but Hagman looked away. He found all that muscle intimidating.

"Well we've been up all night and I'm knackered."

"We can't take the risk of her making a noise and being found by walkers. We'll do it now." Herne's tone allowed no dissent.

"But it's morning. We don't really have to hurt her, do we, not now we've missed Beltane?"

Herne started dressing in fresh clothes as if he was going on a date.

"Nah. We could let her go, but you made one big mistake yesterday. You let yourself be seen. You'd get at least ten years for grievous bodily harm and false imprisonment. She might also try and prove sexual assault, if I can assume that those 'lovely little tits' you've been drooling about weren't flashed at you voluntarily."

Hagman winced. He couldn't understand how Jake could stand calmly in front of the mirror applying after-shave. "And worst of all, when she reports her boyfriend missing, the police might take another, much closer look at that bonfire. Just remember you'll be the last one to be seen with him."

Hagman squirmed in his chair. "I still don't understand why they didn't find nothing."

"I told you, He looks after His own. He's just proved it." Herne made the sign of the Horned God, and then pushed his face close to Hagman's, bracing himself over the chair with his hands grasping the chair arms. He was still naked below his shirt tails, and Hagman recoiled from the contact.

"Listen, if you was part of that fucking church up the road, you'd be running around waving your arms and shouting 'it's a miracle'. We've pulled off a perfect murder because all the evidence burned away, but all you can do is sit there moaning."

"It don't seem right, somehow, killing her. Not like the man. She ain't done nothin'."

"She will do, if we let her." Herne pulled on clean trousers and finished dressing, moving briskly as if he was looking forward to what must be done. "You got us into this, now I'm going to help you finish the job. And He won't want us to leave any loose ends. But we can have ourselves some fun while we do it. It'd be a pity to waste her."

Herne snatched a screw-top plastic bottle of orange juice from the refrigerator and shook some pills into the palm of his hand. "Only one, I think." He dropped a pill into the juice. "We don't want her getting too sleepy too soon, do we? It's more fun when there's a little fight left." Herne shook the bottle to mix the drug and reached for his car keys.

Chapter Forty-Eight

BIRDSONG. FERGUS WOKE to the kind of song that comes from so deep in the throat of a thrush that its richness seems launched from the heart. There had been another noise, an echo of laughter perhaps, but now there was only the tumbling complexity of the dawn chorus. And giggles. High, girlish, angelic giggles. Fergus wondered if he was in heaven, without remembering why he might have thought he could be in heaven. Did they have hangovers in heaven?

Fergus groaned and moved, feeling a dry scratch and rustle underneath him. The giggles came again and he opened one eye. Above him a corrugated metal roof was festooned with cobwebs. There was something he needed to remember, something important about a bad nightmare, but it was fading with the daylight. Fergus turned his head, wincing as his vision speckled with little flashbulbs of pain. Where the metal roof ended, the sky beyond was the fragile blue of a perfect morning. Below the blue stood one of the stable girls, her eyes sparkling with laughter. A name formed in the fog of his brain. Emma. Maybe. Probably. Synapses fumbled blindly in his mental soup, and gradually connected. Emma.

"You must have been well drunk." Emma was enjoying the moment, relishing a story she could tell and retell among her friends. Fergus sat up, blinking at the pain, and wondered where he was. A heavy horse rug slid off him into a gap between bales of hay. He stared at it while his tongue probed at his lips, tasted something foul, and retreated. Hay. Hay barn. Stable girl. He was at the stables.

"How...?"

"Eadlin and Russell brought you back yesterday. My friend Lucy was doing the evening feeds when they came back, and she says you was snoring. They made her promise not to tell anyone, but Lucy's my friend so it's OK. They put you in here to sober up while they went back to the party on the common." The stream of information made no sense. Fergus reached back through the fog for solid memories, finding only images of morris dancing and men in grotesque green costumes. He'd drunk beer at the White Hart, perhaps a couple of pints, but somehow he'd become more pissed than he'd ever been. Fergus slumped back onto the hay bale. There was something crucial that he needed to remember. He ran his fingers through his hair, and noticed his arms.

Fine red scars lay in hoops across the skin. Fergus put his wrists together and the scars matched. Someone had tied him up, and he'd struggled against his bindings. There was a bruise and the puncture mark of a hypodermic in one arm. But no watch. Panicking, he searched his pockets. Fragments of memory started forming in his head.

"What time...?"

"It's only six. I'm on the early shift. Me dad dropped me off on the way to work. You lost something?"

"Watch, wallet, phone, car keys, everything." There was a reason, if only his brain would work.

"So you was robbed. And you missed all the excitement last night."

"Excitement?" One-word questions were about all he could manage.

"Mrs Foulkes and the Vicar said there was a body in the bonfire and called the police. There was cops all over the place. They put the bonfire out and made Eadlin and Russell and Jake Herne and Dick Hagman stay there all night." Emma was almost hugging herself with the excitement of the story. "They was just packing up as we came past this morning. Jake Herne looked well stroppy."

Body in bonfire. Jake Herne. The thing he must remember took shape in his mind, and it had the face of Jake Herne saying "I'm going to fuck your girl." Fergus almost fell off the hay bales and steadied himself against them while the spots in his vision faded.

"Do you have a phone?"

"Sorry."

"Come on, every teenager has a phone." Fergus heard the desperation in his own voice.

"I'm out of credits until payday, if you must know." Emma sniffed, no longer finding the conversation amusing.

"I've got to make a call." Fergus started out across the yard towards the office.

"And I don't have the key to the office, neither. Only Eadlin has that, remember? You'll have to wait till she gets back."

Of course he remembered. The farmhouse was also her home. As Fergus's mind cleared he realised that by the time Eadlin returned to the yard, Herne could be at the Blot Stone.

"Do you have a car?"

"Do I look like I can afford a car? I told you, me dad gave me a lift."

Fergus staggered to a standpipe against the wall of the barn and put his head under the tap, gasping as the cold hit his scalp, but holding himself there until his brain started to work. As the base of his neck began to ache with the cold he straightened, staring at the line of hills, and building a mental picture of the terrain as he weighed up alternatives. About three miles across country to the Blot Stone, four by road and track. Well over an hour on foot, even at his best speed. It would take him as long if he went via Allingley and picked up his car or bike. Plus he'd have to add the time to wake up Mary Baxter so he could fetch his spare keys. But to wait and do nothing was unthinkable. Fergus spun on his heel and strode towards the tack room.

"I'm taking Trooper out."

"What, on your own? Eadlin will go mad!"

"I'll live with it." Fergus hauled the saddle and bridle into his arms.

"You'll bloody kill yourself. You've never ridden anything out on your own before, have you? Let alone a horse like Trooper.

He's well sharp."

"Depends who's riding him. And you sound just like my mother." At that she shut up.

Five minutes later, Fergus had his first battle with Trooper before he even left the yard. Emma laughed at him and called out "I bloody told you so" as the horse spun under him, sensing his tension, and protesting at being put to work before the morning feed. Without the steadying tail of Eadlin's chestnut to follow, this was going to be difficult. When the horse was briefly under control Fergus called over to Emma.

"Emma, when Eadlin gets here, ask her to meet me at the Blot Stone. It's very important."

"Yeah, whatever." Emma was in a huff.

Chapter Forty-Nine

CLARE WATCHED THE dawn spread under the door. Her delirium faded with the dark and her mind came crawling back to her from the nightmare corners, reassembling to stare at that hardening line of light. The pain in her head was now a solid, factual weight that had a label called 'concussion'. The thirst that plagued her was real and of this time and moment, not the waking memory of a dream. It too had a label, and this one said 'dehydration'. Neither the concussion nor the dehydration had an escape. They framed her existence like the wooden walls around her.

In this new half-light Clare cleared the nest of robes to the back of the store and examined her prison. The construction was too substantial for a horse shelter, with an extra security layer of wood that swallowed a blow like a tree trunk. Presumably they wanted to keep their regalia safe. The door moved slightly when Clare pushed at it, and from the far side came the metallic rumble of heavy fittings. She backed against the rear wall, took the two steps run up that the space permitted, and kicked hard at the door at around waist height.

The effort burst like a cymbal clash in her head and Clare staggered back, sinking to her knees and cradling her head in her hands until the pain subsided. The leaden thump of the impact told her the futility of the action. She let her body topple sideways against the door, feeling tears start to trickle down her cheek. One part of Clare's mind wondered where her body had found the liquid for tears. Another part festered with ideas about the scene in the laboratory at the start of the working day. All the research on the Saxon's body was finished, so maybe, Clare consoled herself, they wouldn't notice for days. Yesterday she'd thought of him as Aegl, but today he was the Saxon, and she'd gladly give the bloody Saxon back in exchange for a glass of water and the chance to get out of here.

The sharpness of the light under the door told Clare that the sun was reaching into the valley when she heard the noise of tyres crunching the gravel of the track. She stood, pounding the door with the flat of her hand, shouting as loud as her parched throat would allow. When the engine stopped and the sound of tyres turned into the sound of footsteps she kicked the door hard enough for the locks to rattle on the far side, ignoring the pain in her head.

"Who's a noisy girl, then?"

Clare sagged against the door, sobbing as the hope of rescue collapsed and the bolts were unlocked. She backed away and blinked in the dazzle of light as the door opened and two silhouetted figures filled the space, blocking any escape. As Clare's eyes adjusted, the outlines became Herne and the man who had knocked her out the day before, the Groper, and she knew that her only hope would be to break through them and run. If they were making no attempt to hide their identities, she wouldn't talk her way out of this.

"Naughty girl." Herne looked over her shoulder. "You've made a mess of our stuff." Clare wished she knew how to use psychology to manage a situation. Some people would know ways to defuse the violence that hung in the air like the smell of drying vomit around her. She decided she'd talk to them as an equal, and refuse to accept the role of victim.

"Concussion." Clare's voice was thick, as if she was chewing cardboard, but she was surprised at her own calmness. "It makes you throw up, see? That's what happens when you bash people on the head." She swallowed, trying to squeeze saliva into her mouth. "May I have some water?"

Clare didn't like the way Herne smiled as he held out a bottle of orange juice, but she took it and swallowed, forcing herself to drink steadily rather than show her desperation by gulping. The juice tasted salty but it cut through the stale bile in her mouth as if it was as pure as the morning air wafting in from the door. She handed the empty bottle back, savouring the fruit sugar rush in her blood.

"Thank you." The thanks were deliberate, maintaining the social conventions as long as possible. Clare wouldn't ask them what they were planning. They weren't going to let her go, and the wrong question might trigger brutality. She needed to keep them calm until there was a chance to get past. Once clear she could outrun both of them, even in her weakened state, Clare was sure of that. She could feel the energy surging into her veins from the juice.

"Oh, Dick, you've spoilt her." Herne spoke in the patronising tones of a playground bully, and stared at the side of Clare's face. Clare lifted a hand to touch the dried blood on her cheek. "I'm not sure I want her now."

Clare glared at him, and Herne stared back in silence. The bastard was waiting for something. His eyes were narrowed and he radiated a calculating, predator menace.

Behind Herne, the Groper swivelled his head towards the woods above them, listening. Something had distracted his attention. Then the rippling hoof beats of a cantering horse reached Clare inside the store, travelling fast along the bridle path from the direction of the old yew. Herne had kept his eyes on Clare, and seen the hope in her eyes as her shoulders lifted to shout. In an instant he had spun her so that his plastered arm was across her body, pinning her arms to her sides, and clamped his good hand across her mouth.

"One sound and you're dead." The voice in her ear was utterly convincing. The hand across her face smelt of soap and after-shave, and it gripped her with the confidence of hard muscle until the sound of the unseen rider started to fade away towards the end of the valley. Clare forced the tension out of her body to make herself appear quiescent, knowing that the rider must round the hairpin and return towards Allingley. As she sagged in his arms she felt him nuzzle at her neck, saying "Quiet, girl." Her helplessness seemed to arouse him and the fingertips of his plastered hand stroked at her breast, with the tumescence in his trousers pushing at her back. Clare made no protest, wanting him to feel that she was powerless, while she calculated distances and sounds. She needed to vault the gate out of the field, and run up the track to arrive at the bridle path as the rider was passing. She knew what she had to do. Olrun had shown her.

In the same instant Clare sank her teeth into the hand over her face and grabbed two-handed at the genitals behind her. For one triumphant moment she crushed with all the power that she could muster, but unlike Olrun she released him as he howled and crumpled. As Clare took the first step of her run towards the door the Groper started turning back towards her. At the second step he lifted his arms in instinctive defence, and at the third her stamping kick caught him in the side of the knee so that the leg folded and he yelped and fell.

Clare was free and running, exultation pumping through her veins, with the effects of the night making her stumble as she crossed the grass. No matter; she was clear, and she'd damaged them both enough for her to stay clear. Her limbs would loosen in a moment. But the stumbling became worse and Clare almost fell over the gate by Herne's car, in the way she'd seen Fergus fall over the top gate on the day they found this place. Her powers of motion were fading away from her like sand through her fingers. By the time Clare reached the stream she was staggering, and her run became a living nightmare as her legs moved more and more slowly and the sounds of pursuit came closer. They did not shout at her. There was no sound loud enough to carry to the rider, only two low, feral snarls and footfalls that staggered or limped onto the gravel of the track behind her, coming closer with each step.

Clare tried to call to the rider beyond the rhododendrons, but her voice was no more than an incoherent mumble and her legs slowed to a single, ponderous step as if she was wading through thick mud. The pursuit was close now, no more than a few feet away, and the invisible mud solidified around her legs with each heartbeat. Clare stood swaying for a moment, on the edge of falling, willing the rider to appear at the end of the track. Then her legs became jelly and she sank to her knees so that the first swinging punch from behind passed harmlessly over her head. Still Clare stared desperately at the end of the track where the far gate hung open, but the sounds from the horse and rider had changed. Where there had been the drumming of a fast canter passing above them, now there were irregular palpitations and the scream of a frightened animal. Clare jolted sideways as a fist grabbed her clothes from behind, ripping her shirt as she was dragged out of sight into the clearing.

Above them the pattern of hoof beats became frantic, an irregular drum roll that ended in an animal scream and a heavy thump, as if a body had hit the ground.

Chapter Fifty

FERGUS KNEW THE cross-country rescue mission was a crazy idea, long before Trooper threw him. He was trying to think clearly in a mental soup of swirling fragments of memory. Green men. *I'm going to fuck your girl*. But whose body in the fire? The fevered ramblings became a waking nightmare in which he'd ridden out like some comic-book hero, only to find he couldn't control his horse. The more he tried to force Trooper across country, the more the horse behaved like a seven hundred kilo infant with attitude, leaping sideways away from imaginary threats in the undergrowth as if to show Fergus that he wasn't nearly as good a rider as he needed to be. What's more, he was heading for the Blot Stone but he didn't know for sure where Clare was, even if the field shelter was the only logical place she could be locked up. He'd no weapon apart from a screwdriver that he'd found in the tack room and stuffed into his pocket, and no real plan other than a vague idea that if he reached the shelter first, he could use the screwdriver to release her.

He was able to reassert mastery over the horse when they reached the gallop where he'd raced Eadlin, but perhaps it was just that his interests and Trooper's happened to coincide. They both wanted speed. Fergus was even able to keep the horse in a canter past the yew tree and along the bridle path above the valley of the Swanbourne, but his problems returned as he rounded the corner above the coombe.

Where the valley sides were steepest Trooper came to a complete and sudden stop, snorting and spinning to look up the hill, ignoring Fergus's kicks. A fine underbrush of young birch covered the slope, obscuring the view with a layered tracery of new leaf. There was a hint of movement through the green haze, a shifting of the pattern of grey-brown stems that drew the eye to places that became still as soon as he looked. And there were sounds, muffled thumps like footfalls in the leaf mould.

Whatever it was, the unseen presence was terrifying the horse. Snorting, Trooper backed to the edge of the track until the drop through the bushes to the pond gaped under his tail, so focused on the threat above that he was blind to the risk of falling down the slope. On any other horse it was a moment to use a whip, but Fergus kicked hard in desperation and Trooper shot forwards and sideways, galloping down the bridle path with Fergus hauling at the reins, now struggling to pull the beast back from an uncontrolled bolt.

They'd passed the gap in the rhododendrons by the time he managed to pull up, with the horse rolling its eyes in fear and pirouetting on the spot. If he had to confront Herne and Hagman in this state, they'd probably just stand and laugh at him until he fell off and killed himself. As he fought the panicked animal he glimpsed the tops of saplings swaying, ahead of them now, as a body moved at their base. He had the bizarre thought that they were being herded, the way a sheepdog will herd a flock.

He'd never heard an animal scream in panic before. Nor had he tried to stay in the saddle while a horse rocked back on its hind legs and reared. At the top of the huge buck that followed, Fergus looked down at the track that was suddenly a long way below him, and thought that this was going to hurt. He landed with one arm hooked over Trooper's neck, his face pressed into a hide that was lathered with sweat, hanging far enough out of the saddle to see hooves strike sparks from flints in the path. The next buck dumped him onto his shoulder on the bridleway, with a jolt that punched the air out of his lungs and smashed his helmet against the ground. His vision cleared as he rolled, in time to witness from underneath the mighty leap as Trooper jumped both his body and the wire fence, and smashed through the rhododendrons to land on the track down to the clearing.

* * *

CLARE KNELT WHERE they'd dropped her, slumped over on her knees with the backs of her hands resting on the ground, palms upwards, slack. Some vestige of power in her arms allowed her to brace herself rather than topple onto her side. Her head hung forward, staring at her body. The shirt had been ripped off one shoulder so that it hung in rags down her arm, exposing her breasts, but she no longer had the energy to lift her arms and pull her clothes into decency. She managed to raise her head, feeling it wobble unsteadily, in time to see the Groper aim a kick at her face.

"Bitch!"

"Leave it. Have your fun later. Someone's coming." Herne restrained the Groper before the kick could land. It sounded as if the horse was galloping down the track towards them. Clare supposed that must be good news, but a detached euphoria was settling over her. The scene around her was like a television drama in which she was losing interest, but which was still broadcasting its petty plot.

Now there was a horse running loose around the clearing, looking for a way out, streaked with lather as white as its eyes. This was curious enough to capture Clare's attention and she watched drunkenly as Herne grabbed the trailing reins with his good hand.

"There'll be a rider after it, and maybe others following." Herne struggled to calm the beast. Clare's eyes started to droop, but fluttered open when he spoke again. "They mustn't see her. Run up and tell them we've got their horse and we'll bring it to them. It might be Eadlin," he called after the other man, "this is one of hers."

FERGUS ROLLED OVER, groaning, and pushed himself up onto his knees while the world steadied. He clasped his left arm to his side and staggered to his feet, inhaling deeply, then let out an involuntary cry and fell over again. Deep breathing was another bad idea. Maybe he'd broken a rib. He knew about ribs. The shoulder wasn't working too well, either. He lay on the ground for a moment, breathing as gently as he could, savouring a soothing, crushed herb smell in the grass. A fly buzzed in front of his nose and he watched it dreamily, half tempted to stay where he was, but he groaned, moved his hand under him and pushed the ground away, slowly, swallowing the pain it took to get up. He swayed until the fragments of light and sky and trees assembled themselves into their proper places, and started walking.

Walking wasn't as hard as he expected, if he took it slowly. At first the path had an infuriating tendency to tilt from side to side, but he swore at it, and it steadied. He breathed in small, shallow breaths. It was easier that way. Warm liquid seeped out from under his helmet and trickled onto his forehead. He touched the wetness with the fingers of his good hand as he walked, and they came away sticky with blood.

As he reached the gate it was standing open and he stared, dismayed, at Jake's car parked below at the entrance to the field. The animal shelter beyond was also open.

Fine bloody rescue party he'd turned out to be. Arrived too late, fell off his horse, might have broken a collarbone, probably a rib as well, and couldn't run even if he wanted to. He'd be as much use in a fight as a eunuch in a brothel. And if Clare isn't there, what does he do? Say "Please, mister, can I have my horse back?"

He closed his eyes, swaying, and breathing as gently as he could. Why did it have to be here, of all places? Here, the source of all nightmares? He'd tried to run up that path, once, and blubbered like a baby once he'd fallen over the gate. All his instinct was to walk away, find help, find a doctor. To walk back down it would be lunacy. Fergus couldn't remember the last time he'd prayed, but right now he needed help. He opened his mind, pushing back the terror, seeking the goodness.

The early morning, woodland smells held a hint of grace, an echo of other moments. There was no divine guidance to answer him, just a sense of calm that whispered like the wind in the leaves. It was time to face his demons, real or imaginary. Face the pain, always face the pain. Blood was running down his forehead again and he smeared it away as he reached his decision. Almost crying with the stupidity of what he was about to do, he lowered himself onto one knee, picked up a heavy stick from the debris under the bushes, and used it to push himself upright. It made a satisfying *thwack* when he swung it hard against the gatepost, and did not shatter. Good. He let the delirium carry him downhill, staggering a little with his stick over his shoulder and his left arm trailing uselessly beside him. To his left, through the rhododendrons, he could hear footfalls keeping pace with him, faint enough for him to wonder if they were the sounds of an ally or a threat or simply his imagination. Somehow it didn't matter. There was a flow down the hill towards the clearing and Fergus was part of it, flotsam on a wave of madness.

Voices. Someone was shouting. He could hear Trooper snorting and prancing, and he braced himself for a confrontation as a man came running round the corner from the clearing, limping as he ran, then froze at the sight of Fergus. For a moment they stared at each other. There was something familiar about the squat, paunchy figure. As the man's lips pulled back into a rictus grin that might be terror, Fergus recognised him. Teeth, bogeyman, Hagman. The face that had been covered with green greasepaint turned white as he watched. Fergus lifted his stick and snarled, trying to look as menacing as possible, and wishing his left arm would work.

Hagman's reaction stunned him. The man spun away with a falsetto screech, and splashed through the stream into the undergrowth opposite. Fergus looked over his shoulder to see what there might be behind him to have caused such a reaction, but there was only the empty track climbing back to the gate. He stepped forward cautiously as the sounds of Hagman's flight faded. The blood was still flowing down his face and this time he let it run. He didn't want to let go of his stick.

The sight of Clare stopped him thinking about Hagman. She slumped on her knees at the edge of the clearing, facing the stone, making no reaction to his appearance. Her features were slackening into stupor, dried blood matted her hair and a bruise the colour of thunderclouds spread down her face. Her shirt had almost been ripped off her, and the sight of that abused vulnerability triggered a rage in Fergus he didn't know he possessed. The eruption of anger found voice in a snarl that grew louder as the pain across his ribs became irrelevant and he turned towards Herne.

Herne was leading Trooper across the clearing towards the path, but had stopped at the sight of Fergus, staggering backwards. Fergus lurched at him, his club raised, bellowing. This time, he'd kill. He knew it. No power on earth would stop him bringing the stick down on Herne's head.

"You're dead!" Herne cried, making a strange sign in front of his face, with his two middle fingers folded down to leave the index and little fingers upright like horns. It was an instinctive, protective gesture the way a priest might cross himself against evil. "It's not possible!" His fear was palpable.

It wasn't the sign that stopped Fergus. It wasn't even the betrayal in Trooper's eye at the sight of his friend charging towards him with a raised stick, glaring murder. As the horse snorted and spun away, Fergus was sure he glimpsed a stag in the gap in the bushes, beyond Herne. The image of a grizzled monarch of the woods, crowned with a mighty spread of antlers, was powerful enough to freeze him into immobility. For a fleeting instant it stared at them in the disdainful way a passing adult might look at a children's fight in a playground.

The sight made Trooper frantic. His turn away from Fergus was reversed, and caught between the twin threats of stag and stick the horse reared, screaming, front hooves flailing the air. Fergus staggered backwards to escape the danger, but Herne seemed incapable of movement until a hoof snapped his skull backwards, driving him onto his knees. For perhaps a heartbeat Herne seemed to look towards Fergus, eyes bulging as if they were being forced out of his head, but any intelligence had gone before his body was flung aside and trampled by the fleeing horse. As Herne's body started to convulse, Fergus looked up towards the gap in the bushes. The stag had vanished, so completely that Fergus started to wonder if he had imagined the sight.

At his feet, Herne was making a rattling sound in his throat, as if he was trying to hawk up phlegm to spit. The sounds faded into a rasping sigh as the twitching slowed and stopped, and the body softened into a deeper stillness. Fergus understood that deeper stillness. He'd seen it before.

CLARE KNEW SHE was hallucinating. The boundaries between dream and reality, between past and present, had blurred. Somewhere to her right there was a fight, but it was more interesting to look at the beast in front of her, because she couldn't remember how it fitted into the dream. Stags on helmets, stags on shields, but not stags in a battle. Clare peered at it myopically, wondering what had happened to her glasses. The fight to her right ended with the blow of an axe and she had enough muscle power left to flinch. The sound of an axe hitting someone's head was distinctive. Olrun had shown her that. But Olrun's battle had been in the past and the spatter of warm wetness that hit her arm was in the present. Clare lowered her gaze and looked at the mess drunkenly as it trickled downwards on its way to her upturned palm.

It was becoming harder to lift her head. As Clare looked up it swayed on her neck as if she was a newborn infant. Colours and patterns were dissolving, and she wasn't sure whether she was seeing the toss of an antlered head or the sweep of a sword lifted in salute. Clare wanted it to be the sword. She wanted to see that pattern-welded blade again, the one that his brother Weyland had made. But as she screwed up her eyes to see better there was only emptiness. Her eyes filled with tears at the unquenchable sadness of a last farewell.

A stick dropped into the grass near her. Just a stick? It should be a seax or an axe. A hand reached under her arm and tried to lift her, but whoever it was gasped and gave up after a weak attempt. A warrior knelt in front of her. What was Fergus doing in her dream? And why had he painted the Algiz rune on his face? That looked like blood. Three converging lines of blood. Algiz, not reversed, meant protection or shield. Strong rune, Fergus. Clare approved, but a corner of her mind was cross with him because he might have chased away the stag. She felt Fergus ease her onto her side and turn her away from whatever was on the ground to her right. Cautiously, and with more gasps, Fergus lay beside her, folding her into him with his arm around her back so that her head lay comfortably in his shoulder. His right hand reached up over her back and started stroking her hair. Clare liked that part of the hallucination, even when his fingers snagged in the tangles where blood had dried into knots. Its soothing calm stayed with her as she slipped into sleep, a sleep that held no dreams she would ever remember.

Chapter Fifty-One

FERGUS MEASURED THE passage of time by the angle of the sunlight through the leaves overhead, content to wait for help to arrive. As the sun rose it reached into the glade, dappling the ground with light. He dozed, and dreamed of lovers laughing nearby, until the hum of insects woke him. The sound was focused on the bloody mess under Herne's body, and he tried to get up but the rip of pain across his chest and shoulder told him that he was stuck on his back until someone helped him. As he moved, Clare stirred in her sleep and held him closer. Fergus relaxed, inhaling her presence. Someone would come, eventually.

The sun was near its zenith when Clare stirred, flailing for a moment, panicking until she recognised Fergus. Her face furrowed in concentration, and as her eyes cleared she started to roll away from him although he tried to hold her close. That instinctive movement of recoil hurt. Asleep, she'd pulled him closer, but awake, she pushed him away.

"Don't turn over. There's something there I don't want you to see."

At that Clare struggled harder, too strongly for him to stop her sitting upright and looking around.

"Shit." Her voice was fuzzy.

"I'd have covered him, but I can't get up. You're going to have to help me."

"He looks like a bad waxwork." Clare spoke in the detached way of a casual observer for whom the sight had no personal relevance, and turned back to Fergus, blinking as if trying to remember something he'd said. "What's the matter? Are you hurt?"

"Broken shoulder, I think. Maybe a rib. I fell off Trooper."

This seemed to be all the explanation Clare needed. "I need water. Lots of water."

"Me too. Help me up."

They drank together from the stream, kneeling like animals to bury their faces under its surface. The cold revived Clare and she rocked back on her heels with the water matting her hair and trickling down her throat, and the first spark of intelligence showing in her eye.

"You look like shit, Fergus."

"Have you used a mirror recently?"

"So what happened?"

They were still piecing together what they knew when Eadlin's Land Rover drove fast down the track from the bridle path and stopped in a dusty rumble of gravel. Eadlin and Russell jumped out but froze, horrified, at the sight of Herne's contorted body.

"Bloody hell, Fergus, what have you done?" Russell was the first to find his voice.

"Not me, chief, Trooper beat me to it. You guys took your time." Fergus regretted his flippancy when Eadlin turned aside to retch into the bushes.

"We've been looking everywhere for you two." Russell was unable to take his eyes off the corpse. "We knew Fergus had taken Trooper out solo, but it was only when he wandered back on his own that the girl remembered your message about the Blot Stone."

Eadlin backed out of the bushes, wiping her face on a handkerchief, and stared at Clare.

"Hey, girl, what happened? Where have you been?" Clare was hunched over, holding the rags of her shirt closed across her breasts, with the bruising livid across her face. Gently, as if afraid that Clare would break, Eadlin wrapped her waxed jacket around Clare's shoulders and folded her into a hug. Inside the embrace, Clare began to sob, and Eadlin shushed her like a child. "Hey, it's ok, tell me later. You look like you need an ambulance."

Clare lifted her face from Eadlin's shoulder, and palmed her eyes. "I'll live. Did you bury Aegl?"

Eadlin didn't answer. She was staring over Clare's shoulder at Herne's body.

"Do you mind if we cover him with something?"

Russell went rummaging in the field shelter and returned with one of the robes from the store.

"But what about Aegl?" Clare's voice was insistent. "Did you give him the pagan burial?"

"The Saxon? Nah, better than that." Russell answered for Eadlin as he spread the robe over the body, then bent to twitch vomit stains away from the face. "We gave him a funeral pyre. But we hadn't planned on the Vicar seeing the body."

"You're going to have to bring me up to date, one step at a time." Fergus's confusion was written over his face. "The last I remember was being in the yard of the Green Man."

Russell told him about the rescue from the Jack, and Fergus lowered himself to the ground. For a moment it felt easier than standing up. "It sounds like I owe you, big time."

"But Aegl?" Clare prompted.

"Actually it was Eadlin's idea. She suggested we put him in your place inside the Jack-in-the-Green."

"... and give him a proper balefire. Russell made up the weight with Jake's dumbbells." Eadlin's eyes kept drifting to the lump under the robe. "We thought Clare would be back to share the moment but you didn't turn up."

"We dumped Fergus in the hay barn to sleep it off, but then the police turned up and we couldn't get back," Russell continued. "We was dead scared. Julia Foulkes and the Vicar saw the burning body, see? But then the police couldn't find anything afterwards, which was weird."

Clare giggled as if on the edge of madness. "A balefire! Perfect! Oh, I wish I'd been there!"

"Balefire?" Fergus was floundering.

"A traditional pagan cremation. The sort of send-off his own people would have given him." The hysteria in Clare's voice was alarming. Fergus wanted to stand up and hold her, but there was no strength left in him.

"So why wasn't there anything for the police to find?" he asked, watching how Clare had begun to fidget inside Eadlin's jacket. The question seemed to calm her.

"There was almost no hard skeleton left." Her academic voice. Hard facts. "The acid in the soil had softened the bones. Plus he'd been freeze-dried, so he'd have flared up like dry leather. They might have found some teeth if they'd have looked hard, but nothing much else."

"We gathered some ashes to scatter in the woods, but we were waiting until we found you." Eadlin moved to steady Clare, who swayed on her feet as if she might topple over. "We thought you'd want to do that."

Russell pulled a mobile phone from his pocket. "I guess this time we really ought to call the police. Someone's dead and I dare say Clare will want to press charges against Dick Hagman."

Eadlin looked up. "And where is Dick Hagman?"

"He pissed himself and ran off when I arrived."

"I wish I'd seen that."

"Don't call the police yet." Clare's voice had steadied. "Do you still have the ashes with you?"

Eadlin nodded. "They're in the car."

"Then we're going to have another fire." Clare pulled the battered envelope out of her pocket and held it out to Eadlin. "This is all we found of Olrun at the dig. Can you give her a balefire too? Here? This place was special to them, you see."

Fergus managed to roll onto his knees, and push himself upright. He touched Clare on the arm. "Don't you want to add the tooth?"

Clare closed her eyes as if in pain and pulled the pillbox out of her pocket. She caressed the tooth so tenderly before putting it in the envelope that Fergus wondered if the omission had been accidental. Almost as an afterthought, Clare hooked a coil of blonde hair out of the pillbox and held it looped around a finger. "I was going to do a DNA test. I had this idea that Kate and Olrun…"

"I think she belongs with them." Fergus pulled the hair off Clare's fingers and put it with the fragments.

They built a fire on the scorched site of earlier fires near the Blot Stone, and knelt around it, Fergus self-consciously, the others with reverence. When the fire was established Eadlin started singing a low chant whose words they would never remember but whose cadence was in harmony with the earth itself. As she sang she scattered fresh, green herbs tipped with small, pansy-like flowers over the fire. "Heartsease," she had explained as she gathered the plants from the edge of the field, "although it would have been Banewort to your Saxons." Her mother had called it Love-Lies-Bleeding. As the flowers curled in the heat she laid the envelope on the flames and they watched it flare, releasing a cascade of fragments that were immediately lost in the blazing wood.

When the fire had burned out Clare blended the glowing embers into the ashes Eadlin brought from her car, and the two women scattered the mingled remains on the waters of the Swanbourne. The quartet were quiet as they watched the dust float and fold in the surface of the stream, dissipating until all that was left were one or two charred fragments that floated downstream, tumbling in the ripples.

"You can call the police now." Clare finally broke the silence. "But please, don't tell them about burning the Saxon, just in case I still have a career to go back to."

"I think we ought to let Julia Foulkes and the Vicar know," Russell suggested. "They must think that they're going mad."

"Sure, we owe them that. But only them, please." At the reminder of Clare's escape Fergus tried to put his arm around her shoulders, but she resisted the intimacy and pulled his arm down gently until they were simply holding hands.

"This might take me a while, Fergus." He let his hand drop, hurt.

"But can't you sense what's happened?" Fergus started to lift his arms to gesture at the clearing, but yelped and nearly fell. He took several shallow breaths, with his body folded into a half-crouch while he fought the pain. "Can't you smell it? The clearing is clean again. Pure. It's like a weight has been lifted. It's over!"

"Give me a while, Fergus. This place might be clean, but I'm not, not yet." Clare touched his face, not unkindly. "You only really started to get better when you finally talked about the crash. Perhaps I need to tell you about Olrun and Aegl."

"Maybe I did start to get better then. Maybe it started two months ago when Eadlin let me stroke a horse, but personally I think I really started healing when I fell in love with you."

At that Clare put her hand behind Fergus's neck, pulling him to her so their foreheads touched. It was a start.

Epilogue

Midsummer

PROFESSOR MILES EATON held court in splendid style on the new decking at the Mill House, dazzling a circle of guests with his wit and white linen.

"You've done a magnificent job, absolutely magnificent!" Eaton lifted his arm as if he was about to pat the Mill House's owner on the back, but realising the man was taller than himself he changed the movement and lifted his panama hat instead, waving it at the grounds with their newly re-flooded lake. "So kind of you to invite us to your first garden party." On the fringe of the group Fergus wondered if the 'us' was a regal 'me'. "And you have the water wheel working again!"

"Merely a reproduction, alas, and it drives a small generator instead of a mill, but we're pleased. By the way, I read your excellent paper on the Saxon warrior in the *Journal of Anthropological Archaeology*." The Mill House's owner turned the conversation back to his celebrity guest, deftly demonstrating his erudition in the process. "I'm not an archaeologist but naturally I have a particular interest."

"You're too kind. Sadly, though, we've had to abandon plans for a television documentary. You heard that somebody stole the body? Extraordinary!"

Clare slipped her arm through Fergus's and led him away down an immaculate pathway towards the lake. Other guests were wandering through the gardens, admiring shrubs that had arrived by fork-lift to bring instant, expensive maturity.

"Pompous prick!" she muttered under her breath. "That was *my* paper in the *Journal*. All he did was take out some of the speculative passages. Too fanciful, he said, too romanticised, so he stripped it until it was totally dry and factual, and then put his own name on it. I wouldn't mind if I didn't know I was right."

"But you can't prove it."

"True. Although somehow that doesn't matter any more. It's enough to know."

They paused to greet John Webster, who was climbing the path towards them, doffing his straw hat to Clare.

"Hello, you two. I hoped you'd be here. Have you both recovered?"

"We're fine, John, really fine, honestly." Clare hugged Fergus and beamed at the Vicar to emphasise her point.

"And Fergus, I'm delighted to see you without a sling."

"I've started riding again, as well. Eadlin's hoping that Trooper and I will be competing in the autumn."

"Ah, the horse. Are you sure he's safe?"

"Let's just say we both benefited from a few weeks getting to know each other again."

"Remember, if you ever need to talk..." Webster looked directly at Fergus, the compassion behind his eyes reaching for the soul, saying *I will share your pain, if you'll let me.*

"Thanks, John," Fergus touched the priest's arm, acknowledging the depth of the offer. Webster was one of the very few people he'd ever trust with the screaming time, but a crust was forming over the pit. One day it might stand the weight of conversation. "There was a time when we should have talked, but I couldn't. Now I think I could, but I don't need to, anymore. Some things are best left to heal quietly."

Webster's eyes moistened, and he smiled his understanding.

"How about you, John?" Clare asked. "Were there any repercussions for you or Julia with the police?"

"Not really, although I don't think that it has quite blown over yet. Most people just think Julia was overwrought after Tony's death, and flipped when she saw Jake Herne in a goat mask. It's a bit unfair, but she'll live with it. And thank you both for letting us in on the secret. It's been important for our peace of mind." Webster was perspiring in his clerical collar and jacket, and mopped his face with a folded handkerchief. "I think you should know there are rumours circulating, though, that are quite close to the truth."

Professor Eaton's voice boomed from the decking area above them, enthusing now about the rune stone that 'we' had found nearby. Webster looked up towards the deck, and turned to walk out of earshot with Fergus and Clare, down to where reeds and irises had been planted in naturalising tubs along the edge of the lake.

"I had an interesting conversation with that police inspector the other day. He's still looking for Dick Hagman, and he's sure that there's more for him to discover. He said it was strange to be called out twice in twenty-four hours to the same village, particularly after the previous incidents. Once to a fire with no body, even though all his instinct told him there should be a body, and then again to a body with no fire even though the smell of fire was all around. I hope for your sake, Clare, he never makes the connection with the Saxon."

"Amen to that."

"Have you deciphered that rune stone, yet?" Webster asked, nodding towards the group on the decking.

"Well, there's the stuff we can prove, or at least make a reasonable stab at interpreting..."

"And?"

"There's the stuff I believe, but will never be able to prove." Clare smiled at Webster, gauging his interest.

"I've always found belief more appealing than dry facts." Webster fingered his collar again, pulling it away from his neck to let in some air.

"I think it's rather like one of the memorials in your church. 'Sacred to the memory of...' and all that. Aegl and Olrun had children, and they survived. Their parents' bodies were never found, so when they grew up they erected a stone to their memory in a place that had been special to them."

"You sound very sure."

Clare shrugged. "I'm not, I'm only speculating. But I'm comfortable with the idea. More comfortable than I am with the part of the stone that may be a curse."

Both Fergus and Webster looked at her sharply. Fergus hadn't heard about the curse.

"It's open to wide interpretation, but part of the inscription could mean 'and the damnation of the gods on the foreigners that slew them'. The Anglo-Saxon for 'foreigner' was 'Wealas' but today we'd say 'Welshmen'."

"Dear God. Tony."

Webster sat down heavily on an ornate, cast iron bench beside the path.

"Sorry. Like I said, it's open to interpretation." Clare half-smiled and shrugged before walking over an ornamental bridge onto the dam. Fergus sat with Webster on the bench, concerned by the Vicar's pallor.

"Clare tells me that runes were thought to be very powerful in Saxon times," Fergus tried to explain. "There's some line in a poem about runes being capable of raising the dead."

"Only Christ can do that."

"Yet I'm sure I saw that Saxon when I was trapped in the car."

"You saw an apparition when you were close to death. That's a different thing, and it's not unknown. In fact, there's nothing that has happened in Allingley this year that can't be explained."

"But Tony…"

"Had the heart attack he'd been warned about."

"Or Jake Herne…"

"Thought he could play with the devil, and went mad, homicidally mad. And the village had a bout of collective hysteria due to all the media attention."

"By those criteria, Clare simply has an over-active imagination. But we know differently, don't we John? At Tony's funeral you said this was part of a very old battle. Well, I believe you've just won a skirmish, and you said yourself that you prefer belief to dry facts."

Webster shifted uncomfortably on the seat.

"I hear you're looking for a cottage in the village. I'm so pleased."

The change of subject was too abrupt. It brushed aside truths that Fergus wanted to share, with the priest above all people. He tried to form the sentences in his mind that would describe the supernal moment in the church, but the words eluded him and a comfortable silence grew between them. In front of them Clare ambled over the dam, slender, almost child-like within an oversized T-shirt, and a rush of feeling filled Fergus's chest at the sight of her moving through the flowers. The ability to watch the one you love, without her being aware that she was watched, must be one of the purest of life's joys. Clare paused in the middle of the dam to admire the view down the valley, then turned to squat on her heels at the water's edge, with her face perfectly mirrored in the glassy surface.

Fergus inhaled, seeking the point of calm, needing that elusive wisdom to find the right words for Webster. He wanted to describe the harmony of faiths, the divinity of church and stream.

The Presence was there as he opened his mind, as if it had always been there, strong and vital in this place. But today there were eddies in the harmony, the way a drip of blood will swirl in water, weaving banners of colour into the purity.

A breeze was coming. On the dam it lifted Clare's hair so that it fluttered around her face and she looked up, staring over her shoulder as if someone had called to her. The wind was a mere cat's-paw but as it flowed through the freshly worked gardens it smelt autumn-rich with leaf mould, and laced with salt from the distant sea. Despite himself Fergus shivered.

Beyond Clare's reflected face Fergus saw a flash of white, a scrap of purity half-seen against the sky. And another. As Fergus stared, the glimpses of white grew into great wings that creaked with the slow beat of feathers as two swans flew up the valley. At the far end of the lake the pair soared in formation as they turned towards the water, as dazzling against the backdrop of trees as snow on a distant peak. With infinite grace they glided downwards towards the dam until their wings flared and they met their own reflections in a bubbling rush of water.

Clare was still hunched over, staring up the lake towards the swans, her reflection round-eyed, gamine, perhaps even frightened. The swans slid towards her, bobbing in the wavelets of their own landing, and her image dissolved as the ripples reached the shore. Clare shut her eyes, listening to some inner voice, and rose to her feet in the way one would rise to greet honoured guests. She stood at the water's edge, head down, arms by her side, until the swans stopped close to her, waiting. In that moment Clare seemed as ageless, even sexless, as the stained glass angels in the church. Slowly, she lifted her head and turned her arms palms-outwards, opening like a flower towards the swans and becoming female again as she inflated her chest to speak.

She spoke quietly, serenely even, but her words carried over the water to Fergus with perfect clarity.

"Welcome, sisters," she murmured.

1653: Two plots to kill Cromwell.
One to restore the King.
The other to set the Devil on the throne.

GIDEON'S
ANGEL

"Splendid... Seventeenth-century Britain in all its sweaty, superstitious, blood-soaked savagery, with the bonus of added demons." – *New York Times* best selling author James Lovegrove

Clifford Beal

UK ISBN: 978-1-78108-083-2 • US ISBN: 978-1-78108-084-9 •£7.99/$8.99

1653. The long, bloody English Civil War is at an end. King Charles is dead and Oliver Cromwell rules the land. Richard Treadwell, Royalist, exile, and now soldier for the King of France, burns for revenge on those who deprived him of his family and fortune. He returns to England in secret to assassinate Cromwell.

But his is not the only plot in motion. A secret army run by a deluded Puritan is bent on the same quest, guided by the Devil's hand. When demonic entities are summoned, Treadwell finds his fortunes reversed: he must save Cromwell, or consign England to Hell...

 WWW.SOLARISBOOKS.COM

Follow us on Twitter! www.twitter.com/solarisbooks

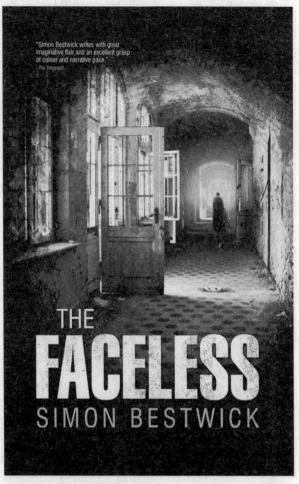

"Simon Bestwick writes with great imaginative flair and an excellent grasp of colour and narrative pace."
- The Telegraph

THE
FACELESS
SIMON BESTWICK

UK ISBN: 978-1-907992-74-2 • US ISBN: 978-1-907992-75-9 • £7.99/$8.99

In the Lancashire town of Kempforth, people are vanishing. Mist hangs heavy in the streets, and in those mists move the masked figures the local kids call the Spindly Men. When two year old Roseanne Trevor disappears, Detective Chief Inspector Renwick vows to stop at nothing until she finds her. In Manchester, terrifying visions summon TV psychic Allen Cowell and his sister Vera back to the town they swore they'd left forever. And local historian Anna Mason pieces together a history of cruelty and exploitation almost beyond belief, born out of the horrors of war — while in the decaying corridors and lightless rooms of a long-abandoned hospital, something terrible is waiting for them all.

 WWW.SOLARISBOOKS.COM

Follow us on Twitter! www.twitter.com/solarisbooks